2 00
/23

EVERMORE

CALL OF THE NOCTURNE

To Melanie,
Thank you so much
for your support
over the years.
I am proud to
call you my friend.
I hope that you enjoy
the book

Scott Christian

Also by Scott Blurton

Suicide is a Tax Write-Off

EVERMORE

CALL OF THE NOCTURNE

SCOTT BLURTON

NASTY | FERRET | PRESS

Evermore: Call of the Nocturne
First Paperback Edition

First published in Canada by Nasty Ferret Press.

Nasty Ferret Press
360 Bell Street South, Apt. 404
Ottawa, ON Canada K1S 5E8

Cataloging data available from Library and Archives Canada.

First Paperback Edition © ISBN: 978-0-9879831-2-1

Copyright © 2012 Scott Blurton
Cover design by Jordan Knoll. Front and back cover illustration by Kevin Bae. Copyright © Nasty Ferret Press.
Editing by Erin Stropes and Amelia Bennett.
Evermore, names, characters and related indicia are copyright and trademark Nasty Ferret Press.

Scott Blurton has asserted his moral rights.

This is a work of fiction. Names, characters, places and incidents are products of the author's imagination. Any similarity to persons living or dead is purely coincidental.

Printed and bound in the United States of America by Lulu.

- ACKNOWLEDGEMENTS -

The genesis of *Evermore: Call of the Nocturne* began in 2000 following a year-long love affair with *The Matrix* by the Wachowski Brothers. Its exploration of a physically and socially constructed world, where even one's existence could be contested, fascinated me with its endless story possibilities. These possibilities were matched by the immense challenge of trying to craft an original and compelling story beyond the wide shadow cast by the Wachowski brothers and their forebears such as William Gibson and Philip K. Dick.

After a couple of years of planning and many dead ends, I finally began writing the manuscript in Fall 2004 while living in Lethbridge, AB. Wanting to escape from the hypnotic glare of my oversized computer monitor, I did much of my writing on a Dell Axim A30 and a portable keyboard inside the hallways of the University of Lethbridge. I would swim laps in the pool and then write for a couple of hours before I went downtown to work as a Technical Support Agent at Convergys. Work-wise, it was the worst of times. However, it was perhaps my productive year as a a writer. It is amazing how much a terrible job can inspire one to write, if only to escape.

After a year of this working hell, I wisely decided to return to University. I enrolled in a Master's Program in Political Science at the University of Ottawa and settled into my new home in the student neighbourhood of Sandy Hill.

According to my computer's filing system, the first draft of *Evermore: Call of the Nocturne* was completed on May 17, 2006. Over the next year and a bit, I re-drafted the manuscript seven times. By August 27, 2007, I finally felt that the manuscript was ready to submit to publishers.

Let's just say that it didn't go too well.

Throughout 2007, 2008 and 2009, the manuscript was rejected by every publisher to which it was submitted. At the time, I told myself that the growth in easy-to-use word processors coupled with the decline of people reading prose fiction had led to publishers being bombarded by manuscripts for an increasingly shrinking customer base. Obviously, brilliant debut works from emerging new writers like myself could be easily lost in the deluge. Now many years older and wiser, I have realized the truth for why my manuscript was rejected. In short, *my book sucked*.

But to understand this fact, I first had to pull myself off the slush pile and re-engage myself in tortuous process of reading every line in book, yet again, change every line to what it was before, yet again, and try to make the byzantine plot more comprehensible, yet again.

But this time was different, because I knew that I wouldn't be submitting it again to a traditional publisher. In 2009, I had become more and more interested in the growing viability of self-publishing my manuscript. The technology had gotten easier and cheaper, e-books were only beginning to take off with the introduction of the Kindle, and just-in-time publishing was just beginning to become an affordable option. But still I resisted. Self-publishing in those days was derided as *vanity publishing*. Besides, I didn't want to do all of this hard work. I wanted a magically guardian angel to swoop in, publish my work and put it on every bookstore shelf in North America. I wanted it easy. I felt I could wait. So what finally changed my mind? What made me finally jump into the no-man's land of self-publishing? Well, that's easy. Let me tell you.

It was the day that Lauren Conrad got a book deal.

Now I haven't got anything against Lauren Conrad. I've never met her, never saw her reality shows, never read her books (New York Times Bestseller!). I'm sure that she's a nice and talented person, maybe even a talented writer. But when I heard about the book deal, I knew that her writing talent had nothing to do with getting the book deal. That said, I also knew that the publisher was making a smart decision. Because of her notoriety, people were going to buy her books. Whether or not they were good or not was immaterial. The traditional publisher gave her the contract because she could deliver buyers.

And that was what has become of the traditional publishing industry. With fewer readers, dropping prices and rising costs, publishers cannot take risks on unknowns. They need proven sellers to stay afloat. There was no room for new, nobody writers like myself. Well, along with the fact that my manuscript sucked. Thus began my journey down the rabbit hole that is self-publishing.

And in that first step comes my first acknowledgement. I owe a huge debt of thanks to Henry Baum, former editor of the Self-Publishing Review and the author of *American Book of the Dead*. Being fairly lost, I had cold-emailed Mr. Baum looking for a recommendation for a copy editor. I understood that my manuscript needed a professional eye and I needed to find someone who wouldn't break my modest bank account. Mr. Baum recommended me to Erin Stropes, who was outstanding.

For a relatively inexpensive fee, Ms. Stropes tore through my manuscript and exposed all of its sores. Every plot hole, every consistency, every over-use of adjectives and adverbs was documented by Erin. She showed me that my novel, well *sucked*, but that it could be fixed. Thanks to her work, I worked through most of 2010 to ensure that the structural issues with the text were resolved. Based on her comments and suggestions, I rewrote a third of the manuscript. When I was done, it was leaner, tighter and far more captivating. It was a polished story.

But since I had changed so much, I needed to send it again through the editing process. This time, I needed a line editor. Since Erin Stropes was occupied, self-published author Todd Keisling recommended Amelia Bennett for her work on his novel, *A Life Transparent*. Again, I was fortunate to work with a consummate professional. Amelia parsed through my script over the Summer of 2011. She tightened it and exposed yet more plot holes that I had to fill. Wading through the mountain of notes and corrections, I finally finished the manuscript, for real this time, on February 15, 2012. It was an exhausting process, but a necessary one. I owe Amelia a large debt of gratitude for taking my polished story and turning it into a polished manuscript.

But as a self-published author, my job was not yet complete. I still needed to commission an illustrator to draw illustrations for the front and back and a cover designer to put it all together. Erin Stropes, thank you Erin once again, suggested that I work with Jordan Knoll on the cover design. Jordan, in turn, suggested that I work with illustrator Kevin Bae. In short, both of them had been outstanding. Kevin has been instrumental in establishing the physically appearance of the character Blue, something with which I had always had trouble. His stunning artwork and his clever composition have visually defined Evermore to the reader. I cannot wait to work with him again. As for Jordan, he has served as my shepherd through the book design process. *Evermore: Call of the Nocturne* would not have been possible without him.

Dipping further into my past, I also feel like to express my gratitude to my Grade 11 English teacher, Mr. Burgess. Mr. Burgess was the first person to encourage my writing and suggested that I begin submitting my short stories to competitions. Without his support, I would never have completed *Evermore: Call of the Nocturne*. I also owe of debt of thanks to Gisèle Baxter from University of British Columbia. Her course on dystopian fiction heavily inspired *Evermore* and continues to influence me to this day.

From the world of film, I would like to thank screenwriters Terry Rossio and Ted Elliott of wordplayer.com, whose articles on story construction proved immensely helpful during the writing of this manuscript. To anyone interested in a writing career, their articles will teach you almost everything you need to know to write fiction. Another major influence were film reviewers Gene Siskel and Roger Ebert. Their television reviews were a must-watch in my young life and gave me an excellent critical understanding of how and how not to tell a story.

Penultimately, I would like to thank my parents. Bob and Betty Blurton have been with me through every step of my life. They taught me everything important that I know and were always there when I needed them. Nobody could have asked for any more from their parents. This book is dedicated to them.

Finally, I would like to thank you the reader. I would to thank you for using your valuable free time to take a chance on a nobody writer and an unknown story. I hope that you enjoy *Evermore: Call of the Nocturne* and that you may be inspired to attempt things that are impossible. For only then can life be lived.

For my parents,
who took so little
so I could have so much.
My debt to you can never be repaid.

- PROLOGUE -

The whites of a child's eyes stared blankly into the monochrome sky. He and six of his friends lay dead upon the ground in a dirty anonymous alley, their lives wilted before they could bud. The flesh of youth, torn asunder by powder and steel, spilled blood into the gutter. None remained to mourn their passing, nor remember their existence. These seven lay quiet in a memorial none would visit, where no trumpets would play. Their graves would not be marked by poppies or immortalized in poems, for they were the dead. Short minutes ago, they lived and saw sunshine glow. Now they lay here in an alley, meat to be cast aside.

Their deliverer, the culler of children, stood five metres away. Her hands squeezed a Beretta semiautomatic, its sights trained straight ahead as she searched for the slightest movement. The reaper stood clad in black, her short brunette hair failing to cover the gleaming blue eyes that stared intensely through the sights. There was an aura of disappointment in her, for there were none left to kill. Her breathing, once controlled, now grew deeper and more laboured. Her hands began to shake and her legs slowly buckled. Nearing exhaustion, she carefully lowered her weapon, revealing a horrible wound to her right cheek. Blood spilled to the floor as her body clumsily tried to heal. A second wound gushed crimson from her larynx. She slumped to her knees, revealing two bullet holes in the wall behind. Decorated with flesh and bone, the holes bled slowly down the wall to the alley below.

Her life leaving her, the reaper bowed towards the concrete, drifting into unconsciousness. This was the manner in which she had always wished to die: victorious in battle. The comforting embrace of nothingness enveloped her, pulling her gently into death. She could no longer feel her wounds and her scars had long since disappeared. Finally, she would know peace.

The leather straps of a single sandal invaded her view. The lady of death raised her weapon, anxious for the rush of war one final time. She aimed without hesitation and pulled the trigger. A car window exploded, scattering shards of glass into the air. The shards tumbled end over end as they fell to the ground, bounced off the asphalt and then lay still. A car alarm roared to life.

CHAPTER ONE

A DAY OF RECKONING

The blare of an alarm clock penetrated the bed cover, adorned with the comic book heroes of a youth long past. Dazed and groggy, Adam rolled over and turned off the alarm, unwilling to hit the snooze button yet again. He sat up on the edge of the mattress and rubbed his temples, trying to rub away the electronic haze that clogged his vision. Collecting himself, Adam stood and gazed at himself into a full-length mirror beside the bed. He smiled as his shaggy hair drooped across his hollow shoulders. He enjoyed looking at himself, using his skeleton of a body—emasculated by lack of exercise and poor nutrition—to flex and pose with an attitude of perfection. In his imagination, he had constructed a hairless body that was sculpted, manicured and tanned to the highest standard. Adam knew that the body he imagined was not his own, but he chose to ignore this fact. He truly believed this fantasy to be his reality. "I am not how others see me," he would tell himself, "I am only limited by my own will." He turned to a poster on the wall and focused on a beefy superhero posing in a dramatic stance. He compared it with the withered form in the mirror and found few differences.

Picking through a maze of discarded clothes, operating manuals and magazines, Adam manoeuvred his way to the kitchen and microwaved some waffles. Eating and dressing simultaneously, Adam succeeded in doing neither well, managing only to spread maple syrup across his creased jeans and hoodie. Finally a close approximation of presentable, Adam strolled to the door of his apartment, stopped and waited. He looked at the clock and listened. The metallic click of another door down the hall was the signal that he was waiting for. With all the coolness he could muster, Adam stepped outside and locked the door behind him.

In the hallway, he feigned surprise at running into Desiree, a gorgeous creature blessed by both genetics and cosmetics. "Well hello Dez," Adam greeted her nervously. "How are you doing?"

"I'm doing all right," replied the statuesque redhead. She suppressed a yawn. "How about you?"

"Same as always. How'd your date go with Ted last night?"

"Oh, Ted," Desiree said with disappointment. "He was great. He was smart, funny, good-looking, but ..."

"But what?" asked Adam with some concern.

"Well, I prefer guys that are a little bit more coarse - tattoos, deep tans and some facial hair. Like, Ted is a nice guy, but he's too waspy, much too ordinary. I'd like to date a guy more worldly, more exotic, more Latin. Yeah, I'd like to date a Latin guy."

"Oh, it's too bad it didn't work out. I'm sure that you'll find what you're looking for."

"Of course I will," she said smugly. "It's what I deserve."

After an uneventful bus ride through heavy showers, Adam arrived at the university bus loop. Incessant raindrops pounded the street. Deep puddles marked the potholes in the pavement. It was on days like today that Adam wished he had a car. He could afford one, but the hassles of car ownership, from insurance to parking, outweighed the advantages. Besides, he needed the exercise. Sprinting from one shelter to another, he finally ducked into the bookstore and out of the pouring rain.

Most of the buildings on campus were connected by way of glass walkways on the second floor. Adam navigated the maze, moving from building to building while he mulled over Desiree's words. Dark skin, exotic, more of an edge, that's what she wanted. He would have to make adjustments.

Entering the Macleod building, he walked down the staircase and into the basement. Recently renovated, the Macleod building had a new face on top of an old frame. Everything looked new and shiny with custom glass and chrome. *It was the least they could do,* thought Adam, *considering the money that his creation was pouring into the university.*

The security guard looked up as Adam flashed his badge. The guard nodded and pushed a button to open the door. Entering the laboratory, he found himself surrounded by silver walls. Everywhere he looked he saw his staff members hard at work at computer desks. He was late as usual, but nobody paid him any mind. He was a programmer. Nine to five was a foreign concept in his world. To his left, he saw a large screen hanging on the wall. The screen displayed a rolling list of statistics: the number of users logged in, the number of zones operational, the Xchange's Composite Index and so on.

Below the large screen, there was a woman with red hair sitting patiently at her desk. She was waiting for him. Beyond her were sliding glass doors. He approached the woman.

"Morning Alice, what's on the docket for today?" he said to his assistant. She insisted on wearing a lab coat just like the others. He had no idea why. They were programmers, not doctors. The lab coats made them look like idiots.

"Morning Adam. The latest requests from the Consortium are in your thoughtbox. The next shift has already logged into Evermore."

"My my, everyone's on time today."

"Everyone but you sir."

Adam ignored her and walked towards the sliding doors. They opened with a satisfying whoosh. Beside them a piece of paper was taped to the wall. On it the words "The Womb" were written in crayon. Adam suppressed a chuckle. It wasn't too far from the truth.

Adam walked through the silver doors into a sea of white. The floor was white. The walls were white. The ceiling was white. Even the backside of the sliding doors were white as they reflected the light. It was a large rectangular white room.

I hate white, thought Adam as he surveyed the landscape.

The white room was filled with about a hundred beds with white sheets. All of them were filled with patrons sleeping peacefully, white headphones resting on their temples.

Adam walked to the far side of the room where there was a little alcove separated by a glass wall and a pair of reflective sliding doors. He entered the alcove to find a soft leather chair waiting for him. A pair of headphones lay on a small table beside the chair. This was his office.

Adam sat down in his chair and looked back through the glass into the Womb. From this side, the one-way mirror separating the alcove from the rest of the room had become a computer screen. Oodles of data flowed across the glass wall as the hosts slept peacefully behind. Adam reviewed the information as it slipped past him. Population: 765,341. Hosts: 37,826. Zones Operational: 52,349. Bugs reported: 37. *Ack*, thought Adam, *my work is never done.*

Adam reached down to the table beside him, picked up the headphones and placed them on his temples. He stared out into the white room. Not a creature stirred, coddled by their recorded dreams. *It was so peaceful,* thought Adam. *What a wonderful way to make a living.* His eyes grew heavy. The stillness of the room was drawing him into sleep. Slowly, the white room blurred into nothingness. When he opened his eyes again, he saw nothing but the following message written in green, a mere six inches from his face.

Login Name: Mmorpg
Status: Administrator
Registration Key: ADM0101
Searching For Record ...

After a short pause, the message changed to navy blue:

Record found.
Welcome back to Evermore, Mmorpg.

He was no longer Adam. He was now Mmorpg.

Mmorpg, pronounced MORG, was not Adam and no one would confuse the two. In this realm, Adam ceased to exist; only Mmorpg remained. But that was okay. He didn't like Adam anyway.

Adam was a peon who sat in a chair all day. Mmorpg preferred to fly. Characters rushed past him as he flew through the code of his greatest achievement - Evermore. The words and symbols that described the lives of millions passed before his cerebral eyes in a waveform of light, sensation and sound. Even at this speed, he missed nothing. Every word, every symbol, every file was fully understood at a velocity that had previously been considered impossible. In this world he was not unwanted, he was not ignored. In this world, he was God. He had no physical body, no visual representation. Instead, he was connected to a world of his own making, able to peer into any corner and listen to every sound. He was nothing and yet he was everything.

****

"It's like he's having a nightmare," said an intern in the university lab, anxious at the sight of Adam's intermittent spasms, which were bouncing with the rhythm of his virtual avatar.

"In a way, that's not too far from the truth," Alice said soothingly.

****

Sightseeing aside, it was now time for Mmorpg to get to work. He opened up his thoughtbox. Thoughts came pouring out. He experienced them all simultaneously, nothing but a confusing mash of sensation. Astonishingly, Mmorpg had long ago learned to differentiate between the recorded thoughts assaulting his brain. He noticed one that caught his attention and pulled it closer to his cerebrum.

It was an image of pink bunny doll.

He examined the attached note. It said that people were complaining about getting bombarded by this message over the last twenty-four hours. Mmorpg did not hesitate. *Junk mail,* he thought, adding it to the spam filter. *I hate junk mail.*

He pulled another thought closer. This one he recognized as a message from the Consortium, the Proxy of the Interior to be exact. It listed off a series of superficial changes for the Downtown Core. This would not take long.

"Kernel: activate god mode," said Mmorpg.

"God mode activated," replied the kernel.

Mmorpg smiled. "Alright hosts," he said, "let's build a world."

Mmorpg motioned up with his hands and the ghostly outlines of the sleeping men from the white room rose up from the floor. He reached his hand out and dragged it back towards his chest and a great city zoomed in around him. A city of glass surrounded by sea and mountains, the Downtown Core was designed as a cross between the great glass monoliths of Toronto and the rugged natural beauty of Vancouver. It was a city of dreams.

But even a city of dreams has its minute flaws. Mmorpg zoomed into a section and found what he was looking for. The intersection between two blocks didn't quite line up properly. It was acceptable, but not perfect. It had to be perfect.

"Downtown East, Downtown Centre," called Mmorpg. "The intersection between Gerudo Alley and Higinbotham Road is a little off. Would you be able to line them up?"

"All flaws shall be washed away," came a voice and the road bent magically into place. Perfect. Mmorpg moved onto the next message.

Mmorpg checked his next message. It was a zone swap. Mmorpg swept the city away with his hand until he found the right section. It was a small theatre in the north-east corner of the city. Its replacement was an Opera House.

Mmorpg raised his hands and drew a cube with his index fingers. The cube glowed green. The zone was one-way now. People could exit but they could not enter. Mmorpg knew that the zone would take a few minutes to empty so he moved on to other matters.

The next message held an image of a building folded in upon itself. As he watched, the image moved. The building swayed back and forth in the breeze. *That's not an error*, thought Mmorpg. *That's Forsythian architecture. It's not* supposed *to make sense.*

Mmorpg ignored it and the thoughtmail disappeared. *The Interior Proxy should really brush up on the latest design trends,* thought Mmorpg, *otherwise he'll just waste everyone's time.*

He moved onto the next message. It was an image of a road meridian. One of the hash marks was three centimetres off centre. It had to be fixed.

"Southwest Peach Station," called Mmorpg. "It's time to do some painting.

"All flaws shall be washed away," came the reply.

Mmorpg filed away the flaws with his hosts for the next half-hour. Each task was accomplished in nanoseconds. Together with his hosts, they could accomplish in an hour what it would take an old-fashioned development team weeks. Mmorpg enjoyed the freedom of his work. Untethered from his frail body, his only limitation was his imagination.

That should be long enough, thought Mmorpg. He swiped his hand in front of his body and the city rushed past him until he returned to the old theatre. The zone was now empty; everyone had left. Mmorpg swiped his hand upwards and a list of items popped up in front of him. Using his fingers, he slid these items up until he found the new Opera House. It was majestic. He grabbed and pulled it in front of him beside the green cube.

Mmorpg reached out and grabbed the cube with both hands. He lifted the cube up slowly.

Before him, the old theatre lifted itself from the ground. Attached to the bottom of the theatre was a square block of asphalt and several layers of dirt. Where the theatre had once stood, there was nothing left. It looked like a cake with a square piece missing.

This one was heavy, thought Mmorpg.

He pivoted to his right, tilting the green cube in the same direction. The theatre block matched the movement, tilting heavily to the right as it moved.

As he turned to the right, Mmorpg squeezed his hands together, shrinking the cube. The theatre block shrank to the size of his hand. He placed the small cube into the items menu and then swiped downwards to make the menu disappear. The theatre block disappeared.

Mmorpg tapped the new Opera House to activate it and made a small green cube with his fingers. Grabbing the cube with his hands, he expanded it until the Opera House grew to the correct size and then placed it into the empty gap. With a satisfying click, the new zone locked into place. Mmorpg let go of the green cube and it dissolved. The new Opera House was open for visitors.

A thoughtmail notice popped up in front of his view. He opened and consumed it quickly, eager to finish his chores. But it was no ordinary change. The Consortium had requested a change to the physics engine. Apparently someone thought that water didn't ripple quite the way it should. They were right. Mmorpg had spotted the problem weeks ago and had spent his spare time pouring through academic journals trying to find a better formula. Finally he had found the answer in an obscure Chinese text. It was long and it was complicated, but Mmorpg was ready to make the upgrade.

"Kernel: deactivate god mode."

"God mode deactivated," said the kernel.

"Kernel: activate debug mode."

"Debug mode activated."

Mmorpg closed his eyes, leaned backwards and dropped into the floor. When he reopened his eyes, Mmorpg found himself falling through a jungle of harsh green letters surrounded by an infinite darkness. He was flying through the code of the physics engine, where the words and symbols that defined the rules for all of Evermore zoomed across his eyes. Even at this speed, he missed nothing. Every word, every symbol, every function call was fully understood at a velocity that had no one could have ever thought possible.

It's a strange sensation, thought Mmorpg, *to manipulate the rules that control a world.* It made him feel like a god.

There it was, thought Mmorpg as he lifted up his palm. The sea of text and symbols stopped in place. Mmorpg pushed his palms forward and then apart. The sea parted way at his gesture. There it was. Mmorpg had found the module responsible for rippling water. He pulled it closer and marvelled at its technology. Mmorpg pinched outwards and the module expanded to fill his vision.

He remembered writing this section many months ago. He used to be so proud of it.

Mmorpg gestured wildly about, like a conductor leading his orchestra. The code danced to his tune: writing and deleting and morphing into a completely new form. Coding in the 21st Century was such a beautiful experience. *It was a shame,* thought Mmorpg, *that very few people could do it.*

And then he was done. The rippling water module had been updated with the best physics science could predict.

"Kernel: deactivate debug mode."

"Debug Mode deactivated."

Mmorpg flew out of the darkness and back into his great city. He landed by a pool and poked the water. The ripples were perfect. He smiled with satisfaction and turned his attention to the outlines of the bed-ridden hosts.

"Good work boys," said Mmorpg. He lowered his hands and the ghostly outlines disappeared back into the floor. "Take a nap," he joked. Nobody laughed. Nobody ever laughed.

Mmorpg was now free to work on his side project. Minimizing Evermore into the corner of his vision, the code warrior opened up his proprietary non-playable character generator. Unlike coding, he preferred to take his time creating non-playable characters, or NPCs, seeing it as more of an art form than the exacting science of programming. "Open A Recent File?" the program asked politely. "Yes!" responded Mmorpg. A human figure appeared before him, but its eyes were dull and dead. Above the figure's head, white text rotated around like a weathervane, spelling out "Ted".

A thoughtmail arrived. *Not now,* thought Mmorpg. Ignoring the thoughtmail, he returned to his project.

Hmm, more exotic, more Latin, thought Mmorpg. With that thought, Ted was transformed into Enrique, a bronze Latin god. His eyes were too wide so he narrowed them. The chin, too thick, grew slimmer. In this manner, all of Enrique's imperfections were chiselled away. Another thoughtmail. It could wait. After a few minutes, Mmorpg was quite impressed with his creation. Desiree would find love indeed. She would find everything that she deserved.

Mmorpg was about to finish Enrique's jawline when he was unexpectedly pulled back into the Womb. One of the supervisors stood sheepishly above him.

"How dare you pull me out like that?" said Mmorpg.

"Sorry sir," apologized the supervisor, "but you didn't respond to any of our messages. We have a situation."

"What could possibly be important enough to disrupt my work?" asked a Mmorpg.

"The safety protocols have failed. One of our clients has lost all brain activity." The supervisor led Mmorpg out of the white room. He saw his staff scrambling around the lab, their nervous energy accomplishing nothing. Nearby, an intern held a cell phone to her ear. Panic seeped into her voice as she spoke.

"Is it a disconnect?" Mmorpg asked her.

"No, she's still connected," said the intern, cupping the phone in her hands. "The father is on the line. He doesn't know what to do." Mmorpg could hear sobbing coming through the phone's receiver. His heartbeat quickened. Adrenaline was rushing into his system. He must remain calm

"Ask him if there's been any physical trauma: a fall, a collision, any physical damage to explain her reaction?" The nervous intern repeated the question into the phone.

"None, sir. He says that they're extremely careful and always take the recommended precautions."

"It can't be. It's impossible!" said Mmorpg. He turned to the supervisor and asked, "What is her location?"

"West 6th Avenue," replied the supervisor.

"No, where is she in Evermore?"

The supervisor checked his screen. "We've used gophers to track her to Zone 1394 in the Underground."

"Seal the Gate, I'm on my way." Settling back into his chair, Mmorpg flashed back into Evermore.

Mmorpg zoomed through a building as he homed in on the body's location. Passing through a crowd of people, he heard the tiniest snippet of each and every one of their lives. He was always unnerved by that; how in a single second there was a universe of lives that could be passed by without a second thought.

He homed in on the location and found her body in the alley. Her torso had caved in. She was just a little girl, no more than ten years of age. She had blonde hair and a white dress. Her feet were bare. Her sandals had fallen off in the struggle. Beside her body lay three small little dolls.

"Oh my god," said Mmorpg.

He felt a thoughtmail arrive. It was from the supervisor. "Did you find her?" it asked.

"Yes," replied Mmorpg.

Another thoughtmail arrived. "How does she look?"

"She looks dead."

Another thoughtmail. "I thought that the security protocols

made that impossible?" asked the supervisor.

"It is impossible. Her father must be mistaken."

Another thoughtmail. "He's on the phone with us right now. He is certain that she is dead."

"That can't be."

"Mmorpg," said the supervisor's next thoughtmail, "our governmental approval is conditional on our technology being safe. Once they find out, they'll shut us down."

Mmorpg thought about all of the years that he had sunk into this project. He remembered all of the sacrifices that he had made. All of his memories coalesced into one single word.

No.

More thoughtmails arrived but Mmorpg ignored them. He knew know what he had to do.

"Kernel: disable logout function," Mmorpg ordered.

"Logout function disabled," replied the kernel.

Mmorpg switched his eyes to purple lens. His vision adopted a purple hue around its edges. He looked at the head of the little girl and waited. His vision faded to black. There was nothing to see.

Just as he had feared, she wasn't registering any brain activity, so he couldn't access her memories. He would have to find another witness. Mmorpg passed through the wall and floated out into the street. He turned his purple eyes towards the first person he saw. It was a young woman, no more than twenty-five years old. His vision faded and he found himself looking through her eyes.

"Rewind," said Mmorpg.

The world before his eyes reversed itself. He could feel the young woman walking backwards away from the alley. Just before the young woman went around the corner. An man with a moustache walked backwards into her view.

"Freeze," said Mmorpg. The young woman's vision froze.

Mmorpg looked intently at the man with the moustache with purple eyes. In the next moment, Mmorpg was behind that man's eyes.

"Reverse," said Mmorpg.

Mmorpg felt himself walk backwards past the alley. Once again, nobody went near it.

There was only one entrance to the alley and there were no exits, so the girl must have entered the alley from this direction. Mmorpg jumped from memory to memory of the people who passed by, searching for the exact moment the little girl entered the alley. He jumped from mind to mind, tracing backwards and forwards, searching for any clue. Had he been wrong? Had he missed something? Could she have entered the alley another way? There! He found it. A blonde woman, on her way to a rendezvous, had spotted a little girl entering the alley. Switching to other witnesses confirmed that it was indeed the little girl who now lay wounded at his feet. She had entered the alley at exactly 1113 hours. But who had done this to her? He must have entered by the same route. Mmorpg pulled back and searched both backwards and forwards, across a lifespan of stored experiences, searching for the perpetrator, anyone else who had entered the alley. He found no one.

His temples throbbed heavily from the strain. Twelve minutes had passed since the emergency had erupted. He had to jack out; there was nothing else to find.

"Lens off," said Mmorpg. All of a sudden, he felt himself pulled back to his office. The room held an eerie calm. He looked up into the eyes of a man that he had never seen before, dressed from head to toe in white. The man spoke, slow and clear:

"The little girl is dead, Mmorpg. We need to talk."

CHAPTER TWO

THE DEATH OF A DREAM

Mmorpg followed the man in white up the stairs to the fourth floor. The pair entered a well-decorated office. A plaque beside the door stated that the office belonged to Director J. Hartford. In the corner sat a soft leather couch. Mmorpg eyed it enviously. The man in white sat down in his chair and invited Mmorpg to sit as well. In the brief pause that followed, Mmorpg examined the director's desk: it was kept tidy and neat. Not a thing was out of place. Even the coffee mug was sitting on top of a saucer. Nobody in Canada did that.

Mmorpg's eyes were drawn to a framed newspaper story hung on the wall. He read it quickly while the director took a sip from his coffee.

NEW DIRECTOR TO COMMERCIALIZE UBC VIRTUAL REALITY TECHNOLOGY

Today, the University of British Columbia Department of Computer Engineering announced that John Hartfield has been hired to direct the commercialization of the exciting Evermore virtual reality technology developed by students. Mr. Hartfield stated that ...

A long breath drew Mmorpg's attention back to the man in white.

"It is a pleasure to finally meet you," said the director.

"Yes sir. This is the first time that I've ever been up here."

"I wanted to met with you earlier but the logistics surrounding the upcoming IPO have eaten up all of my time." The director sighed. "I wish we could have met under better circumstances."

"Did they find the victim?" asked Mmorpg.

"The girl was found an hour ago by her father, who had just come home after teaching his classes."

"He's a professor here?" Mmorpg asked.

"Yes, we were very fortunate. Instead of calling 9-1-1, he called us. Once the ambulance was able to determine that she was no longer connected to the network, she was moved to an isolated room in the campus hospital at our request."

The man in white paused, his voice growing shallow and grave. "I talked to the head of the O.R. department. He said that while they have been able to stabilize her breathing and heartbeat, she is no longer registering any brain activity. While there is no physical damage to her brain tissue, for all intents and purposes she is brain dead."

The full gravity of the situation crushed down upon Mmorpg. His creation had been responsible for the death of an innocent young girl. He felt a sense of betrayal at how his creation and the thousands of hours that he had invested in it could turn on him like this. Everything he had worked all these years to accomplish now lay in ruins. His child would be abandoned by the masses who had once loved her. The electro-synaptic fix that his world had provided would be replaced by another. Technojunkies would gladly move onto other worlds, newer worlds with newer features and newer code, worlds that hadn't killed a little girl. And then the stark realization of what he was about to lose fell upon him. Evermore was the only thing he had. It was the only accomplishment of his life in which he had pride. Mmorpg had created a universe beloved by millions. A universe with an economic base the size of a small country and endowed with thousands of years of tradition and history would be destroyed. As quickly as it had been built, it would crumble into nothingness – lost in the annals of time. All of his work would be forgotten. The end of Evermore would mean the end of him, the end of any chance to leave his mark upon the world. He did not know what to do. Mmorpg sweated profusely. What could he do? It had all ended so quickly.

The face of the man in white eased and softened. There was relief in his voice when he spoke.

"Like I said, we were lucky that he called us. If he had called 9-1-1, there would have been no way to contain this situation. The hospital is aware of our generous grants to their research and will aid us fully on one condition: that we find the cause of her death and ensure that it will never happen again."

"What about the father? He lost a child today," Mmorpg said.

"We will give him our deepest condolences and ensure that he, his family and his children-to-come will be financially secure for well into the future."

"Secure? You're giving him shares in the spin-off?" Mmorpg seethed.

"Yes," answered the man in white. "Yes we are. We are giving him ten percent of the initial stock offering."

"But our people have earned that money. They have spent years working on this project, spending time away from their families, working unpaid overtime to make this dream a reality. That's their money!"

"And without his full cooperation, that money will disappear."

Mmorpg, the dreamweaver, hung his head, unable to find an alternative.

"Besides," the man in white continued, "our biggest problem is not the father, it's the bug that killed his girl. If we are unable to find and neutralize this bug, then all our work will be for naught."

"It's not a bug. I ran a series of tests on the security protocols and they held. She did not die due to an error in the system."

"Perhaps the security protocols were disabled, perhaps by a hacker?"

"No, that's the not the way it works. I designed the security protocols so that they can only be disabled manually at the kernel downstairs or by a signed order from the sovereign. In either case, the fail-safes can only be shut down from my terminal."

"Could it have been affected by a virus - a worm?"

"No, I've checked that too. The tests have not revealed any viral intrusions. Besides, the entire system is designed to prevent such incursions. For an outside user to introduce a virus he would have to hook his brain into a computer and download the virus into his own mind. That's impossible!"

"We trade in the impossible!" snapped the director.

Mmorpg held his tongue, looking only to the floor.

"Could it have been introduced by staff?" asked the director.

"I've already checked all network actions by the staff over the past three weeks - nothing. But even if they had tried, they could do no damage. Only I have access to the safety protocol subsystem. If there was a virus, then only I could have introduced it." Mmorpg looked straight at the director. "Do you think that I would sabotage my life's work?"

"No," the director shook his head, "I don't. But if it wasn't a bug and it wasn't a virus, then what killed that little girl?"

"I traced the memories of those who passed by at the time of the murder."

"Murder?" exclaimed the director. "What makes you think it was murder?"

"The body, or rather the body of her resonant self-image, had been brutally crushed. I saw it myself."

"Did you see her assailant?"

"No."

"He's probably long gone by now."

"Maybe. Maybe not."

"How can you be so sure the killer is still here?"

"If the killer has already logged out, then he's long gone. We'll never be able to find him. But if the killer hasn't logged out then he'll be trapped inside and under our control.

"And how did you manage to trap him inside Evermore?"

Mmorpg shrugged with guilt.

"I disabled the logout function."

"You did what? Now nobody can leave," said the director angrily.

"Exactly, so we know that the killer can't escape."

"But neither can anyone else, Mmorpg. This isn't like changing the colour of a sidewalk. People will notice that they're not allowed to leave. It's hard to miss something like that."

"I've taken care of it."

"Like *heck* you have. When people realize that they can't leave, they're going to start to panic. And once the mob starts panicking, there won't be enough striders to contain them. What are you going to do then?"

Mmorpg looked into the eyes of the director and spoke slowly and carefully. "There is a way."

The director frowned. "What do you mean?"

"Ok, what each user sees in Evermore is a creation of their own mind. The images placed in front of their eyes, the sounds they hear, the scents they smell are all pulled from their subconscious. Their memory forms the RAM of Evermore, reconstructing the world in their own image. But that memory can be accessed more directly."

"And?" asked the director.

"Let's imagine we have one person who really wants to leave. Let's imagine that instead of allowing her to actually log out, we only make her think she's logged out. We pull out the right images from her memory so she thinks she's back in the real world. From her perspective, she'll believe she's logged out. She'll stand up, feel tired and then go to the bedroom to take a nap. A few hours will pass by, we'll find and fix the problem and then we'll log her out. She'll wake up in her bed or chair with her dermals on her head and think that she had forgotten to take them off."

"My god," the man in white gasped in horror. "You're saying that we take control of their mind, that we take away their free will?"

"We don't make them do anything. They think they're doing something, all the while staying safely here in Evermore. When it's all over, they'll think they were dreaming or that they fell asleep after logging out. They'll never know the difference."

"We'll know."

"Hey, I don't like this any more than you do, but it's our only choice. Otherwise, the killer goes free."

The director stared at Mmorpg. "If he's still here."

Mmorpg stared back. "If he's still here, this is our only chance of finding him."

A long silence followed.

"Where did you come up with that?" asked the director.

"It just came to me. Like a little voice in the back of my head."

"Assuming that your strategy holds," said the director, "can you limit it to the Underground? We don't want to violate subscribers."

"I'm afraid that I can't," said Mmorpg. "The operating functions are stored in the kernel and are applied universally to each and every user in Evermore; they are the same whether you're in the Underground or in the Downtown Core. I cannot pick and choose who the functions apply to. But when I learned of the murder, I had the Gate between the Underground and the Downtown Core sealed. If the killer hadn't crossed it already, then he won't be able to now. He's trapped in one half or the other, waiting for us to find him."

"Very well," said the director as he pulled out his cell phone and cupped it to his ear. "Make it happen. And God help us."

"You forget sir. Inside Evermore, we are God," said Mmorpg.

"Mary," said the director into his cell phone, "has our guest arrived?" He nodded to the response. "All right, send her up."

Flipping the cell phone closed, the director returned his attention to Mmorpg. "How much time do we have?"

"Once the Spectacle ends, there will be a mass exodus of people trying to log out. They will find out quickly that they can't leave." Mmorpg glanced down at his watch, reading 10:02 on its outer face. "That gives us about ninety-five minutes, or nine and a half hours in Evermore Standard Time."

"We don't have much time."

"Yes, I know. I'll need to go into Evermore and start an investigation immediately. I'll start with the crime scene."

"That won't be necessary, Mmorpg," said the man in white.

"Why not?"

"We're bringing in someone else to conduct the investigation on the ground - a former detective with the VPD."

"Why did he leave the force, drugs?" asked Mmorpg.

"No, *she* was expelled five years ago after she lost it on the way to a homicide. She saw a group of kids, one of whom pointed a water pistol at her. She pulled out her gun and began shooting. Her partner tried to intervene, but he only succeeded in wounding her.

When the authorities came, they found her lying unconscious in a pool of her own blood; her entire clip had been emptied. Her partner and seven children were dead."

"Yeah, I remember hearing about that. I thought she died?"

"No, but she should have," said the man in white. "After she was stabilized, she was remanded to psychiatric care and released last year."

"How did she come to work for us?" asked Mmorpg suspiciously.

"She doesn't work full time with us - she only takes short-term contracts. I have contracted her services in some of my other enterprises and she has been very effective in fixing critical situations. She's perfect for this type of work – clean, proficient and ... quiet. She has the right background, the right skills and a reasonable price."

Mmorpg looked with apprehension at the director. "Is she safe?" he asked.

"She's a professional."

A thundering knock reverberated through the office door, causing Mmorpg to leap out of his seat in surprise. There were three more knocks, each more cold and lifeless than the one before. Mmorpg held his breath as a shadow slipped underneath the door. The dulled sound of deep breaths came the other side. The hairs on Mmorpg's neck stood on end.

"Good," said the smiling director. "She's here."

- CHAPTER THREE -

THE WOMAN IN BLACK

"Enter," called the director to the figure behind the door. A woman entered. She wore black combat boots, black cargo pants and a black shirt. She was covered by a long black duster that reached down to her ankles. Her dark hair, short and disheveled, hung over her eyes. Upon her left lapel there was a round pin adorned with a red maple leaf inside a blue ring. Mmorpg watched her move silently to the left side of the room. She waited there with her eyes glued to the floor, standing in profile.

"I'm glad that you could come on such short notice," said the director. "May I take your coat?"

The woman in black said nothing, but relented, removing her coat and tossing it to the director, still staring at the floor. Mmorpg noticed her black turtleneck – it was long enough to cover her neck up to her ears and light enough to be suitable for strenuous exercise. He lowered his eyes, becoming more worried as his gaze descended. Her physique was certainly strong, at the level of an elite athlete in its superb shape and form. But her hands disturbed him. Her fists were clenched so tightly that they had turned ghostly white, devoid of circulation. Every once in a while, she would catch herself and forcibly unclench her palms, only to tighten up again when her attention was occupied elsewhere.

The endless flexing of her knuckles had a rippling effect on the muscles of her body, the outline of which Mmorpg could see even through multiple layers of clothing. But she was no man. Her body was not muscle-bound, but toned like a dancer. While he had not yet gotten a good look at her face, Mmorpg felt that her body was fine enough that she could make a decent living on the covers of magazines, rather than working as a soldier of fortune.

"Since time is short," said the director, "I will cut to the matter at hand. We have had an unfortunate incident in which one of our customers has been killed. We need to conduct an investigation immediately and find out how this tragedy occurred and prevent it from happening again."

She only nodded, her eyes never leaving the floor. Mmorpg thought that it was quite peculiar that she never turned her head; she always kept the right side facing away. *Perhaps she preferred her left side,* thought Mmorpg. Some people were like that, always posing to showcase their best angle.

"As is customary with your employment," said the director, "silence on the matter is of the utmost importance. It is imperative that this investigation be strictly confidential. As such, you should avoid speaking on this matter unless it is absolutely necessary."

A sly crook appeared at the edge of the woman's mouth, as if she were privy to some private joke.

The silence of the lady in black clearly unsettled the director. Without acknowledgement, his speech became rushed and impatient. "Your usual fee will be wired to your account—"

Her left eye, icy blue, leapt from the floor to glare at her benefactor.

"The director stopped in mid-sentence, gulped and said, "Double your usual fee."

The eye did not move.

"Tri-triple," he stammered. "Triple your usual fee." The director was now shaking and beginning to sweat. He looked upon his mercenary with the greatest of caution, as if unsure whether his own safety was at risk. Her eye returned to the floor, her head never moving. She opened her mouth and a voice that chilled Mmorpg uncoiled unexpectedly from her lungs:

"Wheeerrrre?" Her cold whisper pierced the air. The lady had spoken, but not with a feminine voice like Mmorpg had expected. Rather, the voice seeped out like a harsh whisper that had been dragged from her throat. The expulsion of breath pushing over her teeth carried her faint word across the room.

The tone of her voice chilled Mmorpg's spine, immediately putting him ill at ease. The director's mouth hung open, unable to summon the courage to move in response. The lady's blue eye shot up from the floor and glared violently at her contractors, while she waited impatiently for an answer. Her eyebrow arched harshly down over the icy iris, shaking in repressed rage. Fighting off the panicked voices from the back of his mind, Mmorpg resisted the powerful urge to flee, drew open his mouth and pushed out an answer with whatever strength he could muster:

"The body ... is in Evermore ... it's a virtual world ... that we manage from this location."

The woman snorted in in disgust and turned towards the exit.

"Not interested," she said.

The director jumped to his feet. "But we're paying you three times your going rate."

"Not interested in searching for little kids. Get a nanny."

"You don't seem to understand," said the director. "We don't want you to capture him. We want you to kill him."

The woman in black stopped in the doorway. Mmorpg looked at the director but remained silent.

"Whoever did this bypassed all of the safeguards that we put in place in order to get legislative approval," said the director. "If this ever gets out, the government will shut us down, destroying years of research and millions of dollars of investment. So you see, the killer is evidence."

The woman turned her head. There was a twinkle in her left eye.

"There can be no evidence," said the director.

The woman grinned.

"I'm in," she said.

"Please follow me," said Mmorpg.

He led her downstairs. The director followed safely behind. The programmers working at their computers perked their heads up as the three of them entered the laboratory. As they walked past the desks to their right, Mmorpg could hear people gasping at the woman's appearance. *This was strange,* thought Mmorpg, *she was intimidating but not grotesque.*

They passed a whiteboard hanging on a wall. Upon its light glossy surface, the words were written in felt-tipped ink.

REMEMBER. Kernel: logout

Mmorpg led the others through a pair of sliding doors and into the Womb. The room was flashbulb white. The ceiling, the floor, the walls, everything was coloured white.

"*Who are they?*" she asked, nodding towards the sleeping men in white. Mmorpg could hear her struggling to push air through her windpipe.

"They are our hosts," said Mmorpg.

They led her into an office enclosed behind sliding doors made of glass, at the far end of the room.

In the middle of the office was a comfortable leather chair, a small table beside it. In the corner there was an empty hospital bed, stark and white. A pair of what appeared to be white headphones rested on top of the hospital sheets while four manacles lay open at the sides. Just ahead on the wall hung a portable whiteboard.

Mmorpg, the director and the lady in black surrounded the white bed. The dark woman kept to the edge of the room, keeping her right side flush with the wall.

"Coffee?" asked an intern as she came from behind them. The director smiled at her as he took a cup. Mmorpg shook his head. The lady in black simply ignored her. The intern waited with the pot politely.

"You'll find him here," said Mmorpg.

The lady in black looked down at the bed. It was empty. She threw Mmorpg an impatient glare.

"It'll be easier and quicker to show you once you're inside," said Mmorpg. "Time inside Evermore moves six times faster than time in the real world. An hour of exposition out here would take only ten minutes in there."

The lady in black looked at the bed.

"If you lie down then we can get started."

She didn't move.

"*I don't lie on my back*," she said.

"Then how do you sleep?" asked Mmorpg.

"*Against a wall.*"

The director turned to Mmorpg. "Can we prop it up against the wall?"

"It's a hospital bed, we can do anything with it."

The director handed his coffee to the intern while Mmorpg hit a switch on the side of the bed. With a mechanical whirl, the bed pulled itself up into an upright sitting position. The director and Mmorpg then moved the bed over to the wall. All the while, the lady in black kept her right side to the white wall.

"Your back is to the wall," said Mmorpg. "Will that work?"

The woman took one look at the shackles. "*No bonds,*" she demanded.

Mmorpg frowned in concern. "We usually don't require the restraints," he offered, "but we have no idea what you're going up against. If there is any struggle, the manacles will prevent you from hurting yourself."

"*No bonds!*" she repeated.

"Very well, we'll remove the restraints. Mmorpg reached down and unlatched the shackles. One by one, they dropped to the floor.

"Is there anything else?" asked Mmorpg.

She shook her head once, only once.

"Before you go in, I'll need a login name to enter you into the system. This will allow us to keep track of you as you move from server to server. What name would you prefer?"

The lady in black turned to face him eye to eye. A coffee mug shattered against the white-tiled floor. The intern gasped in shock, her eyes glued to the right side of the stranger's face. The director showed not the least bit of surprise, but Mmorpg stared with morbid fascination. The silky smoothness of her left cheek was paired with the grotesque monstrosity of her right. The lightness of pale beige skin was interrupted by a broad black-and-blue scar that stretched from just off the corner of her mouth to the cusp of her ear. Her beauty, long ago mutilated beyond recognition, shouted out in agony from behind her scarred shell.

"*Blue!*" came the pale voice of the dark demon before them.

CHAPTER FOUR

CROSSING THE CANAL

"Blue," said the strange frail man in front of her, "this is your key to Evermore." He pointed to the upright hospital bed. Behind him, the intern retreated with pieces of the broken mug. Other than the brown puddle staining the floor, the three of them were alone. "Please take your seat," said Mmorpg.

Blue's left eye darted to the director. The director nodded in approval.

She sat in the upright hospital bed and faced the middle of the white room. Mmorpg picked up the headphones at her side and held them in front of her face.

"These are dermals. They fit over your temples and connect your mind to Evermore. They serve as both receivers and transmitters, able to receive the electro-synaptic images created by your brain as they rattle around your cortex, while simultaneously altering the subconscious imaging in your mind through low-intensity ultrasound radiation."

Blue ignored the prattle. It was a waste of her valuable time. The strange frail man looked at her with an arch to his brow. He had expected a response. She said nothing.

"It'll be more clear in a minute," said Mmorpg with nervous

discomfort. "Put these on." He handed her the headphones like a mother passing a newborn. Blue wondered if his bones would break like a chicken's.

Her glare moved to the headphones in her hand. *"How do I get out?"* she asked.

The frail man motioned to the words written on the whiteboard.

REMEMBER. Kernel: logout

"Normally," said the frail man, "you would simply call the kernel and say …"

"…*logout,*" Blue finished impatiently.

"Right," said Mmorpg. "But to prevent the killer from escaping, we've disabled the logout function. So don't use it."

"So I can't leave?"

"Not until we find the killer."

"Will I feel pain?" Blue's pulse quickened in anticipation.

"Why yes. While our security protocols prevent harm from coming to our clients, we leave the full range of sensations intact, including pain. It's purely cosmetic though. We have found that without it people are unable to suspend their disbelief. When they stub their toe and they feel nothing, their mind won't allow them to accept the illusion."

"How do you want me to kill him?"

"When you log into Evermore," said Mmorpg, "we will assign you a Beretta 9mm. This weapon is not lethal in Evermore. When you shoot someone with it, it'll just knock the wind out of them."

"Only the sovereign can authorize a lethal firearm inside Evermore," said the frail man. "He'll be expecting you."

"The sovereign?" asked Blue.

"The chosen leader of Evermore," said the director. "They have government in there too."

Grunting in displeasure, Blue placed the headphones on her temples and leaned back into the bed.

In front of Blue, the director picked up his cellphone, dialled a number and put the phone to his ear.

"Sovereign Klein," said the man in white. "She's on her way in now. She has been appraised of the situation." Continuing his message, the director turned and left the room. Blue looked back to Mmorpg.

"What you're going to feel is a slight tingling in your temples," said Mmorpg. "Don't worry; it won't hurt, it will just feel like a limb that has fallen asleep. The tingling will spread to your face, then your arms and then the rest of your body. It is only your body becoming numb to all external stimuli, allowing you to become more fully immersed in your subconscious state." The tingling progressed exactly as Mmorpg said it would, starting at her temples and gradually moving down to her feet.

"Now that your body is numb, you will find yourself slowly drifting off to sleep." But Blue did not fall asleep. Her eyes fixated on the sleeping men in white outside the office. They were defenceless, vulnerable to any attack. She could see the cable coming from her headphones stretching to a plug in the floor, allowing whoever was at the other end of the line to be privy to her thoughts and feelings. She fought the blurring white creeping in from the corners of her vision, resisting the oncoming dream state. Her fists clenched in self-defence.

Mmorpg, alarmed by her tension, drew closer and spoke in a hushed tone.

"Some people have a tough time entering Evermore because they have difficulty relaxing. We find that it sometimes helps if the person holds an object that they're attached to, like a necklace or a ring. The younger ones typically use dolls. Do you have anything like this?"

Blue nodded. She reached underneath her pant leg and pulled out a handgun.

Mmorpg jumped back in fear.

"*Don't worry,*" said Blue. "*Safety on.*"

Blue sat back in her seat and stroked the handle of her gun. Gradually her twitching ebbed and her muscles relaxed. The whiteness of the room blurred and enveloped her mind.

And then there was nothing, just a wall of light before her eyes. Her mind drifted, drifted away to a far-off place. A field. A field full of lush savannah grass, untouched and unspoiled. She was running through the field, the tall grass reaching up to her waist. She was happy, running towards something that brought her joy - a person perhaps. But although she looked as far as she could, she could see nothing ahead, just endless savannah over rolling foothills. The elation turned to uneasiness and then to dread. She was not running towards something, she realized, she was running away from something - something horrible, something dreadful, something that brought terror to one half of her heart and rapture to the other. She stopped, turning around to face her pursuer. A two-story silver condominium sped through the grass towards her. With every step she took, it came closer. Too soon, it was on top of her and her vision blurred again.

Her mind refocused and she found herself once again encased in white light. She was standing in a room with mirrors for walls. She looked into one of the walls and her reflection looked back. Beyond her reflection were more copies, stretching on into infinity.

But the figures that faced her were not her own. They had luxurious straight hair that stretched to their knees. They wore a fine pink dress that recalled the glory days of Camelot and Jackie O. Their hands were manicured and their toes had received a pedicure. Their skin was well moisturized and tanned. The reflections were the picturesque vision of domesticity.

This was not her. She looked down at her torso and found soft hands stroking a pink dress.

Blue drew her hand to her face. The black and blue scar was gone, replaced by soft supple skin and a striking cheekbone.

"WHAT HAVE YOU DONE TO ME?" The scream surprised Blue for her harsh whisper had been replaced with a soft and scintillating melody. This only enraged her further.

"I NEED MY SCARS. I NEED MY PAIN. THEY'RE MINE! I'VE EARNED THEM. YOU CAN'T TAKE THEM AWAY FROM ME!" Her yelling had reached a feverish pitch - unable to mimic her former voice, she had settled on an increasingly rising shrill to make her point. She pummelled the mirror with her fists. Shattered glass flew everywhere, scratching her perfect face, tearing her pretty dress into tatters and cutting deep into her sandalled feet. Ideal no more, she was covered in the malice of silicon and sweat.

A ghost floated through the cracked glass wall. Blue stepped back at the sight of Mmorpg.

"Stop, stop, stop, stop," said Mmorpg.

"GIVE ME BACK MY PAIN!" screamed Blue.

"All right," answered Mmorpg. "Just calm down and focus on this." He reached up to his temples and pulled an image from his head. It was a memory of Blue as she once was - dressed in black and covered in scars. Her throat aching, Blue reached out and caressed the image. Beside her the shards of the mirror rose from the ground and out of her body. They rejoined the mirror, rebuilding it just outside her sight. She turned back towards the mirror and looked again at her reflection. But now instead of a domestic homemaker, she faced her true self, complete with scars, bruises, deep wounds and a black duster coat.

"I should have explained," said Mmorpg. "I didn't think you'd react the way you did."

"What happened?"

"This is the Canal. We use it to introduce new users to the way things work in Evermore before they connect to the network. It's sort of like a tutorial. One of the first things that the Canal does is to construct your avatar, your virtual appearance inside Evermore. It does so by pulling your ideal self-image from your subconscious, ensuring that your form in Evermore is a more accurate representation of your inner self than the arbitrary randomness of your physical body. This process is repeated every time you enter Evermore, even if you don't enter through the Canal. No matter what, Evermore will show you the person that you truly want to be."

"No, not how computers work. Your fault. You made me like that."

"Evermore is not a computer. It is a network of shared dreams. This network is constructed and presented to you by three integrated systems: the kernel, the host and your subconscious."

Mmorpg stepped back from Blue as the hall of mirrors melted away. Blue found herself sitting back in the laboratory. The programmers and technicians went about their day without paying her the slightest bit of attention. That was very odd. Nobody ever ignored her. Mmorpg waved his hand and the room rushed past her and then stopped. Blue was standing in front of a large bank of computers without screens. These servers hummed with activity.

"The first system, the kernel, is run centrally from our laboratory. Operating from these servers, the kernel controls all of the rules in Evermore."

"*Rules?*"

"All of the things that can and can not be done in Evermore. How dreams are shared back and forth. How information is stored in the mind. How objects are defined and the physics that they must follow, all of these operations are defined in the kernel."

"*Physics? Like gravity?*"

"Yes."

"*You control gravity?*"

"No, not exactly." Blue watched the bank of servers melt away in front of her. It was replaced by blackness interspersed with small glowing lights. They were floating in outer space.

"The kernel defines objects, formulas, functions, it does not define the data that fills them."

"*Data?*" asked Blue.

"Let's take gravity for example," said Mmorpg. Behind him a reproduction of the solar system appeared. "We define gravity in Evermore using Newton's Law of Universal Gravitation which is $F=G*(m1*m2)/(d^2)$."

The exact same formula appeared in front of Mmorpg as he spoke. Behind him, the solar system enlarged to focus on the sun and the planet Earth.

"Now in reality, G is the Gravitational Constant, m1 is the mass of the first object, m2 is the mass of the second object and d is the distance between them. You can use it to predict the movement of planets around a sun or to predict the gravitational force of a person on earth. In Evermore, this formula is used to predict the gravitational attraction between any two objects inside a specific zone. But in order to make this calculation, you need values for the variables G, m1, m2 and d. The kernel doesn't have this information, all it provides is the formula. The rest must be filled in by the host."

Blue glared at the thin man.

Mmorpg paused awkwardly, unsure whether or not to continue. After a moment, he again found his courage.

"The host is the second system. The hosts take the data structures and formulas that the kernel provides and fills them with the data needed to construct a virtual world."

"*Hosts? More computers?*"

"No, not computers," said Mmorpg. "We needed something with far greater storage capacity."

Blue felt the sensation of falling. The solar system flew up and out of view. From below, the white room rose up to her feet. Recovering from the perspective shift, Blue looked around the room. Just like before, the room was full of sleeping men. Mmorpg appeared beside the head of one.

"In our daily lives, we use but a fraction of the human brain." Mmorpg motioned down to the skull of the sleeping man and Blue could see a three-dimensional pie chart overlap his skull. It notified her that twelve percent of his brain was currently in use. The remaining eighty-eight percent was listed as surplus.

"Hosts, such as the ones in this room, use their excess capacity while they sleep to construct virtual spaces that we call zones."

A three-dimensional video expanded out from the sleeping man's skull and filled the room. Blue was standing in a typical metropolitan city. Skyscrapers lined the sky, the streets were filled with pedestrians and noise filled every inch of her ear canal. The only thing out of place was the city, which was only about three square city blocks wide. Blue could see the streets and the buildings but beyond them was nothingness. One of the pedestrians walked towards the edge of the zone. Blissfully unaware, the pedestrian walked straight into the nothingness and disappeared. Beyond the zone's borders, Blue could make out the smeared afterimage of the girl as she continued walking.

"These zones are then linked together automatically by the kernel to form the world of Evermore."

The sleeping men in white rose up from the asphalt. From each one's mind, a different part of the city grew and expanded into view. More zones fell from the sky, landing with the titanic roar of thunder as they connected with their predecessors. Blue watched the city build itself like a jigsaw puzzle. Each piece had its place, perfectly lining up with its neighbours, only a thin red line dividing them. In the next zone, Blue could see the pedestrian who had disappeared. She was still walking through the city, unaware that she had crossed any special border.

"*So this is Evermore,*" said Blue. "*Not impressed.*"

"No, this is only a demonstration, but Evermore works in exactly the same way. The world is pieced together by a series of zones constructed by sleeping hosts. The hosts provide the data for each zone using the power of their own imagination. In the case of the Canal, Carlos, one of our employees, is hosting this particular instance. Returning to our gravity example, remember that the kernel only provides the correct formula: $F=G*(m1*m2)/(d^2)$. It is the host that provides the variables. To simulate earth's gravitational pull, the hosts will usually create a dummy variable far below the zone's floor to represent the earth's centre of mass. In the canal, I've set up the data for everything in this zone with one exception - your mass. How much do you weigh?"

Blue grunted.

"Fine," said Mmorpg. "Let's see what happens when the host makes your mass equal to the planet earth. Carlos if you would be so kind." Mmorpg snapped his fingers.

Blue heard large cracking noises all around her. She looked up. Every object from every direction was being pulled towards her. The skyscrapers bent over backwards to reach her. The street ripped itself into pieces and rolled toward her. Glass shattered everywhere and flew at Blue like daggers. The ground itself bent and stretched in her direction. The entire universe was collapsing in on the lady in black. But she did not flinch. She stood straight up and glared at the bending world like she was challenging the oncoming maelstrom of carnage.

Mmorpg snapped his fingers again and they were standing on top of a mountain. Standing at the edge, Blue could see the cliff face stretch down for over a thousand feet.

"*If the hosts can do anything, then what do you need me for?*" asked Blue. "*Just have them drop a cage on him.*"

"Because the hosts cannot see him," said Mmorpg. "The hosts can only create and store data using the objects provided by the kernel. They cannot themselves experience the environment that this data creates."

"*That doesn't make sense.*"

"How do you turn a feeling into a variable? How you represent a sensation using a formula? As an example, let's go back to gravity." Mmorpg snapped his fingers and a gust of wind flung Blue off the mountain. She fell quickly down the cliff face. The rising air pushed against her face. Her eyes, struggling to stay open, gushed tears from the assault. Deep inside, Blue could feel the pounding in her chest as the ground rushed up to meet her. Blue hit the valley floor and bounced. She bounced a few more times, the knot twisting in her stomach as the world spun around. She came to stop unharmed. Blue touched the ground and was surprised that it felt like foam.

Mmorpg floated above her. "Can you write me an equation to mimic the sensation of falling? Can you represent the fear of death with only 1's and 0's? No, you can't, and therein lies the problem. We can't simulate human sensation using electronic means. The closest that we've ever come is computer graphics and surround sound. But even with those, the human mind realizes that it's a fake. It rejects the illusion and refuses to suspend its disbelief. We cannot trick the human mind."

Mmorpg snapped his fingers again. They were back in the middle of the city. Around them walked scores of pedestrians.

"So we don't try. Instead, we have the user, the third and final system, interpret the data received by the host using their own subconscious. Our own minds are full of memories, records of sensations that can be drawn upon. These memories are used to interpret the data that you receive from the host to construct the world around you. With their consent, you can see their perspective by using purple lens."

Blue looked at a passing pedestrian and wondered, *Purple lens?* Instantly, her vision tinted purple and zoomed into the pedestrian's head. Blue found herself on the same city street, but everything was different. The skyscrapers were replaced by large gothic structures teaming with gargoyles. The pedestrians were now dressed in garb from the Roaring Twenties.

Blue looked to another pedestrian. *Is this purple lens?* She zoomed into his mind. Now the city looked futuristic with green crystal obelisks for towers and white jumpsuit-clad pedestrians. Every time that Blue thought about purple lens, she would jump into the mind of the person she was looking at. Each time the streets, buildings and people would always be in the same place, but everything else about them would be different.

"Thus everything that you will experience in Evermore,

everything that you see, touch and hear, is a creation of your own mind. Now please note that due to its dependence on your own memories, the world that you see will be unique. This is true for each and every individual who connects to Evermore, even though you all share the same physical space on the virtual landscape. It is a world pieced together by your imagination, a place where your dreams literally become reality."

Mmorpg snapped his fingers and they returned to the white room.

"Do you understand now how it works?"

"Yeah. Kernel makes rules, host makes world and the user sees it all." A slight smile drew upon Blue's face. *"So if they do everything, then what good are you?"* she asked.

Mmorpg smiled. "Kernel: activate god mode," he said.

Blue heard a strange voice. "God mode activated," it said.

Without hesitation, Mmorpg drew a cube with his two index fingers. The cube flashed green as he grabbed the sides with his palms. He twisted the cube to the left.

The world twisted with it. Blue was thrown against the left wall with a painful crunch. Mmorpg twisted the cube to the right. The world tilted to the right and Blue fell towards the right wall. She put out a hand to grab one of the beds as she tumbled past. Her hand caught the hair of the man sleeping in the bed. She held tight, hanging ten metres above the right wall.

Mmorpg turned the cube upside down.

Gravity reversed itself yet again. Blue felt her weight pulled towards the ceiling. She held on to the sleeping man's hair but the strain was simply too much for the bed. It's bolts ripped loose from the floor, flinging Blue to the ceiling with the bed landing right on top of her. Blue threw off the bed and coughed up dust. She started to throw a growl at Mmorpg but then noticed that he was shaking the flashing green cube.

The zone rumbled around in response. Plaster fell from the floor, beds ripped away from their bolts and tumbled end over end across the run. Blue struggled to maintain her footing but she made a beeline for Mmorpg. She was going to put an end to this right now.

Blue leapt for his throat, eager to rip it to pieces. But to her surprise, she passed right through him. Mmorpg stopped shaking the cube and pulled his hands away from its sides. The cube disappeared and the canal came to a stop resting on its ceiling.

"You can't hurt me here. I am the administrator of Evermore. I and I alone can alter the rules managed by the kernel. I am responsible for making sure that everything works, that all of the zones link together properly in the Downtown Core, that the objects and functions provided by the kernel are free of bugs and that the user experience is as seamless as possible. To this end, I am free to manipulate all of the zones in whatever manner I deem necessary. I can spin them, I can shake them, I can cut and rebuild their links to other zones. We call it god mode and I'm the only one authorized to use it. Kernel: deactivate god mode."

"God mode deactivated," said the kernel.

"But these powers have a cost. As the administrator, I am unable to interact with any of the objects placed inside the zones. Gravity doesn't affect me, I pass through objects like a ghost."

Blue picked herself off the ground. Dust and pieces of drywall fell from her shoulders.

"That is why we need you," said Mmorpg. "We need someone capable of carrying out the killing blow. But I can help you. If you can trap the killer alone inside one of the zones, I can isolate it from the other zones by cutting off its links. He won't be able to escape and you'll be able to kill him without any witnesses."

"*Except for you,*" said Blue.

"Except for me," agreed Mmorpg. "Are you ready for this?"

"*Don't worry about me,*" said Blue. "*I don't miss.*"

Mmorpg disappeared and the room began to melt away. Soon enough, Blue found herself alone in a endless room of white. There were no walls. There were no objects. Blue was alone.

But soon enough the room began to change. The white before her blurred away. Indistinct shapes appeared around her but she could not make them out. Her eyes narrowed in concentration, trying to bring the world around her into focus. As her vision cleared, she found herself in a square room.

The walls were gray, with the exception of a thick silver line jutting in peaks and valleys around the room. Every once in a while, the moving line would halt its progress to morph into a small line of text. Blue looked closer at the moving line. "Loading. Please wait," it printed. Blue turned her attention towards the doorway.

The only way out of the gray room was a revolving glass door. The door was sterile, leading to an unknown destination hidden by a powerful light pouring through the translucent glass. However, the door was motionless, blocking her exit. As she approached it, computer text appeared a foot in front of her eyes. The text was in green Arial font and seemed to be pulled directly off a computer screen that hung mere inches from her face. It read:

Login Name: Blue
Status: Guest
Registration Key: TLG0003
Searching For Record ...

No matter where she turned her head or focused her eyes, the message remained firmly planted in the very centre of her vision, making it impossible to ignore. After a pause, the message changed to navy text:

Record found.
Welcome to Evermore.

The revolving door began to spin, inviting her to exit. She approached the door with caution, wary of what might lie beyond, when she heard a noise suddenly behind her. Wheeling around, she found a well-dressed businessman moving towards the doorway. He stopped for a moment, focused on something that Blue could not see and then again moved towards her. Finding his way blocked, he threw Blue an impetuous glare.

Blue threw the suited man through the glass doorway. The revolving door collapsed into a tangled mess of glass and steel. Blue stepped through the debris and over the unconscious man. She had entered Evermore - the place that would serve as her home for the next few hours.

CHAPTER FIVE

THE CONSORTIUM

Blue found herself in the middle of an immaculate urban park. The flat grasslands stretched away from her in all directions until they collided with the imposing towers of the cityscape a hundred metres away. A message popped up in front of her face.

Welcome to Market Square. The Centre of the Downtown Core.

Have a nice day.

Turning around, Blue saw a shallow pond in the shape of an equilateral triangle in the centre of the park. Three narrow paths stretched away from its corners. Each of these paths led to a grand building at the edge of the park about a hundred metres away. The tall building to the west was constructed of square white blocks, each floor set at a slight angle to the one below, giving the impression of a massive corkscrew twisting into the sky. To the east stood a square building constructed entirely of falling water. To the north, a cloud of mist hovered hundreds of feet above the square. The far edge of the park connected these three buildings to form a hexagon. Along this border, Market Square collided with the

Downtown Core, which sprawled out from the park in concentric hexagonal grids.

At the centre of the park, a two-story silver building rose out of the pond. Upon its front rested the crushed remains of a revolving door. Upon this square base stood a doubleclock tower. High above the demolished entryway, the two sets of hands upon its face declared two different times. The white inner hands read 1232 hours. The outer black hands read 10:05. To the right of the building, a golden statue of a balding, portly man rested on the surface of the pond. The statue's finger was lifted into the air as if making a dramatic point, but he said nothing. Blue read the inscription on the plaque bolted into the statue's base.

Asa

First Sovereign of Evermore

There were no other statues in Market Square. The golden figure stood alone and proud, basking in his solitary glory. Blue wondered, only for a moment, what the figure was talking about.

The gold statue moved with an aura of grace and began to speak: "I humbly accept the Consortium's nomination to serve as the first Sovereign of Evermore. I will endeavour to carry out the responsibilities of this office with courage, dignity and honour, to protect our values of peace, prosperity and order. As my first act as sovereign, I would like to introduce a comprehensive reform package to the proposed constitution. For section 24, subsection 3, paragraph ..."

Blue felt an unwelcome presence behind her. She spun on her heels, ready to knock the intruder to the ground, but her arms passed through him like a ghost.

"Wait," yelled the ghost, "it's me. It's Mmorpg." Blue paused. Mmorpg's appearance was radically different. Instead of his pale and pasty frame, she saw before her an attractive Hispanic male in his mid-twenties. She cast a doubtful glance at the dreamweaver.

"*What are you doing here?*" she asked forcefully.

He held his hands up in surrender. "I've taken the form of my avatar to come here and guide you. I'm not needed at my normal duties for a couple of hours."

"I don't need help. I need a gun."

"It's in the holster on your hip."

Blue looked down and sure enough, there was a pistol holstered on her hip. She drew the weapon and examined it. It was a Beretta 92F - a solid professional weapon. She ejected the magazine and thumbed a round into her palm, then held it up for a closer look. The letter "O" was etched upon its side. Blue loaded the round back into the magazine, slapped the magazine back into the gun, and re-holstered the pistol at her hip.

"Good. Now stay out of my way."

"You know nothing of this world," said Mmorpg nervously. "I do. I built it. I know everything about it."

"The only thing I need to know is where to find the target."

Blue heard something rumble. She turned and saw the rubble from the revolving door rolling back towards the entrance. She was surprised. She didn't like surprises.

Mmorpg stole a glance at the debris as it jumped up into the air.

"You don't know what it's doing, do you?" said Mmorpg.

Blue watched as the doorway began to repair itself. The twisted metal frame bent back into shape, the glass shards reformed into panes and the broken chunks of concrete fused together into complete blocks. The revolving doorway had been rebuilt, good as new. Blue turned to Mmorpg and found him smiling.

"The hosts don't like their zones to be trifled with."

"I thought they couldn't see."

"They don't. They feel the change in the data that defines the zone. Their zones are like extensions of their psyches. Damage one part and the host will rebuild it. Make it whole again.

"How long does it take?"

"Every host is different. It depends on their personality. For the Downtown Core, we hire hosts that are extremely obsessive compulsive. We find that they are far quicker in responding to errors, to make sure that all flaws are washed away. As for the Underground, we have no control over the hosts there. Some will rebuild in minutes, others will simply let the damage accumulate until the zone is impassable. It's the wild west down there."

Blue stared at the reconstructed entranceway. In front of it, the suited man picked himself off the ground and brushed off his clothes. Avoiding eye contact with Blue, he walked towards the skyscrapers surrounding the park.

"Now doesn't that seem like something you need to know?"

Blue flared her nostrils, turned and started to walk away.

"*Not important.*"

"Where are you going?" asked Mmorpg.

"*To the sovereign, so I can kill.*"

"But do you know where he is?"

Blue stopped. Her silence gave the Mmorpg his answer.

"Is that information important?"

Blue snorted and turned back towards Mmorpg.

"*Fine. Where?*" she said impatiently.

"Right behind you," replied Mmorpg. Blue turned around and saw at the pond's' northern tip a glass box similar to a telephone booth, but without logos or brands, or for that matter steel.

"And up," Mmorpg added. Blue looked up to a cloud far above them.

Mmorpg led her into the elevator. As the doors closed, an indistinct face moulded itself out of the glass frame. "Welcome to the Consortium," it said in a cheerful voice. "To what purpose do we owe the pleasure of your company?"

"We wish to see the sovereign," said Mmorpg. "We have an appointment."

"Very well," replied the voice. "Access granted. Have a pleasant day." Blue had expected the elevator to move upwards, but instead she found that it remained planted firmly to the ground while she and Mmorpg rose into the air. They floated slowly at first and then accelerated. As they approached the cloud, Blue looked down to see a menagerie of glass superstructures surrounding the square. Looking again at the eastern part of the square, Blue's attention was caught by the building made of falling water. Looking closer, she saw that the building was continually reformed by a central geyser shaping the walls out of water. "That's the Xchange," Mmorpg narrated. "It's the financial market of Evermore - the largest stock exchange in the world, real or virtual."

They rose through the bottom of the cloud, feeling the cool wet air condense on their cheeks. The cloud dissipated, revealing a large greeting room complete with portraits, interactive displays and even a gift shop. Beneath them, cloud vapour solidified into ice and they were able to stand and walk around. A portrait of a middle-aged gentleman with short blond hair and a trim beard caught Blue's attention. As she looked, an annoying voice popped into her head.

"For more information, use yellow lens. For more information, use yellow lens."

How do you shut him up?, Blue thought, *and what does yellow lens do?* Instantly, her field of vision took on an amber hue. Unimportant objects blurred into the background. The face in the portrait jumped out of the painting towards her, rendering its features in more precise detail.

The annoying voice returned with even more sickening exuberance. "Thank you for using yellow lens. The second and current Sovereign of the Evermore Consortium, Richard Klein, first rose to prominence as the leader of a series of demonstrations known as Rouge Revolution. Unifying a diverse coalition of factions from the Underground, Klein brought down the governing Corporate Coalition and enacted equality of rights for all citizens of Evermore. Subscriber or non-subscriber, corporation or individual, all now had representation in the renewed Consortium. The Emancipation of Equality was a key turning point in the development of ..." As soon as she lost interest, the voiceover stopped and the amber hue dissipated.

A man in a brown cloak marched into the room, his arms folded across his chest and his head lowered. As he walked, the muffled sound of clinking chains could be heard. With a hood pulled over his head, Blue could see only a chrome-covered jaw as the man approached.

"Good morning," said Mmorpg. "How fares the safety of the realm?"

"It is quiet," said the cloaked figure as he turned his head towards Blue, "let us hope it stays that way". He looked down at Blue's right hip. "My apologies miss, but you must relinquish that firearm if you wish to enter."

She did not move. The cloaked figure raised his head and met Blue's defiant stare. His green eyes, however, did not flinch. Blue saw a resolve there that matched her own. There was no fear or anger in his pupils. There was only contemplation and peace. He was more than a match for her and they both knew it. With reluctance, she handed over her pistol.

"Please come this way, I will take you to the balcony," said the cloaked figure. Blue and Mmorpg followed him through a grand white hall supported by pillars reminiscent of early Greece and modern America. They walked up a grand staircase carved with images and text from the founding myths and legends of Evermore. From her cursed yellow lens, Blue learned that she was looking at a carver's rendition of Hiru's victory over Beowulf. According to the artist, this victory established the first signs of order during middle acts of Evermore's Second Age.

They came upon a balcony overlooking a great chamber below. The balcony was adorned with plush red carpet and brass railings, giving them an unobstructed view of the action. In the house, the representatives were engaged in a fierce debate. They sat on utilitarian square podiums that extended out of the floor. It appeared that each member's podium was at a different height. Their suits were tinted in two different colours, red on the left and blue on the right. Peering down into the chamber, Blue spotted a woman in a red suit speaking to the rest of the assembly. She was younger than most of the Consortium and was very pretty: tan skin, straight black hair and narrow brown eyes hidden behind round spectacles. She spoke with a flustered tone.

"—With a deficit due to the overly optimistic projections of growth by the previous government. These miscalculations were exacerbated by rapid increases in government expenditures. To resolve this financial crisis and ensure that the fiscal health of Evermore remains secure, the following programs will be cut or postponed indefinitely: the JTF project-" Roars of disapproval came from the right side of the chamber. "-the Bedrock implementation project, legislative expansion into the Underground and all research into the intellectual property initiative known as R3X." The chamber was becoming raucous, a chorus of "Vendu, vendu" coming from the right. The speaker's seat was slowly but steadily sinking towards to the floor, as were those of her colleagues on the left. The blue seats, however, were rising towards the ceiling, none faster than that of a man in the front whose features matched the statue Blue had seen outside. When she briefly wondered who he might be, the word "Asa" appeared in yellow text above his head. Beside him, and rising just a touch slower, was a young man in a dark suit with a sombre look upon his face.

Blue's attention returned to the speaker as she finished her speech. Her conclusion was blunt, lacking in the subtlety and manoeuvring common to her profession. Her speech was jeered mercilessly from the right, interspersed with cries of "Shame" and calls for her resignation. However, the left side of the chamber applauded in support, led by a beaming young woman of Indian descent and British bearing in the back row. The woman, identified as "Jie" by yellow text, smiled meekly to her supporters and returned to her seat.

Speaker after speaker stood up before the chamber and gave his or her thoughts - first from the right and then from the left. With each passing speaker, the blues grew stronger and bolder with their attacks. The red defence became more agitated and confused, unable to blunt the momentum of the rising right.

Finally, Asa rose to speak before the chamber. The members gasped in both excitement and concern. His podium, now towering above the assembly, moved forward and faced both his allies and his enemies.

With a glint in his eye, he raised his hands and addressed his now captive audience. "Dear friends and colleagues. It is an honour to speak here before you, today of all days. A man's greatest wish is that his words and deeds may influence those around him, and in some small way influence the course of events for the better. I have been silent, resting my tired mind and letting a new generation of leaders," he motioned to the red faction, "have their chance to govern without interference.

"But I can remain silent no longer. For what we have seen today is no less than a betrayal of our founding principles. A step back from progress, from the pursuit of our dream of an Evermorian nation, unified not only by law and organization, but by purpose. A nation that will reflect not only our ambitions and aspirations, but our very souls. If this betrayal is allowed to continue, if we are unwilling to punish this government for its callous disregard of our needs, then the dream of Evermore is truly dead. I chose to speak today because this day is of such vital importance to the future of our land. For it is today that we will bring down this government and save our country."

He received a standing ovation, his popularity pushing the height of his podium above even the balcony where Blue and Mmorpg sat. His charismatic speech, short yet effective in highlighting the fears of many in the population, pulled scores of members in the middle of the chamber. Blue briefly wondered why the representatives in the middle were switching sides. The yellow lens was only too happy to explain with yellow pop text:

The Consortium is divided equally into three different groups. The Klein Coalition, currently in government and dressed in red, occupies the left side of the assembly. The Corporate Coalition, the official opposition, is dressed in blue and sits on the right side. In the middle sits representatives of Evermore's Internet Service Providers or ISP. In order to maintain control over the Consortium and thus pass legislation, the governing party must hold the support of more than half the members of the assembly. Likewise, the opposition must gain the support of over half the members in order to defeat the government and take power. Thus the parties are constantly seeking each others support to protect their interests. However, since the ISPs are the most divided, they usually split their support between the Klein and Corporate Coalitions who in turn compete for power.

As Blue wondered how to turn the yellow lens off, she watched the ISP representatives move one by one from the left side of the chamber to the right, their suits changing from red to blue. The party in red was on its heels, clinging to a two-seat red majority. Asa was on the verge of returning to power. The position of sovereign, the most coveted title in the land, was up for grabs.

From the middle of the red left, surrounded by his supporters, the man from the portrait, Richard Klein, rose to speak.

"Dear friends, today is indeed an important day. For today is the day we must decide between two visions of Evermore: the myths of the Corporate Coalition, or the reality of our present situation.

What my good friend Asa sees as a dream, I see as a nightmare. The quest for a singular consciousness that will somehow define the varied nature of millions of people, each with different needs, dreams and ambitions, will lead only to despair and frustration. There will be a sizeable minority within Evermore who can not and will not conform to this idealized version of our state. Rather than pulling our so-called 'nation' together, it will rip our country apart. The 'dream' of Evermore is not fusion, it is not unity, but the acceptance of the strange multiplicity of peoples who have chosen to make Evermore their home. They fled a world that could not appreciate and understand them. They have fled ideology, they have fled uniformity, they have fled domination. In their place they have chosen heterogeneity, hybridity and acceptance.

"Dear friends, my predecessor is correct. Today is indeed a very important day. For it is today that we choose to embrace the future, rather than long for the past. It is today that we let go our monistic fantasies and accept our humble reality. It is today that we celebrate the country we have, rather than pine for the nation we want. For only then can our people find liberty and justice – as friends, as brothers and as equals. Thank you."

As he returned to his seat, the chamber filled with a deafening roar that could not be stilled for ten minutes. While he had spoken, Klein's clear arguments and rhetoric raised his seat as they lowered Asa's. For a while they were neck and neck, but Klein's conclusion powered him towards the ceiling as Asa was reduced back towards the blue throng. The fence-sitting ISPs returned to the fold and Klein's coalition was secure for another day. Filled with the sounds of both acclaim and criticism, the chamber slowly began to empty. The cloaked figure led Mmorpg and Blue out of gallery. They followed him down the hall and into a beautiful wooden office.

"Please come in and have a seat," said Klein, gesturing to two oak chairs sitting in front of his wide birch desk. The cloaked figure retreated to the darkness of the corner. The office, in contrast to the ice that defined the rest of the building, was comprised entirely of wood. "I prefer the feel of wood," said Klein. "It just seems so much more natural, don't you think?"

"I'm afraid that we don't have much time, Sovereign Klein," said Mmorpg.

"Yes, I've received your communiqué, Mr. Mmorpg. I am well aware of the situation. Desperate times call for drastic measures."

Klein eyed Blue from head to toe. "So you're the urban mercenary."

She nodded.

"I can't stress to you enough the importance of your task. If word of this murder were to leak out, it would cause the populace to panic and further pressure the Consortium to disenfranchise the Underground community. You must accomplish your task with efficiency, but also with discretion. There are many here who would use such a situation for their own advantage. You must be careful. The crime scene has been sealed off and will only be visible to the two of you. Use your green lens; the arrow will lead you there. Do not speak to anyone about the facts of this case or divulge this information unnecessarily."

"Yes sir," replied Mmorpg.

"I want you to work with *Arthur* on this assignment," said Klein.

"Whatever for?" Mmorpg demanded.

"He knows more about Evermore than anyone else. He has studied every group, every server, every trend. He knows this place inside and out."

"True, but in an attempt to destroy this country! He doesn't care about our problems. He has dedicated his life to shutting this place down. If Evermore collapsed, I can't think of anyone else who would be happier."

"Perhaps, but the information that he has accumulated will be invaluable in finding the perpetrator and bringing an end to this crisis as quickly as possible."

"Why would he help us? How could we trust him to not use the situation to his advantage? How can we ensure that he is under control?"

"By giving him this," said Klein, handing an envelope to Blue. Mmorpg instinctively reached for it, then drew back as the letter passed through his incorporeal form. Blue took the letter and deposited it inside her coat, the thick seal of the Sovereign of Evermore brushing her fingertips. "Deliver that to him if he gives you any opposition. It is for his eyes only."

"What is it?" asked Mmorpg impatiently. He began to pace.

"A grant to cover all of his research for the next five years."

"What if that's not enough?" asked Mmorpg.

"Then you will give him whatever he wants," said Klein.

"Fat chance."

Sovereign Klein sighed. "Mmorpg. We have a killer stalking our shores. Every moment we waste is another moment in which he can kill again. It is my opinion, and thus the opinion of the people of Evermore, that Arthur's help is essential in finding the killer. If you are unable to put your ego aside, then perhaps we should speak to your director."

Mmorpg's shoulders slumped in resignation. "Fine," he said. "We'll bring him on board."

Klein settled back into his chair, sighing. With a forlorn look he asked Mmorpg, "Do you think she suffered at all?"

Mmorpg closed his eyes and looked towards the ground. "I don't think so, but I can't be sure."

"I thought that your security protocols protected against this sort of tragedy," said Klein, a hint of anger edging into his voice.

The eyes of the dreamweaver narrowed. "If someone found a way through my protocols, we will find out how they did it and plug the hole. The gate has been sealed and locked. Whoever caused this is trapped inside the Underground. More than likely, he is one of your supporters."

"That is possible. Then it is best for both of us to find the person responsible, and quickly." Klein pulled a photo from his desk and looked at the picture of the victim. It was a little girl no more than eight years of age. "A life not yet begun, unable to defend herself," mused the sovereign, "destroyed by those who should be protecting her." Klein sighed and rubbed his temples. He looked up to Blue and Mmorpg.

"Will there be anything else?"

Blue turned her head and glared at the cloaked figure.

The cloaked figure reached inside his coat, pulled out the Beretta and placed it on the table.

Klein didn't move. "Ah yes," he said, "you want the right to kill my citizens, a right that not even the striders possess."

Blue nodded.

"I've read a great deal about you." He reached into his desk and pulled out a folder. "Nine years with the VPD. Sterling service record. You were well on your way to captain. Apparently, you are also very tough." Klein pointed to her face. "Those wounds would have killed a lesser man."

Blue did not react.

"I only have one question Ms. Blue—"

"*Just Blue.*"

"So tell me, Blue. When you slaughtered those poor children like dogs in the street, did you enjoy it?"

In an instant, Blue leapt over the oak desk. As she landed beside the sovereign, her hand shot from her side like a shotgun blast and clenched tightly around Klein's throat.

Instantaneously, she felt the cold edge of a blade across her neck. Out of the corner of her eye she could see the hilt of a sword grasped by cloaked figure's metallic hand. A small chain hung from the sword hilt, its end disappearing into a small slot beneath the cloaked figure's wrist. Her eyes returned to the defiant sovereign before her.

"Be careful mercenary, striders are not to be trifled with. Especially ones as skilled as Strider Ryu."

"I am the least of my kind," said the cloaked figure.

Blue held tight.

"*They were a threat,*" she said. Despite her vice-like grip around his throat, Klein continued to speak.

"The children were unarmed, playing hockey in the street. I read that the last three cried as they begged you for their lives." Her grip tightened as the sword dug deeper into her neck.

"*You wouldn't understand.*"

Klein's eyes narrowed. "I understand enough. You are a sick, twisted psychopath, as much of a danger to my citizens as any killer. If this was any other day, I would have never let you step onto my streets. And I certainly would not give you an activated firearm. But these are not ordinary days. A killer stalks our country and must be brought to justice."

Klein picked up a pen. The top of the desk lit up, revealing an executive order embedded into its face. Klein signed his name in light at the bottom of the document.

"I, Richard Klein, Sovereign of Evermore, hereby authorize the use of lethal force by Firearm #17681375. The user bearing this firearm is to be considered armed and dangerous."

Klein looked up at Blue.

"Take your weapon and get out of my office."

Blue picked up the gun, ejected the magazine and pulled out a round. She held it up to her eyes, noticing the letter "X" etched into the bullet casing. She smiled, loaded the cartridge back into the magazine, and slapped the magazine back into the gun.

"I tolerate your presence here only because of the insistence of your benefactor and the seriousness of the crisis that we now face," said Klein. "Don't mistake my tolerance for acceptance, or my passivity for weakness. Evermore is for those who wish to start anew in peace and harmony. We have no place for predators like you. Get the job done and get out."

A tense silence fell. Blue slowly released her grip. As she did so, Strider Ryu drew back his blade, revealing a new wound for the collection of the lady of death. For the longest moment, Blue glared at the leader of the virtual world. Wearing fury upon her brow, she holstered the Beretta and walked out of the room, brushing past a white, spiky-haired individual waiting outside. Blue lived without remorse, seeking only the exhilaration of her assignment to cover the stains of a troubled mind.

CHAPTER SIX

THE GREAT GATE

Mmorpg and Blue rode the elevator down in silence. Blue's pistol, now lethal, rested in the holster on her hip, waiting to be used. Out of the corner of his eye, Mmorpg watched Blue rub the grip with her finger, salivating at its cold, serrated touch. She noticed his wandering eyes and pulled her hand away from the pistol. She kept her head low, watching the rising skyline with numb detachment as they dropped gently to the ground.

"Was that really necessary?" he asked.

"*It's always necessary,*" she said.

The elevator reached the ground and they stepped back into Market Square.

"Green lens," said Mmorpg. Before him, he saw a large green arrow leading up Malon Mall and straight through the retail district.

"*Green lens,*" Blue repeated. Mmorpg saw her irises turn a soft shade of green. From her reaction, he knew that she had also seen the arrow. Together they walked up Malon Mall.

The retail district looked like any other shopping district in any other major city. There were stores and shops of all types and varieties lined up on each side of the pedestrian mall. The only difference was that no two people would see the same assortment of stores. While a single shopper would see about a hundred shops as they walked the three blocks that made up the Malon Mall, in reality there were at least five thousand. Rather than give every business their own space, which would make the shopping district the size of a small city, the Consortium decided to have the retail outlets share the property. In other words, all the businesses occupied the same geographical space. The consumer would only see and could only enter those retail outlets that best suited his individual tastes. As Mmorpg walked down Malon Mall, he saw shops for computer programming, technology, software training and dating services. Blue saw stores dedicated to firearms, self-defence, violent films and action figures. Even if they chose to hold hands and enter the same store, they would see two completely different interiors, two different sets of sales representatives and two distinct sets of products. Malon Mall was a shopping nirvana of overlapping consumerism.

While the stores changed for each shopper, the crowd that filled the street was constant no matter the perspective. The street was packed with shoppers criss-crossing from store to store, arguing with one another and rushing to buy some collector's item that would be worthless within an hour. Blue bristled at squeezing through the crowd and being forced to touch so many people. One man swore at them as they brushed by, but ducked his head when Blue turned around with blazing fire in her eyes. When they came to the end of the district, Mmorpg passed through the last of the crowd and spread his arms out to celebrate.

"Even without a body it's nice to get some personal space. Makes you feel free again, doesn't it?" he said.

No response.

He turned around and found himself alone. "Blue?" he asked, searching the crowd. He finally spotted her looking into the window of the last store on the block, a specialty store focused on home networking supplies. He came up behind and said, "We don't have time to sight-see." But she did not move. Curious, he switched to purple lens.

Mmorpg felt his perspective forward into Blue's head. As a purple hue tinted Mmorpg's vision, the electronics storefront before him morphed into an art gallery. On the window before him, words were etched into the glass.

The Sanctity of Death, by Palette
A portrait of the symbolic rendering of conflict within the
human race.

The words faded away along with the rest of the window, the background and everything else save for three solitary figures clad in black. They stood in a triangle, staring at each other with an intensity somewhere between hate and fear. In each hand, each man had a pistol. The men kept their weapons trained on one another, ensuring that none of the three were uncovered. But every few seconds, as if in accordance with some rule, the combatants would change their targets, manoeuvring to get an uncontested shot. If they wanted to cover all their bases, they would train a gun on each of their opponents. If they were particularly afraid of one individual, they would train both guns on him alone. Round and round the Mexican stand-off went, until two unfortunate souls made the mistake of training both their guns on each other at the same time. The third did not miss his opportunity, firing both his barrels at his vulnerable opponents. His first opponent made the mistake of trying to cover the unmarked man as he leapt backwards away from danger. The bullets from three barrels hit him square in the chest, sending him tumbling to the floor. His second opponent was wiser. He rolled out of the way as the bullets passed overhead.

The two remaining combatants continued to fire at one another. Simultaneously attacking and dodging, the pair dove to their left, criss-crossing one another as they emptied their chambers. Neither missed, the slugs slammed deep into their torsos, throwing one into the wall and sending the other spiralling through the exhibit window.

Silence fell for what seemed an eternity. And then the vignette reversed itself in meticulous slow motion. The bodies pulled themselves from the floor. They flew backwards through the window as it rebuilt itself and returned to their original positions. The ballet began again, but this time, the actions and results were different.

Mmorpg heard Blue's voice. "*Stay out of my head,*" she warned. Mmorpg gulped and turned off the purple lens.

Mmorpg lurched backwards into his own body. Blue turned around and glared at him with her raging propane eyes.

"I only did it to find out why you had stopped. We don't have time for manners. Every second counts."

"*Stay. Out. Of. My. Head,*" said Blue.

Blue pulled herself away from the gallery and continued down Malon Mall, brushing past a young couple holding hands. Mmorpg following behind her.

****

Jonah and Indira's hands pulled apart as a lady in black brushed past them. They stood and watched as the scary lady walked away with a shorter man in tow.

"She must wear the pants in the relationship," thought Indira.

"Poor guy," thought Jonah back.

They smiled at one another and took up each other's hands again.

"So what would you like to see now?" asked Jonah without moving his lips.

"I want to go to that store over there. Can you see it?"

Jonah switched to purple lens. "I can now," he thought.

They walked over to the store, a perfect couple holding hands. He was white, tall and handsome with a slight tinge of red in his hair and soft freckles upon his cheek. She was brown and beautiful with long legs and an endless ocean in her eyes.

The store they approached specialized in cheap T-shirts with clever phrases. "I rolled a saving roll" said one. "+3 to charisma" said another. Indira laughed and Jonah smiled. The shopkeeper, a large burly man with a thick beard, spotted the little black boxes they had attached to their hips.

"You're not supposed to have those," he warned.

"We know," said Indira, her lips moving this time. She motioned to Jonah and smiled. "But I like to hear what he thinks." Jonah smiled but so too did the shopkeeper. He had seen this before.

"It may bother the Consortium but it doesn't bother me. How long have you two been soul steady," he asked.

Jonah and Indira looked at one another. "About three months," Indira said. Jonah blushed.

"I don't know how you do it," said the shopkeeper. "If I had to listen to my wife's thoughts, I would go nuts."

"Oh you get used to it," said Indira.

The couple looked through a few of the shirts and then moved on. All of a sudden, Jonah froze in place with his head perked up like a prairie dog.

"What is it?" thought Indira.

"That's Casey Finnegan!" thought Jonah.

Indira followed Jonah's eyes to a tiny woman with short, bleached hair. She was standing alone in the crowd talking to herself.

"Who's Casey Finnegan?" asked Indira.

Jonah looked at her incredulously. "How can you not know who ... oh that's right. She's Canadian. Casey Finnegan is one of the top thloggers in Evermore."

Indira looked curiously at the small woman in front of her.

"She beats people?"

"No. Not flog, thlog. It's short for Thought-Log. You see we can share our thoughts with each other by posting messages on the thlogosphere. If people like what you post, then they will follow your thlog."

"So it's kind of like a diary that you share with everyone?"

"Yes, exactly."

"Why would you do that?"

"Well, it's a way to keep everyone informed about what you're up to and what you think about current events."

Indira smiled. "You Canadians are very strange."

"Oh come on. How do you communicate with each other in India?"

"We talk to one another."

"Okay, but with thlogging you can share your thoughts with thousands if not millions of people. And because they're thoughts, not text or video, you can read them almost instantaneously. You can listen to thousands of thlogs in the amount of time it takes to drink a cup of coffee."

"By why would you want to do that?"

"Because by listening into what everyone is posting, you can understand everything that's going on in Evermore. It's hard to explain. It's like you're a part of something greater than yourself, like you're participating in a greater society, sharing ideas back and forth."

Indira place her hand on Jonah's cheek.

"I hope you don't share *everything.*"

Jonah smiled as he put his hand on his soul box. "No, some thoughts are only between you and me."

Indira turned back towards Casey Finnegan. "So if anyone can thlog, then what makes her so special?"

"She thlogs about politics at the Consortium. She used to write a blog in Ottawa called *Queensway Confidential* but moved to Evermore and began thlogging a couple of years back. She's funny, insightful and a brilliant researcher."

"So is that what she's doing now? Thlogging?"

"Yeah, let me show you. Follow my vision."

Indira agreed. "Purple lens," she said.

A purple hue suffused Indira's view and she found herself looking back into her own face. She was seeing the world through Jonah's eyes now. Like an echo, she heard him say the words "gray lens". A gray filter overlapped the purple hue to form a dull purple tint. Before her, a vast array of gray columns appeared. She saw Jonah reach out with his hand, grab one of the columns with his fingers and pull it towards them until it completely filled her vision. Inside the column, pictures zoomed by as random thoughts entered her consciousness. People complained about their day, remarked on current events, or came forth with clever thoughts about life in general. At first the flood of thoughts almost overwhelmed Indira. But she soon grew accustomed to the onslaught. It was amazing. Indira felt connected to everyone in Evermore in such an oddly personal way.

"I see what you mean," she thought. "But where is Casey Finnegan?"

"She's here," thought Jonah. He reached out with his hand and pushed away the columns. With a swipe to his right, he brought up a list of profiles: thloggers that he was following. He brushed through these with his hand until he found Casey Finnegan. Her picture had the mischievous smirk of a leprechaun.

"Let's see what her last thlog was," thought Jonah. The response came back instantly.

"Why is Jonah standing behind me? Perhaps he and his girlfriend are stalking me? How rude! Most people have the common decency to introduce themselves first."

"Lens off," said Jonah. The gray tinge disappeared from Indira's vision. She could see Casey Finnegan turned around with a smirk on her face.

"Lens off," said Indira, and just like that she was back into her own body. Casey Finnegan approached.

"You know who I am?" asked Jonah.

"Yes," said Casey Finnegan, "you thlog about life in the Underground. Weird place. I should visit more often."

"I didn't even know you followed me," said Jonah.

"Well when you get to a couple thousand, it gets a little harder to keep track of." Casey Finnegan turned to Indira. "And you must be Indira."

"You know me too?" asked Indira.

"Jonah won't stop thlogging about you," said Casey Finnegan.

Jonah blushed and immediately tried to change the subject.

"What are you doing here? Don't you usually cover the Consortium?"

"Not today. I'm heading down to the Spectacle to catch the Goddess Pageant. Do you have any favourites?"

"Vanessa," chorused Jonah and Indira.

"That's what everyone says," said Casey Finnegan. "At this rate, there may not be much of a story to write. Oh well. There's nothing else interesting happening anyway. Other than the Spectacle, it should be a pretty quiet day."

****

After a couple more blocks of towering skyscrapers, Blue and Mmorpg came upon a subway entrance, its steps descending below the street. Inside the station, they found a smooth and bare subway tube without any tracks. Blue frowned at the empty tube.

"*Where are the tracks?*" she asked.

The sight of an incoming train soon gave her an answer. Floating off the ground, dozens of white cars barrelled into the station at high speed. Blue felt a whoosh of air as the cars came to a stop instantly in front of her.

"This is ours," said Mmorpg, motioning to the car at the end. Unlike the other cars, the car marked "The Gate" was painted completely black, as if in warning. The car hovered for a moment, then lowered itself to the ground and opened its doors. Blue followed Mmorpg inside and saw hideous orange seats with seat belts.

Mmorpg was almost giddy with anticipation. "I've always loved riding the train," he said as he reserved a seat at the front of the car. Blue snorted in disgust at his childlike exuberance. She remained in the middle of the car, grabbing the passenger bar above her with one hand.

"Uhhh," said Mmorpg, "you might want to sit down and buckle up."

Blue ignored him.

A soft beeping noise notified them that the doors were closing. In a lurch that lasted only a second, the train accelerated to its top speed, hurtling down the poorly lit tunnels at a lightning pace.

Mmorpg was beaming. "Here comes the junction," he yelled. Blue looked out the window of the car and saw the junction approach. But instead of the one or two directions that she expected, there were no less than seventeen different paths. Before her, the train uncoupled and broke apart, each car heading down a different path. Blue grabbed the bar with both hands as the black car careened downwards, deep into the dark abyss of the unknown.

The solitary car plummeted down the tunnel. Lights placed every few metres whizzed by in a blurry flash. Although the car was falling headfirst down the tube, Blue still felt gravity pulling her to the floor of the cab rather than face-first into the bow of the car. As they fell, the car picked up speed and momentum, transforming the yellow lights that lit up the tunnel into a continuous incandescent stream. The seats shook from the air resistance, vibrating to an unheard musical beat.

Blue dared to look up ahead and found herself staring into a dead end. The car carelessly sped towards its doom, seemingly eager to smash itself into pieces at the bottom of the tunnel. At the last moment, the car swung up like a fighter jet pulling out of a dive. The centripetal acceleration pressed Blue down towards the floor. Her hands, still gripping the rails, ached from the strain. Propelled by the fall, the car barrelled through the tunnel. The car jerked to the right. The momentum threw Blue against the side. Into a tight semi-circle the car spiralled, twisting to the left like a corkscrew. Blue felt herself pinned against the wall. She pulled on the bar, every muscle in her buddy straining against the force pushing against her.

And then the car lurched backwards and Blue felt herself thrown forward. Her hands slipped from the bar and she rolled to a stop on the floor. Flat on her back, she looked up in time to see the car doors swoosh open. She glared at them with wounded pride.

A buoyant Mmorpg skipped over to her with a wild grin on his face. "I never get tired of that ride," he said as he floated out the door. After a moment his head popped back into the car. "What are you doing on the floor?"

Blue grunted at him. She pulled herself to her feet and stepped outside.

Before her stood the Great Gate of Evermore. Dividing the Downtown Core from the Underground, the Great Gate served as both a symbolic and literal division between the paying and non-paying clients of Evermore. Built on the only link between these two halves, the gateway was heavily reinforced with anti-intrusion countermeasures and guarded by a pair of cloaked striders, one on each side.

The gate itself was extremely large, forming a circular vault ten metres in diameter. The vault was adorned with a series of locks, bars and chains that gave the impression of invulnerability. Painted in army green save for the words *Tuum Est* etched in white, the gateway towered above all those who would approach it.

Blue and Mmorpg walked towards the strider at the gate. He looked them both over through irises the colour of amber, then let them pass.

"Has anyone else passed through here today?" asked Mmorpg.

"Yes," responded the cloaked strider, his words cold and distant, "Hiru's squad entered about an hour ago."

"Excellent, was that all?" asked Mmorpg as he floated past.

"No." Mmorpg stopped in his tracks and turned to the strider, who added, "He entered about a half hour after Hiru."

"Arthur?"

"Yes, that was his name. He would not give me his purpose, but he had been authorized by the sovereign to cross."

Mmorpg frowned. "Perfect," he muttered under his breath. "And no one else?"

"No other is allowed to cross. None shall cross the threshold while I am here."

"Thank you for your help," said the dreamweaver as he walked through the gate. But he didn't float through it like he had before. Instead, the gate stretched around him like taffy. After he moved through, Blue watched the gate ooze back around his point of entry. She approached and cautiously examined the gate. The threshold appeared to be constructed out of steel and iron, yet it had stretched around Mmorpg.

She reached out and touched the giant door. It was soft to the touch and melted before her fingers, allowing her to push her fingertips deep into the door. Blue paused, then tried to pull back her fingers. She could not. The door had hardened around her fingertips and trapped her hand.

Blue pulled at her hand only to feel it get sucked further into the door. She resisted, attempting to brace her legs against the door, only to find them sinking into the soft steel. Struggling against the vacuum, Blue was dragged mercilessly into the vast unknown beyond the Great Gate.

CHAPTER SEVEN

THE UNDERGROUND

Blue toppled through the gate awkwardly as the metallic substance peeled away from her skin. Mmorpg and another strider were waiting for her on the other side. Steadying herself, Blue turned and cautiously touched the gate again. This time, the iron and steel were hard and cold to the touch. There was no going back.

Mmorpg led her to a giant staircase that descended for about thirty metres. The stairs were divided down the middle by three-foot high railings and surrounded by walls of bright white tile.

The bottom opened into a small foyer before narrowing again into a long horizontal tunnel. At the end of the tunnel they found a glass revolving door, the word *Bienvenue* carved into the wall above.

"Beyond these walls," said Mmorpg, "lies the future of Evermore." And without another word, they stepped through the entrance and walked outside.

The "future" of Evermore was a remarkably quaint 19th-century European village. Built with cobblestone, brick and mortar, and surrounded by a bright blue sky, it contrasted heavily with the ultra-modern Downtown Core. Where the glass monoliths of the Downtown Core were cold and imposing, the quaint buildings of the Underground were warm and welcoming. Blue felt a sense of community around her, a bond connecting each and every person here in a way incomprehensible to the world above. Everybody here seemed to know and care about one another in a manner completely foreign to Blue. Here, everyone moved a lot more casually, strolling through the cobblestone streets, stopping to chat with others or simply relaxing on the benches. Instead of the panicked hustle and bustle of Malon Mall, the square held a slower, more relaxed pace of living. It was as if life was precious and not to be rushed.

They were in the middle of the village square, which according to yellow lens, was named Daisy Plaza. A series of small cobblestone streets sprang out of the square and cut randomly through the village.

Off to her right, Blue heard laughter, running footsteps and the sound of rubber meeting wood. Turning, she found a group of children armed with long, wooden sticks. As they ran up and down the street, the children continuously knocked three rubber balls back and forth between them. Yellow lens informed Blue that they were playing something called "Striderball".

Blue followed Mmorpg on a winding tour of the town. Through streets, parks, cafes and playgrounds they marched. Mmorpg led Blue to a lonely brick wall, floating forward and passing through like a ghost. Blue stopped and stared intently at the solid wall.

Mmorpg stuck his head back out through the wall.

"Come on in. The wall's just to keep everyone else out." His head disappeared.

Blue stepped cautiously into and then through the wall, accompanied by the sensation of a curtain draping over her body. She found herself in a long, narrow alley covered in soot and grime. There was nobody there. Blue followed the alley. First it turned left, then right. She turned a final corner and found Mmorpg waiting for her at a dead end. At his feet lay the body of the little girl. Torn strands of blond hair covered the victim's face. She was barefoot and wore only a small white dress. Blue's instincts kicked into high alert. Something was wrong, something other than the body.

"I'll leave the two of you alone," said Mmorpg as he moved towards the exit.

"*But we're not alone,*" said Blue.

She drew her pistol as she spun around, aiming up high against the wall.

But her target was blocked by Mmorpg.

"STOP! DON'T SHOOT HIM!" yelled Mmorpg.

Blue lowered her weapon and stepped around Mmorpg, her eyes trained up high on the wall. She saw what appeared to be a man growing out of the wall.

"*What is that?*" she asked.

"You've seen them before but not from this side," said Mmorpg. "That is a host."

The host was embedded halfway into the wall. As he breathed the wall followed the rhythm of his chest. His arms were spread out wide but the fingers disappeared into stone. His hair stretched up and became sky. His feet stretched down to the alley and formed the ground. The world around them grew from the host's body, like the branches of a tree.

"*You said they just build the zones, that they can't experience the places they create.*"

"They can't. Maxwell there cannot see, hear or feel anything in this zone. These are sensations that you, the user, must fill from your memories. However, that does not mean that the hosts do not exist within the spaces they define. To create these zones, the hosts have to be logged in and present. Think of them like they're acorns. When an acorn germinates, it puts down roots and a tree grows up from the ground. You can't see the roots, and they can't see you, but without them the tree would wither and die. It's like that with the hosts, they are the roots of Evermore's zones. In each zone, there is a host just like Maxwell. The zone, and all the objects that define it, grows directly out of him."

"*Why were you so afraid?*" asked Blue.

"Under no circumstances are you to pull your weapon on a host."

"*Why? What happens when I shoot them?*"

"That's not important and we're wasting valuable time. We hired you to hunt down a killer, not to ask questions."

"*No, you hired me to kill. Don't ever forget that. And be careful whelp. Some people I'll kill for free.*"

"I'm sorry but every second counts. We cannot afford to waste any more time."

"Then get out of my way."

"Okay. I'll be waiting on the street. Please, work quickly. Mmorpg floated back around the corner, leaving Blue alone to do her work unmolested.

Beside the body were three dolls. Blue kicked them out of the way and bent over the carcass. There were signs of struggle everywhere. Bruises stretched across her hips and waist. Her right cheek bore the signs of a beating. Looking at the side of the alley, Blue saw footprints walking up the wall. The footprints matched the victim's feet, off of which which several toenails had broken. At the last footprint, she found tissue from where the victim's head had struck the wall.

Blue examined the little girl's neck. It bore a deep abrasion around it from some sort of cord. Looking more closely, Blue was able to make out a strange indentation among the abrasions. The indentation was incomplete; only one section of the outline was visible. Blue could see a line with a straight edge leading to a semicircle. The number 4 was etched in reverse inside the semicircle. Blue reached into her pocket and removed a small yellow can. Opening it, she pulled out a ball of green modelling clay. Pressing the plasticine to the indentation on the victim's neck, Blue took a mould of the impression. She carefully returned the clay to the yellow can and placed the can inside her coat.

Blue believed that, during the struggle, the perpetrator had strangled the girl from behind. The little girl attempted to escape the choke hold by walking up the wall, but the attacker dragged her back to the ground and finished her where she now lay. There were no fingerprints, no traces of the killer himself in this virtual landscape. Blue had the body and the method, but not the man. More information would be required.

Perhaps this Arthur character could help, she thought.

She hated to depend on anyone for assistance, but in an investigation, information about the area was vital. She knew nothing about this theatre of operations and despite his bluster, she could tell Mmorpg knew little more. Time was also of the essence. The longer they took to investigate, the colder the trail would become. She needed to hurry or she would miss the chance for violence, a chance she relished more than her fee.

****

Mmorpg waited outside while Blue worked. He passed the time watching people walk by. After a couple of minutes, Mmorpg spotted a woman wearing a Victorian-era gown approaching. She had luxurious red hair and was carrying a wicker basket of apples. Struck by her classic beauty, Mmorpg stared. The red-haired woman glanced at her watch and said, "That time already? I have to put the food on for the kids. Kernel: logout."

Mmorpg watched in horror as the wicker basket fell to the ground and the apples came tumbling out. The red-haired woman went limp, her head falling back onto her shoulder while her body remained standing, frozen in place.

With the words "Kernel: logout", she had activated the logout function that had been disabled by Mmorpg. Instead of waking up in the real world and cooking dinner, her mind was now trapped inside her avatar shell. Imprisoned within her own mind, she would sense nothing wrong. She would dream that she had logged out and then feeling tired, had logically chosen to go to bed. The function had worked exactly as Mmorpg had programmed it, but he never considered how it would look up close. With a single word, all the life had drained out of the vibrant woman, leaving only an empty husk behind.

Mmorpg reached out and touched her cheek. Her skin was cold and empty to his touch. Mmorpg glanced around quickly to make sure that they were alone. She was too conspicuous. Someone was bound to notice that something was wrong. Mmorpg cradled the red-haired woman in his arms and moved her to a nearby bench.

****

As Blue searched for more clues, a splash of water caught her eye. She spun around and saw a man cloaked in water. Each movement the man made caused a ripple in the fabric like a drop of water in a still pond. Blue caught only a quick glimpse of the cloaked man before he disappeared around the corner. Blue sprang to her feet and sprinted in pursuit. Following the walls, Blue burst through the drape hiding the alley and back into the street, searching for the cloaked figure as the drape slid back into place. He was nowhere to be seen. Turning to her right, Blue saw Mmorpg laying a red-haired woman down on the bench.

"What are you looking for?" asked a surprised Mmorpg. She gave the area another look before responding.

"*What did you do to her?*" asked Blue.

"Nothing," said Mmorpg. "She fell asleep sitting up on the bench. I was just laying her down so that she would be more comfortable."

Blue looked at Mmorpg suspiciously and then scanned the area, looking for the man with the cloak of water. She glanced down at the sleeping woman and then glared back at Mmorpg.

"*Where is Arthur?*"

"It's going to take us time to find him. It's going to take more time to convince him, time that we don't have. Do we really need to get him involved?" he pleaded.

"*Yes.*"

"Fine," he sighed. "We'll gopher him." He led her back towards the square. "But be warned. That man is as dangerous to Evermore as any killer."

CHAPTER EIGHT

THE DISORDER OF THE 733T

"How do we find him?" asked Blue, her frustration growing with each passing minute.

"Since we know his username, A*r*th*u*r, we can find him by using a gopher. The gopher protocol was used extensively in the days before the Internet to index the vast journal collections of universities so that they would be easier to find. As the World Wide Web expanded, they were for the most part replaced by spiders, which collected information to be stored in massive databases accessible by high-speed search engines, such as Google. We use gophers in the Underground because people here are highly sensitive to the collection of personal information that a spider would entail. Some fear that a proliferation of spiders would usher in an era of Big Brother-like surveillance, but they're just being paranoid. The bigger issue is that the Underground is so complicated and is growing so fast that it would be impossible to store all of the data that spiders would collect. For example, every time you and I move, the servers would have to be updated with our new locations, any changes to our personal appearance, the amount of time that we've been logged in, et cetera, et cetera. The physical resources required to maintain these servers and continually update the files for several million users are far beyond that which is economically feasible. Gophers have a far easier time adjusting to the rapidly changing conditions of the Underground than do spider-based search engines."

Mmorpg moved away from Blue and stood silently in the middle of the quiet street, staring into space. Below her feet, Blue felt the street crumble. Burrowing out from the pavement was a pudgy little creature that appeared to be constructed from aluminum foil. It chirped excitedly and twitched its nose at Mmorpg.

"Find Arthur," commanded Mmorpg. With a cheerful chirp, the creature jumped out of its hole and waddled joyously down the street from which they had come.

"*What good can one gopher do?*"

Mmorpg smiled.

"I take it that you've never owned rabbits."

To Blue's surprise, the gopher split into two at the first intersection. And then again at the next pathway. The gophers were multiplying exponentially, one for each conceivable branch in the Underground. Within a matter of minutes, they would cover the land.

"*How long?*"

"Ten, twenty minutes tops," Mmorpg replied. "But hopefully we won't need him." He floated towards a run-down antique store. "Hyperlink 1774 to 1924," he said to the door. The door remained still. Mmorpg turned back to Blue. "I've been thinking about it, and there's only one person with the motive to pull something like this. I can't prove it but my gut's telling me it's him."

"*Guts are only good for spilling. Who is it?*"

"His name is Beowulf and he lives inside this door. He's heavily armed and extremely dangerous, with both the will and the means to carry out such a heinous act. Whenever trouble is afoot in Evermore, he is always at the centre of it."

"*Need more than your gut.*"

Mmorpg sneered. "Would you prefer to wait for the gopher, or would you like to get this over and done with?" He passed through the doorway. She opened the door and looked inside. There was nothing there. Blue hesitated. From far inside, Blue heard Mmorpg's familiar voice.

"Come on. What, are you afraid of the dark?"

Blue stepped inside.

As the door shut behind her, Blue found herself covered in darkness. She listened for Mmorpg's footsteps but heard only the whisper of silence. As her eyes adjusted to the darkness, Blue made out a faint point of light in the distance. Feeling along the walls, Blue walked slowly towards it.

As she walked, she felt the hardwood floor beneath her feet slowly change to mossy undergrowth. Stepping out of the darkness, Blue blinked as the light blinded her. Once her eyes readjusted, she found she had stumbled into a western boreal rainforest teeming with trees and vegetation. She looked back towards the open door of the antique shop, and saw instead a rotting outhouse, its door swinging shut. Mmorpg called from up ahead, "Over here, it's this way."

Blue made her way through the thick brush to a clearing where Mmorpg was waiting.

"*Where are we?*"

"We are in what I hope is the final refuge of Beowulf," said Mmorpg. "His home is known as Mecina, even though the location always changes. It has been deserts, oceans and barren arctic landscapes. Today, it hides within this forest. Which is just as well, virtual frostbite is extremely unwelcome. Come!" he said. "Our tormenter is this way."

They forced their way through the inhospitable brush as the dreamweaver spoke. "Beowulf and his bandits have always been a thorn in our side. They move from place to place, looting and stealing wherever they can. We've been trying to force them out of Evermore for some time. For every host we shut down, they find a new one. For every door we close, they open another. But this time, we have them cornered.

"They moved into this area about three days ago. Once I located them, I deleted all of the links from this zone to any outside area save the door we just came through. And I made the door one-way. They are trapped." Mmorpg stumbled over a rotting log. "Ouch, the trail should be up ahead. It will take us to him."

"*Why would they kill her?*" asked Blue, "*and how?*"

"They must have had another sleeper cell in the Underground. A backup plan. If the main army was trapped, the cell would kick into action. Start killing people as a bargaining chip to secure their escape."

"*Have they ever killed before?*"

"No, but they've never been trapped like this before. They are desperate and will do anything to avoid exile. But it won't work. We will never be bullied by such barbaric behaviour from these savages. The striders will be here soon to finish them off. The 733t, as they like to call themselves, are about to make their last stand." Mmorpg walked around a tree and came face-to-face with the tip of an arrow.

"Don't believe it," said an archer. Blue saw three more attackers surrounding them. Without hesitation, Blue sprang into action. She jumped in front of Mmorpg and knocked the bow away with her left hand. Blue locked her right leg behind the archer's knee, grabbed his shoulder with her right hand and slammed him hard to the ground. A second soldier attacked, swinging his sword in long, wide arcs. Ducking under the blade, Blue grabbed the swordsman's right hand, swung it low across her body and snapped his wrist. She then pivoted around, grasped his belt with her left hand and slammed his body upside-down into the trunk of a tree. With a resounding crunch, half the trunk splintered away, spilling shards of timber onto the thick bed of moss.

The remaining two attacked together, one with an axe and the other with a ball and chain. Blue drew her pistol and took aim. She smiled with glee.

"ENOUGH!" commanded a voice that suggested immense power and control. The two remaining ambushers halted and lowered their weapons. Blue stood defiant, weapon drawn, eager for the next challenger.

The man stepped out of the brush. His fiery eyes demanded obedience. He looked at the gun in Blue's hand.

"For what purpose do you bring a weapon of death into our land? To kill my people?"

Blue looked back for Mmorpg and found him peeking out from behind the tree.

"We seek a murderer," said Mmorpg. "A man who feels nothing

at the slaughter of defenceless children. A man who would do anything to save his worthless hide. A man like you, Beowulf."

A flicker of understanding crossed Beowulf's eyes and his shoulders drooped. After a brief moment surveying the ground, he looked at the invaders and his wounded men. "Follow me," he commanded with a soft, yet authoritative voice. The ambushers picked up their winded comrades and followed their leader. Blue and Mmorpg shot each other a look and then fell in behind.

The path meandered through the woods for many minutes. During this time, Blue examined the stature of her would-be opponent. Beowulf walked with purpose, his broad shoulders carrying the burdens of many others. He kept his eyes on the path and his brow furrowed in concentration. He held his arms close to his chest like a monk, walking with an authority that seemed to be bestowed by a higher power. This man was certainly a force to be reckoned with.

The brush surrounding the path dispersed and they found themselves approaching a small village. The village itself appeared to have been pulled out of the fourteenth century. The huts were built of straw and stone and had a temporary feel about them - as if the inhabitants expected to move at any moment. The children played tag in an adjacent clearing while the women, clad in baggy work dresses, worked around the home. They cooked meals, mended clothes and looked like they were preparing for some sort of harvest. Blue dismissed their activity with a snort.

Beowulf led them to the very back of the village towards a large cloth tarp covering what appeared to be a pumpkin patch.

"What is the meaning of this, Beowulf?" said Mmorpg. "Why have you brought us here?"

"Beowulf," sighed the samurai king. "I have not heard that name for a long time. My people now call me Massoud."

"*The Lion of Pashtun*," said Blue, to everyone's surprise.

Breaking the silence, Massoud said, "Yes, that is correct." He looked at her intently. "I am not the man you are looking for, but I have met him."

"And how did you manage to meet him?" asked Mmorpg.

"Because," the king answered, "he tried to kill me." Massoud pulled back the tarp. It was then that Blue realized that Massoud had no hands. With his stumps, Massoud motioned to six bodies lying underneath the tarp. Blue quickly examined the corpses. Most of them seemed to have fallen from a single blow that had crushed their bodies. Only one had been able to withstand more than a single strike. The final victim had received a vicious beating all over his body, but the beating had not killed him. Blue bent down and picked up the victim's head. It had been knocked clean off.

"They sacrificed their lives so that I might escape. They gave up their youth, their hopes and dreams, so that I may continue." Massoud took the head from Blue and looked straight into its face. "None gave up more than my protégé Three Rivers. He was the finest of my warriors, always eager to help those in need. He was the last to fall; I could hear his screams as I ran through the woods." He returned the head to underneath the tarp. "And thanks to your 'security' protocols"—he glared at Mmorpg—"I will never see him or his brothers again." He allowed the tarp to fall back into place.

"*So you ran? Coward.*"

"I have greater responsibilities than my pride or your respect. I have to protect my people. My warriors understood that. And because of the threat that this killer represents, my people must once again flee."

Blue could see that preparations were already being made to evacuate the area. Homes were being pulled down, bags were being packed and crops were being rolled up for transport. But she saw no transports and no pack animals to carry the supplies out.

"How can we believe you?" asked Mmorpg. "How can we be sure that you had nothing to do with it?"

"Do you believe that I would do something like that? Slaughter a defenceless little girl? I have done some horrible things in my past, but I am not capable of that. We are nomads, not savages. The one who did this"—he motioned to the tarp—"can not be swayed by soft words or cold reason. He has no purpose other than to kill." Blue's breathing deepened. "He lives for chaos and destruction, eager to destroy the lives of all who cross his path. I have seen him fight with a fury that can not be matched or overcome. Not even the striders would be able to overpower him."

The breathing of the lady of death had become very slow and strong.

"The worst was the manner in which he approached us. He didn't run up to us or try to surprise us through an ambush. We saw him coming from a great distance. And we waited as he calmly strolled up to us. And yet we did not run. There was a deliberateness to his manner that was unnerving. Even though he walked with such patience, you could sense a great tempest within him, like the calm before the storm. And yet, we were too fascinated to run away. We were too curious to see what he had," he looked forlornly again at the tarp, "and too anxious to see if we could match him."

"*Weapon?*" asked Blue, thinking back to the cord that had strangled the little girl.

"No weapon," responded the king. "The damage he did, he did with his own hands. He had opportunities to arm himself with the weapons of the fallen. He refused them all. He killed them all with only his hands and his feet."

"Why not use a weapon?" Mmorpg wondered aloud. "Wouldn't that make it easier?"

"Yes, but there is something else at work here. He was certainly enjoying himself, that is true. But that's not driving his mayhem. He has some goal, some purpose that he pursues without question. I think that he might not even know or care what it is, but he chases it nonetheless. There was a pride to his work - a quest for the challenge it presented, perhaps a trophy. When I had reached a safe distance, I looked back to see the fate that had befallen my 733t. I saw their bodies lying sprawled upon the forest floor. And in the middle of the killing fields, I saw him holding up my heir apparent, the man I had trained like my own son. He held him by the throat and looked into his eyes before he knocked his head from his shoulders. It should have been me."

The ground shook beneath them and a gopher popped its head out from the soil. It began to chatter in the synthetic binary whine of a dial-up modem.

The dreamweaver quickly deciphered the message. "Arthur's where?" Upon the gopher's chattering response, Mmorpg stood up and looked towards the north side of the village. "He's with who?" A series of screams emanated far off from the north.

The booming voice of Massoud filled the air. "733t! CONVERGE, NORTH SIDE."

From the woods behind them sprinted a throng of warriors, rushing to take their positions at the front. The warriors appeared to be from all corners of the earth. Some dressed with taste and care, others did not. The samurai armour that Massoud favoured was present, but everyone had their own style. There were even some that did not appear to be human, complete with various and disturbing deformities. The army marched through the village. Mmorpg and Blue followed in their wake.

They came to the north side of the village, where Massoud's men had formed two lines: swordsmen in the front and archers at the back. While Mmorpg simply passed through the lines like a ghost, Blue had to push her way to the front.

The lines formed at the edge of a great red cliff overlooking the prairie to the north. The fields had been freshly harvested in anticipation of evacuation. The remaining workers were fleeing back towards the village from the rather slow advance of six unarmed figures clad in brown cloaks. The cloaked invaders moved slowly, deliberately across the fields and towards the cliff. Like geese, they formed a V, their leader at its point. He raised his hand and the advancing army of six came to a stop, a mere five hundred metres from the cliffs. Massoud began to speak, even though there seemed to be no one to speak to.

"For what purpose have you invaded our home again, Hiru?" said Massoud. Blue looked out onto the great plain. The lead figure was moving his lips, but he was too far away for the sound of his voice to carry. Blue wished that she was closer and at that moment her vision turned red. Her sight zoomed in on the cloaked speaker until it looked like she was standing right in front of him. Not only could she see him clearly, she could also hear his words with perfect clarity.

"... ensure that you, Beowulf, have fulfilled the vow you made to me so many years ago," said the cloaked figure.

"I have honoured that vow, Hiru, unless you are too blind to see. I serve my people and their needs, and no other."

"You have stolen from many to serve the needs of a few. There is no honour in this nest of thieves," said the man called Hiru.

"Then you have forgotten much. You have let your position sour your judgement. My people are without equal in this world, surpassing even your precious striders."

"They live on the backs of others. They take what is not theirs and return nothing to society." As the cloaked man motioned with his right hand, Blue could make out a chain looping up from his wrist and over the shoulder to a large hump in the cloak behind his head.

"The very field you stand on is a testament to their hard work and character. My people have a dedication to life that not even you could approach."

"It is time for them to leave. It is time for them to go home, by order of the Consortium."

"The Consortium," spat Massoud. "My people have never supported them or their authority. Why should they bow before their laws?"

"Because the Consortium has brought order to what had been chaos. It has created a society where we can all belong."

"Belong? They have created a world just like the one my people have fled. They can't go back to that. Order cannot be imposed from the top down; it must grow from the bottom up, as a tree grows from its roots. Among my people, order has never been imposed, it has collectively been agreed upon. We have no need of an outside authority to fill a role that we already fulfill ourselves. We don't need the Consortium, and we don't need you."

"That is unfortunate," said the cloaked figure in a melancholy tone. "I have no choice then but to serve you and your followers with W3C protocol 802.11w. You and your kind have been sentenced to expulsion, to be carried out by our swords."

"So be it, squire," said Massoud defiantly. He reached his stump of a right hand into an oval sheath on his belt. With a click, Massoud raised a black rapier bound to his wrist that had the word *Mifune* etched into the hilt. As he brought the blade forward, a thousand and one arrows flew from the bows of the archers behind. The arrows soared over the plain in a great arch and fell upon the army of six. None hit their mark, harmlessly striking the ground below. Massoud ordered another volley, to no effect. The cloaked warriors were simply adjusting their position to stand in between the falling arrows as they slowly advanced to the base of the cliff.

Massoud pointed his sword towards the ground and drove it

into the soil beside him. The soil shook and crumbled. From the ground beneath them rose their steeds. Some were built of roots and leaves; others were formed of rock and mud. Every horse was different, but Massoud's was by far the most spectacular. His horse was formed of translucent crystal, spilling rainbows of light. The steed had eyes of diamonds sparkling brightly across the land.

Together the cavalry stood against the the advancing army of six. Massoud raised his sword again.

"Artillery!" he ordered.

Blue heard the rumbling thunder of wood grinding against timber and steel. She turned and saw an artillery barrage of massive tree trunks flying in the air above her. The trunks were an attack of brute force. The logs tumbled end over end as they flew over the battlefield. The cloaked army halted its advance, unsure of how to proceed against this new and unpredictable weapon.

As the timber fell towards the advancing army, the two biggest trunks collided and exploded like a bomb, firing sharp pieces of wooden shrapnel in every direction. Unable to avoid or dodge the bombardment, the striders drew their swords and threw off their cloaks in a single motion. The chaos of the bombardment was met with the clean hollow whisper of their everblades.

The striders fought with immense broadswords, tall as a man and wide as a skull. The striders were linked with their everblades by a chain that stretched from the hilt of the blade to a slot in their armour below the wrist.

The striders formed a defensive ring with Hiru in the lead, cleaving the trunks into pieces with their blades and using resonance trails to deflect the shrapnel. This type of battle was extremely demanding. As soon as they had defended themselves from the first volley they were faced with a second, leaving them no time to regroup. The chaos of the barrage was slowly pulling them apart, forcing them to fight on their own.

As Blue watched a five-metre chunk of timber glance off Hiru's shoulder, she heard Massoud order a third and final volley. Blue looked back towards the woods from which the projectiles were being launched and used her red lens to zoom through the trees.

Far into the forest, about half a kilometre, she discovered a full battery of catapults. As Blue watched, the catapults launched the trunks into the air with such turbulence that nearby trees were knocked down.

As the third volley was launched, Massoud pointed his broadsword towards the striders and yelled in a voice that few would disobey, "For the Homeland!" With a jubilant battle cry, the 733t rode their steeds over the cliff. The thundering hooves of the cavalry roared as they rode down the embankment with grace and power. They rode without fear. They rode as one. They rode towards battle, kicking up a cloud of dust that blocked Blue's view.

The third salvo hit the striders hard. Now separated, they were far more vulnerable to attack. Hiru moved like a gazelle, working his way from one strider to another, aiding their defence at the very time they most needed it. But the barrage had taken its toll. A trunk deflected from a subordinate struck Hiru in the left arm, breaking it in two. But Hiru continued, cradling his injured arm close to his chest as he fought with one good arm.

The cavalry charge tore up grass and soil as it picked up speed across the plain. The horsemen rode as a unit, maintaining line and focus. As they approached the battered striders they unsheathed their weapons, a wide variety of blades, clubs and axes. With each step, the horsemen gained momentum. With each passing moment, their power grew like the rising sun. But like the sun, their power and advantage would soon fall. Their timing had to be perfect.

And so it was. The 733t hit the striders at the very moment the trunk barrage subsided. The striders had no time to recover before facing the surging 733t.

****

The cloud of dust and debris that signalled battle blocked the action from the eyes of Mmorpg. Even with red lens zoomed in, he could not see the striders through the dust storm.

"Who could have survived that?" No response. The dreamweaver zoomed out and turned to find that he was now alone. Blue was nowhere to be seen.

Amid the chaotic sounds of battle, Mmorpg could make out a sound of sliding clay. Peering down the cliff, he saw Blue, pistol drawn, skidding down the cliff face on the heels of her boots.

****

Blue used the momentum of her fall to propel herself forward at full speed across the plain. She had been held quiet without the narcotic of violence and destruction for far too long. The exhilaration of battle and the rush of death fed her sprint towards the dust cloud. She could feel the screams of pain and victory, the clang of metal on metal and the scraping of bone and sinew. Before her, people were fighting and falling, living and losing, battling for everything yet gaining nothing. Before her was nothing but chaos, and she lusted for it. Her blood lust fuelled her flight. She ran straight into the heart of the maelstrom and was enmeshed in the dusty fog. Within the dust bowl, she glimpsed a man in the distance, cloaked in water, walking across the field.

Inside the storm, Blue could only make out vague shapes in battle. She could not distinguish friend from foe. This was of little consequence to her, as she did not care who she killed. Just to her right, she could make out two figures fighting off a horde of attackers, their chains rattling in the dust. Without hesitation, Blue jumped into the fray, attacking indiscriminately, driving away the 733t attackers.

The two striders turned, offering thanks to the stranger who had aided them. Their gratitude quickly turned to surprise as Blue redirected her assault, firing off round after accurate round at her new targets. Had the striders been less skilled, the slugs would have met their targets in the back of their skulls. Instead, the bullets deflected harmlessly off the resonance trails of their blades.

The male strider threw his blade at the approaching Blue. She arched her back away from the attack, watching the blade fly by her head with the steel chain still attached to the hilt of the sword. As Blue dodged the attacks of the male strider, his female counterpart moved in close with a series of fast one-handed swings with her broadsword. Unlike the weapons of the other striders, the blade was broken in six pieces and held together by a chain that ran through the middle of the sword.

The pony-tailed warrior swung her weapon not like a sword, but like a heavy whip. She threw heavy, fast and unpredictable swings at the woman in black. As Blue avoided her attacks, the male strider pulled back on his chain, narrowly missing Blue's jugular with the boomeranging blade. On went this dangerous dance, the female strider fighting in close with support from her male counterpart while Blue stayed on the defensive, avoiding blow after blow. The pair tried a simultaneous attack, with the female swinging a low strike from Blue's right and the male throwing an attack from the left. But the arc of his strike was too wide, allowing Blue to wrap the chain around her left arm as the blade passed harmlessly overhead.

Using her right boot, Blue blocked the female's low strike and pinned the sword to the ground. A yank on the chain wrapped around her arm pulled the male off-balance. With the excess slack, Blue used the chain to wrap up the shocked female strider. As the male stumbled into range, Blue threw an elbow to his gut to double him over, wrapped the back of her leg around his neck and forced him down till his face was inches away from the blade beneath her foot.

Blue grabbed the female warrior by the throat and swept the legs out from underneath her. She fell back into an arched position that left the female strider utterly defenceless, a 9mm Beretta pointed into her face.

The two striders were at Blue's mercy.

For so long, she had waited to feel this, the rush of battle. She had endured the boredom of introductions and speeches, of explanations and exposition. She had lived in that prison for too long, her natural inclinations bound by the principled society, her passion chained by the weakness of others. No more. Now she was free, free to experience the only thing that made life worth enduring - the adrenaline pumping through her veins.

But as soon as she had found it, as soon as she tasted it, she could sense it slipping away. The battle was ending around her as the 733t retreated. The danger had passed. There was nothing left to fear, for there were none left to fight. The adrenaline glow leaked away. The exhilaration that she had sought for so long seeped away far too quickly. *No. No.* She needed that rush. It hadn't lasted long enough. She needed more. She needed far more. She could not go without it again.

She scratched the trigger of her Beretta, fantasizing about the strider's face exploding before her eyes. With a gun in her face, the female strider's expression was resolute. Her death was coming; she faced it well.

The shiver of steel touched the back of Blue's neck. Turning her head, Blue saw a large silver blade as blank as the sky rake across her neck. She stared along the blade and found its owner.

"Who are you, and do you fight for Evermore?" asked Strider Hiru.

"*Blue*," she replied defiantly. "*I fight for whoever pays me.*"

"So you're the mercenary," said Hiru. "Drop your weapon and release my comrades or you will lose your head along with your contract."

"You can't kill me," said Blue. "But I can kill her."

"Yes that is true," said Hiru, "but with one swing, I can banish you from this realm. Is that what you want?"

Blue hesitated for a moment. "Not yet," she said. Blue lowered her pistol and freed the striders. The female strider fell into a coughing fit as she pulled the chain from her neck. Hiru released Blue and looked down at the coughing strider.

"Strider Eva. Your opponent won because of your inability to see past your own pride. You and Strider Siegfried have fought too much together."

The male strider stepped forward.

"It's my fault," said Strider Siegfried. "I underestima-"

"Silence," said Strider Hiru. "Your dependence on one another has made you overconfident. You take foolish risks and depend on your partner to bail you out. I will not be around forever to protect both of you from your mistakes. From now on, you will fight separately." The two striders hung their heads in shame.

The battle over, the remaining striders converged on their leader. Hiru examined them, checking for any injuries while complimenting their successes and chiding their errors. "Are there any prisoners?" he asked.

There was one. Hiru was led, followed by his kin and then by Blue, to a spot near the middle of the great prairie. A body lay there, caked in bile and mud as it gasped its final breaths. Its features were a perverse mutation, a split between human and reptile. The creature had beady grey eyes, green scaled skin and a forked tongue that hissed at its conquerors.

"Shall I finish it?" asked one strider.

"No," responded Hiru. "She would want to see this."

They turned to the west, where Blue could make out two

shimmering figures moving slowly towards the battlefield. As they approached, Blue could distinguish between the two by using red lens. The one on the right was a man, about thirty years of age with dark brown spiked hair and sporty wraparound sunglasses. He wore light blue jeans and a white short-sleeved summer shirt, over a red T-shirt bearing the word "Canada" in white. From a black box clipped to his slim dark belt, a pair of headphones plugged into his ears. Adding yellow lens revealed him to be "Arthur": the man she had been sent to find. Holding his right hand was a woman yellow lens could not identify. She wore a traditional brown chador, only her large brown eyes exposed by the blue half niqab that covered her face. Her clothing and manner were soft and serene. As the woman approached, Blue's pain and rage seeped away. By the time she faced the unknown woman, Blue felt completely at peace, unaware of the fury that had consumed her soul so short a time ago.

The prone body spat up bile and phlegm, cursing at the striders with both viciousness and sorrow. Green liquid began to ooze out of its pores.

"It's grotesque and repugnant," said a strider.

"Put that foul creature out of its misery," said another.

"She's crying," corrected Arthur.

Blue peered in closer to the body. Tears streamed down the mutant's face and slowly washed the dirt and grime away.

"dear child," said the unknown woman, cradling the mutant in her arms. "why do you cry?"

The mutant's voice broke through sobs. "I can't go back. I can't take it anymore."

"is it really that bad where you came from?"

"You ... you can't understand. You don't know what's waiting for me! You don't know what I have to go back to!"

The motherly figure paused for a moment to reflect. With a sigh of comprehension, she leaned close and said softly, "unfortunately child, i do understand what waits for you. all of us have felt the same. the difference between us is that you will face reality sooner, for you are far braver than the rest of us. we shall hide here from the outside while you must face it."

"But I don't want to face it!" whined the 733t. "I can't!"

"ahh, but you must, child. you must face it far earlier than you wish, and for that i am sorry. i wish i could take all your pain and troubles away, child. i really wish i could bear them for you."

"I'm scared. I'm scared of them."

"i understand, child, we all fear. but you will face your fears and be stronger for it. you have so much for you out there. it will be tough, it will be trying, but you will make it. you will look back upon your time here as the lost years, years that you can never get back."

The creature sobbed. "But I like it here. Everyone I care about is here, everything I cherish is here. This is my home, this is where I belong."

"what is your name, child?"

"My name is Prairie Wind."

"what is your real name?"

The 733t paused for a moment, struggling to remember. "Susan?" she said cautiously.

"no, Susan. this is not your home. this is a halfway house, a place to rest and collect ourselves before facing our fears. this home is only meant to be temporary. there is so much more for you to enjoy than this world can offer."

A smile flowed across the face of the 733t. "Do you really think so?" she asked. Blue looked again at the creature. The once grotesque warrior now seemed timidly pretty. With every passing moment, the dirt and grime fell from her face. The small, beady eyes widened and softened. Her sharp fangs shrank to pearly whites and dimples appeared on her cheeks. As her features improved, her body sagged; her wounds were overcoming her spirit and she was passing away before their eyes.

"yes, i do, child," said the motherly figure as she hugged Susan. "as you pass from this world to the next, please know that you will never be short of people who love and care about you. your life will be full of laughter and cheer, complete with memories that will fulfill you to a ripe old age. bring the joy that i see in your eyes and touch every soul you meet in a way that makes their lives special. for our value is not our clothes or our money or our image, it is the joy that we bring to the lives of others. and i sense great joy in you."

"Thank you," laughed Susan. "Thank you so much."

"thank you, child," said the motherly figure as the child died in her arms. "thank you for facing what the rest of us cannot."

The motherly figure laid the body down on the soil and backed away. The striders and Blue sat in silence as the soil churned up and swallowed the body. Strider Hiru, Susan's blade in his hand, stuck the edge into the ground, leaving the hilt to mark the place where she had fallen.

Blue stepped forward towards the motherly woman. "*Who are you?*" she asked.

Beneath the soft silk of her niqab, the woman smiled. "i am the one who brings peace to those who most desperately need it."

"*Your name?*" Blue asked.

"generally, my children call me the earth mother but that is not my name. only you know my real name. you need only to open your mouth and my name will come forward. so i ask you: what is my name?"

There was a slight pause. Then, "*Your name is Terra,*" said Blue.

"that i am child. it is a pleasure to meet you."

"*How did I do that?*" asked Blue.

"everyone has their own name for me. in my experience, each child's name for me reflects what he or she desires most—" She wheeled around and stared across the flowing plain, as if hearing a cry for help. "i must go," she said. "there is a soul in tremendous pain. i must help him."

Blue heard a rustle in the grass to her right. She turned to watch a man in sunglasses draw closer to Terra. He placed his arm on her shoulder affectionately.

"Good luck," said the man as they hugged. "We'll see you soon." The Earth Mother floated across the plain like she was on a pocket of air and slowly disappeared over the horizon.

The man in sunglasses turned towards Mmorpg and chuckled in amusement.

"Nice body Mmorpg. Who you trying to impress this week?"

"Take off," replied Mmorpg.

The stranger turned towards Blue. A wave of disgust washed over his face.

"So," he said, "you must be the mercenary."

CHAPTER NINE

THE PRINCE AND THE PRINCESS

"Enter," commanded the sovereign. Jie, his beleaguered protégé, entered solemnly, head hung low. "What can I do for you, Jie?"

She dropped an envelope on his desk.

"I am submitting my letter of resignation, effective immediately on this date at 1402 hours."

"May I ask why?" asked Klein in a soothing voice.

"I am no longer able to perform my duties as a representative of this government," she said.

"Are you ashamed of us, young Jie?" mused Klein.

"Far from it, sir. I have brought nothing but disgrace to your government. I do not wish to destroy through my incompetence the work you have accomplished over these last few years."

"Your incompetence? Nonsense. This coalition has held together because of you."

"How can that be true? The coalition almost fell apart today while I was speaking. Why, if you hadn't been there..."

"Which is exactly the point. One day, I won't be there. One day, I won't be able to speak for our cause. Is there any point in maintaining the coalition if it will only fall apart once my career is over? Nothing lasts forever, Jie. All careers, no matter how successful they are, must end. That is why we must always prepare the next generation to take our place. To step up and take charge when they are needed. That is what I am preparing you for."

"But I have failed in every portfolio you have given me. I have done little but discredit this government. I have become a joke to the opposition."

"They tease what they fear, Jie. They see what you are capable of and fear the skills you will one day master. They know that the more experience you get, the less likely they are to regain power. You are the next generation. You will soon lead millions into the future. That is why I have given you such tough portfolios. That is why you have had to handle every controversy that has hit this coalition. To prepare you, to train you for the coming time, when I will leave the stage. A leader who leaves without handing off the torch risks not only his party's fortune, but everything he has accomplished during his time."

"There are better speakers than I. They are better able to defend your legacy."

"*Our* legacy, Jie. There are better speakers, but they have become too accustomed to power. They have forgotten about the people who placed them there, the people they are sworn to defend. The common touch has been lost by everyone here except you. *You* have not forgotten where we came from and *you* have not been corrupted by power. While others placate themselves with status, you seek out the constituents, ever anxious to represent their needs. Our power is not based on polls or popularity; it is based on our connection to a people who have been rejected by the outside world, a people whose needs and wishes are completely ignored, a generation that needs and wants validation. If you lose their support, then the government will fall."

"There must be others ..."

"No, there is no one else. The fate of this government will soon rest in your hands, far sooner than anyone thinks. That is why I must be so hard on you now. That is why you must face such adversity. So that when the time comes and everything is on your shoulders, you will be ready."

"I'm scared of disappointing everyone," admitted Jie.

"As long as you stay true to the cause," said Klein, "I will never be disappointed in you."

Jie understood, and left without saying another word. She wandered the towering halls of the Consortium lost in thought. Was she ready? She thought about the consequences if she failed. The Corporate Coalition back in power. Everything they had accomplished over the past five years destroyed, the needs of their constituents ignored for a generation. Jie shuddered at the thought.

A man approached. Jie did not smile at him, and he did not smile back at her. Their faces remained still and distant.

"Good morning Ms. Wan," said the man as he drew near.

"Good morning Mr. PRNC," returned Jie.

They walked past one another without another word. The exit drew near. Jie's mind remained silent.

She looked up at the ceiling and dreamed of a life without worries, free of responsibilities and pressure. She dreamed of being a dancer.

****

Vanessa stepped towards the stage cautiously. She felt dwarfed by the massive coliseum that surrounded her. The Chrysalis was the pinnacle of the arts scene in the Underground, but for now it was only an empty shell.

She worried. Her style of singing was so personal, so deeply heartfelt, that she worried its impact would be lost in such a vast venue. Still wearing the black spandex and pink tank top from her three hour rehearsal that morning, she examined the stage where her career and all her life's prospects would be decided by a single five minute performance. It was by no means a fair indication of her talent, but she had understood the risks and the probability of failure when she started on this road three long years ago. It would be decided tonight, in front of millions, whether her life had been worth living.

Tonight. The word hung over her like a dagger. She wished only for it to be over, to know where she belonged — one of the most beautiful and seductive creatures ever known to man, or an ordinary woman living an ordinary life.

Now she stood at the base of the stage. Her dark brown hair, originally shoulder length and curly, straightened and grew down to the tips of her bare feet. Like the tentacles of an octopus, the hair pushed down on the floor and pulled up on the stage to lift the beautiful Vanessa onto the platform. As she walked towards the centre of the stage, her hair retracted and returned to its curly state.

Vanessa turned and looked out into the empty auditorium, trying to imagine what it would look like with millions of people cheering. She could see an electric crowd, hanging on her every breath and watching her every move. The attention flattered her, making her feel beautiful, wanted and valued. She had the attention of everyone in the theatre and held every soul who laid eyes on her in rapture, save for one.

He stood hidden in the crowd with his back to her, face encased in shadow. Ignoring the attentions of millions of others, she focused on him. She intensified her focus, willing him to look at her. But the harder she tried, the further he drifted away into the shadows, a love she could never reclaim. She screamed out to him, calling for him to return, begging for him not to leave her alone.

"What have you done with your hair?" said a raspy voice from behind. Vanessa snapped out of her dream and turned to face her matron, the woman known only as Lamare. Lamare was in her mid forties, with the look of a once-beautiful woman unwilling to accept the inevitability of time. She hid her aging form by draping it in an attractive gold sari, but could not hide the aging of her face. Her once supple skin had been stretched and pinched to the point where her visage was more of a caricature than a face. Buried underneath a mountain of makeup, Lamare seemed desperate to erase every day and hour from her complexion.

"What have I told you about curls? Curls make your body look wider and fatter. Long straight hair will make you look thinner."

"But they're not curls," complained Vanessa, "they're butterflies." Lamare stopped short, peering closer. Sure enough, each strand of hair was shaped to form a small butterfly that fluttered with joy. Vanessa pouted at her mentor. "I like them."

"Well," Lamare huffed, "they still make you look fat. Straighten them out." Disappointed, Vanessa lowered her head as her dark brown hair uncurled and the butterflies disappeared. "Oh, stop pouting. You can grow them back after the Spectacle."

Vanessa's face beamed with expectation. "No matter what?"

"No matter what," responded Lamare, grinning slyly as Vanessa hugged her. "Now precious, what song are you performing tonight?"

"Call of the Nocturne."

Lamare furrowed her brow. "Are you sure about that? Perhaps we should go with something a little more upbeat, more catchy; something with pizzazz and pop."

"Yes, I'm sure. I've thought long and hard about it and the song captures exactly what I want the crowd to feel when I'm on that stage - the loss, the loneliness, the need to be loved."

A forlorn look fell upon Lamare's face. "What is it?" asked Vanessa.

Very gravely, Lamare said, "Avideh has chosen 'Walking in the Air'."

"By Howard Blake?"

"Yes, I'm afraid so."

Vanessa now understood why her patron was so worried. Avideh was a beautiful singer. "Walking in the Air", with its scintillating melody and operatic finish, would showcase the full range of her stunning voice. If Vanessa chose a more contemporary tune, she might be able to blunt Avideh's strength through popular sentiment. With 'Call of the Nocturne', she would be challenging her rival at her biggest strength – heartfelt melody. She closed her eyes for a moment to consider her decision and weigh her doubts, but she could not change the song. She tried reasoning with her emotions, trying to overcome her feelings with strategic logic, but her heart simply failed to listen. She had to do her song. She had spent far too much time on it to give up on it now. It was her song to sing.

"I'm going to sing 'Nocturne'," said Vanessa.

"Are you sure that's wise?" asked her patron.

"Tonight," Vanessa promised, "I will give a performance that no one will forget."

Vanessa's stubbornness surprised Lamare, who was more accustomed to docility than defiance from her protégé.

"Fine! Don't listen to me," she snorted, "it's only your career."

Vanessa, noticing that Lamare seemed hurt, moved forward to comfort her, but Lamare stepped back, saying only, "Remember, you have to make an appearance at the Globe in half an hour."

"I can dance?" Vanessa beamed like an excited little girl, her hair curling back into butterflies.

"No dear, you are meant to be something that everyone wants but can never have. On the dance floor, there are no divisions, no distinctions, no superiors. You must make an appearance but you cannot dance or mingle. You are on display. Don't forget your station, for if you associate with those below you, you devalue yourself to those above."

Vanessa nodded. "I understand." Her hair fell lifeless to her sides. "I'll go get ready," she said listlessly, slinking off towards the changing rooms.

Lamare examined her motion critically. "For goodness sake Vanessa, don't walk like that. You walk like a man. Walk the way I taught you." She demonstrated for her protégé. "Deity was far too generous with your hips, so you might as well use them."

Vanessa nodded and walked away, careful to put her full weight on each step to accentuate the motion of her hips, her soul forever trapped by a cocoon of her dreams.

****

Jonah and Indira held each other as they watched waves crash upon the shore. They were just north of the Downtown Core in a large park that slowly sank into the sea. To their right stood a crystal building, approached by none: The Hall of the Striders. To their left, people congregated on the boardwalks stretching out across the sand. Behind them, a layer of leafy trees framed the setting. Indira and Jonah had chosen a spot away from the others. They sat on a small hill just before the grass met pure white sand. Indira sat in front, leaning back into Jonah's embrace. They sat quietly, watching soft waves roll upon the white shore. Finally, Indira broke the silence.

"Is this what Canada is like?" she thought.

"No," thought Jonah. "It's mostly shopping malls and houses that all look the same. We have cities, but they're not as clean as here. We have parks, but they're far away. How is India?"

"It's hot and it's full of people. I love my country but it's not like this. It's beautiful but it's not perfect. Here everything looks like a painting."

"Yeah, it's beautiful. I know that you love the Underground but today I wanted to give you something special."

"How much did the Day Pass cost you?" she thought.

"Don't worry about it," thought Jonah. "It doesn't matter."

"If you could, would you visit me?" asked Indira.

"Do you think your father would let me?"

"No. Do you think your mother would let you go?"

"No."

Silence followed.

"So where do we go from here?" she thought.

"I don't know," he thought.

"We're going our separate ways, aren't we?"

"No, we'll still see each other."

"I don't mean right now. I'm sure that right now we'll see each other all the time. But over time, we'll grow apart. We'll both go to school and meet other people and we'll simply drift away."

"We don't have to," thought Jonah.

"Jonah," she thought, "do you expect that you'll have a virtual girlfriend for the rest of your life? We're soul steady, but at some point we have to be together."

"We are together."

"I mean in the real world. I can't have a relationship with an ethernet cable forever. At some point it has to become real."

"Let's just try to enjoy today," thought Jonah.

Silence followed.

"Why couldn't you have been born in India?" thought Indira.

- CHAPTER TEN -

ARTHUR

"Yes," replied Blue, *"I am the mercenary."*

"Then it is true," said Strider Hiru. "There is a killer loose among us, preying on the weak and powerless." His gray eyes glistened with indignation. "Why weren't we notified? We have heard nothing from Strider Aeris."

"Our discretion was a necessity," said the voice of Mmorpg as he floated up behind them. "If we had mobilized the striders, the danger would have been readily apparent and the population would panic. Without due cause or need, everyone would have rushed to leave, cashing in their bonds, selling their stocks, removing as much value as they could. If the threat were known, the entire economy of this world would collapse."

"Would that be such a bad thing?" asked *Arthur.*

Mmorpg made a move to answer when Hiru again interjected. "We have dedicated our lives to the protection of Evermore for generations. Now there is a threat greater than we have seen since the dark days of Deity, and we weren't notified because you were worried about stocks and bonds."

"Without those stocks and bonds, there is no Evermore."

"I have defended this land for my entire life. Evermore existed before the days of commerce, before the reign of the Xchange. There would still be a land without them. The most important aspect is the people. *They* are Evermore. Without them, there is nothing to defend."

"Which is all the more reason to keep them calm and unsuspecting. What would be gained by inducing panic?"

"You still could have kept us informed. For what purpose do we keep Strider Aeris at the Consortium as a liaison? If we had known the situation, we could have conducted our own sweep discretely without raising suspicion. Instead, you bring in an outsider. An outsider with, from what I've seen" — he glared at Blue — "no sense of discipline or honour."

Mmorpg shook his head. "It was not my decision to make. That authority belongs to the sovereign and the director."

"I don't know of any director," said Hiru.

"That's because his authority concerns the operation of Evermore from the outside," said Arthur. Mmorpg nodded as Arthur continued. "The director controls the world of Evermore from outside, and the sovereign controls the world from the inside. Between them, these two men hold both physical and psychological power over the realm."

"They have restrictions placed on that authority," said Mmorpg.

"Yes, of course; parliamentary procedures, responsibility to shareholders, blah, blah, blah. But centralized power, however restricted, is always dangerous. The pursuit of absolute power lies within each and every one of us – a natural instinct, if you will. What we have is never enough. We always thirst for more: more money, more power, more love. It matters not what we have, but how much more we might win. That is the quintessential human condition. It is not bound by conventions, rules, or in our case, flawed security protocols."

Mmorpg looked away uncomfortably.

Arthur, however, was not going to let him off lightly. "As I remember," he said, "you were resolute that your security protocols were perfect, invulnerable to attack and infection."

"They *are* perfect," said Mmorpg vehemently. "There were no holes, no back doors, no weaknesses that could be exploited."

"Then how is this situation possible?" asked Arthur. "Why do we find ourselves going to such extreme measures? How is it that someone has died in this world; not the death and re-spawning that we're used to, or the exile of the poor soul now lying beneath us, but a death that claims us in both this world and the other?"

Mmorpg grimaced. "I don't know," he said, shaking his head. "I just don't know. After the incident, I triple-checked everything; it all seemed fine. There were no viruses, no Trojan horses, no penetrations of the protocols. The safeties worked exactly as designed."

"The victims may disagree with you," said Arthur with righteous pleasure. "But no matter, this has been coming for a long time."

"What do you mean?" asked Hiru.

"When building a prison, one can't be too surprised when people start to knock down walls."

"This isn't a prison," shot back Mmorpg, "this is a utopia where everyone can be exactly who they want."

"Exactly, people can be whatever they want. They can choose their appearance, they can choose their personality, they can choose their friends and so on. They can change and mould every aspect of their lives."

"And what's wrong with that?" said Mmorpg.

"They should be focusing on their real selves, not living in a fantasy."

"But that's not their *real* selves. That's their body defined by the cruel hand of God. Why should some people have an advantage throughout their entire lives simply based on their genetics? Some child are born smart and beautiful. Others are born ugly and stupid. It doesn't matter what they do. Their fate is decided at birth. How is that fair?"

"I never said it was fair, just that it's real. Through Evermore, you have raised a generation of children who are unable to cope with their identities in the real world. For them, the real has disappeared or faded away. You haven't freed them from their genetic limitations, you have imprisoned them through their dependence upon their created selves. They can't go back, they can't return — just like the girl that the striders just expelled. You have trapped them here forever."

"But they are happier here," said Mmorpg. "What is wrong with that? We are not just permitted happiness, we are entitled to it. Why should some people have all the breaks while the rest of us live in the shadows? If some people find their true identity here, then so be it. If some people change their outward appearance to reflect how they feel, then let them. How can any harm come from that?"

"We are all born with faults, Mmorpg," said Arthur. "The most crucial part of life is the hard work and dedication it takes to overcome those limitations. Removing our limits artificially does not free us, it robs us of anything to pursue."

"To pursue? Before we built this land, drug use and crime were at record levels. We were raising a generation that fried its brains on juice and stole to pay for its habits. In the years since, those social evils have all but disappeared. We give a bigger high than any drug, at a cheaper cost, without long-term damaging effects. Suicides, teen pregnancies, vandalizing, bullying - all down. Murder, assault, rape – nonexistent. Evermore, besides serving as home for the disenfranchised, also makes the outside world a far better place to live. Our customers are refugees who have stumbled upon a paradise, a modern Zion."

"But one day they will have to leave and then what will they do?"

"By then," said Mmorpg, "they will have the confidence in themselves to lead full and successful lives. If not, there is no reason they can't stay here. The economy is booming and will surpass the GDP of Canada next year. People can work here, make real money, pay all their bills online and live their entire lives here online. Life here is so much more fulfilling, they never have to worry about growing older, having enough time, doing chores, or ..."

"Dying?" asked Arthur, raising an eyebrow.

Mmorpg thought for a moment. "There are theories," he said.

"You are beginning to sound too much like the clerics."

"It may be possible," said Mmorpg, "but no one has risked it."

"And for good reason," said Arthur. "We are human. We are supposed to die. It is the single act that makes every other moment of our lives precious. Without it, life is meaningless, just a boring trudge towards infinity."

"No, death is pointless. It has no value. No sane person of sound mind and body would choose death."

"No, they have it foisted upon them. By fate, by God, or by their reckless belief in your so-called security protocols. Your egotistical belief in your own programming ability has resulted in death. Your failure to acknowledge the danger of the virtual world has bred a false sense of security that people have paid for with their lives. You are ultimately responsible for every soul who will lose his life today due to your incompetence."

"No," said Hiru in a commanding tone. "The killer himself is responsible. Even if Mmorpg left open a door, it was still the killer's decision to walk through it. He is the one we must focus on." Both Mmorpg and Arthur stood silent, bowing their heads in agreement.

Hiru motioned to the other striders. "We will hunt for the one responsible, and we will be discrete about it. No one will panic and the killer will not know that he is being tracked."

Arthur broke his silence. "I will join you. I must see the full extent of this society's foolishness."

"No," Mmorpg said. "Your aid has been requested."

"By whom, may I ask?"

"The request comes from the sovereign himself."

"The sovereign. Hmmph," snorted Arthur. "He has no authority over me. Has he become so delusional to believe that I would help him save this deluded world?"

"He said that you would be more than willing to help us."

"And what, pray tell, makes him believe that?"

Mmorpg glanced over at Blue. She reached into her duster, pulled out an envelope and handed it over to Arthur. He examined it carefully. Arthur opened the envelope and pulled out a piece of white paper. He unfolded the letter and read from the top. His face went white with shock, eyes open wide with excitement. He calmed himself, folded the paper in half, placed it inside the envelope and deposited the envelope safely in his pocket.

"That's very generous of the sovereign," said Arthur. "But it's not enough."

"What more could you possibly want?" asked Mmorpg.

"Answers," said Arthur. "I want the truth. From you."

"Like what? Particle effect generation? Compiler theory?"

"I want to know what happened to Gibbs and Chiu."

Mmorpg froze.

"Out of the question," he said and turned to leave. "We're out of here."

"I'm not interested in exposing you, Mmorpg. I just want to know what happened to them. To satisfy my own curiosity. I won't go to the cops."

Mmorpg paused.

"How much is the IPO expected to be worth?" asked Arthur. "Millions? Tens of millions? How much will you lose if we can't find the killer?"

"We don't need you. We have our own leads."

"If your leads brought you here," said Arthur, "then what good are your leads?"

Mmorpg turned and looked Arthur in the eye.

"If you help us find and stop the killer, I will tell you about Gibbs and Chiu."

Arthur smiled and said, "I'm in."

Mmorpg glanced down at his wrist, where Blue noticed a watch for the first time. This doublewatch had two faces: a black inner face in the shape of a circle, surrounded by a white outer face in the shape of a ring and adorned by twelve black Roman numerals. The watch held two pairs of hands. The hands moved at different speeds and read a different time. Looking closer, Blue could see the inner hands read 1529 hours in white Arabic numerals. The outer hands, only their tips visible against the white of the outer face, moved at a much slower pace. For every six seconds that passed on the inner face, only one passed on the outer. Forever trailing the white hands of the circular face, the black outer hands were eternally stuck on 10:34.

"We had better get moving," said Mmorpg. "We need to find him before he kills again."

"Only if the killer is stupid," said Arthur. "He's probably logged out by now."

Mmorpg said nothing.

"But you're right. We had best get started." Arthur turned to say farewell to the striders but found that they were no longer there. They had slipped away unnoticed.

"Bollocks," said Arthur. He winced at the word.

"Mmorpg," he said. "Did I mention how much I hate your

language filter?"

CHAPTER ELEVEN

THE GLOBE

Arthur led Blue back through the forest, walking a different path through the woods than she and Mmorpg had taken earlier. Mmorpg floated above them like a ghost. Instead of the run-down shack, they came upon a door carved into a tree. The face of the door was a continuation of the tree's bark, save for the deep etching in the wood that marked its frame. If Blue had not been standing right in front of the door, she would never have realized it was there. When Arthur pulled on the handle, the door fell off of its hinges. Arthur smiled.

"The 733t are ingenious at finding new ways around your restrictions," said Arthur. He stepped through the door and into a short, lighted tunnel. "Their innovation knows no bounds."

"Neither does your arrogance," said Mmorpg.

The pathway was circular and shallow, forcing them to crouch . The wood around them glowed golden-brown. With the scent of cedar in her nose, Blue could see the tree's luminous rings follow her as she walked. They moved through the doorway at the other end and found themselves back in the village,

"*Where are we going?*"

Arthur looked up into the sky and watched it fade quickly

towards night. "We're going to see a friend of mine," he said reluctantly.

"Who?" asked Mmorpg.

"A friend," smiled Arthur.

"*Where is he?*" asked Blue.

"He runs the Globe, down in the club zone."

"You mean Marcony, don't you?"

"Well, he goes by several names."

"That's by necessity. We keep trying to ban him."

"It's pretty hard to ban someone from the Underground."

"Well nigh impossible," said Mmorpg. "What business do you have with the daimyo?"

"*Daimyo?*"

"Head of Evermore's criminal underworld?" said Arthur. "He always has his ear to the ground. Hears things no one else does. Sometimes, he hears things no one else wants to know."

"Sounds awfully dangerous," said Mmorpg. Blue's eyebrows perked up.

"Oh he's harmless," said Arthur.

"*Nobody's harmless,*" said Blue.

"As long as you don't threaten his data trafficking ring, you'll be fine. He's a teddy bear. The only one in his crew that worries me is his second-in-command. That guy is kinda scary."

Arthur led them through the village until they came upon a stone staircase. The staircase descended into a large lake surrounded by ancient brick and mortar. As they approached the water's edge, Blue could see the staircase continuing down to the bottom of the lake. She balked.

Without hesitation, Arthur and Mmorpg dropped into the water and were swallowed up by the waves. Blue's body began to twitch. Clenching her teeth, she grunted and followed her companions down into the water.

In the clear blue water, light diffused into beautiful waveforms on the lakebed below. Blue found it odd that she did not float, but was able to keep her footing and walk through the water as easily as if it were air. Visually, it seemed they were surrounded by the panoramic beauty of the lake floor. But physically, they moved as if on land. Blue could feel the water as it rushed past her body and pulled back her hair, but she did not get wet and had no problem breathing.

"The wonders of the virtual nirvana of the human mind," said Arthur.

"*Nirvana?*" asked Blue.

"Oh, that's right; you're a n00b." Arthur immediately felt his head jerk back. Out of the corner of his eye, he saw Blue holding the back of his neck with her left hand, eager to snap it in two.

"It means that you're new to this world, unfamiliar with its culture. It's a statement of fact, not an insult."

Blue hesitated, then released him.

"Nirvana is the Evermorian conception of heaven," said Arthur as he rubbed the bruise now forming on the back of his neck. "A place where all pain is forgotten and where we all live in a family of eternal peace."

"*Does it exist?*"

"No, it is a myth propagated by the clerics of the covenant. Their belief is that if one lives his life by the code – their code - then he will be rewarded with eternal life in Nirvana."

"*So it's heaven?*" asked Blue.

"Not exactly. The covenant believes that Nirvana, rather than being a corporeal place, is here among us. Those who gain entrance to Nirvana are able to feel the emotions of all who live in Evermore. You feel their pain, elation, successes and failures. In essence, you experience the lives of everyone simultaneously, living in an infinite network of connected souls."

"*Why would you want that?*"

"Our generation has access to the most advanced technology that humanity has ever seen. We can communicate to someone thousands of miles away in an instant. And yet, no generation has ever felt more isolated. We live our lives in silos, ill-equipped to connect with others in any meaningful way. And so for many people, the covenant's promise of an eternity of shared emotions is appealing. It has always been that way. Heaven has always served as an opiate for the masses."

"You don't believe in heaven?" asked Mmorpg.

"I don't believe in anything that deludes people into thinking there's a better life than the one they have now. To fool someone into maintaining an unsatisfying life in the vain hope that the afterlife will bring contentment is morally repugnant. We should be improving the state of our lives and the lives of those around us, not sitting around dreaming of a fictional paradise."

"Then why do you study something that doesn't exist?" asked Mmorpg.

Arthur smiled. "Because to understand a people, you must understand their beliefs, no matter how strange they may seem. Perhaps if you had spent half as much time thinking about the people who come here as you do about your technology, maybe this nightmare could have been avoided."

Mmorpg sniffed in protest and turned to Blue.

"Do you believe in heaven?" he asked.

"*I believe in heck.*" She grimaced at the invasion of the language filter.

"Yes, they have one of those here too," said Arthur.

The staircase led them down a dark pathway surrounded by flowing kelp. As they walked into the darkness, luminescent fish appeared, softly lighting the passage ahead. Before them was a rumble of activity, barely noticeable at first but growing as they approached. Two bioluminescent towers rose slowly above the kelp. They were both carved out of wood. The one on the left had a crow on the top, wings spread wide, with large eyes gazing out through the water. The tower on the right had its top carved into the shape of a bear, snarling at all who entered. The wooden crow, steeped in the visual tradition of the Haida Gwai, flapped its wings and watched the approaching duo with suspicion. The bear growled at them initially, but soon grew bored and fell asleep.

"The twin towers of Pier 21 and the home of the Blue Mile," announced Arthur with a pinch of drama. The towers framed a passageway leading to the port. As they passed the poles, Blue felt the warmth of the lake retreat from her body. Turning around, she found herself staring at a wall of water. The towering poles delineated a barrier between the lake and the zone of Pier 21, keeping water out and air in. Blue followed the barrier as it stretched up and over the pier, forming a protective dome above the small city. Just like a lake, waves moved across the entire surface of the dome.

The crow was still watching Blue, its deep prowling eyes examining her. As the water drained from her ears, the collective dissonance of a hundred songs and a thousand voices invaded her mind. She looked towards the sound and saw a long pier extending far off into the distance. On both sides of the pier, hundreds of establishments floated safely upon the watery floor of the dome. This was the Blue Mile - a selection of night-time entertainment venues unmatched in all of Evermore. As they walked along the pier, they saw every imaginable variation of club, bar, pub and studio. Here was a place for every person, a crib for every gang, an atmosphere for every demographic. It was here in one place for all to enjoy.

At the end of the mile, at the very head of the pier, stood their destination - the Globe, a silver sphere sixty feet in diameter set on a small square base. A bulging black man, identified by Blue's yellow lens as Henry (pronounced on-REE), stopped them at the door. His bald head made his large frame look even more gargantuan. "VIPs only," he said, glaring at Arthur.

"So the princess has descended from on high to mingle with us commoners. I take it that this VIP list excludes me?" asked Arthur.

"Especially you," said Henry.

Arthur gave just the smallest hint of a smile.

"Unfortunately, I'm here on official business." Arthur gestured towards Mmorpg and Blue. Henry looked at them and then turned back to Arthur.

"Don't care. Nobody goes near her without my say-so."

Blue snorted in impatience and attempted to walk around Henry.

"Hey Freak! Aren't you listening to me?" said Henry as he grabbed her arm. "I said no one goes near her without ..."

Henry's head slammed into the wall. Henry found that his left arm was pinned halfway up his back. The sensation in his shoulder was not pleasant. Blue drew close to Henry's ear.

"*I love the sound of broken bone,*" she whispered.

"Let him go, Blue," said Arthur. "He's just doing his job."

"*Nobody grabs me,*" said Blue.

"Please," said Arthur. "Let him go."

Blue tossed Henry aside, the way inside now clear.

"I'm sorry about that Henry," said Arthur as they walked past him. "She's new."

Henry gave them a final warning: "Stay away from her, she wants nothing to do with you."

"The feeling is mutual," muttered Arthur.

"Are you stalking someone?" asked Mmorpg.

"No," said Arthur. "It's a long story. Do you really want to hear it?"

Mmorpg looked at his watch. "Not particularly."

The entrance opened into the building's small, dark, rectangular base. The floor was covered in a dense white fog while a dark blue hue stretched across the walls. A slow beat bounced off the smooth metallic walls as Blue, Arthur and Mmorpg eased forward, searching for life. Their eyes moved upwards, as did the whine of an amplifier. At the height of its pitch, a harsh chord poured out of three pulsating streams of light suddenly appearing in the ceiling above.

The three streams, coloured green, red and yellow, stretched forward towards the dark horizon. The trio followed the streams until the glowing chords were replaced by a slow riff, alternating colours flashing from the ceiling above. As the music intensified, the display illuminated a blank, open stairway in the darkness ahead. Together they ascended, following the pounding notes towards a large silver sphere. Without hesitation, Arthur and Mmorpg melted into the sphere. After a moment of careful observation, Blue followed.

As Blue stepped into the bottom of the silver sphere, the roar of thousands greeted her. With the light oscillating in time to the music, Freezepop's "Less Talk More Rokk" kicked its psychotic scales into high gear. Around the entire inner surface of the sphere, people danced to the rhythm of the music in defiance of gravity. They were egged on by dry mist illuminated by the pulsing rainbow notes that poured out from vents at their feet.

The music pulsed out of a smaller white sphere spinning weightlessly in the middle of the room. Inside stood the DJ, spinning tunes as he watched each and every part of the globe. As his eyes flowed across the dance floor, the DJ could feel the emotions of the crowd: their hopes and fears, their worries, and their collective need to cut these feelings loose. The music moved in time to the vibrating emotions of the dancers on the floor. The wavelength of the treble and bass formed a barometer of the crowd, marking the swing of their souls.

The floor thumped with the feet of these dancers, an organic mass of mayhem flowing to the heartbeat of the song. They moved as one like the tide of the ocean, rising and falling in peaks and valleys as the song rose and fell through its musical scales.

While Mmorpg floated above, Arthur and Blue made their way through the crowd. They walked up the inner surface of the globe towards an office that lay at the apex of the sphere. The throng of dancers, endlessly distracted by the beat, slowed their progress but paid them no mind.

For Blue, being trapped in a sea of people was simply too much. With each bump or jolt, her anger grew. Visions of dismembered corpses and anguished screams filled her eyes and ears. With her rage came an almost imperceptible sense of anticipation - a hunger for violence.

The club was melting into the viciousness of her subconscious, drenching the walls of her mind in blood, gore and tinsel. But her clouded mind was distracted when the world around her flipped to hypercolour. No longer confined to the misty floor, the scaling notes now moved from person to person, turning their hosts into fluorescent silhouettes as they passed. As the tempo quickened, so too did the oscillation of glowing notes, passing through the entire colour spectrum as their hosts multiplied.

Far too quickly, Blue was surrounded by pulsating human light bulbs, swapping neon colours until the raging beat reached a stroboscopic pitch, forming a flashing rainbow. The world around Blue went dark. She snapped back half a second later, catching her balance as she stumbled. Arthur looked over in concern, but a quick glare from Blue's icy blue eyes drove his eyes forward. After Blue had righted her balance and returned her attention forward, she noticed that 'Less Talk More Rokk' had moved into its first verse, the pulsating notes had returned to the floor and a clearing was opening ahead. When they approached, the heads of all around them turned towards the clearing, their eyes held in rapture.

In middle of the clearing, a princess rose from the neon mist. Her dark brown hair flowed like a river down the back of her body and onto the floor, sweeping away the mist so that her luxuriously bare and delicate feet could walk unobstructed. If the masses were captivated by her hair, they were awestruck by her mystifying algae-blue eyes and tanned Chilean skin. She walked with the grace of a ballerina and the power of a runway model, crushing the hearts of men with but a single glance.

Everyone within sight of her instinctively wanted to hold her, to bring her as close as possible so the euphoria of her inner aura would envelope them, cover them with the love they had sought for so long. But none dared approach her. She was a goddess they were fortunate enough to see, but could never touch. Her eyes skimmed over the crowd, falling upon Arthur. They betrayed a moment of surprise and pain before she recovered, bearing him no further heed and continuing her march through the masses. The crowd converged on the clearing in time for the first chorus.

Mmorpg turned to Arthur. "So you *are* a stalker," he said.

"Forget you, Mmorpg, and forgot your language filter," said Arthur.

Arthur bowed his head and led them to the oval office at the apex of the globe. As Blue followed Arthur in, she found gravity continuing to change. Just as it was within the globe, here in the office her weight was pulled towards whichever surface was closest. She walked up the curling wall on the right side of the room and looked to her left. She saw a crystal desk lying perpendicular to her, its feet on the floor to her left. At its base, the stomping feet of the dancers pounded the glass. Around the desk, five dangerous-looking men had taken up various positions on the room's interior surfaces. Their eyes were locked on the closest target, Arthur, who approached the desk from the ceiling. Walking around the curved walls, Blue followed him. If there was going to be any action, it was clearly going to converge on Arthur, so that's where she wanted to be.

Arthur took a long spiralling path around the room as he approached the desk. They stopped in front of the crystal desk, Blue's eyes skimming its blank surface before coming to rest on the back of the cushy chair behind it." Blue followed, the world spinning around her as she walked.

"This place never fails to trip me out Marcony," said Arthur.

"My compliments to the host, as always."

The chair swivelled to face them, revealing a pale-skinned man with square glasses. A look of surprise flashed upon Arthur's face.

"Hello Arthur," said the man with square glasses. "Welcome back."

"Hello Toland," said Arthur. "What are you doing in Marcony's chair?"

"Wondering what *you* are doing here," said Toland.

"We just came to visit Marcony. We can come back later." Arthur turned towards the door.

"I don't think so," said Toland. The door clicked as it locked. "I think that we should have a talk."

Arthur turned back to face Toland. "About what?" he said.

"About the narc you brought with you." Toland stared at the floating Mmorpg.

"Marcony discussed opening up a club district in the Downtown Core," said Arthur. "He asked me to introduce him to Mmorpg to work out what updates would be needed."

"And you needed muscle for that?" Toland turned his head towards Blue, who returned his stare.

"It's a dangerous world," said Arthur.

"Not nearly enough," Toland motioned towards Mmorpg, "thanks to your rules."

"Marcony did well enough."

"He did okay. But we could do better. I never understood why he sunk so much money into this place. We don't make a dime off of it."

"He was always fascinated by Forsythian architecture."

"It's interesting that you say that. I'm more fascinated by Forsyth's ideas than his architecture."

"Forsyth was an architect, not a philosopher," said Arthur.

"Architecture is merely an abstraction of ourselves. In earlier times, we were at the mercy of our environment. Then we gained the ability to reshape and remake our environment to suit our desires through the use of mud, brick, wood and steel. It gave us the belief that we could control our lives, that we were masters of our destiny. But it was just an illusion. Architecture was the consolation prize. We could change the world around us, but we remained its slaves."

"We need our limits."

"Limits are unnatural. Forsyth understood this. He saw beyond the limitations of physical necessity and saw the beauty of the ideal - an image to be pursued for its own sake, free from restriction."

"Freed from the limitations inherent in physical design," said Arthur, "he went mad. He was unable to reconcile the paradoxes of his designs without the structure that the physical world provided. He could not paint the picture without the frame, nor build a building without structure or purpose. He died penniless, driven insane by his ideas."

"He died free. He dared to dream of a world without limits, a world without the unjust hand of God. A world where we are free to make our own way without anything holding us back. As architecture, it is madness. As an idea, it is freedom."

"Freedom without responsibility to others is tyranny."

"Enforced responsibility is tyranny. Freedom without rules is liberty. Only individuals should have the right to make choices, not societies. Take your narc over there: we live under the tyranny of his regulations. His security protocols prevent human nature from expressing its true self. Instead, we live in enforced civility."

"There are just some things people shouldn't do."

"There is nothing that we shouldn't be able to do. It is in our nature to overcome such barriers. Take our criminal enterprises for example. We can get around most restrictions that have been put in place. Our ability to do so creates a market opportunity."

"Data smuggling," said Arthur.

"Among other things," said Toland. "However, we keep running into one persistent problem. It is very difficult to run a criminal empire without killing anyone. That is the one restriction that we have never been able to bypass, and it creates a major challenge in our line of work. How do you keep people in line if they're not afraid for their lives? If you give out a high-interest loan, what incentive does a person have to pay it back?"

"If you were legitimate, payment wouldn't be a problem."

"That is true, but that would leave the market opportunity untapped, free for someone else to exploit."

Toland reached down beside him and picked up an ash baseball bat.

"No, the black market isn't the issue. The issue is that we can't enforce our contracts. People are only honest when they fear death. It is in our nature."

Toland walked out from behind the desk and approached one of his goons.

"Fortunately, we have found some alternatives."

Toland swung the bat and struck the goon in the back of the head. With a loud crack and an anguished cry, the goon fell to the floor. Toland stepped on top of him, beating his lackey repeatedly. The goon's screams bounced around the office but were drowned out by the music. Soon, there was only a whimpering moan. Toland stepped away and let the lackey get to his feet, unharmed.

"You see," said Toland as he returned to his desk, "we are only able to induce pain. It is the only method we have to keep people in line."

Toland smiled at Arthur.

"Until today," said Toland.

One of the thugs reached behind Toland's desk, picked up something limp and tossed it at Arthur's feet.

"Marcony," said Arthur. Marcony's mouth lay disturbingly ajar, his tongue resting limply at the side of his mouth. Mmorpg turned away in disgust. The head had been beaten relentlessly. Blue ignored the battered remains of Marcony's face and focused instead on the red scar that encircled the neck. Just like the little girl, he had died of asphyxiation, not cranial trauma. His visage had been smashed in after his death.

"We were a little confused when we found him here this morning," said Toland, "so I had someone in the real world check up on him. To my amazement, he was found dead in his bed, still jacked into Evermore."

Feeling with her fingers, Blue found another indentation on the neck alongside the red ring scar. She could see the flat edge again, stretching down to a jagged lip. Blue pulled the yellow can from her coat. The thugs watched her carefully.

"Subsequent examinations by our people could not explain why he had died in the real world," said Toland.

As Blue pushed the plaster to the scar, she felt the floor beneath her rumble. Looking through the glass, she saw the dancers in the adjacent Globe jumping up and down on the floor in rhythm. Beyond them, the DJ's booth began to spin in the centre of the sphere.

"By all accounts, his body was healthy," said Toland. "His brain, however, was gone. It was like someone had just decided to shut off his mind. Without life support, he didn't survive for long."

"I'm sorry for your loss."

Blue worked with the plaster. Making sure to line up the straight edge of the indentation with the mould in the plasticine, Blue pressed down and recorded the little lip at the bottom. The crowd beneath continued to jump towards the spinning DJ booth. As the crowd took one final leap, the DJ's booth flashed white.

"I'm not," said Toland. "I would have done it myself if I had the chance. And that's what makes this such an exciting breakthrough for our industry."

After her eyes recovered, Blue saw that the crowd was no longer standing on the glass floor of the Globe, but spinning around the white DJ booth holding each others' hands. The crowd followed the DJ booth wherever it turned. If the booth spun right, the audience spun right. If it spun left, they spun left. Like planets around the sun, the dancers followed the spin of the white DJ booth.

"You see," said Toland. "His murder opens up so many possibilities. Someone killed him inside Evermore. That means the power to kill exists here. As my demonstration showed, it is a power I don't yet possess. It is a power I must have. Our growth as an industry depends upon it. And judging from your coincidental appearance here, you know a lot more about it than you're letting on."

"We don't know what you're talking about," said Arthur.

Blue returned the yellow can to her coat pocket. As she stood, the DJ booth flashed back to black. The dancers landed back on the glass floor with a loud thud. They screamed in adulation and raised their hands up towards the spinning sphere.

"You've always come here alone," said Toland. "And yet today you bring with you the administrator of Evermore *and* hired muscle. You know something and you're hiding it from me."

Blue turned her attention back to Toland.

"We know nothing," said Arthur.

"I doubt that very much."

The goons drew closer. Blue reached down slowly to her holster. Her eyes caught Mmorpg. He shook his head.

"Don't worry," said Toland, "we can't kill you. But we have ways to make you talk."

The thugs around him pulled out electric whips from their sleeves. The live current crackled in the air.

Blue pulled out her Beretta and pointed it at Toland. Toland laughed.

"And what are you going to do with that pea shooter? Bullets can knock you around but they don't cause much pain. Electrical burns, on the other hand, they're excruciating."

Mmorpg floated up alongside Blue. "Put it away, Blue," he said, "or we'll take it away."

Both Toland and Arthur threw him a curious look. The goons moved to encircle Blue, their whips crackling with anticipation. Below, Blue could feel the glass floor rumble from the jumping dancers.

Mmorpg held up his ghostly hand. "I promise," he said, "you'll get what you need." Toland's lackeys came in closer. Now all of them were standing on the glass floor.

Blue lowered the weapon to her side.

"Too bad," said Toland. "I was just starting to be impressed. Take her."

The goons raised their arms to strike just as the glass beneath their feet flashed white. The floor stopped rumbling.

Blue pulled the trigger. The bullet smashed into the glass and stopped. The goons froze in place.

Toland laughed. "I can't decided what's more pathetic. That you actually tried to shoot yourself in the foot, or that you missed?" said Toland.

An impish grin appeared on Blue's face.

"I don't miss."

Cracks in the glass streaked out from the bullet wound. The floor shattered, spilling everyone down into the dance floor. Only Mmorpg was left floating behind.

Blue felt her weight lurch to the right as she was pulled around the black spinning DJ booth with the crowd. She turned headfirst into the flow and picked up speed. Dancer after screaming dancer flew past. She ignored the mindless cattle and accelerated around the spinning sphere. Finally, she found her prey. There were three of the them floating around Toland. The goons flailed helplessly as they tried to adjust to the whirling sensation of gravity wrenching their stomachs into knots. Toland barked orders with little effect. She sped towards them.

One of the thugs saw her, but it was too late. She pulled out of her dive and smashed his face with the hilt of her gun. *One down.*

The crunch alerted the others. A goon desperately tried to swing his whip at her but missed. An elbow to the jaw put him to sleep. *Two down.*

She felt a wire wrap itself around her left arm, and burning pain roared up the limb. She ignored both the agony and the smell of roasting flesh, focusing instead on the whip's master. Blue wrapped the whip further around her frying arm, bringing him in closer. She reached up, grabbed his head with both arms, and smashed her knee into his face. Teeth spilled into space. *Three down, Toland to go.*

A punch grazed her cheek. She turned and Toland grabbed her throat.

"I own this town," he screamed, "I have the weapons and the muscle to hunt you down. What have you got?"

Blue pulled his hands away from her throat and placed her knees on his chest.

"*Timing,*" she said.

Behind her, the DJ booth flashed black. Gravity returned to normal and the dancers fell back to the curved floor. As they crashed into the floor, Blue's knees drove Toland's torso deep into the glass. He was out cold. *Four down.*

She tossed the whip away.

"*Get a real weapon,*" she said. She turned and made her way towards someone groaning in the crowd. She found him, pulling himself groggily to his feet, but it was just another thug, not who she was after. She drove her elbow down onto his unsuspecting head. *Five down.*

She followed another groan. As the crowd parted, she finally found Arthur on his hands and knees. She reached down and grabbed the back of his neck.

"*Get up*," she said as she yanked him to his feet. Mmorpg floated down beside them. The stunned look on his face said it all.

"*Good enough?*" asked Blue.

"Yeah," said Mmorpg. "Good enough."

The three of them left the Globe and returned to the pier.

"That's not going to make things easier," said Arthur as they walked up the pier.

"*Problem's solved,*" said Blue.

"No you don't understand," said Arthur. "We just made an enemy of the one guy in the Underground you don't want to tick off. He'll be coming for us."

"*His funeral.*"

"No," said Mmorpg, "he doesn't want us. He wants the killer."

"So we're in a race against Toland to find the killer first," said Arthur.

"And we're running out of time."

"What do you mean—"

Arthur was interrupted by sobbing as the three of them reached the entrance to the pier. Before them, dozens of people had collapsed to their knees, shedding tears of sorrow.

The closest was a young man with flowing blond hair. Arthur crouched beside him.

"What's wrong?" asked Arthur.

The boy struggled for words. "Sh-Sh-She's dead. He killed her."

"Who's dead?" asked Arthur.

The boy sobbed, growing seemingly younger before their eyes. "The Earth Mother," he said. "She has abandoned us."

CHAPTER TWELVE

THE END OF THE EARTH MOTHER

They rushed back to Daisy Plaza at top speed. In the square, a great crowd had formed. Some were standing, others wept on their knees. Pushing through the masses, Blue and *Arthur* made their way to the centre of the square, afraid of what they would find. Mmorpg, on the other hand, rose into the air to get a better look.

There lay the broken body of the Earth Mother, known to each by a different name, but beloved by all. Her chest, struggling for each breath, was crushed in upon itself as though hit repeatedly by a jackhammer. Her eyes were slowly losing their spark, replaced by a coating of oncoming death. Her niqab had been ripped from her face, exposing all who gazed upon her to the unending torrent of their sorrow.

Looking upon her bare face, Blue grimaced in agony as she fought to hold back tears. *Arthur* let himself go, teardrops streaming down his cheeks as he cradled her limp form. Mmorpg floated above with nothing but a quivering lip.

"Why?" *Arthur* sobbed, barely able to speak.

"i could not help him," said the Earth Mother in soft, painful gasps. "so much pain, so much anger. i tried to help him." She coughed painfully. "so much pain, i could feel it from far away. i searched for him for so long. i found him, but i could not take away his suffering. he would not let it go."

"*Who is he?*" asked Blue, "*What does he look like?*"

"he lies undecided on the edge between fear and hate, pain and fury, sorrow and rage. someone has hurt him deeply and his anger is limitless. i could not heal him, i could not tame him. he will never stop until all love in this world is spent."

"We will stop him," said Arthur. "I swear it."

"what will happen to my children?" she asked, "who will take care of them now ..." And with those final words, the Earth Mother, the matron saint of all within the land of Evermore, the one that everyone could turn to when they were at their end, the only one who could ease their suffering, was gone.

"From the depths of Nocturne we deliver you," chanted a figure from the crowd. Arthur turned to see a cleric, robed in black water, his voice vibrating through a thin vertical slit in his rigid triangular hood. "May she find peace within your arms in the Nirvana that she earned by serving others."

"Her place is not with you," shouted Arthur into the growing wind. "She would want to stay close to her children."

"It is not up to us to question the indomitable will of Deity. His word is our bond." The cleric raised his staff.

"*I know you,*" muttered Blue, drawing the cleric's attention, "*I've seen you before.*"

The cleric slowly twisted his hood towards her. Pointing the staff at Blue with his white bony fingers, he said, "Your time will come soon, heir of destiny."

Arthur clutched the body of the Earth Mother tightly. "You can't have her," he said, "the Earth Mother belongs to us all, not to your cult."

Still pointing his staff at Blue, the cleric rotated his head and his attention slowly back to Arthur. A long and tense silence followed. Blue felt for the hilt of her pistol upon her hip.

Without warning the cleric made the first move, swinging his staff towards Arthur. Blue immediately drew her pistol and fired, but her bullets were blocked by a rising wall of broken pavement that followed the arc of the staff's swing. As the asphalt rose, it spilt sulphur and dust into the crowd. Arthur staggered back in surprise, moving out of range of the swinging staff. But the cleric wasn't attacking with his staff, he was drawing with it.

The arc of the silver staff and the pavement that followed it coalesced into a shape. The shape grew four legs, dripping with the crumbling soil from beneath the paved street and began to stand. Its boar-like head curled out from beneath its body and snarled at Arthur as he stood between the creature and its objective.

"A golem!" Arthur yelled.

Mmorpg's jaw hung open at the sight of the creature. "How did he do that?" he said.

Blue fired round after round at the creature to no effect. Annoyed but unhurt, the golem charged Blue, butting her backwards and knocking the weapon from her hands.

Arthur stepped forward to intervene, but the golem's tail, a construct of electrical cable, struck back at him, carving up the pavement and kicking up dust between Arthur and the body. Arthur fell to the ground, pinned by a slab of pavement. The corpse of the Earth Mother lay unprotected.

With a squeal of elation, the golem charged forward and grasped the Earth Mother gently in its mouth. Looking nervously for any new threats, the golem backed up slowly into the hole from which it had been born and disappeared. The cleric moved to follow. Arthur struggled against the weight of the rock. He could not let them get away. Slowly the slab began to move.

Before the cleric could reach the crevice, Mmorpg dropped down in front of him. "How did you do that?" Mmorpg asked. The cleric stepped back in surprise at the sight of a ghost. Before he could recover, a bullet struck his hand, knocking the staff from his fingers. Three more slugs struck him in the back. Mmorpg turned to see smoke rising from the barrel of Blue's Beretta.

The staggering cleric collapsed in a heap upon the pavement. With one final heave, Arthur pushed away the asphalt slab and pulled himself to his feet. Covered in white dust, Arthur ran to the fallen priest. "Where did you take her?" Arthur asked. "What have you done with her?"

"We have given her a place where she can find rest eternal, peace from the world of chaos and men," the cleric gasped.

"Where is the Cathedral? You must have taken her there."

"No, the Cathedral is for the living who wish to be saved. Nirvana is for the chosen dead. Deity is gracious, but also discerning. Only the most worthy individuals are invited to the bliss of infinity."

"And how do we find Nirvana? How do we bring her back?" demanded Arthur.

"She can't be brought back," gasped the cleric. "The trip is one way. One must pass first through the depths of Nocturne to grasp the beauty of Nirvana. You"—he looked at Arthur and Mmorpg —"will not make the trip. But Heir of Destiny—" he turned to Blue—"you will make the journey, though we cannot see if you will pass through the night of Nocturne or become trapped within it. We can only see the path, we cannot see the destination. Continue your quest. Find the man with the key. Follow his path to Deity. There you will find either peace or war."

As the cleric spoke his final words, his hooded head fell slowly back to the ground. Upon his final exhale, the cloak of water that covered him rippled out, the liquid gushing onto the street. With one final spasm, the figure dispersed into a torrent that flooded the ground around them, leaving nothing behind but mud.

Mmorpg glared at Blue. "WHAT DID YOU DO?" he screamed. Blue showed no remorse.

"*Got tired of waiting,*" said Blue.

"So she let him go. What's the big deal?" asked Arthur.

Mmorpg turned to Arthur and caught his tongue.

"Nothing," he said.

The crowd, driven away by the struggle with the cleric, returned cautiously. Arthur turned his attention from Mmorpg to the crowd. "One of them must have seen who killed her," said Arthur, "someone must have seen something." But as he tried to question the returning denizens, he was struck by an obstacle - anger. Everywhere he turned, he was met by rage. Rage at having lost the one person who brought significance and meaning to their lives.

With every question he asked, their answers grew shorter and their fury rose. Instead of getting answers, Arthur was getting the crowd to ask the same question. *Who was responsible?* Most had seen nothing, some had seen the propane fire of the killer's eyes and others had noticed a strange man wearing an Akubra. One had seen a man wearing a brown leather jacket even though it was a warm day. Individuals said many different things, but the mob was coalescing into a single mind.

"What happened?" said one.

"They took her," said another.

"Who?" said a fourth.

"Those three there!"

"That ghost!"

"The woman in black!"

"The guy in sunglasses!"

"He was holding her when she died!"

"He was helping her!"

"Was he now?"

"No. He was killing her and making it look like he was helping her!"

"He killed her?"

"They killed her!"

"They took her away from us!"

"They must pay!"

"We had better leave," said Mmorpg, but as he turned to Blue his face fell in horror.

Blue walked towards the approaching crowd with the gun in her hand and a smile upon her face. Her chest heaved with deep, long breaths.

"Shooting them won't do any good," said Arthur. "It'll just knock them down.

"No! Don't shoot them!" yelled Mmorpg. "Let them go!"

Arthur turned towards Mmorpg with a curious frown.

****

Blue scanned the faces of the crowd as they closed around her, looking for one she liked. Finally, she saw her target. Rage and violence in his eyes, her target sprinted towards her with shoe in hand. She liked his face. It reminded her of a father ready to spank a child. She raised her Beretta at his head.

A loud crunch roared from the street beneath them. As a wave of loose pavement swept past, the crowd jumped back from Blue.

Lowering her weapon, she turned and found Arthur holding the cleric's staff. He pointed the staff at the crowd.

"Get away from us," he said, "or you'll be next."

The mob turned and fled without argument.

"Blue," said Mmorpg, "we have to go before more come."

Blue turned away and listened to the street. Even as the first mob ran away, she could hear a second mob, this one much larger than the first, bearing down on them. She smiled again and scratched the trigger.

"We have to leave," ordered Mmorpg, "Now."

Blue ignored him. She had waited long enough for the ecstasy of violence. She would wait no more. This crowd would do.

"I'll take it away," said Mmorpg. Arthur looked at him with curiosity.

Blur stopped. She looked longingly at her pistol, then back at Mmorpg. Dropping the staff, Arthur watched Blue caress her gun. With great reluctance, Blue holstered her weapon. She turned to meet Mmorpg with a scowl on her brow.

"Let's go," ordered Mmorpg. The second mob was closing in.

Together, they raced to the nearest door and crashed through it. The crowd followed them with a vengeance, eager to exact penance. They raced from doorway to doorway, jumping from one server to another with the crowd in hot pursuit. No matter how many zones they rushed through, the crowd still followed.

Through each portal they passed, the landscape became stranger and more disorienting. They passed through a world of sixties technicolor, full of people wearing bright smiles and colours that seared one's vision like a sunset. The next was a cantina full of an amazing collection of aliens and robots who gawked at the fleeing party as they ran past. Finally they ran into a monochrome film noir world where everything was stylish and everyone a caricature. They ducked into a diner, ignored the cackling waitress and fat, dirty cook and burst into the bathroom. There were a series of numbered stalls, beginning with one and ending with seven nearest the door. They hid in stall number two, where they waited and held their breath.

Blue could hear the mob explode into the monochrome world, some staggering, others retching from the forced perspective of the previous landscapes. She heard a cry of disappointment and the pitter-patter of feet moving away from one another. The crowd was spreading out. The footsteps of some entered the diner. A garbled conversation between the mob hunters and the waitress ensued, unintelligible to Blue.

Footsteps slowly made their way to the bathroom door. As the door creaked open, Blue heard two individuals step into the room. Blue and Arthur moved their feet from the floor so they could not be seen under the stall door, while Mmorpg rendered himself invisible. Blue readied herself, gun in hand. A mob of hundreds would have been an exciting challenge, but a pair would be easy. The only challenge would be neutralizing them quietly. The searchers moved down to the end of the line of stalls.

"Do you hear that?" said one. "I can hear her whispering."

"Kick it open," said the other. The bang of a kicked-in door followed. They moved to the next one. BANG! Empty. They moved to each stall in succession, kicking it open and finding it empty.

The hunters moved to the next stall and kicked it. But it would not open. They kicked it again, but it would not budge. The hunters paused for a moment, stepped back and rammed their shoulders into the door, breaking it off at the hinges.

...

Nothing. Blue could hear nothing more from the hunters. They were strangely quiet. She peered under the stalls and saw their legs, quivering with fear. Their breath was jagged and uneven. Slowly, they stepped away from the stall. With each step they took the less their feet shook. The hunters backed out of the restroom and quickly left the diner.

Blue opened the door slowly, leading with her pistol. They were alone. Motioning to Arthur to remain in the stall, Blue stepped out, turned and looked in stall number three.

Her breath grew cold. Before her was, for the most part, an ordinary restroom stall, complete with toilet bowl and toilet paper dispenser. Unlike the other stalls in the restroom, this one was perfectly clean. The porcelain gleamed as if it were freshly polished; there was not a speck of dirt or grime remaining.

On the wall above the toilet bowl was a hole, big enough for a man to crawl through, boarded up clumsily with plywood. The surrounding tile was ruined by fingernail scratches and words written in crayon. The words were cluttered and messy, sometimes written over top of one another as if scrawled by an impatient child. As her blood ran cold, Blue read the markings.

"*STAY AWAY!*" warned one line. "*DON'T GO IN!*" read another. Blue read as many as she could bear: "*WHERE ARE YOU? STAY AWAY FROM ME! come out, come out little piggy. NOT BY THE HAIR OF MY CHINNY CHIN CHIN. where can you go? WHERE CAN I GO? WHERE CAN I GO? and then the prince rescued the princess. DON'T COME IN! no one can ever know. STAY AWAY! so that's why the chicken crossed the road. I'M ALONE. NO ONE IS COMING TO RESCUE ME. and lived happily ever after. WHERE'S MY EVER AFTER? WHERE IS MY PRINCE? WHERE IS MY CASTLE? kuwabara, kuwabara. HE'S COMING! kuwabara, kuwabara. HIDE ME PLEASE! kuwabara, kuwabara. PLEASE, PLEASE, PLEASE, PLEASE, PLEASE. WHY HAVE YOU FORSAKEN ME? hush little baby don't you cry...*"

The writing trailed off in a smudged scrawl. Blue caught her breath. Her heart pounded against her chest plate, anxious to break through. Her legs shook.

A soft slow moan could scarcely be heard through the hole before her. It cried for something, anything. The moan turned into heavy, forced breathing. Each gulp struggling for air. It sounded like someone was drowning, the panicked gulping of air as water slowly filled the lungs, the wet, squishy sound of approaching death. Strange marks covered the plywood blocking the hole. As the gulping turned into soft gagging, she stepped forward to read two small words carved into the wood.

help me

Blue's skin crawled with goosebumps. The hole was now quiet and lifeless. She stepped back slowly into the restroom and closed the door, resting it upon the broken hinges to once again seal stall number three.

"Is it clear?" asked Arthur.

Blue did not respond.

"Is it clear?" he asked again.

"*Yes,*" she said, "*it's clear.*"

"Mmorpg," said Arthur. "Show yourself."

Mmorpg reappeared in the corner. Arthur lunged at him.

"The gun is live isn't it?"

"I don't know what you're talking about," said Mmorpg.

"You were more afraid of her than the crowd," said Arthur. "Can she kill them?"

"Well, she has to have the ability to defend herself."

"Can she kill them?" asked Arthur.

"*If I couldn't kill, I wouldn't be here,*" said Blue.

"What?" said Arthur. He turned to Mmorpg. "What have you done?"

"To ensure that she will be able to take down the killer," said Mmorpg, "we have exempted her firearm from the security protocols."

"How is that even possible? You've always said that your safeties were impenetrable."

"They are. This is a programmed exception."

"But what's to stop anyone from simply hacking your protocols and engaging the exception?"

"The exception can only be authorized by the sovereign. The only other way for the protocols to be disengaged is for me to turn them off for everyone."

Arthur paused. "Are you saying that the sovereign authorized this?"

"Only the sovereign can grant the individual the right to kill. It is hand-coded right into the kernel. It cannot be hacked, it cannot be side-stepped. Only the sovereign can overrule the security protocols."

"Does the Consortium know?"

"No," said Mmorpg. "Due to national security concerns, the Consortium has not been notified that the exception has been granted."

"Well, it won't take long for the Earth Mother's death to reach the Consortium," said Arthur. "They'll put two and two together soon enough. What then?"

"Let me find out," said Mmorpg. He disappeared, leaving Blue and Arthur alone.

"Where do you think he's going?" said Arthur.

Blue said nothing. She just stared at stall number three.

CHAPTER THIRTEEN

THE WAR ROOM

Jie walked past the ice pillars and towards the large oak door, its gold-lettered label reading "War Room". She pulled open the heavy doors and entered.

She saw a political partisan's dream: a flood of data pulled up on every wall. Instantaneous polls, the biographies, loyalties and voting habits of delegates, opposition strategies and simulated focus groups. All were projected as an interactive hologram upon each of the four walls. In the middle of the room, upon a maple table, stood the Helix.

The Helix was the political equivalent of the society's DNA. Based on the Holmes theory of belief structures and political mobilization, the Helix was a simulated representation of the social bonds of every person in Evermore. Everyone in Evermore was represented by a dot in the Helix. From there, they were connected to other individuals according to their social bonds, their shared beliefs and their political ideology. For example, if two individuals believed that the state was an intrusion upon their personal lives, then they would be connected on the Helix by a line, the density of its colour representing the strength of the bond. Thus the Helix represented a three-dimensional map of the nation's political society.

The strongest bonds pulled the links together like magnets, forming clusters that represented the various social groups that penetrated modern society. From this Helix, the parties in question could tailor their messages and adjust their policies to attract the maximum amount of support.

Public support for each of the three parties was marked by an overlapping and coloured nebula (red for the Klein Coalition, blue for the Corporate Coalition and green for the ISPs) that split the Helix into a constantly shifting rainbow. The greatest concentrations of clusters were near the middle of the helix, and it was these "swing clusters" that the parties fought to influence, for they would determine who would ultimately hold power over the Consortium itself. The clusters further away from the competitive centre were known as "solid blue, green, or red clusters," depending on their support for one party or another.

However, not all clusters were within these three competing demographics. Some clusters were so far out of the mainstream, and so disconnected from the centre, that they were strategically irrelevant to the major parties and thus left to themselves. For the most part, they were harmless. But there were two growing white-coloured clusters at the north and south ends of the Helix. So far, no party had succeeded in attracting these groups. The main problem was that they couldn't figure out what unified these groups. The growth rate for these two clusters predicted they would soon become the key to political power in Evermore. Whichever party could identify and co-opt this social demographic would rule Evermore well into the future.

"Thank you for coming," said Klein.

"Thank you. How bad is it?" asked Jie.

"Particularly worrisome," said Klein. "Kinsella, would you mind telling her what you told me?"

"Of course sir." An overly-groomed young man stepped out from behind Klein. "I fear that the Waffle may be becoming too difficult to handle."

"Burke's faction."

"Yes, they have gained the support of another two members of our coalition: Munro and Davies. That brings their total up to thirty-six. This has coincided with a rise in their popular support, as you can see in the Helix."

Jie looked at the Helix, noting how the red dots in middle of the Helix were relatively stable. No matter how the blue and green dots surged and ebbed, the red dots that represented their support held steady. Their outside flank was holding.

"At first glance," said Kinsella, "it appears that our outside flank is secure. We are holding our own against the Corporate Coalition and the ISPs. But if you divide our popular support between us and the Waffle, you get the following."

The image changed, showing the yellow growth of the Waffle contingent consuming the red base of the Klein Coalition as it marched towards the centre of the Helix.

"They've outflanked us at our base of support and are squeezing us into an isolated ghetto in the centre," said Jie.

"Exactly," agreed Kinsella, "but that's not the end of it. Look at this." He motioned to a hologram on the wall. Polls filled with questions and answers, percentages and analyses filled the screen, updating every minute. "According to the polls, people see our coalition as too conciliatory to the needs of the ISPs and Corporates. The Waffle has been gaining on the issue of values. Our supporters are starting to believe that the Waffle reflects their values more than we do. While we've been occupied trying to hold the political centre, they've more than happy to mobilize our base."

"That's never a good sign," said Jie.

"They're also seen as more trustworthy in dealing with the opposition," said Kinsella, "and have a ten-point lead in generating new ideas. In all of these critical areas, they have become the de facto opposition, playing all sides against the middle. There is, however, one critical area where we still have an edge - leadership. Our constituents trust Klein as sovereign by a 3 to 1 margin over Burke. When you include the leaders of the Corporate Coalition and the ISPs into the analysis, Klein leads with 57%, followed by Asa at 20%, Mici at 9% and Burke at a mere 6%. Our constituents see Burke as untrustworthy and manipulative, eager to play the system for his personal gain. It is this characteristic that has slowed the Waffle's growth over the past two days. Without our reputation for leadership, the government would have fallen by now."

"What about the white clusters?" asked Jie. Can we expand our support to them?"

"Now is not the time to try to expand our support. We must defend our base or see our coalition dismantled."

"All while not losing the middle," said Jie. "That's a tall order. What would you suggest?"

"I feel that we have no choice but to go negative on him," said Kinsella.

"You always want to go negative," said Jie. Klein laughed.

"Well, half the battle in politics is kicking the *birthday cake* out of the other guy." Jie and Klein suppressed smiles. "I hate that language filter," said Kinsella before continuing. "But in this case it's doubly necessary. Burke has kept himself out of the spotlight so as not to adversely affect his faction's growth within the Klein Coalition. People, eager for a change, are embracing the Waffle without worrying about Burke's weak leadership. We have to change their perceptions and the easiest way to do that is by bringing up the issue of leadership. We have to link the Waffle to Burke. If we can make it a choice between Klein and Burke, we will win every time."

"Why are you asking for *my* consent? The sovereign is right here," said Jie.

"Because, Jie," said Klein, "I have made you president of the coalition and head of political strategy. It is now your call to make."

"Why thank you, sir. But are you sure I'm ready for that?"

"Of course you are," smiled the sovereign. "Now, what is your decision?"

Jie hesitated.

"I agree with Kinsella. It's the best way to head off the Waffle."

"It may not matter," Kinsella said as he stared in surprise at the Helix. "Our leadership advantage has just evaporated."

"What?" chorused Jie and Klein. "How could that change so quickly?" They looked at the polls and saw that Asa had climbed to 33 percent support, overtaking Klein at 31. Burke was close behind at 26 percent and Mici had fallen to 5 percent.

They glanced at the Consortium seat projections and saw that Burke had gained another 24 representatives. He now controlled 60 of the Klein Coalition's 100 seats. With the support of either the ISPs or the Corporate Coalition, Burke could now bring down the government. Looking back at the polls, they found two new entries:

credibility, with Burke leading at 40%, and security, with Asa leading at 43%. Klein was a distant third in both polls.

"What could have caused such a sea change of opinion in five minutes?" said Kinsella.

"There's something on the thlogs," said Klein and they all switched to gray lens.

The gray portal rushed up to meet their eyes. They did not have to search for long to find out what was causing the commotion. In a flash, they found themselves before the wreckage of Daisy Plaza, ripped apart and covered in broken chunks of asphalt, wire and glass. The panicked thoughts of the correspondent piped into their ears. "Chaos erupted this morning in Daisy Plaza when the matron saint of Evermore was, according to witnesses, kidnapped in broad daylight."

"Who's he?" asked Jie.

"Ken Hendrick," said Kinsella. "He's a thlogger employed by Marcony's crime syndicate."

"How many assailants were there?" commented another thlogger.

"There are conflicting reports of the attack," replied Ken. "Some say three people were involved. Some say four. But every witness has agreed that there were at least two assailants. No descriptions of the suspects are available at this time, people are too..."

"Why would a crime syndicate keep a thlogger on the payroll?" asked Jie.

"Because if you can't kill a man, the worst thing you can do to him is destroy his reputation," said Klein.

"And for that, you need a megaphone," said Kinsella. "That's Hendrick."

They returned their attention to Hendrick's report.

"...witness contends that the matron saint spoke to the attacker, causing him to break down into tears. We believe that this may have provoked the attack. Another witness argues that a scuffle broke out and two people held the victim down to the ground. There apparently was another scuffle and the pair knocked her unconscious and made off with her body. At this time, the Earth Mother has not been recovered."

They flashed to another thlogger. It was a woman with bleached blonde hair and a devilish look in her eye. The profile surrounding the thought identified her as Casey Finnegan.

"It doesn't matter where it came from," said the sovereign. "It's everywhere now."

"Purple lens analysis from the witnesses have been unable to reveal footage of the attack or the kidnapping. However, it has captured footage of the last two individuals seen with the Earth Mother before she disappeared."

The three of them saw Arthur bent over the Earth Mother.

"The first suspect has been identified as Arthur, 28, a doctoral student in political science from the University of British Columbia and a well-known critic of Evermore society."

Next, they saw an image of Blue staring at them with a dangerous smile.

"The second attacker remains unidentified."

They heard a male voice come from off-screen.

"And how are the bystanders coping with the shock of the attack?"

At this time," said Casey, "the bystanders are constantly asking when authorities are expected to arrive. They don't seem to realize that there *are* no authorities. No fire department, no police, no military can be called on, because we have never had a crisis such as this. The striders are supposed to protect us, but where were they when we needed them today? The Office of the Sovereign has thus far provided no comment about the matter."

Flash. A different profile popped to the top, one they didn't recognize. "A new break has occurred in the investigation. By cross-referencing the witnesses' memories with the Evermore member database, thloggers have identified the second assailant in today's attacks as 'Blue', an outsider to our country admitted earlier today. No other biographical information was stored in her file. Further investigation revealed that she received access to Evermore through an unlimited pass granted by the Office of the Sovereign. For what purpose was the Office of the Sovereign handing out passes to outsiders? What explanation does the sovereign have for bringing a dangerous outsider that we know nothing about into our country? Was the sovereign involved in the kidnapping. Despite repeated attempts, we have been unable to get a comment from his office."

Flash. They had returned to the first thlogger. He surveyed the scene of the crime

"Right now it's calm," thought Ken, "but some witnesses are inconsolable. They believe the matron saint was not kidnapped, but killed."

"That's ridiculous," came a user comment. "You can't die in Evermore. It's impossible. They must have gotten confused when she was knocked unconscious."

"Most likely yes," said Ken. "But then again, I've never heard of anyone getting knocked unconscious either. It's been a very strange day down here in the Underground. I think I speak for everyone here when I hope that the authorities are able to rescue her soon. She has touched the spirits of so many. An entire nation prays for her safe return."

Flash. It was Casey Finnegan. She was watching a press conference by Asa. The streaming thought was carried to them as she watched.

"Today we have lost a national treasure. Explanations are warranted," bellowed Asa. "For too long, we were secure in the promises of our sovereign and his assurances that the striders would be enough to protect us. He promised us that no harm could ever come to us. And now today we find that our hope, our light, has been taken from us. The people deserve answers. Why was this dangerous outsider given access by the sovereign? What is her purpose here? And what role did the government have in the kidnapping? Someone must be held accountable for this travesty. The sovereign of this great nation can no longer hide from his responsibility. He can no longer hide the truth. He must come clean or his government will fall."

The trio flashed back to the Office of the Sovereign. Kinsella, with a stunned look on his face, walked over to the walls and silently re-read the polling information. After a couple minutes of uneasy silence, he turned back towards Jie and Klein. His face said it all.

"What is it?" said Jie.

"It's over," said Kinsella.

"Over? What do you mean?" asked Jie. Klein did not look surprised. Instead, he had the manner of a man who had been expecting this for some time.

"We no longer have the support needed to maintain power," Kinsella said. "By these numbers, either Burke or Asa could seize control at the next assembly."

"There must be something that we can do," said Jie. "We can lobby. Work the representatives back to our side."

"There's no time. The Consortium convenes again in less than ten minutes. There's simply not enough time to mobilize our political base. There's nothing that we can do. It's over."

"I refuse to stand here and do nothing while this government collapses. There must be some solution to this problem."

"There is," interrupted Klein. Both his colleagues fell silent, bowing to his will. "When the Consortium next assembles, I will give a full explanation, take full responsibility for my decisions and resign my post as sovereign. I will put forward a motion that Jie should lead a non-partisan caretaker government until this crisis is resolved. They will follow my final request."

"I'm not sure about that" said Kinsella. "Everyone thinks that she's been kidnapped. If you tell them she's dead and there's a killer on the loose in Evermore, all *heck* will break loose."

"We don't even know if she's dead," said Jie.

"She's dead," said Klein. "The public will figure that out soon enough. The only thing we can do now is to get ahead of the story."

Jie was beside herself. "Absolutely not. That would end your political career. There must be another way."

"All careers end, my dear. It's how we choose to go out that makes all the difference."

Kinsella massaged his chin in deep thought. "Yeah," he said, "that could work. At the very least, it would buy us time to reorganize our political base and pull together our coalition."

Jie shook her head. "No, I can't. I'm not ready for this."

"Yes, you are," said Klein. "You have been ready for a long time but you have simply not wanted to believe it. There's no more I can teach you."

"It's not your time to go," argued Jie. "We need you."

"No you don't," said Klein. "We are all ready to move on."

"What will you say, sir?" asked Kinsella. "Shall I have a speech prepared?"

"Leave that to me," said Klein. "But make sure you use the time I'm about to give you wisely; we won't get a second chance."

"Of course, sir. Good luck."

Klein smiled at Jie.

"You are ready," he said.

"Thank you," Jie said. "Thank you for believing in me."

"It is your time. Make what you will of it. You won't be able to accomplish everything you would like, but you will be able to make a difference."

There was a knock on the giant oak doors. "Two minutes, sir," said a muffled voice. Klein looked down at Jie and nodded. And with that, they opened the door and moved to the floor of the assembly. Side by side they walked, the past and the future of Evermore marching towards their destiny.

****

Blue and Arthur sat inside the restroom, waiting for instructions. Their cover had been completely blown. Everyone thought they were responsible for the kidnapping of the Earth Mother. Any attempt to move around the Underground would invite more attacks. Unable to move, they were forced to endure an uncomfortable purgatory, sitting still in a lavatory as the minutes passed like hours. Blue thought about stall number three and the horrible voices that had called to her. Arthur's thoughts were somewhere else.

"*Any word?*" asked Blue.

"No reply yet," said Arthur. "The thoughtmail said that the sovereign had stepped into the Consortium. He won't be available for at least another ten minutes."

"*What do we do now?*"

"Nothing," said Arthur. "Toland's cronies have backed us into a corner. We can't go anywhere without causing a panic."

"*Smart move,*" said Blue.

"I just hope the sovereign can fix this before Toland finds the killer."

"*Killer could do us a favour.*"

"Death's not to be wished on someone lightly. Toland is human, just like the rest of us. He doesn't deserve to die."

"*But if Toland could kill, would he deserve to die then?*"

"If Toland had the power to kill, not even God could save Evermore from itself. Power is impossible to hold onto in Evermore. Eventually, it'll spread out to the masses - for a fee of course."

"*So would you kill him?*"

"No," said Arthur. "There's too many killers as it is. One more isn't going to make it better."

Blue sneered with satisfaction.

"*Weak,*" she said.

Arthur took a step back from Blue, and they said nothing more.

In the absence of conversation, Blue's mind receded into the depths of her consciousness. There, she found a bathroom sink. A rancid bathroom sink, well worn with the passage of time and lack of regular maintenance. The fumes of rotting mildew thrust themselves into her nostrils. An array of shaving gels, aftershaves, deodorants and utensils in the growing field of male grooming lined the shelf. She looked down into the sink, expecting to see water, or hair, or small bits of stubble collected around a clogged drain. Instead, she was met with the sight of her own blood pouring from her wrists. She held her hands up to her eyes and watched the crimson syrup creep down her arms. A gasp came from her left, from the bathtub. Holding her hands up like a surgeon, as if afraid to get them dirty, she slowly turned towards the bathtub and came face to face with the first victim.

The little blonde girl lay lifeless in the empty tub, looking up at the ceiling with grave eyes set in a crushed face. For reasons she did not understand, Blue almost wanted to apologize to the corpse before her. She wished she could speak to the little one whose life had passed far too soon. To ask what death felt like. To ask if she had finally found peace, if all would be forgiven and forgotten. To ask for redemption from the evils thrust upon us in our daily struggles.

To her surprise, the head of the girl turned towards her. Her mouth opened as if to speak. But instead of pouring out words, the jaw fell off as a rat crawled out of her mouth. The bloody rat looked up at Blue and grinned.

"... brought meaning into my life," Blue heard Arthur say as she was pulled back into reality—or pulled back from reality, she wasn't quite sure. But she was sure that Arthur had been talking for quite some time. "She brought meaning into *our* lives," he said. "She gave us a love and understanding that none of us had ever felt before."

"*What did you call her?*" asked Blue.

Arthur thought for a moment and then said morosely, "I called her Faith. I don't know why. What did you call her?"

"*Terra,*" she said.

"The names were always different, unique, but the feeling was the same. From her, there sprang a well of love and undiluted caring we all so desperately needed. Unconditionally, without reason or context, that woman loved us for no better reason than to bring us peace. There was no greater goal, no mission statement, no bottom line with her." Arthur hung his head. "To be without her is to live in darkness, lost in a sea of black, struggling to be found." He paused. "Have you ever felt like that?" He turned towards Blue, but Blue ignored him. She lost herself in melting walls no one else could see. Unknown screams filled her ears.

****

They entered the chamber together, Klein and Jie, ready to face the onslaught that awaited them. As they entered, a great murmur emerged from the assembly as politicians plotted and schemed.

Klein was unafraid. He strode in like a conquering hero, ready to meet and defeat any challenger. Jie wore her pessimism like a mask for everyone with eyes to see. Together they marched towards their positions among the fractured coalition. There were fewer than sixty left. Defeated and demoralized, they waited for the government to fall.

As they took their places, the podiums rose to their respective levels of public support. The Corporate Coalition towered above the demoralized Klein Coalition. But Klein saw something that sparked hope.

The Waffle wasn't there.

Neither Burke nor his dissident group had taken their seats. Thus they could not join the opposition. A small grin spread across his face as he did the math. As his podium slid forward,, he straightened his spine and looked defiantly up at the opposition above him. When he spoke, it came out like the roar of a lion with the hidden fury of a wolverine.

"As Sovereign of Evermore, I hereby execute my executive

prerogative of *session fermé*. Hence, today's assembly will be closed to the public."

As the public galleries melted into the wall, the lighting of the chamber dimmed, encasing the Consortium in the shadow of a full media blackout. Cut off from the public, the seats of the representatives lowered to the floor. Now everyone was equal.

"There had better be a good reason for this," called out Asa. Klein ignored him and began to speak.

"Today we find ourselves in the midst of the greatest crisis we have ever faced. There is a killer among us, moving from zone to zone, killing as he pleases. He has killed the Earth Mother—" a gasp roared from the assembly, "—a loss we all feel deeply. But she is not the first victim and she will not be the last. He does not kill with a purpose. He does not kill for a cause. He kills because he enjoys it. Death and murder are merely a game to him, racking up lives as if in pursuit of some perverted high-score. When faced with such a threat, I acted immediately and without hesitation. I instructed the Order of the Strider to seal the Great Gate, trapping the murderer within the Underground. Over the past morning, they have been scouring the Underground in search of this monster. They have tracked every lead, followed every trail and soon enough they will find him.

"In order to assist their search and bring a different perspective to the manhunt, I personally enlisted the aid of Arthur, the most knowledgeable expert on our realm, and Blue, who worked for many years in law enforcement within the seedy underbelly of Vancouver's Downtown East Side. Their services were necessary to maximize our chances of catching the perpetrator and bringing this crisis to a peaceful conclusion. And yet, at this time, when the country needs strong leadership, when we need a united government, this is the time that we are bombarded by the ambitions of the few at the expense of the many. By those who feel their personal power is far more important than the threat now stalking our land. This is not the time for leadership squabbles. This is the time for leadership. We can never forget who really matters - the people, both from the Underground and from the Downtown Core. Both living and dead, they are the ones that we are sworn to protect. Lest we forget."

The seats shifted, even if they did not rise. The Klein Coalition was regaining its strength, but would it be enough to withstand the bombardment about to come? Asa rose to his feet to speak amidst great applause.

"You are right, Mr. Klein, to say how important leadership is in times of crisis. But so is trust. We entrusted you with the protection of our people. We trusted you to be open and truthful with us about the challenges that this nation faces. We thought our saint had been taken from us, that she had been kidnapped. Only now do we learn that she has been murdered and anyone in Evermore could be next.

"We trusted you and you let us down. You admit that you knew of a grave threat risking the lives of every man, woman and child in Evermore, and you did not feel compelled to notify the Consortium of this threat. Instead, you put our lives in the hands of a group of outsiders - a secret organization that doesn't answer to us, an extremist who wants to shut us down and a mercenary from the outside world. Your cure is worse than the disease.

"The death of the Earth Mother was a tragic blow to our country, a blow that may be irreparable. But what pains me most is that in the moment of our greatest peril, in the moment of our greatest threat, you chose to keep this information to yourself, hoping it would blow over, hoping no one would find out, hoping for a painless solution. You have betrayed the trust of a nation and thus I have no choice but to put forward a motion of non-confidence in both your government and your leadership. I urge the Consortium to pass this motion so we can form a strong and accountable government able to meet this new menace."

Asa sat down to thunderous applause. Representatives shouted at one another as they argued. The podiums shifted back and forth while the coalitions wavered indecisively.

Klein rose again. "I did what I had to do, not only to protect us from the killer but also to protect us from ourselves. If I had broadcast the full extent of the crisis, the people would have panicked. We all know that to be true. That is why this must be a closed session. If I hadn't closed this session, the killer would be aware that we were on his trail and disappeared to threaten us on another day.

"The objective now is to minimize the loss of life and to

maximize our chances of catching the perpetrator. If my government is to fall for protecting the citizens of Evermore, then so be it. I put my faith in the confidence of this chamber. If I am unable to retain your confidence, I will resign. But if I retain the confidence of this house, I must demand your full and complete cooperation to bring this matter to a satisfactory conclusion. Can the opposing member give me such an assurance?"

Asa rose to take the bait. "If the sovereign maintains the confidence of this chamber, then we will recognize his authority and support his leadership to address this issue. If not, then we will accept his resignation."

Holding back a smile, Klein stood again. "But I must ask all of you," he said, "do you have the one hundred and fifty-one votes necessary to topple the government?"

For the first time, Asa realized a key ingredient to his plans was missing. Burke and his forty-member strong Waffle were nowhere to be found. Their seats remained empty and useless to all. Asa had forgotten a key and unique aspect of Consortium parliamentary procedure.

Without Burke or his Waffle, Asa did not have the votes to engineer a defeat and Klein knew it. Klein, instead of offering his resignation, had gone on the offensive, hitting the Corporate Coalition for using the crisis as an opportunity to grab power. Asa could accept the hit in the polls if he could engineer the defeat of the Klein Coalition, but he needed Burke to show up.

Asa stalled for time, hoping Burke and his crew were merely late. But as he pushed his speech far beyond its shelf life, it became hopeless. The Waffle were missing. Finally, Klein forced a vote and the tally told the whole story. Yes: 121; No: 147. Asa was unable to garner the absolute majority needed for the non-confidence vote. Klein's government had survived once again.

Jie was jubilant. This last-minute reprieve had given them the most precious of political commodities—time. With that precious time, they could lobby support back to their side. They could use the momentum of the failed coup and Klein's accusations of political expediency to rebuild their public support.

In dejection, Asa rose to his feet to speak. "As agreed, this chamber will give the sovereign our utter and complete support in resolving this crisis. But I must ask the sovereign how we are to keep this crisis under wraps. The kidnapping of the Earth Mother's body has been broadcast to the four corners of Evermore. Even as we speak, our offices are being flooded with despondent inquiries. What are we to tell them?"

"Leave that to me," said Klein, with the full confidence of the Consortium behind him.

CHAPTER FOURTEEN

LAMARE'S COUNSEL

From the dressing room, Vanessa could still see the stage. It looked so big and she felt so small. In just over three hours she would be on that stage, her life's ambitions dependent on two minutes and fourty-nine seconds. She went through her performance again and again in her mind, replaying every note and humbling herself with every flaw, every mistake.

They will see right through me, she worried. They will see that I am no angel, no goddess, but a simple scared little girl, just as lost as they are. They will see me for the fake I am and turn their backs on me.

"They will do no such thing," responded Lamare. Vanessa was never subtle in her feelings. Unguarded, her every thought could be read by simply looking upon her face. Controlling her visage in public took enormous effort and strained her terribly. She did not like to put on an act. She no longer had the energy for it.

"I'm tired," said Vanessa, the strain beginning to show. "I don't belong here."

"Two million people seem to think differently. They have voted for you again and again with their feet, their lungs and their admiration."

"Then why must I be so cruel to them? Why do I have to manipulate them?"

"You know why. If you were to treat them the way you want, you would become worthless in their eyes. They're not in love with you because you're accessible or kind, they're in love with you because they think that you're above them. They think that you're better than them. That's the attraction. Everyone needs someone they can put on a pedestal, someone they can admire but are never allowed to touch. You must manipulate them; you must hurt them because that is what they want. They want to be hurt. They want heartbreak. They want to feel the loss of a love far greater than themselves. That is your role, your life."

"But I'm tired of it. I'm tired of pretending. I wish I could just open up to someone and be myself with them and no longer have to hurt anyone."

"Would you like to go back? Before I moulded you, you were nothing. No one paid attention to you. You were just a fat little girl no one cared about."

"One person did."

"An insignificant person. Get a hold of yourself. You are forty-five minutes away from infinite adulation, from being the face of the most beautiful dream that anyone has ever known. You are forty-five minutes from rising above all this, from joining the elite, from spending the rest of your short life in the best company that money can buy. You will be taken care of in times of trouble and living it up in times of plenty. You are so close. Don't blow it now."

"Maybe this isn't what I want."

"Then what do you want?"

"I don't know," said Vanessa, crouching down onto the floor. "I don't know what I want. Do I have to decide now?"

"Yes, you do," said Lamare. "You, like all women, come with an expiration date. These are the best years. The years when you will receive the most attention and respect. Your time in the sun is short, so don't waste it dilly-dallying around. You have to make your mark before you get old, before you are yesterday's news, before you are tossed aside with the garbage. You don't want to be left to rot by your lonesome, looking to the next generation to correct your mistakes and retake the steps you've missed or were too foolish to follow. You have an opportunity all of us would kill for Vanessa. Don't blow it."

Vanessa was near tears, but held up against the pressure. She remained silent for a long moment, her face contorted by doubt and indecision. Sniffling, knees clenched to her chest, she looked up at Lamare — her counsel, her mentor, her caregiver — with large, tear-filled blue eyes and said, "Thank you for everything you've done for me. I won't let you down. I know sometimes I don't seem to appreciate what you've sacrificed for me, but I do. I really do. It's just that it's so hard. I'm always acting. I'm always someone else. It's like I'm standing outside of myself, looking in with such a critical eye. I feel...lonely. I feel alone."

"I know, child. Living in adulation is lonely. Being unreachable means you can never be touched. But you will also never feel pain or loss. You will never feel heartbreak or rejection. You are a crystal ballerina, forever young and beautiful, but cold and hard to the touch." Lamare reached out to put her arm around her protégé, but hesitated and pulled back, leaving Vanessa coiled up upon the floor.

"Is it worth it?" asked Vanessa.

"Absolutely," answered Lamare. "You will never regret it." She opened the closet to reveal a sparkling white dress, adorned with small shards of crystal and diamond. "It will be dark in the theatre tonight," said Lamare. "Make sure you stand out."

"Thank you," said Vanessa as her matron left the room.

Vanessa pulled herself off the floor and walked over to the breathtaking dress. Removing it from the hanger, the pop princess dressed herself carefully, making sure that she didn't dirty or tear the fragile fabric. She looked in the mirror and the mirror looked back at her. The image facing her seemed so much more confident, passing its hands through its hair so sensually that Vanessa could only watch with envy. *I wish I could do that,* she thought.

But you can, replied her image.

But I'm not that confident, Vanessa protested.

Of course you are, you have always been, it's been inside you waiting to come out, said the image.

But how can I keep hurting them, pleaded Vanessa. *I saw a boy crying at the Globe because I wouldn't talk to him.*

You're not hurting them, you're entertaining them, corrected the image. *The rush they get will haunt them for the rest of their lives, affect every relationship they have and follow them to the grave. So enjoy it. You want to be me? Then enjoy your power. Salivate with lust for attention. Feel the rush of unrequited love sweep over you, flushing doubts from your pores and unnecessary compassion from your mind. Who are you? You are* perfection. *You are the visage of both beauty and love, an Aphrodite for the ages. None who gaze upon you will ever forget it. You are the morning star, bringing light into the farthest reaches of their souls and heartbreak into the deepest depths of their lonesome hearts.* You *are everything. They* are nothing. *They are meaningless to you and your dreams, for you are their centre, the aura bringing meaning to their lives. You are the light that illuminates their dungeons. They are your minions, your legions and you are their queen. While they live their short insignificant lives, they are there to remind you of one thing: you are Helen to their Troy; you are their world. And they will spend their lives loving you eternally. For you are a goddess!*

Vanessa, holding her hands in her hair, looked into the mirror again and was surprised at how little difference there now was between them. She looked out again onto the massive stage and thought of the millions who would come to watch her. She thought to herself how small the stage seemed and wondered whether it would be able to contain her.

CHAPTER FIFTEEN

THE MEMORIAL IN MARKET SQUARE

Jonah and Indira walked down the street hand in hand. A small crowd walked with them. Their heads were held low. They did not say a word. They were in mourning.

Jonah felt Indira squeeze his hand. He looked over at her. She threw him a sympathetic smile. "How did she help you?" she thought.

Jonah dropped his eyes to the pavement and walked silently. After a moment he thought, "She helped me talk to my father. I was always too frightened to talk to him. To tell him how I felt. But she showed me that he was just as scared as I am." He walked silently.

"How did she help you?" he thought.

She thought very carefully about what to think next.

"I cut myself," she thought.

"Why did you do that?" he asked.

"I don't know," she thought. "I guess on some level it made me feel better."

"How did she help you?"

"She told me that we only find meaning when we dedicate our

lives to someone else. It is only through others that we find our purpose in life."

"I like that," he thought.

They came to an intersection and met another small group moving to their left. Both groups joined and continued in the same direction. The crowd was quiet and still.

"What did you call her?" Jonah asked.

"I called her dost."

"Dost?" he thought.

"It means friend."

He thought about what to say carefully.

"I called her Larry," he thought.

Indira struggled for words. Finally she started to giggle. "Larry?" she thought, "Why do you call her Larry?"

"I have absolutely no idea," Jonah thought. "Do you think it means anything?"

"I hope not," she thought while giggling.

Jonah looked up and saw that the small group they had been walking with had become a mob. People poured into the street from all directions and joined the march. Everyone wore expressions of sorrow and regret.

The river of people came upon the edge of Market Square. A barrier of volunteers awaited them. As they passed, the volunteers handed them a small lamp and a pack of matches. A small candle lay within.

"What is this?" asked Indira aloud.

"It's a dimmer lamp," said the volunteer. "You'll see in a moment."

Together they walked into the middle of Market Square, the heart of the Downtown Core. They could see people pouring into the square from all directions. It seemed everyone in the city was there. The crowd grouped together peacefully with dimmer lamps in hand. More and more came until the square was full. Still more came, taking their places in the overflowing streets.

Jonah looked up and saw blues skies and sunshine. It was always clear and sunny in the Downtown Core. Always perfect weather. It was made that way.

In their hands, the dimmer lights began to glow. But it did not glow with light. It glowed with dark. The dimmer lamp sucked in light and created darkness. Thousands upon thousands of dimmer lamps sucked in the light from above. Market Square fell into night with only the blue sky above remaining light. But the candles were still unlit.

Indira took a match from her book and struck a flame. So too did everyone else, and they lit their lamps. From the darkness came a thousand points of light. Blue sky above, darkness below and light within, the crowd stood in peaceful assembly and prayed for the Earth Mother's safe return.

Without provocation, someone began to sing. Another joined her and then another. Soon the whole crowd sang together. They sang in thanks for the guidance the Earth Mother had given them. They sang for her kind and understanding heart. They sang for her deliverance from harm. Indira pulled Jonah in close and hugged him. She cried for no reason at all. He could say nothing, for there was nothing to say.

The crowd sang for many minutes. By mourning together, their loss seemed easier to bear. The Earth Mother had taught them well.

But the song was broken by a murmur spreading through the crowd. As the murmur grew closer, Jonah could see people's expression turn from sorrow to joy, from despair to hope. As the words reached Indira, a smile broke out upon her face. The Earth Mother was safe, she heard. Everything was going to be alright.

CHAPTER SIXTEEN

THE COVENANT

"Are you two alright?" Blue and A*r*th*u*r heard Mmorpg's voice pour into their heads at the same moment.

"We're fine as long as we stay in here," answered A*r*th*u*r.

Mmorpg reappeared before them. "Fortunately, that's no longer necessary," he said. "Klein has leaked a series of rumours suggesting the Earth Mother's death was a major world event."

"*A major world event?*" asked Blue.

"Periodically," explained Mmorpg, "online-world developers will activate one or more significant plot points that seriously alter the user experience. They are used from time to time to shake up an online world that's become too static."

"In other words," said A*r*th*u*r, "they're telling people the Earth Mother didn't die, it's just part of an elaborate story meant to entertain them."

"*Are the cattle that stupid?*" asked Blue.

"You would be surprised what people will believe," said A*r*th*u*r, "especially if it's leaked."

Blue frowned.

"What do you mean?" asked Mmorpg.

"If Klein had come out and said this was all a story, then

nobody would believe him," said Arthur. "The public are far too cynical about politicians and their motives. However, by leaking the information, Klein makes it look it was a truth hidden from the public. People think they get the inside goods they weren't meant to see. I suppose the next step would be for them to leak that they're disappointed their plotline has been spoiled by the previous leak."

"That came out about five minutes ago," said Mmorpg.

"Like a fiddle," said Arthur. He grinned as if impressed.

"*So it's all just a story?*" said Blue.

"Well, it's not like we haven't done this before. In the early days of Evermore, we orchestrated major world events all the time to keep people interested. However, as Evermore grew bigger and more complex, major world events became more and more difficult to organize. In fact, the last one we used was the introduction of the Great Gate you passed through earlier. We used it to separate the Underground and the Downtown Core areas."

"Which in turn segregated the paying and non-paying users of Evermore," added Arthur. "Those who could afford to pay would have access to the more privileged Downtown Core, full of designer content. Those who could not afford to pay were left to their own devices. But the Great Gate was just one part of a larger plot. To justify the Gate and the segregation it entails, the developers crafted an elaborate plot involving demonstrations, grand speeches and the eventual fall of Asa's government."

"That's inaccurate," said Mmorpg. "We had nothing to do with that. The decision to install the Great Gate and bring universal suffrage to the non-paying avatars of the Underground was made due to the demonstrations led by Klein. We did not create the crisis to justify separating Evermore into two halves. It was an adjustment made due to user feedback."

"Perhaps," said Arthur, "but how are we to know for sure? For all we know, the murderous rampage we're facing today could be an elaborate plot to liven things up and justify a major change to the online world – higher subscription fees perhaps?"

"Nonsense. I saw the bodies myself. This is not a plot. This is real, and real people are dying."

"Well, we won't know for sure until this plot plays itself out," said Arthur. "So did people believe the leak?"

"It looks like it. Everyone has calmed down and gone back to their daily lives. Some commentators are calling it the most interesting plot twist they've seen in years. Anyway, you should be able to move freely now. The people may not fully trust you, but they should leave you alone."

The trio left the bathroom and walked through the diner. Blue's head jutted from left to right. She kept one hand beside her holster.

"What was Asa's reaction?" asked Arthur.

"He tried to get through a motion of non-confidence, but it failed to reach quorum."

"That's fortunate for Klein. I would have thought he'd have been skewered alive once the story broke." The pair was on the street now, at the crossing of Main and Elm.

"That's part of the reason I'm contacting you. The Waffle have disappeared."

"Really?" exclaimed Arthur. He glanced at Blue in surprise, but she was staring listlessly down the street, paying no attention to him. Arthur returned his focus to the conversation. "Was that how the Klein government survived — the Waffle simply failed to show up?"

"Yes. At first we thought it might have been part of their political strategy, but they can't be found anywhere. We fear the worst. Do you have any other leads to follow?"

"No, we've pretty much run into a brick wall here. I don't know where to turn next."

"Then search for the Waffle. We need to find out what has happened to them."

"Alright, we'll send a gopher. As usual, it'll take some time."

"But we must hurry." Mmorpg's voice was uncharacteristically pleading. "Today's events have everyone spooked. They're even considering cancelling the Spectacle tonight."

"Fat chance," said Arthur sardonically. "It's too valuable to the sponsors, certainly worth a few measly lives."

Arthur turned away from Mmorpg and called a gopher. The gopher popped up through the street with a cheerful chirp. Arthur gave the happy creature its instructions. The gopher went on its merry way, chirping a song of gracious servitude as it began cloning itself.

"Arthur," said Mmorpg, "our clients' lives are our top priority."

"If that was the case," said Arthur, "you never would have created this place."

For the first time, Arthur wondered where everyone else had gone. The zone was completely deserted save for them, empty of the frantic activity that was its norm.

"That's completely uncalled for," said Mmorpg. "We have taken every effort to protect our citizens. We've launched an investigation, hired Blue and even brought you on board. We are doing everything we can."

"No," said Arthur, "you're just trying to protect your investment. You people couldn't care less about—hmpphh!"

Blue's left hand wrapped tightly around Arthur's jaw, shutting his mouth.

Mmorpg and Arthur followed her eyes and saw a cleric standing mere feet away, staff in hand. Blue remained still, leaving her weapon in its holster.

"Fear not," said the cleric, his face hidden by the hood of the cloak. "I come not for conflict, but for a request."

"Request?" asked Mmorpg.

"The Caliph has requested your presence at the earliest convenience."

"Only if it means returning the body of the Earth Mother back to where she belongs," said Arthur.

"No, he requested only the presence of the Heir of Destiny, but you two may wait in the Cathedral, if you like." The cleric returned his attention to Blue. "Heir of Destiny," he said, "would you grant this request?" Blue nodded her head solemnly.

"Follow me please, I will lead you to the Cathedral."

"I have been searching for the Cathedral for years," said Arthur. "Where has it been hidden all this time?"

The cleric turned to his left. Arthur followed his gaze to find a grand cathedral standing before him, carved in the classic baroque style of old Quebec. Its tower lorded over him with both power and beauty. Its breathtaking majesty stretched far beyond its worn, elderly stones. Its giant oak doors, guarded by two clerics, stunned Arthur into silence.

"The Cathedral has been here all the time, heretic. But only a true believer can find it. Those driven by fear, lust or cynicism will search forever for its doors to no avail."

"Rather innovative," was Arthur's only reply.

"How on earth would you program that?" said Mmorpg.

"With all due respect, Ghost of Evermore," said the cleric, "some things must be taken on faith."

The cleric turned towards the guards and gave them a simple nod. The giant oak doors opened graciously by themselves. The cleric slowly led the group through the giant doors and into the darkness. But there was nothing there. The group found themselves upon an empty lot. Before them rose the floor, stone by stone, giving them a place upon which to walk. Before their eyes, walls built themselves piece by piece from the floor to the ceiling. Majestic pillars grew from the floor and stretched upwards, forming arches that joined floor, wall and ceiling.

Ancient marble shaped itself into arrays of figurines and statues of religious heroes from decades past. At their feet, words, passages and illustrations were etched by an unseen hand, creating passages of religious verse and beautiful illustrations of a god-like being. He was tall, broad and strong. His frame seemed able to weather any challenge and carry any burden - a powerful protector of all beneath him. But there was a secondary image that caught Arthur's attention. Hidden in the background was another figure. White and pasty, her face was covered by long, straight auburn hair stretching down to her ankles. She looked so distant and yet so familiar. So sad and yet content. In contrast with Deity's boldness and strength, she was the epitome of duality, always in two places at once, holding two emotions in check. She seemed infinitely more complicated, more interesting.

The walls were finishing their building process, but there were no windows within them. On cue, shards of coloured glass flew past as if carried by a spring wind. The shards blew into the gaping holes in the wall, filling them with stained glass portraits of pain, love and suffering of the one true Deity.

Each pane chronicled one of the steps of Deity, numbering twelve. But the centrepiece, the thirteenth pane, stood above them all. Inside was Deity himself, staff in hand, welcoming back the woman Blue had seen drawn on the floor. She looked sullen and sad as she returned to his bulging arms.

From nothingness came benches, chairs, candles and clerics. Several of them glanced at her and muttered incoherently as they turned away. Most kept quietly to themselves and their study of the testament.

"Welcome to the Cathedral," said the cleric. "This is our home. Without it, we would be lost forever."

"Why is it hidden?" asked Arthur. "Do you have something to hide?"

"No, it is to protect us from those who don't believe. Those who seek to destroy us simply for the sake of argument. Those like yourself."

"Where have you taken the Earth Mother?" demanded Arthur.

"Caliph will answer all of your questions," said the cleric. He turned towards Blue. "He is waiting for you."

"Good," said Arthur. "I have many things to ask him."

"As I said before," said the cleric, "your presence is not requested, but you may wait here while Caliph speaks with the Heir of Destiny."

"And what am I supposed to do in the meantime?" Arthur asked impatiently.

"Do what you usually do. Listen to your tortured souls." The cleric motioned to Blue and she followed his shimmering cloak of water past a golden chair that had settled in from the ceiling. The cleric led her behind the curtain and into the inner sanctum, leaving Arthur alone with his headphones.

Both Arthur and Mmorpg were left standing by themselves. Mmorpg looked at Arthur and said, "Forget this! I want to see what they're saying." Without another word, Mmorpg floated towards the curtain and passed on through.

Arthur wandered over to a nearby bench, sat down and proceeded to lose himself in the infinite consciousness streaming from the soul box on his hip. From that box, Arthur poured through the thoughts of a generation, voluntarily broadcast. The topics were varied and disorganized. It took a trained ear to make headway through the synaptic collage. Those in pain or misery poured their thoughts onto these bulletin boards, documenting their limited successes and continual failures. Expressing their deepest fears and greatest dreams, they came together in a forum of both the lost and the found. There they found something they could find nowhere else: someone willing to listen, someone willing to care. And Arthur would lose himself within their worries and their loves, drowning his consciousness in the streaming thoughts of all those who chose to broadcast them. He heard some people were using the black boxes to go "soul steady", to share their most intimate thoughts with one another for twenty-four hours a day, both inside and outside Evermore. He thought that it must be nice to be so close to someone.

A thlogger, known only as Chameleon, was one of Arthur's favourites. Today, Chameleon was posting very rapidly, eager to get out every raw emotion trapped inside. His posts were always entertaining, but as Chamelon poured out his thoughts, Arthur heard an echo. He kept hearing the words spoken twice, once from the headphones and then again from somewhere inside the Cathedral.

Arthur logged out of the forum and listened. After a long pause, Arthur heard the familiar tone of Chameleon's voice. Turning around in his seat, he saw Chameleon for the first time. Even though Arthur had been privy to his thoughts for quite some time, the person he saw was a stranger. Chameleon was on a bench behind Arthur, speaking to a cleric who had taken the unusual step of pulling back his watery hood, revealing a youthful black and bald head. Trying not to draw attention, Arthur eavesdropped on their conversation.

"... but you must understand, contentment is not a result but a choice," said the black cleric. Yellow lens revealed his name to be Luther.

"But I was told if I lived my life a certain way, bought certain things, I would be loved and happy. I would never be lonely and afraid. But I'm not happy; I'm miserable. I am always alone and I am always afraid."

"Of course, so are we all. Happiness is made of none of those things. Happiness is not a product you can buy. It is a choice. We choose whether or not to be happy, to enjoy what little time we have. You are miserable and alone because for some reason you wish to be miserable and alone. You get something out of it. A certain pride, an expression of your individualism perhaps."

"But what can I do to get past that?" asked Chameleon. "I want to be happy, but I don't know what to do. How do I change?"

"No, you don't seem to understand," said Luther. "It's not something you change. You change your clothes, your hair, your voice, your personality. You have always tried to become someone else. You believe if you become this other person, then you will be happy. You believe that someone else has all the answers, but..."

"But I want to be *perfect*," interrupted Chameleon. "I want to lead the perfect life. I want to have the right clothes, the right job, the right girlfriend. I want everything to be perfect. Why can't everything just be perfect?"

"Perfection is a mirage. It is only perfect if you believe it to be so. It is a choice for you and you alone. You can continue to be perfect, to be something that you are not. Or, you can let it go and try to find happiness and contentment within yourself, not as an image but as your true self, not as a dream, but as reality - as a true reflection of yourself and no one else."

"But I can change, it's easy. I can do better. I can learn more and become better. I'm a late bloomer, I'll hit my stride soon enough and then everyone will love me. Everyone will respect me. I will be perfect one day. I will adorn magazine covers, be a celebrity guest on day-time talk shows. Everyone will know me by name and appreciate all I have done. People will watch my biography on TV and dream of living a life like mine. Eastwood didn't become famous until he was thirty-four. Nobody makes it until their thirties, it'll be the same for me. I'm just waiting to be discovered, for my genius to be seen for the brilliance it is. It is only a matter of time. It is only a matter of time until my life is perfect. A matter of time," Chameleon repeated to himself soothingly.

Luther sighed deeply. "My friend, you simply don't understand."

****

Blue was led into the back of the church. The cleric stopped in front of an iron door. He looked at her worriedly and spoke.

"Beyond this door lies the Caliph, the hand of Deity. Do not speak until spoken to, and never forget the power he holds within his hands. He is the instrument of Deity's will and the cup of Deity's knowledge. Do not fail to respect him or the absolution he represents. Deity does not smile kindly upon the unbeliever."

"He'd better respect me or I'll break his neck."

The door opened on its own accord. Blue stepped inside. She entered into a sleeping chamber of sorts, but instead of walls she saw images. Images of hope and despair, love and loss, screaming past her on all four sides at a solid sixty frames per second. Lying in the middle of the room, watching the images fly by, was the Caliph.

His appearance was not what Blue had expected. In fact, he did not even appear to be a man. Instead, Blue found herself looking at an extremely elderly woman lying in a hospital bed, arms helpless at her sides and sucking in a lifeline of intravenous fluid. She appeared to have been in a state of immobility for quite some time. Her sustenance on an IV had robbed her of every ounce of fat on her body, while her paralysis had atrophied her muscles to the point of non-existence. Without filler, the wrinkled skin constricted tightly around her skeleton, making it appear that her body had collapsed in upon itself. Where her chin had been, the mouth merely sank in the remains of her neck.

Unlike the rest of her body, her eyes were still full of life and fear. They stared out from her sunken face to gaze upon her guest. The eyes glistened, hypnotically demanding Blue's attention.

An unfamiliar voice popped into Blue's mind. "Tell me," it said, "Heir of Destiny, what service may I provide for you today?"

The words surprised Blue, for the invalid's lips never moved. *"You know me?"* she asked.

"Of course I do," responded the Caliph. "I have seen you many times before. Whether that was really you or just an image in my head is beyond my ability to comprehend. Does my appearance surprise you?"

"Yes, I thought the Caliph was a man."

"That would depend on who's looking. I am the articulation of your faith, a representation of your belief in a higher power. Apparently" — she looked at her decrepit body with large, vivid eyes — "your faith is weak."

"Faith is for the weak," said Blue.

"Tell me," asked the Caliph, "do you believe in the concept of god? In this world or another, in any way, shape or form?"

"No," said Blue, a hint of anger in her voice.

"Then you are most certainly unique among your kind. While most people don't subscribe to a particular organized religious group, the vast majority do believe in the concept of god - a nameless, shapeless entity of omnipotence that loves them and cares for them no matter the sin or situation. You are different. The possibility that you could be dependent on anyone else, mortal or immortal, deeply angers you. Even now, you wish to strike me for the words I speak. To crush me for speaking any measure of truth. Perhaps that is why you see me in the form of an old and decrepit woman. No one could harm the old and weak, not even you."

"Don't bet on it."

"I don't intend to, but pay attention." The Caliph motioned with her eyes to the surrounding hallucination. "From here, I can see the lives of everyone in Evermore simultaneously. I can feel their insecurities eat away at them. Their limited successes bring me a jubilance beyond their own, for they are both my children and my masters. Look at her," commanded the Caliph, and the hallucination focused on Vanessa, preparing for the Spectacle. "She can never bring herself to approach the one she loves. She tells herself lie after lie about him, trying to prove his unsuitability. But he's always there, stapled to the back of her mind. She toys with herself as much as she does with any man, while he believes that he is in love with a woman that is above him, beyond him. She has hurt him deeply and he can't forgive her. Instead, he has dedicated himself to attacking the underpinnings of the society that puts her out of reach. He lashes out at our society, our lives, when really he wants to lash out at her. To hurt her in the same way she has hurt him. Love makes us do some very silly things, Heir of Destiny. These two are trapped by their inability to see what truly matters. They will be alone, or be with someone who will be no more than satisfactory. And that is how they will live their lives, trapped in a void of mediocrity."

"Why are you showing me this?" asked Blue.

"To help you understand a very simple concept. We all believe that we are singular, alone and unique. We cannot see how truly connected we are. We are not alone, but complex parts of a whole we can't even begin to comprehend. You believe you are alone among your kind, that you are an original character. In some ways you are. But in many ways you are not, Heir of Destiny."

"Why do you keeping calling me that?"

"Are you not familiar with the term? I thought it would be obvious by now." The Caliph looked up to the windows and blinked twice. The streaming visions of the Caliph's children dissolved to reveal twelve stained glass paintings.

The Caliph looked at the first one, beside the door. Blue followed her gaze. "In the beginning, there was only Deity and Destiny. After much wandering they found each other, as shown in the first window." Blue saw an image of a man holding the hand of a saintly female figure, who wore a white cloak and looked shyly at him over her slanted nose. The second window showed Deity, a beam of light flying from his extended fist into the air. The third window showed the woman cradling a infant giraffe.

"The second and third windows chronicle the creation of Evermore. Deity was responsible for rocks, trees, the physical landscape of the world. Destiny was the one who created all life within that realm, including us.

"The fourth window chronicles the dawn of the magi, when our ancestors first entered this land. You can see Destiny bringing them bread to survive the torturous early years. In the fifth painting, the magi are thriving, but new problems arose. Bored with peace and prosperity, the magi raised pointless questions over which to argue. We call this era 'the Great Debate', where the magi shown in the sixth painting debated amongst themselves over who was the one true god: Deity or Destiny. Unfortunately, this conflict was unresolvable. In the seventh window, the magi have divided themselves into two groups — those who worshiped Destiny and those who prayed to Deity."

Blue looked at the figure of Destiny and saw a tear streaming down her cheek.

"Why does she look so sad?" she asked.

"Because she worries about her flock for the pain they inflict upon themselves. She laments our inescapable human need to divide ourselves, to find conflict where there should be peace, war where there should be love. 'Destiny's Lament' is one of the most enduring images of our faith."

Looking at the same window Blue's eyes moved to Deity, who

appeared fearful and angry.

"Deity was jealous that any would choose his wife over him. As you can see in the eighth window, this led to the War of the Magi."

Blue looked to the window and saw Deity leading his flock with a sword of gold. Destiny, however, hung her head in disappointment, her eyes hidden behind her hair.

"In the ninth window, Deity stood victorious over the field of the dead, the remaining kneeling before his might; Destiny was gone. In the tenth window, we find Destiny hidden deep in a cellar. She clutches a young child with unparalleled love and tenderness.

"The eleventh window shows the discovery of Destiny and her forced exile from Evermore. Note how in the painting, the baby is hidden from Deity's sight. She took the baby, leaving only its blue bow, and left this realm never to return. The final painting is known as 'Deity's Regret'. As you can see, Deity has realized the error of exiling the woman he loves and his unknown child." Blue looked at the final stained glass window. Inside, she saw Deity looking out towards the horizon. He held a blue ribbon in his hand.

"*Did she ever return?*" asked Blue.

"No," said the Caliph, "and she never will. The child, however, will return. Our histories stipulate that one day the Heir of Destiny will return to the land. And I believe that day has come, for you are Destiny's Heir - the one who shall step through the shadows of Nocturne and the heights of Nirvana to bring about the end of the world."

"*The end of the world?*"

"The destruction of this realm and all who inhabit it, leaving only the Nirvana of shared consciousness, the fusion of experience and emotion. When we shall finally discard our human husks and become one soul, together for evermore."

"*You're crazy.*"

"Alas, you cannot understand. You have become so trapped in your shell that you cannot see the truth surrounding you."

"*Why me? Why do you think it's me?*"

"The symbolism of the colour blue is no coincidence. It is your birthright, your name, the scar upon your cheek."

"*I was not born with this. This was done to me.*"

"Not in this realm. Not in this time, Blue, Heir of Destiny. Your fate has been decided."

"*Fate is just an excuse to be weak, to let others control you.*"

"So you say," mused the Caliph. "So you say."

"*Why have you been following us, interfering with us?*"

"First of all, we had to be sure it was you. We've had our hopes raised before and our spirits disappointed. Second, we had to prevent you from facing the demon who haunts these lands."

"*The killer?*"

"We are all killers, Destiny's Heir. But you seek to face him too soon, far before you're ready."

"*And when will I be ready?*" asked Blue with a hint of malice.

A long sigh came from the living corpse before her. "You must first pass through the burning shadows of the Nocturne, where you will be cleansed of your sins and debts. As you pass through the realm from which none have returned, you will face unspeakable horrors and visions that will haunt you. But pass through it you must, as it is foretold. Upon passing through the Chamber of Souls you will find the gates of Nirvana, heaven upon earth. Pass through and you will come face to face with the glory of Deity himself. He will either embrace or destroy you, depending on how pure you are."

"*I am not pure.*"

"So you say. The Nocturne will cleanse you, but will it be enough to meet Deity's approval? That is for the moment undecided."

"*And Destiny?*"

"Destiny cannot be found in this world. She has left, never to return."

"*I don't have time for this. I've got work to do.*"

The old woman smiled and Blue saw she had no teeth. "Then you will fail, and that we cannot allow. You must first pass through the trials and win the approval of Deity. Only then can you face the killer you seek and bring upon us the end of the world. Go, Heir of Destiny, lead us to the dawn of a new day."

"*And the people who will die, what about them?*"

"Tragic, but unavoidable. Tell me, are you really that concerned about their lives?" asked the Caliph.

"*No,*" answered Blue calmly, "*I'm not.*"

"Nor should you be. You are far more precious, Heir of Destiny. For within you, all our fates are sealed."

"*No. I will face him and I will crush him.*" Fury poured out of her blue eyes.

"No, dear child, you will fail and all will be lost."

"*I don't fail,*" said Blue.

"Without faith, you already have," said the Caliph.

"*Let me tell you about my faith,*" said Blue as she moved closer to the bed. "*Let me tell you what I believe.*" Blue placed her thumbs on the Caliph's eyes. "*I could crush your eyes like raisins without a second thought. God won't stop me because there is no god. There is no one protecting us. There is no one watching over us. We are alone and must fend for ourselves.*"

"Let her go Blue," said Mmorpg. Blue turned to her right and saw Mmorpg appear out of thin air.

"*How long have you been listening?*"

"Long enough. Let her go or I'll take your gun away."

Blue hesitated.

"Let her go. You'll have someone to kill soon enough."

Blue released the Caliph's eyes.

"Did God not stop you," said the Caliph. "Know this, Deity has a plan for all of us, including you. No matter what you do, it shall come to pass."

Blue turned walked away.

"Remember," called the Caliph. "Embrace the fall, for only then can we find salvation."

****

Arthur grew impatient waiting for Blue to return. He flipped through his lenses, trying to gather as much information about this place as possible, since he might never get to visit again. He synaptically recorded every detail, every name, every byte of data he could find on the Cathedral and its inhabitants. "Great," he said to himself. "I may have to add another chapter to my thesis."

"That is not your major problem." The voice came from behind him. Arthur turned and saw a masked cleric slowly approaching.

"For a long time I have watched you. I have seen you walk from one end of this land to the other. You have spent your life in search of the truth, but you have always found failure."

Arthur cocked his eyebrow. The cleric continued.

"Despite your efforts, illumination has eluded you. You have failed because your search for truth is instead a search for meaning. You search for meaning because you have always found yourself alone. You have always found yourself lost. And you are lost because you are living a lie."

Arthur frowned, his discomfort growing.

"You have never wanted to admit it to yourself, but the face you wear is not your own. It is a mask you have created to make sense of the world, to make sense of yourself. But it is an illusion, a mirage. And it is preventing you from discovering your true self."

Arthur's teeth clenched behind his lips. The cleric drew closer.

"For all of your life, you have sought truth, you have searched for meaning and it is finally within your grasp. But first you must remove your mask and look upon yourself with new eyes."

With an open palm, the cleric raised his hand towards Arthur.

"Take my hand and I will show you the truth. I will show you who you truly are."

"I know who I am!" The words exploded from his chest, its intensity leaving Arthur's voice broken and staggered. The Cathedral faded away and Arthur found himself surrounded by faceless silhouettes. They were laughing at him, mocking his accomplishments and deriding his never-ending list of failures. But he would show them. He would be the one to eclipse them all. At the end, he would be the one laughing at them. That was the way it was meant to be.

The faceless silhouettes faded away, and Arthur found himself back in the Cathedral. The cleric was gone. He glanced around, searching for his tormenter. But the cleric had disappeared; Arthur was alone again.

Blue appeared from behind the curtain, followed quickly by Mmorpg. They were eager to leave. They walked to the great wooden doors, which opened at their command.

"What did he say?" asked Arthur.

"*Waste of time.*"

"We need to keep moving," said Mmorpg. "What's our next step?"

"The gopher will lead us to the Waffle," said Arthur. He frowned and looked up and down the street.

"That's strange. It should have come back by now."

CHAPTER SEVENTEEN

GRAVES OF THE DISSIDENTS

"Can you track the gopher's progress?" asked Mmorpg.

"Not a problem," said Arthur.

Arthur switched to green lens. Condensing time, he watched the dotted green line of the gopher's progress. It stretched out from the Cathedral door and off into the distance, multiplying infinitely. The mashing of overlapping gopher trails from host to host was simply too complex to differentiate as anything more than a green blob of activity, but soon enough the trails coalesced back into a single gopher. It returned to its master by the shortest possible route, but then something changed. The path of the re-formed gopher deviated, zigzagging from host to host with no logical pattern, as if it were fleeing. The chase led back towards the Cathedral, slowing back into real time as the gopher approached.

Arthur looked up ahead. "It's coming, from the alley."

Sure enough, the gopher came running out of an alley thirty metres in front of them. It had a noticeable limp in its hind leg that was forcing it to sprint sideways like a ferret. As it approached, it let out a screech of warning to its masters. Arthur stepped forward. The gopher jumped into his arms and began to chatter rapidly. "I can't understand binary," said a Arthur. "Show us where you found the Waffle." The gopher continued to chatter away. "Mmorpg?"

Mmorpg furrowed his brow in concentration, "Strange, it keeps talking about a spider but spiders haven't been used for almost three ye—"

With a screech, the gopher bolted from Arthur's lap. Sensing danger, Arthur turned around and found himself face to face with the snarling mandibles of a mechanical spider.

The snarling spider leapt past him in pursuit of the gopher. The gopher led it away, then used a sewer grate to slip by the arachnid and double back. But in its injured state, the gopher couldn't outrun its hunter for long.

The spider closed on the helpless gopher in an instant. Trapping it with eight metallic legs, the spider mounted its aluminum prey and reared its head back for a fatal bite to the skull. But instead of the aluminum flesh of the gopher, the spider bit the hardened steel of a 9mm bullet. The round crushed the mouth and exploded rusted innards out the back of its body. A puff of charred powder rose from the barrel of Blue's semiautomatic. She smiled with satisfaction.

The gopher, struggling with its wounds, slumped to the ground. Arthur went to its side and pulled it to his chest. "Where are the Waffle?" he asked. "Did you find them?"

The gopher nodded and then slumped still. After a moment, its body fell into pieces. As they watched, the pieces formed themselves into an arrow on the ground, pointing west. It began to move, leading them towards the gopher's final search.

"*What was that?*" asked Blue, glancing back at the spider's mechanical innards as they walked.

"A spider," said Mmorpg. "They were used in the early days of the Internet to crawl along whatever network they could find, collecting information from each site's meta tags. This information was added to the massive databases used by search engines to improve access to the web. We used them here in a similar vein, crawling from zone to zone, host to host, collecting information about what, when and where."

"*But you said ...*"

"Yes, we decommissioned them about three years ago. As the

Underground expanded, the overhead in storing the data that the spiders collected was astronomical. We simply couldn't keep up. We gave up trying to keep track of it all. Instead, we created a registration system for the Downtown Core and left the Underground to its own devices."

"A wise decision," said Arthur. "Too much centralized control is never a good thing."

"In this situation, it simply wasn't feasible," said Mmorpg. "Since then, only one plausible alternative has been suggested—"

"And rejected," interrupted Arthur. "The R3X protocols are too risky."

"Since then," said Mmorpg, throwing a glare at Arthur. "We've used gophers for searches in the Underground. In the Downtown Core, every citizen, every building and every blade of glass is stored in our central servers for instant query. The kernel uses it to decide who can enter the Downtown Core."

"It can also be used to track individuals without their knowledge," said Arthur. "That's why I prefer the Underground. I don't get that same sensation that someone is watching me."

"We don't spy on our clients," said Mmorpg, "We locate individuals only when necessary to serve their needs. But you are right about the Underground, finding anything down here is impossible without the gophers."

"You just have to know your way around," said Arthur. "But that doesn't explain why the spider was attacking the gopher."

"Maybe it was sent by Marcony?"

"To slow us down? Could be. But if he did it would have left some tracks. The wreckage of the spider should still contain its embedded code. Or more accurately, the wreckage is the code. Mmorpg, can you decode it?"

"Well, it's in machine code, so I'll have to pass it through a decompiler to convert it from machine code to a high-level language. With the source code in hand, I can pull information from the spider's registers and match them to their corresponding variables inside the program. One of those variables will store the username of the avatar who dispatched the spider, but only if the right register hasn't been destroyed. It can be done, but it'll take quite some time."

"*Do it,*" said Blue.

"But what is so important about the Waffle that someone would go to such great lengths to stop us from finding them?" asked Mmorpg.

"There's only one way to find out," said Arthur, turning to the green path before him. "Follow the arrow."

The arrow led them into an industrial area, full of shiny new buildings. But it was empty, not a soul could be found.

"*What is this place?*" asked Blue.

"The future," said Mmorpg.

"*What?*"

"It's a pilot project recently started by the Consortium," said Arthur. "You see, they have this crazy dream about turning Evermore into an economic superpower. They believe they can build a virtual economy big enough to match the United States and China."

"Economic self-sufficiency is a perfectly valid goal," said Mmorpg.

"Not when you're stealing it," said Arthur. "If the Consortium planned for economic growth through innovation, creating new products and services, that would be fine. But that's not what they're doing. Instead, their strategy is to virtualize already existing jobs and bring them inside Evermore. That is the point of these industrial zones. The Consortium sets up these industrial zones in the Underground, free from the taxes and regulations of the real world. They then invite companies in to set up shop. Service jobs, the backbone of modern economies, will be virtualized and then transferred here. The employees will no longer have an office. They will simply jack into Evermore and come here to work. The companies will save millions in infrastructure costs, dodged regulations and unpaid taxes. These savings will be pocketed, with a small percentage going to the Consortium."

"That's not true," said Mmorpg. "The corporations still live in the real world. They will still have to pay taxes."

"No they won't. With globalization, corporations became multinational, moving from country to country to find the most competitive tax and regulatory environment. Imagine what will happen when these multinationals take the next step and become virtual corporations, when they move their business and all of their employees into Evermore. How do you tax something that doesn't exist? Tax revenues will plummet and so will the capability of government to provide services to their citizens."

"What about the major savings? With a virtual economy, you would no longer need roads, you would no longer need infrastructure. Everyone would live and work from home. Governments would save billions."

"Not enough to offset the losses. Governments still need revenues to provide services that can't be virtualized, like health care, public safety, even national defence. Besides, humanity was not designed to live in a box."

"Humanity has always adapted to an ever-changing environment. How is this different then-"

"*Would you girls shut up*," said Blue. "*We're here.*"

The arrow led to a simple square building, exactly like all the others in shape, size and colour. Whereas every other building vibrated with the uniform march of droning productivity, this one was quiet. No sign of activity was evident. The door, instead of being secured and guarded, was left ajar. They entered cautiously, Blue holding her pistol ready at her side.

They found themselves in a security checkpoint. The walls were a neutral colour, denoting safety and security. The carpet appeared to have been chosen according to the principles of feng shui: an attempt to bring serenity and purpose to a place dedicated to mindless productivity.

All was well but for the crumpled remains of the security turnstiles. Their debris lined the floor. Up ahead, Arthur could see one of the turnstiles embedded in a wall about twenty metres away. They stepped through the wreckage and followed the hallway as it jutted to the right, bringing them to the main floor.

It was a building without walls or rooms, only cubicles as far as the eye could see. Instead of typical cubes, the room contained row upon row of computer stations, with three foam walls giving privacy to the computer, but not its user. They were the pinnacle of productivity, maximizing both space and discomfort. The arrow led down the middle of the vast chamber, passing a sea of workstations.

In the middle of the room, they came upon a crushed

workstation. The soft fake wall, the plastic desk, the entire cubicle lay in pieces. Soon they saw more signs of damage. A battle had happened here – one that was heavily one-sided. None of the victims had gotten far.

But there were no bodies, there was no blood.

"Where are they?" asked Arthur.

Blue looked down at the ground. Arthur followed her gaze and saw something etched into the carpet: two sets of five marks, creating ten grooves that moved off to the right. The grooves were the same width as fingers. They followed the grooves, as did the arrow. It led them to a wall they had not seen before. Along this wall, a door was left ajar.

Stepping inside, they found themselves standing on a catwalk above a huge warehouse. Below them, the catwalk descended in a square spiral staircase. Arthur went to the edge and peered down to find a drop of about three stories. A dusty concrete floor lay below him, marked by a small crater where each of the bodies had fallen. From that spot, the carcasses were dragged again through the dust. Following the trail, Blue and Arthur saw it at the same time — a graveyard of about thirty bodies. Collapsed, broken and twisted, the bodies were carefully positioned into letters. The gopher's arrow pointed right to the bottom of the message:

HELP ME

"*There's no blood?*" asked Blue.

"Of course not," responded Arthur.

"*There's never any blood?*"

"That would be by design," said Mmorpg. "You see, parents wouldn't be so eager to allow their children access to Evermore if they had to worry about blood and gore. The same goes for profanity and nudity – all eliminated by our obscenity filters."

"My god, is this them?" said Arthur.

"Yes, we've found the Waffle," said Mmorpg.

"*Not all of them,*" said Blue.

"What do you mean?"

Blue reached down and picked up a whip constructed of electric cable. The broken whip sparked in protest.

"Toland's men?" asked Mmorpg.

"She's right," said Arthur. "I recognize a couple of the bodies from the Globe. They were all wearing the same suits."

"What were they doing here?" asked Mmorpg.

"Meeting with the Waffle I suppose. I didn't realize Marcony had that type of reach. He must have been bankrolling them for some time. Using them to open up loopholes in the law he could exploit. That might explain the spider. I've underestimated him. Marcony had far more influence then I thought."

"And now Toland has his connections, and he's using them to find out what we know."

"Not from this group."

"We'll have to dispatch someone on the outside to check on their bodies."

"You mean cover them up. Can't have your future shareholders finding out about this, right?" said Arthur.

"They already know, but they prefer to believe Klein's leak. The director has already received several hundred inquiries from investors saying they can't wait to find out how it ends. Our expected initial stock offering has almost doubled since this crisis became public. We're now the hottest ticket in town, and everyone wants a piece of the action."

"How touching," said Arthur. "Now could you tell me why I'm about to puke? I don't have a real body here."

"Because your mind is telling you that you should feel sick after what you've just seen."

"Of course it is. I hate this place."

"No one forced you to be here."

"Yeah, I know." Arthur pulled himself away from the edge of the cakewalk.

"Where's Burke?" asked Mmorpg.

"I see him," responded Arthur. His eyes fell on a body with white, spiky hair. "But if the killer has targeted the Waffle, there's no reason why he wouldn't go after the rest of the Consortium, maybe even after Klein."

"The Consortium has four striders at the ready, which should be more than enough. Besides, he would have to get through the Great Gate first, and it's impenetrable when it's locked down."

"That's what you said about your security protocols. A lot of good they did us."

"They didn't fail," said Mmorpg.

"The corpses might disagree with you, my friend. We can't assume anything is the way it should be."

"You're not here to waste our time with your opinions," said Mmorpg. "You're here to help us catch the killer as fast as possible. Every minute we waste arguing gives him more time to kill again."

"Well, to find the killer we need a lead," said Arthur. "It's tough to find leads without witnesses.

"Maybe he knows something?"

Arthur wheeled around to look at the target of Blue's gaze. There, on the warehouse floor, he saw only corpses. And then he saw it - a body twitching at the edge of the word HELP. The body crawled slowly away, changing the word to HELF in the process.

Arthur sprinted down the circular metal stairwell. Blue beat him down easily, leaping from the catwalk three stories to the ground. She landed with a hard *crunch*. The impact of her soles broke the concrete where she landed, and flakes of crushed rock sprayed out as she took the first few steps towards the survivor. The writhing body clung to life.

Arthur sprinted from the stairway and switched on his purple lens. He didn't have much time. The purple lens focused on the future corpse, leaving everything else—including Blue—blurred and irrelevant. His vision drew closer and closer to the victim, endlessly closer, until he entered the man's nostril.

And then he saw the world through the dying man's eyes. He saw Blue looking down at him as she examined his body. Standing behind her was the frozen form of Arthur, motionless during an unfinished step forward. He pushed the rewind button in his brain.

The purple lens produced images of spectacular clarity. The first images were of Blue walking backwards away from him into a converging cloud of dust, kneeling down and leaping up with perfect grace and strength. Then he pulled himself back into place, facing away from the walkway. Much time passed where nothing happened. And then he could feel the vibration of being dragged, but he was unable to see who was dragging him. He was pulled to a group of bodies at the foot of the stairwell.

Some time passed again and he was thrown up at high speed, bouncing off the railing of the catwalk. He was pushed by his feet back into the office, his fingers erasing the ten grooves before him, but his head was limp to the side, he could not see his mover. Finally, he came to his resting place, behind a demolished desk.

Seconds passed. Looking forward, he could see his fellow coworkers but the killer was blocked by flying debris. An electric whip flew past him, along with the pieces of a desk. The co-workers would rise up from the ground and meet the killer's fist as time moved in reverse.

If only he could see the killer's face.

As the killer moved away, the co-workers stood frozen in place. Their heads were tilted to the side, as though they slept standing up. Finally, his body began to rise off the ground. Arthur slowed the replay. He didn't want to miss anything. He pulled up and through the desk, the scattered pieces re-forming behind him. He fell back to his feet, looked forward and saw a blur pulling away from him.

Freeze frame, thought Arthur.

The rewinding stopped.

The image stood before him, waiting to be seen. A man was frozen in mid-charge. His head was lowered like a bull, his face hidden behind the brim of his brown Akubra hat. He wore a brown jacket with a high collar, blue jeans and brown steel-toed hiking boots. He was unarmed. Behind him stood the wreckage of desks and the bodies that had filled them. The one thing that stuck out to Arthur, more than anything else, was the navy bandanna wrapped around the brim of the killer's hat. Arthur recognized it as the Earth Mother's niqab.

Plus yellow lens, thought Arthur.

Like a filter, the yellow lens was placed on top of the purple lens, creating a dirty reddish tint over the scene before him. Arthur focused on the perpetrator, ignoring the names of victims popping up in yellow all around him. Finally, the killer's name appeared above the brown Akubra.

5B4A5446362E305D556E64656369646564

The vision began to blur. The image before him began to melt away. Arthur knew the truth, the witness was dying. He had to leave. If he was in the witness' mind when he died, his mind would die too. Arthur had no interest in becoming a vegetable.

But there was one question still bothering him. Why hadn't they logged off? A killer could ambush a single person before they could react, but not an entire room of people. At the first sign of trouble, everyone would have logged out of Evermore and disappeared. The killer should have faced an empty room.

Arthur hesitated as the edges of his vision melted towards the centre.

"Rewind," said Arthur.

The memory pulled back further until Arthur could see other co-workers standing in front of him. Some of them were Waffle. Some of the them were men in dark suits holding electric whips. They were watching the killer enter the room.

"Play," said Arthur. He could feel a hot sensation at the back of his skull.

The memory played itself forward. His co-workers watched in stunned silence. The killer walked to the first victim and smashed his head into a desk.

The group shuddered in surprise. Arthur's left eye became murky as the image turned to tapioca. He didn't have much time. He closed his left eye and watched with the right.

One of Toland's men attacked with the whip. Its crackling blue arc bounced harmlessly off the killer's shoulder. The killer tore his head clean off with a punch. Everyone started to scream.

The field of vision in his right eye became smaller as the outer edges became milk. He could feel the back of his brain burning.

The killer walked up to the third victim. The victim put up his hands and screamed "Kernel: logout". But the victim was not pulled out of Evermore. He did not disappear. Instead, his body shuddered. His head slumped to his shoulder. The killer slammed his head and his body into the floor. Two more victims tried to escape, but both shuddered and slept instead. The fear spread through the rest of the crowd.

"We can't get out," said one.

"Oh my god, we're trapped!" said another.

The vision in his right eye was gone as the image turned to mush. Arthur smelled kerosine as his brain burned. Despite the screams coming from his dying mind, Arthur heard the last victim's final words.

"Please God. I don't want to die," she said.

"Lens off," commanded Arthur.

Both the yellow and purple lenses flickered off, returning Arthur to the warehouse beside the pile of bodies. Arthur coughed in fits, even though he had no lungs with which to breath. His brain throbbed with pain. He looked over at the body of the last victim and watched as it shuddered and went still. He had gotten out just in time.

Nearby, Blue was hunched over the upper torso of Burke, examining the neckline of the Waffle's dead leader. Zooming in with red lens, Arthur could make out an odd indentation on Burke's neck – a jagged edge leading to a lip at the bottom and the number 1 in reverse at the top. Blue rose and returned a yellow can to the confines of her coat.

"What did you find?" asked Mmorpg.

"What did you do?" said Arthur.

Mmorpg didn't look surprised.

"What do you mean?" he said.

"They couldn't log out," said Arthur. "They tried to log out, but they couldn't leave. They would just fall asleep. The killer massacred them because they couldn't leave. You disabled the logout function didn't you?"

"Calm down. It was the only way we could guarantee the killer wouldn't escape," said Mmorpg. "If he logged out, there would be no chance of tracking him down."

"I knew it" said Arthur. "I knew there was something strange about how worried you were about time. You were always pushing us to move faster. That didn't make any sense when the killer could log out at any time. The best you could do would be to find out who he was and prosecute him in the real world. I never realized you would actually try to trap him inside Evermore with millions of innocent people."

"It was a necessary step to make sure he didn't get away. It was the only way to protect our users."

"No. If you wanted to protect your users, you would have gone public and shut down Evermore. You would have suffered some losses, but you would have protected them from the killer."

"If we had shut everything down, he would have simply waited until we reopened and killed again."

"So instead, you trap your users inside a cage with the murderer. They can't leave, Mmorpg. There's nowhere for them to run."

"We've done everything in our power to protect our users," said Mmorpg. "Their safety is our number one concern."

"No, you've done everything to protect your investors. I *knew* it. I *knew* one day you guys would go too far. I just never realized you would let people die so you could maintain your stock price."

"That's not what this is about."

"So I assume that Evermore's upcoming stock offering never came up once then?"

Mmorpg remained silent.

"I thought so. I'm done." Arthur pulled out the envelope from his coat pocket and threw it onto the ground. "Nothing is worth this. I want to log out."

"I can't let you do that, Arthur," said Mmorpg.

"Of course, you've disabled the logout function. Turn it back on, Mmorpg."

"Not until the job is done."

"That won't save you. Once I get out of here I'm going straight to the cops. I hope you like prison, because you're going to be there for the rest of your life."

"As will you," said Mmorpg. "If you go to the cops, you will be charged as an accessory and you will be convicted. We will make sure of that."

"I had nothing to do with this," said Arthur.

"You accepted payment on our behalf. You knew there was a killer, yet you didn't go to the cops. Instead, you took our money and have been helping us cover it up."

"That not...—that's not how it happened."

"Once you took that envelope, your neck was on the line just like ours. You are an accessory, Arthur, whether you like it or not. If we shut everything down now and get the police involved, the killer would just disappear and wait for another opportunity. No. We have to stop him right here, right now."

Arthur said nothing.

"Now you have two choices. You can contact the police and go to jail, or you can pick up that envelope and help us track the killer down."

Arthur hesitated.

"How much time do we have?" he asked.

"It's 1630 hours in Evermore Standard Time," said Mmorpg. "The Spectacle will end in about three hours. "Once it's over, millions will attempt to log out at the same time. After that, it will be nearly impossible to keep this under wraps."

"You have no idea what you've unleashed," said Arthur.

"The people will understand."

"No, when people realize they are trapped in a world with a killer, keeping this a secret will be the least of your worries. You are going to have massive panic. Your so-called 'superior' society will rip itself into pieces."

"I know."

"No you don't. You don't have any idea of what you're dealing with."

"Arthur, I am very aware of the stakes. That is why we have to find the killer as quickly as possible and bring him to justice."

Blue cocked her Beretta.

"*Have you girls stopped whining yet?*" she asked.

Mmorpg turned towards Arthur.

"That's depends," he said, "do we have a lead?"

Arthur bent down and picked up the envelope. He returned it to his coat pocket.

"We have a name," Arthur replied, "but it makes no sense. It's just letters and numbers." He repeated the name to Mmorpg.

"That's an odd name. It's in hexadecimal."

"Hexadecimal?"

"Yeah, it's a list of seventeen digits marked by base-16 numbers rather than the base-10 we're used to," explained Mmorpg. "They're typically used in pairs in computers so it translates to '91, 74, 84, 70, 54, 46, 48, 93, 85, 110, 100, 101, 99, 105, 100, 101, 100'. Can I send a gopher to track it?"

"No," said Mmorpg, "the gophers are programmed to track alpha-numeric characters through a markup language. They won't know what to do with a base-16 number."

"Hmmm," said Arthur.

"Do you have any ideas?"

"No, not on the name. I have scores of theories, but nothing that puts the pieces together. Has the Spectacle started yet?"

Arthur moved towards the door. The others followed him.

"Just started," said Mmorpg. "Where are we going?"

"We're going to see an old friend - Palette."

"Palette? What are we going to get out of that lunatic?"

"Perspective," replied Arthur as he and Blue left the building. "We need a fresh perspective."

CHAPTER EIGHTEEN

THE OPENING ACT

Vanessa stood backstage, watching the opening act of the Spectacle. On stage was a band she had never seen before, playing a song she had never heard. But instead of four men playing instruments, they were themselves the music. Flowing like the northern lights, floating on the bass and pounding on the beat, the band did not play the song – they *became* the song. Much like the opening scene of Disney's *Fantasia*, they stripped the music of all physical structure, allowing the audience not only to listen to the melody, but to feel it with all of their senses.

Vanessa watched the crowd, scanning the faces row by row. The seats were only about half full; people were still coming in. It was the final act everyone was interested in– the Goddess Pageant. First and foremost, they were here to see her and Avideh, to find out who would rise above them all to join the best and brightest of their world. Vanessa's hair stretched in preparation.

"Calm yourself, child. It's bad luck to view the audience before the performance," said the motherly voice of Lamare.

"I know, but I want to be used to it before I go on," said Vanessa as she brushed her hair.

"He's not here," Lamare said.

"Who?" Vanessa feigned ignorance.

"You know who," chided her patron. "I'll tell you again — don't get mixed up with him. You can do so much better."

"I know."

"He has no status. He has no position here. He can do nothing for you."

"I know."

"Then why do you look for him?"

"I'm not looking for him. I'm looking at the crowd."

"You have many talents, dear Vanessa. Subtlety is not one of them."

"But I never talk to him. I leave him alone and he leaves me alone. That's fair." The ends of Vanessa's hairs stood on end as if possessed by static electricity.

Lamare frowned.

"You ignore him too blatantly, as if to make a point."

"Don't be silly," said Vanessa. "I have no interest in him. None at all."

"Then why do you have this?" asked Lamare. Vanessa turned to see her patron holding a black box and a pair of foam headphones. A soul box.

"What is that?" asked Vanessa innocently.

Lamare shook her head.

"You know what this is. I found it in your closet."

"So what if it's mine? Maybe I find the thoughts of others comforting. Maybe it helps me sleep."

"It's only tuned to one frequency."

Vanessa's face remained aloof, but her hair, pulsing momentarily in surprise, gave her away.

"How long have you been listening to his thoughts?" scolded Lamare.

"Not long," said Vanessa, eyes to the floor. While her hair curled into 9s, a small grin drew itself upon her face.

"What are you smiling about?" said Lamare.

Vanessa's smile broadened. "He thinks about me," she beamed.

"Irrelevant," said Lamare. "He is irrelevant. You are above him. Do you want to be trapped here?"

Vanessa's smile vanished, her hair falling limp to her sides. "No," she said softly, shaking her head.

"Then get your head out of the clouds and focus on the task at hand. There is no prize for second place. You either ascend or you fall. Which is it going to be?"

"Ascend. I want to rise." And as she said the words, her hair rose and constructed a fortress of beauty upon her head, revealing her luxurious neck and ears.

"Then go down to the performers' lounge. One of the judges is there. This is the perfect opportunity to make a good first impression."

"Which one is it?" asked Vanessa.

"PRNC. The only one that matters."

"He's here?"

"Downstairs. But you better hurry, before Avideh gets the same idea."

Vanessa moved quickly towards the performers' lounge, looking back only once to see Lamare taking her soul box away, probably to destroy it. Vanessa wondered when she would hear his voice again.

Encased at the base of the Chrysalis' spire, the performers' lounge was relaxed by most standards. A simple table was set up for beverages. Even though drinking was not necessary to survive in Evermore, it provided a comfortable social convenience, giving people a prop with which to relax. The room was littered haphazardly with chairs and couches. Walls were plastered with pop-culture posters emblazoned with the latest fad.

The music was kept upbeat and low in volume, creating an atmosphere that encouraged conversation. Various performers stood and sat, trying to relax before their curtain calls.

PRNC sat in the middle of the room. He was the closest thing to royalty that Evermore had. Well educated, handsome, with the right combination of pedigree and populism, many saw him as a potential sovereign. He was Evermore's most eligible bachelor, the cream of the crop.

As Vanessa entered, everyone's eyes moved to her, save for his. He would not be so easily charmed. Instead, he busied himself in conversation with two women seated on the love seat across from him. The first woman was tall and thin. Her skin, painted by the sun over generations upon the Somalian shore, was a bold and sensual black that commanded attention. Her eyes glinted green and her pearly whites glowed even more brightly against her dark skin. Her hair, shoulder length and fine, shimmered as she smiled and laughed at PRNC's jokes.

Vanessa recognized her. She was a princess, a prospect for next year's competition. The VIP section would be full of them, fighting for attention. The competition had not even begun, and the next generation was already working to replace her.

The second woman was less glamorous, but made up for it with spunk. She was the singer and drummer for an all-girl punk band playing at the Spectacle. She wore spiked purple hair, heavy mascara and piercings all over her body. She engaged PRNC with wit and humour.

Vanessa, uninterested in talking to anyone else below her station, had little else to do but listen to the conversation and learn as much about PRNC as she could. She found an empty couch behind them and sat down. But she did not sit on the couch itself and directly face them; no, that would have been too obvious. Instead, she sat on the back of the couch with one side of her hip, so she would be perpendicular to the conversation and thus less intrusive. From here, she tilted her head fourty-five degrees, half to the conversation at hand and half away. She smiled a sly grin to herself, impressed by her subterfuge.

As noted before, subtlety was unfortunately not one of Vanessa's strong suits. Though brilliant in her mind, her thinly-veiled deception was obvious from her awkward perch to her lack of activity. Even her hair gave her away, acting on her emotions rather than her commands and tilting towards PRNC like flowers towards the sun.

PRNC noticed right away and smiled. His companions took a moment to register the arrival of another participant. The black woman gave a confused look to PRNC, who smiled at the situation and winked to let her in on the joke. The black beauty smiled and settled back into her seat, ignoring Vanessa's eavesdropping.

PRNC decided to take the conversation in a different direction, to satisfy the curiosity of his new guest. Up until then, they had been talking generalities: life in politics, debates on topics of a dubious interest, and finally dating. He seized upon the topic like it was his own; deciding to have some fun with it and see how much he could get away with.

"No," he said, in response to an inquiry from the beauty, "it is usually best not to lie to a woman. They're so skilled at detecting deception that they easily pick apart the lies of an amateurish male. In most cases, it's just best to be honest and leave it at that. If she can't handle it, there's always someone who can."

"Unfortunately," responded the singer, "there seem to be a lot of men who are very good at deception. Therein lies the problem. There's so much deception going on that when a nice guy comes along, it's impossible to tell if he's the genuine article."

"Tell me," said PRNC, "if you had to choose between a nice guy and a fun guy, which would you choose?"

"Fun," the two women said in unison.

"Exactly. A wise man once told me that people get exactly what they're looking for. You both could find some really nice guy who'll put you on a pedestal and raise your 1.3 kids like a perfect husband and father, but you would be bored out of you skulls. What you really want is an exciting guy, a guy for whom every day is an adventure. Where at any moment you could end up anywhere and be doing anything."

"Yeah," they both agreed. The black beauty added, "Life was not meant to be boring."

"Absolutely right. We need the unexpected, that's what makes life worth living. It is what we don't see, what we can't predict, that makes life exciting and fun. Now, have either of you two ever dated a man like that?"

"Not yet," they said again in unison, captivated.

"That's a shame," said PRNC.

The opening act came down into the lounge. Vanessa had expected them to transform into their human forms, but they remained as instances of light. They moved through the room and engaged in conversation, the colour of their light changing to match their mood. The set must have gone well, for the four band members beamed with bright rainbow colours.

"I'm next," the singer said. She bounced towards the door. "Wish me luck."

"Good luck," said the model, smiling. Vanessa admired the

white shine of the model's perfect teeth.

"It was a pleasure to meet you, Ms. Turner," said PRNC, extending his hand. "Knock 'em dead."

"Naturally," said the drummer before she bounded up the steps.

"You had best get prepared," PRNC said to the black beauty, "the competition in the stands will be very fierce tonight. I wish you luck."

The black beauty seemed a bit taken aback by his attempt to end the conversation politely, but she recovered quickly, curtseying before moving towards the dressing room.

PRNC slowly turned towards Vanessa. "So tell me," he said sardonically, "is it your habit to eavesdrop on the conversations of others?"

Shock flashed briefly across Vanessa's eyes, but it was soon replaced by the cool detachment that defined her image.

"Of course not, whatever are you talking about?" she asked innocently.

PRNC grinned. "Exactly what I thought. I see your legendary subtlety has been greatly exaggerated."

"Ridiculous," she said, "I was merely sitting by myself. I wish to be at peace before my performance."

"Of course you were," said PRNC with a small smile. "Then I had best leave now and allow you to find your 'peace.'"

"Oh, it's too late for that now. You've already disturbed me," Vanessa lied. "You might as well stay around and entertain me to make up for it."

He grinned. "Sure, why not?" he said. "I haven't got anything better to do." He sat down in his chair and leaned back casually. "So tell me something about yourself, Vanessa. What's your story?"

"You know my story."

"No," he said, "I know the official version. Both you and I know that's not what we'd call entirely accurate, is it?"

"Of course it's true," she scoffed. "I am nothing more than I appear to be. Honest," she batted her eyes.

"Do you have any brothers, sisters?" he asked, bemused.

"None. I am the only one of my kind." Vanessa turned her body away from him, but not too far away. She suppressed a smile.

"I see. Then is it your habit to sit all by your lonesome before a performance?"

"Of course," she looked away from his intense hazel eyes. "I like my solitude."

"For a girl who's supposed to be the most popular celebrity in the land, you certainly spend a lot of time by yourself," he smirked.

She pretended to sneer at him with condescension.

"I think," he continued, "it's all a sham really. I think you're not as pretty or as engaging as your reputation pretends. I think this is all just a marketing ploy. It used to be that the Goddess Pageant was about finding the most stunning and provocative woman in the Underground. Now it's about the one who can run the best marketing campaign, who has the best manager or patron."

He smiled at her.

"Why should we choose you?" PRNC asked. There was a twinkle in his eye. "What makes you so special that we should ignore everyone else? That we should ignore those who have longer legs, bigger curves, a better voice? What makes you a goddess?"

Blush rushed to Vanessa's cheek. She looked him straight in the eye and said, "When I am on the stage, I will show you why I am a goddess."

"You better," he grinned. "I hope you're a lot more interesting on stage than you are in person, or else you'll be stuck down here forever."

"You won't be able to take your eyes off me, Mr. PRNC, I promise you that," said Vanessa. Standing up haughtily, she strutted out of the room with her hair in hot pursuit, the dark strands dragging themselves reluctantly away from PRNC.

CHAPTER NINETEEN

THE ART OF WAR

Blue, Arthur and Mmorpg approached a building made of black glass. Like a tumour, the rectangular base of the building multiplied and stretched out in all directions in a fractal pattern. Upon its entrance, the words "The Studio – 1142 Forsyth Park" were etched into the glass. Oblong and staggered, the building was the perfect home for an art gallery.

"Are you sure this is a good idea?" asked Mmorpg.

"If you want to catch the killer quickly, we need to know where he will be, not where he's been," said Arthur. "We need to understand his motivations. Palette can help with this. He's always had strange perspectives on things."

"That's because he's an artist. They're always a little weird," said Mmorpg.

They entered a dark hallway, glass cases on either side filled with vignettes depicting artistic violence. Men armed with guns, knives or only their bare hands were locked in struggles for survival that were both frightening and beautiful. Their battles were captured in super slow-motion, the scene spinning around with the cinematography of a virtual camera designed to always show the best view of the action. These were live recordings of performance art.

"*I've seen this before,*" said Blue.

"Yes, he has a gallery down on Malon Mall. He is very good, and well compensated for his work."

"So how is his strange perspective going to help us?" asked Mmorpg.

"There is a pattern to these crimes, something that doesn't make rational sense. I can't see the pattern, but perhaps Palette can. If there's something there, he will be able to see it. He understands the mind of an artist far better than I."

"We're hunting for a killer, not an artist," said Mmorpg as he floated past a figure getting its head chopped off with a bloodless blow.

"It's surprising how often those two personalities coincide," sighed Arthur.

Arthur turned towards Blue but found her attention focused on something else entirely. Inside the final glass case at the end of the hallway stood an emaciated figure encased in a strong black exoskeleton. It looked like a robotic ninja. Its feet, covered by a metallic slit-toe tabi shoes, seemed almost amphibious. But what surprised Arthur was the head. Instead of a face or a mask, the head was a round steel helmet. Alone in the centre of the helmet was a single red crystal eye. While the shell was silent, Arthur could sense malevolence radiating from its slight and starved frame. At the base upon which the cybernetic ninja stood was a label: "Coming Attractions."

Arthur pulled his attention away from the case and towards a pair of silver doors at the end of the hallway. A message was written on them with a paintbrush: "From Nocturne to Nirvana."

Blue stepped forward and pushed open the doors. As the large doors creaked open, the three of them entered the chamber.

They found themselves in a large square glass room, surrounded by walls of silver. A thin sliver of water trickled down the walls and collected in a shallow pool stretching across the reflective black floor. In the middle of the room stood four square pillars coloured silver like the walls. Between the pillars, a golden "N" was etched upon the opposite wall. Another pair of doors rested below it. Arthur looked to the left wall and saw a golden "W" just below the ceiling. To his right, he saw a golden "E". Arthur turned around and saw yet another golden character above the entrance behind him. It read "S".

"Was he afraid we'd get lost?" asked Mmorpg.

"It must have some artistic meaning," said Arthur.

He took a closer look at the wall. On the surface, there were shallow grooves shaped like fractals. The physical tattoo stretched across the room, around the floor, up the pillars and across the pillar. The pattern was everywhere.

"It's beautiful," said Mmorpg.

"It's unusually peaceful for Palette," said Arthur. "Something must be wrong."

"Has the killer come for him too?"

Blue drew her weapon and held it ready at her side.

"*Stay here,*" she said as she stepped forward into the pool.

The water was only about an inch deep. Arthur watched as she moved slowly towards the pillars, always careful to check her angles. She pivoted around the pillars to the side, making sure there was no one hiding behind them. It was clear. She continued her circuit, moving around to the north side of the chamber. She disappeared for a moment from Arthur's vision, then reappeared behind the pillars. She was alone, framed for Arthur by the pillars in the middle of the room. It was safe. There was nobody there.

Arthur moved forward and stepped into the shallow pool.

"*Stay there!*"

"Nobody's here. Palette must be in the back."

He continued forward. Blue moved angrily toward him. As she stepped in between the rear pillars, her foot sank into the floor and hit something uneven. Blue looked down with a curious look on her face. She then looked up.

Arthur looked up. In the ceiling, he saw four well-dressed goons hiding in the alcoves in between the pillars. They pulled out their whips.

"Ambush!" yelled Arthur as Blue raised her weapon. Below, thugs jumped up out of the water in between the pillars with whips in hand. Four more dropped from the ceiling. Blue turned to bear her sights on the nearest target and fired. Arthur heard a cry and watch the goon fall to the black floor with a splash.

A thug from the ceiling landed in front of Arthur and pulled back his arm to strike. Arthur ducked and felt crackling coils whip just above his head. Blue knocked down another attacker with an elbow to the face, then aimed her gun once again. But a coil wrapped itself around her arm. With a yank, her weapon was knocked away. The Gun! Arthur pushed past a goon and ran towards the fallen weapon as it landed between the pillars. Before he could reach it, he felt burning coils wrap around his neck.

Arthur thrashed about as someone pulled him closer, binding his arms behind his back with the electric whip. Everywhere the coils touched, his body screamed in agony. Arthur could see nothing but white light. He felt like he was going to black out.

"Keep them conscious, you morons," he heard someone say. "We have a lot to talk about."

Arthur felt the current decrease, the burning sensation retreating from his skin, still he saw nothing but white. He was pushed forward. He must be beyond the pillars now.

"On your knees," commanded a voice.

A swift kick to his legs forced him down to his knees.

"*Lucky,*" he heard Blue say. "*No leverage.*"

The coil relaxed and pulled itself from his skin. As the white faded away, Arthur found himself face to face with Toland and a short, pudgy Chinese kid with round spectacles. However, the spectacles were no ordinary glasses. The pattern upon their lens was always changing. As Arthur watched, the pattern went from the clashing blades of duelling samurai to a bullet-storm ballet of gunmen shooting at one another. The glasses themselves were an artistic medium, endlessly transmitting the thoughts of the artist to his eyes. The visions Arthur saw could only belong to one person.

"Palette," said Arthur. "I would like to introduce you to Toland. Toland, Palette."

"Yes," said Toland. "Mr. Palette and I were having the most interesting conversation."

"It's a shame we interrupted. We can come back later?"

"Where's the other one?" asked Toland.

"I don't know," said Arthur. "He must have run." Arthur looked to his right and found Blue kneeling beside him. Almost every inch of her body was covered in electric coils. "He was always a bit of a coward."

"That's too bad. He's going to miss our little reunion. A second chance to finish our conversation."

Palette remained silent.

Toland turned to Blue and nodded. Electricity shot across her body. Her muscles spasmed violently. She gritted her teeth and glared back at Toland. Arthur whiffed the putrid smell of burning flesh and turned away in disgust. From his peripheral vision, he saw seven large men protecting Toland. Three of them had significant damage to their faces. There was an eighth lying motionless on the floor.

"You two are going to tell me everything you know about the killer," said Toland. "I want his name, I want his location and I want to know how to bring him to heel."

"You think you can control him?" asked Arthur.

"Every animal can be tamed. All it takes are the right tools." Toland nodded his head again.

More current scorched through Blue's body. The electricity snapped her head back as her body shook. Saliva started running out her mouth.

"That's enough," said Toland. The current stopped. Blue fell forwards and spat out a mouthful of foam. Her scorched wounds were beginning to smell like charcoal.

Toland looked past her and saw the goon lying still upon the black floor. "What's with Williams?" he asked. "Is he taking a nap?"

"I don't know," said one of the well-dressed thugs. "It looks like he's unconscious."

From this angle, Arthur could see a bloodless bullet hole in Williams' head. Thankfully, the wound was mostly hidden by his hair.

"Well then wake him up. I'm not paying him to sleep."

Toland returned his attention to Blue while one of his guards went over and kicked Williams repeatedly.

"Let's try this again," said Toland. "What do you know?"

Blue raised her head and smiled with a surprising glee.

"*HURT ME MORE!*" yelled Blue.

"As you wish."

More current burned through her body. The convulsions were

far more violent this time. Her back arched and her shoulder blades clenched together awkwardly. Every muscle on her body was taut, but she didn't scream. She just kept holding that scary grin upon her face.

Toland waved his hand.

The current stopped and her body slumped forward. The electric whips, held taut, kept her kneeling.

"You are certainly a tough nut to crack, darling," said Toland. He turned towards Arthur. "Let's see how tough your friend is." Arthur's body shuddered in anticipation.

"*Krnmpaktvtcodmmph*," mumbled Blue as a pool of saliva poured from her mouth.

Toland turned back towards her. He knelt down, grabbed her chin with his hand and pulled her face up to meet his gaze.

"What was that?" he asked.

Blue smiled and looked beyond him.

A voice from behind Toland rang out, "She said 'Kernel: activate god mode.'"

Toland turned around and saw the ghostly form of Mmorpg floating in mid-air.

"God mode activated," spoke the kernel.

Mmorpg drew a green cube with his index fingers.

"Grab onto something!" yelled Toland.

Mmorpg grabbed the sides of the cube and twisted.

The room twisted in response. Arthur's feet left the floor and he fell towards the ceiling. He hit the roof with a thud and felt the coils loosen around his neck. He threw off the whip and turned towards Blue. Her captors hit the ceiling hard, but they held the coils tightly wrapped around their prisoner. Toland and Palette ran to the northwest pillar and grabbed on to the little grooves on its surface.

Before Arthur could react, the world twisted again and they all fell towards the floor. Blue's bonds came loose as her captors hit the ground. She pulled the coil away and elbowed one of the goons in the face. Pushing away the pain, Arthur jumped to his feet and ran to the northwest pillar. Toland and Palette were still holding on above him. Their feet were dangling towards the floor. Arthur grabbed onto the groves and wrapped his legs tightly around the base. He wasn't going anywhere.

One of Toland's men lifted his head up with a dazed look in his eyes. Blue stomped on his face with her foot, putting him to sleep. Seven to go.

Blue was free, but still unarmed. Around her, the guards jumped to their feet, pulling their whips into the attack position. She spotted one of the thugs hanging on to the west wall for dear life. He was unarmed, too.

Mmorpg spun the cube along its diagonal. The room bent to his demands, spinning end over end from one corner to the other. The southwest dipped down while the northeast corner rose up. Blue ducked a sparking coil as it whipped by her head. She ran down towards the west wall as it dropped. As Arthur watched, she ran to the wall and then ran up to the wall towards the unarmed goon. The unarmed man stood up on the wall, relaxing as he returned to his feet. He turned around just as Blue drove her shoulder into his chest. The impact slammed them both into the west wall. The thug's head snapped and his body went limp. Six to go.

Arthur felt his weight pulled towards the southwest corner.

As Blue got to her feet, another attacker ran in and took a swing at her with his whip. She fell backwards to dodge the attack and kicked out at his legs. He fell on top of her and they scuffled as they rolled into the southwest corner of the ceiling.

Arthur felt his weight pulled towards the southeast corner. Blue grabbed the thug's whip hand and snapped the wrist with a satisfying crack. He screamed in pain as their weight was pulled to the northeast corner. He grabbed onto a groove in the southeast corner as Blue pounded him in the head. The water fell from their corner and sprayed across Arthur as he held onto to the pillar.

The guard grabbed onto one of the grooves as Blue pounded on his head. Their feet dangled off the wall and towards the pillars. Finally, Blue grabbed the man by his hair with her right hand, pulled up her left foot and stomped on his one good hand. He screamed and let go. As they fell towards the now horizontal pillars, she turned him around in mid-air. They smashed into the southwest pillar. Blue made sure that the goon's face struck first. They separated. Blue dropped into the space between the pillars while her victim fell unconscious towards the floor. Five to go.

Wedged in between the western pillars, Blue slid down to the floor. Her foot clipped Arthur's arm. He gasped in pain, but held on tightly to the pillar. The room had just rotated a full 360 degrees, and it wasn't stopping.

The goons surrounded the pillars and Blue retreated to the inside. Arthur felt his weight pull again to the southwest corner. The guards jumped in between the pillars striking their whips at Blue. Bracing herself against the walls of the pillars with her limbs, Blue retreated towards the centre of the room, dodging strikes while dealing out punishment with her fists. As the water rained up towards the ceiling, one of the thugs got a little too close. Blue let the whip wrap around her arm as she grabbed the guard's neck with her free hand. In a single motion, she twisted his neck and pulled him up and past her, so his back faced the ceiling. She let go of the pillars and put all of her weight on his chest. Together, they fell towards the ceiling. She drove the thug's back hard into the roof, leaving a deep crater and an unconscious body behind. Four to go.

She turned and came face to face with Toland, still holding onto the top of the northeast pillar. He ducked his head behind the pillar as Blue drove her fist into the glass. As the rain fell towards the northeast corner, Blue heard a swooshing sound from below. She turned and saw one of the guards sliding up the northeast pillar towards her. As he slid, the goon's feet clipped the fingers of Palette. Palette yelped and let go, falling towards the east wall.

Blue sprinted down the pillar towards the oncoming attacker. She dove over his feet and smashed her fist into his chin. The goon's body went limp and fell towards the northeast corner. Three to go.

Arthur watched the guard hit the corner wall and roll with the turning gravity. He saw Palette, holding onto the east wall and watching the fight continue in the centre of the room. Palette's jaw gaped in awe.

Wedged in between the pillars, Blue battled with the remaining three guards. They surrounded her and attacked with flailing strikes while the room turned. As rain fell down to the floor, Blue braced her arms against the northeast and northwest pillars, slid down five feet and surprised one of the thugs with a kick to the face. He fell and crashed into the floor beside Arthur. Two to go.

Arthur's attention turned to another body sliding across the floor. Williams' dead and open eyes stared at Arthur as he slid towards the southwest corner. Arthur heard the sound of metal sliding on wet glass. He turned and saw a small black object sliding past him.

It was the handgun.

Arthur moved to grab it, but it slipped past his grasp. It joined the unconscious guard in the southwest corner. As the room turned, the gun slid up the corner wall and became wedged in one of the grooves. The body of poor Williams kept on sliding around the room.

Arthur turned back to the battle above. Blue ducked a swing from an attacker below her. She dropped to all fours and held onto the southwest pillar. The pillar rotated down towards the horizontal plane. The thug leapt down towards her, his whip ready to slash across her face. She found her balance, pivoted and threw an uppercut up to meet him. The punch broke his jaw. The whip slipped from his hands. The thug slumped forward, resting momentarily on the horizontal southwest pillar. Then he slipped off, fell and smashed into the middle of the south wall just above the silver doors. One to go.

Arthur felt his body lurch towards first the ceiling then the east wall. William's body fell with the water and collided with Toland at the top of the northeast pillar. Toland looked down at William's body and saw the bullet hole in his head. He blanched in disgust. Arthur turned back towards the southwest corner and saw the gun still lodged in the groove.

The gun came loose and fell towards the centre of the room. As Blue and the final goon grappled between the pillars, the gun fell across them, bounced off the goon and fell towards the east wall.

Blue saw the gun. Toland saw the gun.

Blue turned towards Toland and their eyes met. Toland looked down at the bullet hole in Williams' head and then back at Blue. She kicked out the goon's legs and dropped towards the gun.

Toland understood everything.

"Get the gun! Get the gun!" he screamed.

Blue and the final guard smashed into the east wall, just out of reach of the gun. The impact knocked the guard's electric whip from his hand. The gun slid towards the northeast corner of the floor. Blue and the guard tumbled after it as they fought.

Arthur felt his weight lurch down towards his feet as the gun bounced on to the floor. While Blue and the final thug fought in the corner, Arthur felt the world continue to spin. His weight lurched once again towards the southwest corner. Rain fell from left to right. The gun slid towards the northeast pillar. Above, Toland let go of his grip and slid down the pillar towards the approaching gun.

Blue kicked out the thug's legs and threw the both of them towards the gun. As they slid towards the northeast pillar, she pinned the his head to the floor and put her weight on top of him.

Toland and the gun hit the bottom of the northeast pillar at the same time. Coming to a stop straddling the pillar, Toland reached down and grabbed the pistol. Arthur saw delight shine in his eyes.

An instant later, Blue drove the goon's face into the pillar. Knocked unconscious, his body's fell through the pillars and towards the southwest corner. Blue caught one of the grooves and hung onto the northeast pillar. Her legs dangled across Arthur's line of sight.

Toland stroked the black gun in his hand.

"Why would I need a killer when I can kill with my own hands," he said.

He looked down towards Arthur and smiled. Arthur felt his stomach lurch towards the ceiling.

"I guess your help is no longer needed." Toland pointed the gun at Arthur.

Blue reached up, grabbed Toland's shoe, and pulled. They both fell up the pillars and smashed feet-first into the ceiling. Blue grabbed Toland's hands and they wrestled for control of the gun. Arthur felt his weight lurch again to the northeast. Blue and Toland rolled into the ceiling corner. The water rained down from the ceiling. Blue pinned the gun against the corner while they slid down the corner to the floor. Arthur felt the rain falling from the northeast as his weight was pulled again to the southwest. Still in the northeast corner, Blue and Toland fought for control over the pistol. Toland had two free hands but Blue kept the gun pinned to the wall. As the room turned, their weight shifted towards the pillars in the middle of the room. Their legs pulled off the wall and hung out in space.

Toland's grip slipped on the gun. He had two hands, but Blue had leverage.

"No! No!" yelled Toland as the weapon slipped from his fingers. Blue grabbed the pistol, then elbowed Toland in the head. Toland shrieked and fell. He grabbed onto Blue's leg and hung on.

The room stopped spinning. Arthur looked over and saw Mmorpg holding the green cube still.

"I'll give you whatever you want," said Toland.

Blue cocked the pistol.

"*I already have what I want,*" she said.

Blue raised her right foot and kicked Toland in the face. He fell, bouncing off the pillars to join his unconscious guards below.

Blue uncocked the pistol.

Mmorpg rotated the room back to its original position. Gravity returned to normal as Arthur let go of the pillar.

"Kernel: deactivate god mode," said Mmorpg.

"God mode deactivated," spoke the kernel.

"I thought you weren't supposed to do that when people were still in the zone," said Arthur.

"We didn't have much of a choice. Toland had you both dead to rights."

"But now he knows about the gun. That's the worst possible thing that could have happened. What if he had gotten his hands on it?"

"*Then I would have killed him,*" said Blue.

Arthur paused for a moment. "Why didn't you kill him?" he asked.

"*Because I wanted to kick him in the face.*"

Their argument was interrupted by applause echoing off the ruined walls. Palette dropped down from the east wall.

"Brilliant performance," he said with the excitement of a child. "Ms. Blue, your reputation precedes you."

"What did you tell them, Palette?" asked Arthur.

"Everything. They arrived just before you did. They asked me about the killer and I told them everything I knew, but they understand nothing. They're not like your friend here." Palette motioned towards Blue. "Her art form is exquisite."

"*Art?*"

"Violence," said Palette while opening his arms, "is our earliest form of artistic expression. Far before we could paint, we could kill. We took the skeletons of our prey and the skulls of our enemies and wore them as trophies, used them as protection against the spirits and displayed them for status. Violence binds us together like no other art form; it is something we all crave."

"Thankfully, it doesn't have much of a place in today's world," said Arthur.

"Civilization has made our lives so much safer to lead, true, but it has robbed us of so much primal beauty. For example, Ms. Blue, when you fought just now, what did you feel?" Palette grinned. Footage of Blue fighting Toland's men flashed across his glasses.

Blue thought for a moment.

"*Joy*," she said.

"Yes. Of course you did. It's because we enjoy violence. It is our opium rush against the tedium of society. The morality of civilization crushes down upon us, suppressing our natural instincts, dulling our sensations, dampening our ecstasy. Have you felt the weight of false morality upon you, squeezing the joy out of your inner self, holding back the rage and disgust inside, making you feel like an animal when you just want to be free?"

She gasped for breath. *"Every day."*

"I envy you, Ms. Blue. Despite the limitations of civilized society you have still found an outlet for your urges. How fortunate is one who is paid to kill."

Palette motioned towards the gun.

"Can I touch it?"

Blue handed the weapon to Palette. He took and cradled it like a newborn.

"You and the killer are the only ones here who have been given the power to kill. To kill for pleasure is a trait that separates us from the rest of the animal kingdom. Only we are so depraved. It is that depravity that defines us as human. But in here our humanity is caged, trapped by the power of technology."

Palette handed the weapon back to Blue, who returned it to her holster.

Palette smiled. "I wish that I could feel what you feel. Instead, I am limited to a simulation, to painting with flesh and sweat."

"But no blood," said Mmorpg floating above.

Palette grimaced. "Of course, no blood. How I loathe your obscenity filters. It severely limits my colour palette. Nonetheless, it has allowed me to focus on the movements themselves rather the results." He looked up towards Mmorpg. "Any hope that the filter will be removed any time soon?"

"Nope," replied Mmorpg. "I've deeply encoded it in the kernel. There is no way to dodge it inside Evermore."

"Such a shame," said Palette. "My opus shall never see the light of day. My life's work lies trapped deep within my skull, with no audience to please." He smiled. "Just like your killer."

"What do you mean?" asked Mmorpg.

"Ask her," said Palette, nodding towards Blue. "She knows of what I speak. The quest for violence not in the pursuit of blood, but as an end to the bondage of our minds." Palette turned to Blue. "Each punch, each bullet sets you free. It allows you to escape the torturous journey of your own consciousness. But only for a moment, then the solid steel bars of morality slam shut around you again. This time, the bars are closer. There is less room. The cage closes in around you and it squeezes the air from your lungs."

Palette took a step towards Blue.

She felt the tips of her fingers massage the holster of her 9mm as Palette approached.

"Just like now. You wish to strike, but you hesitate." He took another step. "You lust to kill, yet you do not act upon your natural instincts."

Another step.

"You are held in bondage by your own fears, hiding from your wretched dreams."

His face drew even to hers, flames flickering upon his flat plastic eyes.

"It is like a nightmare that you...can't...wake up from. You can't leave the nightmare behind."

Palette turned abruptly and joyously bounded away. "And so it is with him."

"How do you know this?" asked Arthur.

"Your target and I speak the same language, the language of art. Some use paints, others keys on a piano. We use flesh and bone to create our masterpieces."

207

"And what is his masterpiece?" asked Arthur.

"I do not know yet. I see the path, the arc of his brushstroke, but I cannot see the grand design. I do not see his motif."

He turned back to Blue. "He is very much like you, but with one major difference - he is truly free. He does what you can only dream of doing, unbound by the conventions of justice. He is free to express himself - unrestrained, unedited and uncut."

"*Where is he?*" demanded Blue.

Palette ignored the question. "Each artist needs an audience to appreciate their genius and understand their message. It is an audience we must build. An audience we must cultivate for our professional and personal gain. Your killer is indeed penning a masterpiece, but only his audience will understand its meaning. Only they can see into his soul."

"*Where is he?*" Blue repeated, her nostrils flaring with impatience.

"More important is to understand where he *will* be, to see where his brush will land next."

"At least we know his name," said Mmorpg.

"His name," exclaimed the child artist. "What, pray tell, is his name?"

"It's gibberish," said Arthur. "It's not listed in the registry."

"By any chance, is it in hexadecimal?"

A look of slow surprise dawned upon Arthur's face. "Why yes," he said, "it's hexadecimal. How did you know?"

"Then you should seek the Graduate; he will find your killer." Palette bowed slightly, politely signalling the conclusion of their conversation. Smiling, he said, "The leaves of UBC are very beautiful this time of year. And, dear angel of mercy," he said turning to Blue, "may you find peace in the burning embers of purgatory. Burn bright, burn short and take as many people down with you as you can." Blue ignored him and moved towards the door. Arthur looked at the unconscious bodies of Toland and his men.

"Are you going to be alright when they wake up?" asked Arthur.

"I've already told them everything I know. What more can they do to me?"

"Take care Palette," said Arthur as he followed Blue and

Mmorpg to the door.

The artist called after them, "Art can be understood not through explanation, but through introspection. The only truth you will find is that which comes from within. And that which consumes you."

He smiled after them as hearts danced across his eyes.

CHAPTER TWENTY

LUTHER'S REPRIMAND

The hallowed halls of the Cathedral, adorned with coloured glass and finely crafted architecture, surrounded a troubled man wearing the robes of a cleric. His name was Luther.

Luther sat quietly in his pew while yet another wayward soul poured out his dissatisfaction and shame. Within Luther's mouth, he restrained a yawn. Everyone who came to him had the same problems. They were all missing something, some eternal piece they had lost along the way. Each and every time, he told them what to do, he told them what to buy, but they always returned.

"Did you buy the right shoes?" Luther asked out of habit.

"Yes, I bought everything in the catalogue. The hat, the shoes, the clothes, the house, the car, all sanctioned by the Covenant." The man raised his fine shoes, showing off the blurred mark of the Covenant proving the footwear was proper.

"Do you have a wife and kids?" asked Luther as he scratched his bald, black head.

"Yes," the man answered, "a boy and —— girls." The exact number was lost to Luther. He found it increasingly hard to focus on the irrelevant minutiae of his parishioners' lives.

"Uh huh," Luther nodded.

"I've gone through the catalogue backwards and forwards. I've consulted the good book, I've listened to you."

"And?"

"It's done no good. I feel this emptiness inside of me, eating me from the inside out."

"Are you sure you have everything?"

"Yes," said the man, "but yet I still can't see it. I know the mark is there, but I can't make it out at all."

"Of course," recited Luther. "'Only a true believer can see the mark of the Covenant and understand what it represents. It is the ultimate symbol of enlightenment. For those who can see the brand of Deity are destined to live forevermore at his side in the glorious sunrise of Nirvana.'" Luther quoted the passage monotonously, as the words themselves had lost all significance. The words had simply become painkillers to the poor, unenlightened souls who foolishly searched for meaning in their lives. Luther had once been among them, full of hope and confidence, eager to understand the world around him.

But that was a long time ago. Now he just went through the motions, over and over again, twenty-four hours a day. His only escape was when he could rattle off prayers and lessons without conscious thought, leaving him free to explore new worlds. New worlds far removed from the one that held his fate.

"Can you see the mark?" asked the believer, holding up the blurred brand upon his smartly tailored sleeve. "What does it look like?"

Luther wanted the see the brand, he tried to see the brand, but he could not. He might have been able to see it once, long ago, but no longer. Deity's touch had long since left him. There was only a blur where his faith had been.

"Yes," he said, "I can see it. But it does little good to tell someone what it looks like, or what it represents. You simply would not understand. It would be like describing shadows to a blind man."

"Then how do I see it?" the worshipper asked. "How do I find the mercy of Deity?"

A long pause followed, Luther's eyes looking longingly at his feet.

Finally, he pulled his heavy head up, looked the man in the eye and admitted, "I don't know." The poor man seemed stunned by the confession, even more so when Luther motioned to a cleric at the other side of the room and said, "Check with him, I'm sure he knows."

As the man left to seek his answers elsewhere, Luther dropped his head to his knees in hopelessness. Almost immediately, the gloved hand of another cleric fell upon his shoulder. Through the thin slit of his hood, the cleric spoke.

"Cleric Luther. Your presence has been requested by the Caliph. Please do not keep him waiting."

Luther nodded in defeat and slumped towards the inner chamber.

Excommunication, the punishment for those who have lost their faith. The excommunicated were content to sit at a fork in the road, seeing the choices that Deity lay before them as pointless. He once swore he would never join their ranks. How Luther wished he could swear now — it would show a passion that he had long ago lost.

The great Caliph stood waiting for him in his inner chamber. Like a majestic leader of centuries past, he held his gemstone staff tight and straight with an air of authority. His aged neck, skin pulled tight to the bone, held itself up with dignity. The ever-knowing Caliph stared straight at Luther with both disappointment and contempt. Unlike his disciples, the Caliph wore the colour red upon his robes. Deep in the halls of the Cathedral, it had been rumoured that his robe had been hand-stitched by Deity himself. Of course, since Luther had long since lost his faith, the stitching was nothing more than a blur. When the Caliph open his mouth, he spoke with a strong yet civilized tone.

"So tell me, Cleric Luther," came the calm yet condescending voice, "what seems to be troubling you?"

Luther bowed before his spiritual leader, his eyes to the floor.

"I have lost my way, your Excellency," said Luther. "I still think there is a Deity, but I no longer believe."

"Have you been reading the book, a passage every day?" asked the Caliph.

"Yes, I read the book, a passage a day. But every day the words grow hazier. The book doesn't bring the enlightenment it once did. The sentences blur together until they all become the same."

"Then focus more intently. Meditate on your teachings."

"I've tried, but the more I try the more my eyes wash over the text. I can read the passages, but I can no longer understand the words."

"And yet, you are still able to conduct your ministry?"

"It's become so routine. Everyone comes to me and asks the same questions, over and over again. I give the same answers, the same directions, the same path, again and again. The lips move, the tongue speaks, but the mind is silent. I could do this job in my sleep."

"Job? Your ministry is a responsibility from Deity, not a simple job to be slouched through eight hours a day. Your devotion must be resolute. Your efforts must be limitless. Your faith, unshakeable. So tell me, Cleric Luther, can you continue to uphold these principles?"

Luther held his breath, carefully looking for any other answer than the one that lurked on his lips. He knew what his fate would be, but he could not lie to his mentor, his guide, his father of everything incomprehensible, unknowable and inconceivable.

"No, I can't." He sighed. "I'm sorry."

"I'm sorry too, my brother," said the Caliph. "I am disappointed." He stepped towards his pupil. "I had such high hopes for you. The word of Deity dawned upon you like a supernova. Before that moment, your youth was wasted in the pursuit of electronic paralysis through the medium of games, movies and music - living your life as an avatar of someone else's script. Gleefully accepting the role of consumer, a patron saint of the electronic arts, you wasted your youth on the dream of being someone else. An actor, an athlete, a model, it didn't matter what it was, as long you were famous. As long as everyone knew who you were and worshipped the ground upon which your feet came to rest. But that faithless dream could not come to pass, not for everyone. You were a compass without a map. Here, you found a path, you found a spiritual oasis where before you had known despair. The Covenant gave you hope—and more importantly, purpose."

"I have lost my purpose. I pray to find it again."

"Are you aware of the consequences of your lack of faith?"

"Yes I am," answered Luther, eyes closed, head hung awaiting the axe of the executioner. "And I am prepared for excommunication."

"Normally, excommunication and the spiritual exile it entails would be appropriate. But I sense something different for you."

The Caliph paused.

Luther tilted his head up, waiting for the other shoe to drop.

"Tell me, Cleric Luther," continued the Caliph, "have you heard of the legend of the last magus?"

"Yes, your Excellency," answered Luther. "I read about it in the Book of Chapters."

"Can you recite the tale?" asked the Caliph.

"Of course, your Excellency." Luther recited the passages from memory, paying more attention to the words than usual.

"The magus was the very last of his kind. He walked the land for seven years in search of Deity. One day, he came upon a door — a door that terrified him greatly. He called it the Luminati Aurora, the pathway to both heaven and *heck*. Swallowing his fear, he entered the gateway and fell down into the darkness of Nocturne.

"Buried in the shadows of the Nocturne, he spent another seven years fighting his demons, face to face with his greatest fears and trespasses. For another seven years, he fought to pull himself out of the oily darkness. Shedding his own metaphysical filth, the magus found himself blinded by the light of Nirvana, the endless luminescence of pure souls.

"He found himself in the presence of Deity — the first and only mortal to bask in his light. So great was the impact of this experience that the magus could not move or speak for yet another seven years. When he could finally bring himself to move, Deity spoke to him without words.

"Deity told the magus he would one day return to the sanctuary of Nirvana, that he would one day feel the presence of Deity again. But before he could do so, he would have to return to Evermore and build a Cathedral — a Cathedral that only those with faith could find. He was to build a Covenant to study and pass on the word of Deity to those willing to listen. Then one day, Deity promised, one of the magus' followers would be allowed to return — to know forevermore the grace of Deity. Forevermore."

"Your memory serves you well. Last night, I had a vision. The vision had no words or characters. It had neither story nor plot. The vision contained one and only one image - the Luminati Aurora. The black hole that leads to the endless tar of the Nocturne. It filled my dreams."

"What does it mean?" asked Luther.

"It means that the time has come for another to pass through the Lumunati Aurora, face his demons in the Nocturne and pass into the magnificence of his Deity for all eternity. I believe that it is you who must make this journey."

"Why me, your Excellency?" came Luther's careful reply.

"You missed an important part of the legend, Cleric Luther, for it is written that the journey will be taken not by the strongest cleric, or the most devout, but by the one who has lost his way. Only by completing the journey through doubt can the soul of the last magus, and by extension the souls of all humanity, find salvation. You have become lost, my child. It is time to find your way."

Luther's shoulders lifted at the Caliph's words. Hope returned to his face as he gazed up at his master.

"Where shall I find the Luminati Aurora?" asked Luther.

"With that I cannot help you, for no one has found it since the days of the magi. You must wander the land until it finds you. Like the Cathedral the magus constructed, it will come upon you when you are ready to enter. Now rise, my disciple."

Luther rose slowly to his feet.

"When shall I see you again, your Excellency?" he asked.

"Only the Lord Deity our saviour knows the answers. Go to him in peace." The Caliph turned his back to Luther, signalling that it was time for him to go.

Luther turned around and walked slowly out of the inner sanctum. As he passed his fellow clerics in the main hall, he avoided looking upon their faces, afraid of betraying their faith. The giant oak doors opened at his behest, creaking with immense age and weight.

Luther stepped outside and looked around with no idea where to go. Finally, he choose a direction and walked ahead, unsure of what he would find.

****

From the opposite direction approached a different man. As he walked, the heels of his brown boots crushed the asphalt beneath him. With each step, and the expulsion of rock and dust it caused, he grew stronger.

Crunch. Crunch. Crunch came the sound of his steps as the pavement disintegrated beneath his feet. He pounded the ground with tremendous force, yet he was only using a fraction of his strength. To him, his steps were soft and easy. But to others, the pounding of his feet and the asphalt tracks he left behind were terrifying. To him they were simply collateral damage on the way to his destination, the Cathedral none could find.

He had finally found it, and now he approached the house of worship with glee. His pace quickened, his boots now kicked up slabs of asphalt as he sprinted towards the Cathedral.

He was nearly at the giant doors before the two guards spotted him.

Even though they had never laid eyes upon him before, they recognized without question the nightmare that approached. They could see in his eyes the searing hate and anger that could not be controlled. They rushed to the doors, vainly trying to close the gate before the maelstrom hit.

But it was too late.

CHAPTER TWENTY-ONE

WELCOME TO SPECIAL COLLECTIONS

The morning dew hung over the campus as the trio approached the gothic towers of the UBC Main Library. The library was surrounded by a square complete with a fountain, soft grass, and trees imported from Japan. Rising from the soft grass, a short doubleclock tower read 1945 hours in white and 11:17 in black. The entire scene, the serene garden stretching out before the aging library structure, was but a mirage. The garden, the trees and the morning dew were all brilliantly designed to engender contemplation and introspection.

What could not be seen were the endless arrays of 1s and 0s, spatial algorithms and neural transmitters that constructed the scene before them. The world's first truly virtual university, serving over a million students a year without any signs of overflowing its capacity, the University of British Columbia in Evermore was a carbon copy of its namesake's in all its early 21st century glory.

Inundated by corporate sponsorship and aggressive grants from the federal government, the university campus in the real world had begun making investments into its information infrastructure, yielding great returns. The original Main Library that stood before them had long since been torn down in the real world, the history of brick and mortar replaced with the power of glass and wires. The new facility contained state-of-the-art technology that allowed universities from the around the globe to share and transfer information with immense speed.

At about the same time, the new computer engineering building was constructed three blocks away. This new structure was also considered quite impressive due to its advanced computing labs and its pilot project with the department of political science. Graduate students in this project investigated the growing phenomena of MMORPGs - massively multiplayer online role-playing games.

Examined from both a sociological and technical standpoint, the growth of these games in complexity was awe-inspiring. For political scientists, the opportunity to test their hypotheses in a virtual lab was too good to pass up. For engineers, the promise of building a better world of their own design, in a digital format, beckoned. To improve educational opportunities and to speed up the research process, the students of the new computer engineering complex were given access to the impressive broadband capacity and server space of the library commons. These various decisions created momentum, an opportunity for levels of innovation unseen since the earliest days of the Internet. Into that stream stepped Mmorpg.

"This is where it all started," Mmorpg reminisced to his companions. "It's been a long time since I've been here."

"I thought you worked there," asked Arthur.

"Yes, but it hasn't looked like this for a long time, not since my undergraduate days. The library was demolished for the commons, and the hill by the bus loops was torn down for expansion. It's a different place now."

"True, but it still has that wonderful West End scent," said Arthur. "The smell of endless rain."

The granite steps, worn from eighty years of rainfall and the fashionable footwear of students, squeaked beneath them as they walked up the stairs. The stone temple opened its doors to them in welcome. Inside, the smell of old and mouldy texts instantly overwhelmed their senses, forcing the pair to fight back the tears in their eyes.

"They got the smell right too," said Mmorpg.

They found themselves in an entry hall. The walls had been painted green many years ago and had slowly faded as the decades wore on.

"*Why so old?*" asked Blue.

"I prefer the old mould to the new glass," said Mmorpg. "It always felt like the place had a soul."

Buried in the stacks following the hallway, they found an elevator that looked like it hadn't been used in decades. Its green paint was chipping away, and the cables were old and worn. The old iron of the green stacks creaked as they passed, sagging under the weight of the texts upon its shelves. The three of them entered the elevator cautiously. It groaned under their weight. Mmorpg looked up worriedly at the fraying cables.

"They don't build them like this anymore," said Mmorpg.

"Just like your spiders," said Arthur. His brow frowned in curiosity. "Did you find out who sent the spider yet?"

"No," said Mmorpg, "I've managed to de-compile the spider's machine code into IR code. That was the easy part. Now I have to feed it through an idiom detector to simplify the code before it's analyzed. Decompilation is such a problematic process. It's automated, but it's extremely slow."

"How long?" asked Arthur.

"In Evermore Standard Time? About five hours."

"How long before the end of the Spectacle?"

"Just over two hours."

Arthur shook his head. "Yep, they don't build them like that anymore."

The ancient elevator doors opened with a mechanical whine and the trio stepped out on the sixth floor. A sign told them that they were now in Special Collections. In its original incarnation, UBC Special Collections had been responsible for safeguarding the oldest and most precious texts in the UBC Library. Great care had been taken to protect books, atlases and scriptures that were, in some cases, several hundred years old. But such priceless texts had long since been translated into the cold 1s and 0s of the universally accessible digital milieu, and the originals locked safely away never again to face the damaging gaze of the curious. In Evermore, UBC's Special Collections was focused on a completely different type of precious information.

There was a standard reception desk: a chair behind a table with a glass shield. It was equipped with a slit for submissions and a silver bell. Arthur sighed and rang it three times in succession.

An eerie silence fell over the room. Blue started to stroke the Beretta beneath her coat, but Arthur rolled his eyes dismissively. "He always has to be dramatic," he complained.

"You have some very undependable friends," said Mmorpg.

Arthur snorted in response. He rang the bell again, two short rings that hung in the air far longer than before. The ding-a-ling of the bell stretched out into eternity, rising slowly in pitch until it was a nearly imperceptible whine.

Before their eyes, the quaint and comfortable office began to transform. The materials that lay before them slowly became pixelated, blurred and then transformed. The chairs, tables and desks bent into a flat pane, as if the pixelation was forcing their three-dimensional view into a two-dimensional universe. As the furniture moved, however, the pixels remained in place, giving the impression that they were now looking at an image moving over an old television screen. All perspective had been ceded to the beauty and simplicity of a flat and simple world. A world that could be easily understood, easily categorized and easily mastered.

Mmorpg glanced with confusion at Arthur. Blue stood silently, showing neither surprise nor alarm. Arthur, however, was completely caught off guard. He had never seen this before. "René?" he asked.

"Good evening Arthur," came a synthetic voice, "it's been a long time since you've called me by that name." The voice was odd. It spoke each word as if it had been recorded separately. It had difficulty transitioning smoothly between the words like ordinary speech. The voice sounded like an old computer reading aloud.

The blocky image in front of them vibrated as the voice spoke. Arthur strained his eyes as he examined the image. Instead of a person, Arthur saw only the pixelated equalization of the speaker's synthetic voice. Horizontal bars spiked up and down with the bass, tone and pitch of the audio signal.

It could no longer be considered a human voice, so distorted that the only hint of humanity remaining was the slight sardonic tone that mocked its guests.

"My god René," Arthur gasped, "what have you done to yourself?"

"Forget me from a past life, serial pessimist. What you see before you is my crowning glory. The man you once knew as René has long since disappeared from my data banks."

"What do you mean?" asked Arthur.

"You were always a bit on the slow side my friend. If you must know. I have shucked off my mortal coil. I have downloaded my consciousness into Evermore."

"That's impossible," said Mmorpg.

"Apparently your friends are even thicker than you are," said the Graduate.

"No, it's not possible." said Mmorpg. "You can't download your consciousness into a host."

"Who said anything about a host? This is the world's biggest virtual library. Do you really think you could store all of that information in someone's mind?"

Arthur searched for any trace that remained of his dear friend. As the audio ghost before him spoke, he noticed a distillation of colour within the equalization bars. Straining his eyes, Arthur finally found what he was looking for - a subtle outline of the face of his old colleague: soft, cherub-cheeked and innocent.

"So you've downloaded yourself into the library's database," said Arthur, "and lost your humanity."

"You say that like it's a bad thing."

"You have become nothing but the bytes of a server, trapped inside a prison of hard disks and data registers. You are nothing more than ones and zeros now."

"Everything can be defined by those two digits," said the Graduate. "The opposite sides of the same coin, off and on, yes and no, existence and nothingness. They contain within them all knowledge, all logic, everything of value that humanity has created. I *am* the one. I *am* the zero. Thus, I have become the pinnacle of the human race, merging with the exponentially-growing data that streams through our homes, our cities and through our very consciousness. We are drowning in a volume of information from the date of our birth to the twilight of our deaths, endlessly gasping for air. Only now can I understand it all."

"Our struggles are an essential part of our humanity. When you are engulfed by the waves, you must learn to swim, or you will drown," said Arthur.

"Or you can become the water," countered the Graduate, "and flow to worlds that you could never hope to discover. I have become one with the data that controls our world. I understand every concept, every theory, every thought that has passed through existence. No topic escapes me now. There is nothing I can't understand. I have been reborn as the grail of knowledge and the ark of wisdom."

"Wisdom is the application of knowledge, not its accumulation."

The distorted face of the Graduate, hiding behind the equalization of his voice, let slip a hint of surprise. "I do not recognize this quote. Who said it?" it asked.

"You did," said Arthur, "many years ago."

"Hmmph, that was a long time ago," chortled the Graduate. "You cannot comprehend the breadth of what I have become."

"But you've limited yourself to everything that's come before. You have lost your ability to create something new, something groundbreaking, something that would be remembered. You know everything, but have become nothing. What good is understanding all there is, if you are powerless to use it?"

"Powerless? No. My knowledge has given me a portal into the future, a window into what is to come with the precision of Euclidean logic."

"But what of human experience?" argued Arthur. "Love's first kiss, the birth of a child, the anticipation of Christmas day. The maze of emotional highs and lows that we experience every day. In your quest for total knowledge, have you not given up something far more precious?"

"I have lost nothing more than the urgings of animals. Now I see and understand everything. But are we so different? We have both chosen a virtual life over a real one. Our only difference is that I've accepted my choice, while you foolishly deny yours. How long have you been here? You stand there in moral piety, endlessly blathering on about the evils of a world inside which you spend your entire life. Actions speak louder than words, you hypocrite. Your arguments, while wearing the mask of rhetoric and fear, lack the force of your own convictions. You still say the words, toe the rhetorical line, repeat your arguments again and again, but you have become just like the rest of us. Comfortable in your position here, you are afraid to return to the pointless existence that is reality. Me, I have made the leap. Whereas I was once René, the illegitimate son of a world to which I didn't belong, now I am simply data. No names, no past to hold me back from an eternity of perfect knowledge and wisdom."

"Enough of this," said Mmorpg as he waved his hand dismissively. "You know why we are here."

"I can read Evermore like a book. Of course I know what you seek."

"*The killer,*" said Blue. She breathed in deeply and exhaled slowly. Her shoulders rose and fell in anticipation.

"Yes, you will find the killer," it said, its audio reverberations pulsing towards Blue, "but are you prepared to face him?"

With fire in her eyes, Blue glared at the Graduate. He chuckled and looked back to Arthur.

"You have a number for me?" it asked.

"Yes," replied Mmorpg. "It's a hexadecimal number: 5B4A5446362E305D556E64656369646564. It's not listed on any of our registries."

"Of course not," replied the Graduate with condescension from its voice. "They only began to sort avatar data structures by character strings in the Third Age. In the First and Second Ages, before the Great Migration, before the Consortium, before the society that we so dutifully cling to now, they used a primitive ASCII coding structure."

"Of course," said Mmorpg. "It's been years since we've used that. I never even thought about that."

"*Who is he?*" demanded Blue.

The Graduate smiled and his electronic body swirled in front of them:

5B4A5446362E305D556E64656369646564

"ASCII Code uses two Base-16 numbers to define each character," said Mmorpg. "So if you divided up the string into groups of two..."

The letters in front of them stretched as hyphens fell in between the characters.

5B-4A-54-46-36-2E-30-5D-55-6E-64-65-63-69-64-65-64

"...which according to the ASCII table, translates to..."

[-J-T-F-6-.-0-]-U-N-D-E-C-I-D-E-D

"...[JTF6.0]Undecided," finished Arthur. "He has a JTF tag?"

"That he does," said the Graduate as he returned to a electronic haze.

Arthur shot a look at Mmorpg. "That tag is reserved for the JTF project. How did he get a hold of it?"

"I feel pity for you my friend. All you can see are the shadows upon the wall."

"Fine. Be that way." said Arthur. He turned to leave.

"Illumination can arise from but a single question. Ask yourself this: why does he kill?"

Arthur stopped.

"Palette told us why he kills. He's an artist sending a message."

"But what is the message?"

Arthur turned back towards his old friend. The Graduate was grinning.

"I don't know," said Arthur. "I haven't figure that out yet."

"Then ask yourself this: the targeted victims of which you know, do they share any trait?"

Arthur thought long and hard. As the pieces slowly clicked into place, his face lit up with illumination.

"Power," a smile curled across Arthur's lips. "Beowulf, Marcony, the Earth Mother, the Waffle. They all had power."

"But what about...," started Mmorpg.

"Bright lad," interrupted the Graduate. "For once, you are seeing the bigger picture."

"Thank you Réné," said Arthur. "You've been extremely helpful."

"What is it?" asked Mmorpg. "What do you mean?"

"I'll explain later. First we have to get to the Spectacle."

"Why?"

"Because that's where he's going to be," said Arthur.

"*About time,*" said Blue. The three of them turned to leave.

"Congratulations," said the voice, "you are one step closer to discovering the identity of the killer."

"We already know who he is," said Arthur. "It's Undecided."

"Is it now?" came the muffled reply as the two-dimensional equalization melted back into furniture, leaving them alone with more questions than answers.

CHAPTER TWENTY-TWO

THE COUNTEROFFENSIVE

Kinsella walked into the Office of the Sovereign, his eyes alight with good news.

"What is it?" asked Klein.

"Blue and *Arthur* have discovered the identity of the killer."

"That's excellent news. Have they found him yet?"

"No, but they've dispatched a gopher. With a positive ID, it's now only a matter of time before this matter is put behind us."

"Hopefully no one else will be hurt," said Klein.

"Of course, sir."

Klein arched a brow at the glee of his political advisor.

"What was his name?" Klein asked.

Kinsella grinned. "[JTF6.0]Undecided."

"JTF?" asked Klein.

"The very same tag."

"As I recall, tags have to be authorized by the government."

"That is correct."

"And [JTF6.0] would be under the JTF program."

"It was reserved for the sixth iteration of the program." Kinsella's smile grew.

"The program created by my predecessor?" said Klein.

"Yes indeed, sir."

"The program that we put on hold when we formed government?"

"Yes sir."

Klein jumped from his seat. "Call the Consortium to rise," he commanded as he strode with energy towards the exit. "This oughta be fun."

"It's already done."

Klein barged through the giant oak doors that represented the link to the past, down a hall evoking the renaissance, and into the great present of the Consortium. There his coalition waited for him, asking amongst themselves why the sovereign would face the opposition attack so soon.

The opposition benches filled up chaotically as delegates rushed back from their offices. The public galleries were dark and closed as the session fermé was still in effect The opposition earnestly took their seats and grinned confidently at the sovereign. Their leader Asa silently watched Klein walk towards his silver lectern. Asa looked worried. Klein smiled. His rival had good reason to be afraid.

Sovereign Klein stepped behind his lectern, waited for the hustle to subside and began his speech.

"Ladies and gentlemen of the Consortium, I bring news, both good and bad, to our hallowed halls. Through the efforts of numerous dedicated citizens of Evermore, the identity of the killer that has been stalking our streets has been revealed. But what is most surprising to me and what should concern us all is not the name itself but its paternity. The killer is the progeny of years of misguided efforts and broken dreams. The killer is the end result of an administration so obsessed with foisting its vision upon its people that it barely paused to consider the monster that it was creating. Dear sirs and madams, the name of the monster who kills without remorse or shame is none other than [JTF6.0]Undecided, the illegitimate child of the JTF project enacted by the previous government."

"We have been led to believe," he continued, "for as long as I can remember, that our sanctuary would be threatened, that the lives of our children would be in peril, unless we built an army. We heard theses arguments over and over again. 'Fear the Underground, for we cannot control them. Fear the different, for they hate our way of life.' Taking advantage of our collective weakness, a platform of fear and insecurity was foisted upon us. The JTF project has never been necessary, and was born of the imaginations of those who seek to legitimize their power through the strength of arms rather than the strength of persuasion, through force of threat rather than the force of will.

"This country has pulled together all its disparate elements, not for greed, not for power, not for security, but due to the belief that we can be more than the sum of our parts. As a society, we have always believed we can accomplish more together than we ever could apart. This bond was built by the will of the people, not by the force of an overbearing state. The previous administration forgot this and spread the lie that we were weak and vulnerable. They argued that what we needed was not a nation governed by consent, but a state ruled by fear.

"They initiated the JTF project, and in doing so created the very threat they had warned us about for so very long. A member of the JTF, uncontrollable by us, is hunting down the peaceful citizens of our humble land. It kills without thought. It kills without remorse. Its only purpose is to destroy all we hold dear. For that we must thank Asa and the Corporate Coalition."

Murmurs of shock spread across the crowd. Asa's seat lowered itself while the seats of the Consortium flowed and ebbed across the floor in the endless dance of coalition building and breaking. Klein's coalition swelled with the ranks of ISPs wishing to avoid blame for the crisis.

"We must take strong action. With the identity of the killer revealed, it will take only minutes to discover his location. I have ordered the striders to stand by at the Great Gate for confirmation of a final location. I remind you all that the Order of the Striders has never—individually or collectively—lost a battle in the recorded history of Evermore, dating back to even the Second Age. They are the finest warriors Evermore has to offer, and they will not rest until our homeland is safe"

Klein motioned up to the balcony where Aeris and her striders were standing.

"Until this manner is resolved, I would encourage everyone to remain here at the Consortium under the protection of Strider Aeris and her squad. The political leadership of the country must be maintained. In this era of crisis, the people will be turning to us for hope. We must maintain a united front against the threat that endangers us all. We must remain strong and resolute in the face of danger, calm and sure in our responsibilities. I will require the help and support of each and every one of you before the day is out. Today, in the face of annihilation, we will stand together. To Evermore, may the Deity protect her."

Klein finished his speech to thunderous applause, his seat high above the super-majority of delegates marshalling below him. Never before had the Klein Coalition held such power in the white halls. Even some members of the Corporate Coalition had joined with the government. The few that remained outside formed a weak and demoralized opposition. The political battle was over.

Regardless, Klein sighed at his greatest triumph. He knew such unity wouldn't last forever. *Soon the battle will start again.* His eyes fell upon Jie, clapping meekly far below him. *And it will be for her to fight it.*

****

Jie clapped weakly as she searched the now sparse opposition benches. Her eyes fell anxiously on the empty seat of PRNC.

Amid the applause, Asa rose to speak. Klein sat down to listen to his old adversary.

"Given this latest development, we recommend the Consortium investigate the JTF program immediately and ascertain if there have been any security breaches. I must say that the JTF6.0 tag of the killer is unusual, as the program itself had only progressed to version 3.0 before its cancellation. However, we will diligently examine the program for an explanation. In the meantime, we will give our full and complete cooperation to the sovereign until this crisis has been resolved. Our members will remain here under the protection of Aeris and the Order of the Strider. However, one of my members, representative PRNC, has left the safety of the Consortium to serve as a judge of the Goddess Pageant in the Underground. I would like to request to the Consortium that someone be dispatched to pick him up and return him to the safety of this chamber."

Jie sent a thoughtmail to Kinsella back in the War Room. "How did PRNC get past the Great Gate?" she asked. "We've had it locked down since this morning."

The response came back immediately. "As a leading member of the Consortium, he has the authority to pass through the Great Gate at his own discretion. Restricting the movement of ordinary citizens across the Great Gate is fairly routine, as that is its primary purpose, but to stop a ranking member of the Consortium from passing between the two realms would have immediately caused alarm. Instead of believing the crisis was scripted, people would have figured out something was wrong, seriously wrong, and started to panic."

Furious, Jie looked up to see Asa returning to his seat, awaiting Klein's response. A quick glance at Klein told her everything she needed to know. Klein would reject sending someone due to manpower concerns. All the resources they had must be aimed at stopping the killer as soon as possible, with a minimal loss of life. Dispatching someone away from that duty to rescue an important member of the aristocracy would put others at risk. Besides, there was no indication he was in serious danger. He was in as much danger as everyone else in the Underground. Why should he get preferential treatment?

Jie understood the arguments and knew that in the big picture, Klein was right. On a personal level, she knew that doing nothing was wrong. It was ultimately their fault that he was now in serious danger. It was up to them to resolve it.

Before Klein could stand to respond to Asa's request, Jie rose. The Consortium turned to her in surprise. She spoke with an authority she had never felt before.

"As the Proxy of Finance, I can assure the leader of the opposition that we will spare no expense to protect the life of his deputy. Let it be a symbol of the common front we all must forge today to overcome this crisis. Individually, we are as weak as a strand of wool. Bind us together in common purpose, and our nation becomes unbreakable. We will stand together on the extraction of PRNC. We will stand together against the killer. And we will stand together for our country. For now. For tomorrow. For Evermore."

Jie returned to her seat surrounded by thunderous applause. Her chair rose up towards towards her beaming mentor. Klein patted her on the back as she stopped alongside him.

"Great speech, but you may have overextended us. We can't waste the striders on just one man."

"It's ok," said Jie. "I know exactly who to send."

– CHAPTER TWENTY-THREE –

LA CHANSON D'AVIDEH

As Blue and Arthur neared the Chrysalis, they had to fight their way through the throng of people gathering in anticipation of the next goddess. The crowd had come from all four corners of the Underground for this blockbuster event. The fashion was as varied as the crowd, with varieties of blaxploitation, space-age retro and other deformities of pop culture. The mood of the mob was upbeat and excited. They were ready for a celebration.

Blue pulled Arthur through the growing mob, resisting the urge to reach into her holster. Her frustration melted into awe as the spire of the Chrysalis came into view.

The Chrysalis itself was a marvel of Forsythian architecture. Every year, the Chrysalis morphed to fit a different theme, never taking the same shape twice. This year, the Spectacle had decided on an Atlantean theme. In response, the Chrysalis had become a giant conch shell, its flaring pink lip stretching up from the top like a fin. Approaching from the rear of the Chrysalis, Blue and Arthur found a giant spire reaching out and over them. Looking up at the spire, Blue saw a series of whorls extending from the narrow apex to the broad base of the Chrysalis, not unlike a giant pyramidical drill. Upon each whorl stood a crown of five blunted spines. Zooming in with red lens, Blue could make out windows and doors upon each of the blunted spines. Looking even closer, she saw a Persian woman sitting relaxed at a table, drinking from a cup and saucer.

"Incredible isn't it," said Arthur. "The spire is not actually part of the theatre, but an executive hotel added onto the end. The performers and dignitaries will each have a room."

"*Will our target be up there?*"

"No. According to Klein's thoughtmail, PRNC will be backstage waiting the start of the Goddess Pageant. That's this way."

"*You're sure that he's next?*"

"Absolutely."

Blue and Arthur moved beneath the giant conch shell. The Chrysalis was held up by three thick legs. The first two were at the rear of the Chrysalis and connected to the back of the shell. The third leg was at the the front of the giant shell, leading up like a ramp to the entrance.

"*So what's the plan?*"

"Get in. Get PRNC. Get out."

"*And if the killer gets to him first?*"

"Then you take the killer down."

Blue smiled at that thought.

As they walked underneath the base of the Chrysalis, its ivory walls surrounded them, encasing them in a dull white light. Various aquatic antiquities were strewn along the exterior of the theatre to give the appearance of entering the long-forbidden and sparkling world of Atlantis. There were coral reefs, pitched tridents, chirping seahorses and a strange crab with a Jamaican accent. Only the mermaids were missing.

Arthur and Blue pushed their way through the mob and past a circular entrance marked with words of greeting. A couple of young men protested against their cutting in line, but once Blue crushed their fingers, the crowd magically parted way.

Blue felt a laser scan her eyes.

"Welcome to the Chrysalis Ms. Blue," said a happy voice. "The Spectacle is a once-in-a-lifetime event that can't be missed. How will you be paying for the ticket today? Bank, credit card or Easy2Pay?"

"*Go away.*" Blue kept walking towards the entrance.

"That's too bad. I hope that we will see you again soon."

Blue found herself standing at the exit.

"*What the?*" Blue whirled around. Everywhere she turned she found an exit. The entrance had disappeared. She felt a tap on her shoulder. She turned to found Arthur standing beside her.

"Just pay the man."

"*With what?*"

"They probably set up an Easy2Pay account for you. It's what most people use here."

"*Fine. I'll buy one.*"

Immediately the voice jumped back into her ears.

"Welcome to the Chrysalis Ms. Blue. The Spectacle is a-"

"*Easy2Pay.*"

"Thank you. The Chrysalis management is not responsible for any or all psychological ailments that may arise as a result of the performance. This includes tricotillomania, agoraphobia, post-traumatic stress disorder, phronemophobia, separation anxiety, intermittent explosive disorder, ophthalmophobia, stasibasi-phobia ..."

Blue grunted and followed Arthur up a coiled walkway that appeared before her. The staircase led up into the bottom of the shell.

The voice of Mmorpg chimed directly into Blue's eardrums as he floated through the wall beside them.

"You better be right," said Mmorpg.

"He'll be here," said Arthur.

"How can you be so sure?" asked Mmorpg.

"Because I know what he's hunting for."

They entered the main arena and were struck by the spectacle of hundreds of thousands of people moving to their seats. Hearing the soft roar of the ocean, Blue looked around the cavernous pink interior of the Chrysalis, her eyes falling upon the closed clam stage that was its centrepiece.

"We're just in time," said Arthur. "The opening acts have just finished. The Goddess Pageant is next."

Blue could see that Arthur was right. The stage was expanding in anticipation of the final act.

"Mmorpg go up high," said Arthur. "See if you can scan their faces."

"There's millions of people here. How am I supposed to find him."

"He'll be near the front of the stage. He kills with his hands. He'll need to get in close."

Mmorpg turned translucent as he rose above the crowd to his position.

Blue turned away and scanned the faces of the hordes as they brushed past her. Her fingers rubbed the hilt of her Beretta in anticipation. A large whooshing sound drew her attention skywards.

To a grand roar of approval, the top of the arena began to move. Slowly it uncurled itself with the groaning steel of a mechanical titan. With an air of monumental effort it uncoiled into place, adding hundreds of thousands of additional seats to meet the demands of millions of fans. As the upper half of the shell opened, it morphed in shape and size, pushing and rotating around and above the main stage so that no space with a decent view was left unused.

Blue saw the ceiling of the Chrysalis filled with row upon row of luxurious seating, as far as the eye could see, in rotating seats that had the comfort of a recliner but took up the space of a stool. She wondered to herself how many people could fit in this beast of an arena.

"Two million," said Arthur, anticipating her question. "There were two million people at last year's competition."

"*What's its limit?*" asked Blue

"There is no such thing as limits here. It will expand to accommodate all who buy tickets. That's what it's doing now, growing in size to match the demand."

Blue swivelled her head in all directions, scanning the crowd for her target. She saw only a flood of faces, flowing past one another like water as they moved to their seats.

"*There's too many,*" said Blue.

"He'll be here," repeated Arthur.

"He had better be," said Mmorpg.

They made their way to the front of the stage, passing row upon row of the fortunate souls who had been able to secure a front row tickets. Their smugness was pointless, however, due the ingenuity of Forsythian architecture. At every seat, no matter the location, would appear the view most desired by its occupant. If the ticket holder

CALL OF THE NOCTURNE

wanted to be close, he could count the nostril hairs of his favourite singer. If he wanted some space between himself and the music, then the view would adjust accordingly. The location of the seat had no bearing on the quality of the view; it was merely a status symbol - something to brag about with your friends after the concert, showing the ticket stub for proof.

Blue wondered to herself as she passed the vapid stares of the faceless masses, *Who are these sheep?* Immediately, the yellow lens kicked in, displaying the names of everyone around her.

Annoyed, she ignored the name tags and pushed on forward through the crowd. But just behind her, beyond her field of vision, was a man hidden behind the mundane chic of styled hairdos and designer clothes. The number "5B4A5446362E305D5-56E64656369646564" floated just above his hat. As the man walked away, the tag rotated around in translation, revealing the golden words: "[JTF6.0]Undecided".

Blue stopped and turned around in an instant, staring behind her.

But there was no one there.

Blue's eyes darted left and right but she found nothing but the mindless masses. Grunting, she turned and followed after Arthur.

With Mmorpg following overhead, Blue and Arthur broke through the crowd and approached the judges table. Arthur wasted no time. "Mr. PRNC," he called.

Three heads rotated to look at them. The woman in the middle was in her late 30s, her best days evidently behind her. The man on the left was early 40s and portly in a cheerful, Santa Claus type of way. But the man on the right was impeccably dressed, composed and self-satisfied. PRNC was a difficult man to ignore.

"Yes, what is it?" asked PRNC.

"Sir," said Arthur. "May we speak with you privately?"

"Of course. Asa said you would come."

The three of them moved out of earshot of the other judges and the surging crowd.

"I understand that you are to escort me back to the Gate," said PRNC.

"That is correct sir, my name is Arthur and this is—"

"I know who you are. But I'm afraid that I've made a commitment here that must be fulfilled."

"But you're exposed here. You can't be protected," said Arthur.

"I'm in the same position as everyone else. We're all under threat here. Why should I get special protection or an escort to safety while everyone else must face this monster? Besides, he's as likely to kill me as anyone else on his random rampage."

"It's not random," said Arthur, "everyone that he's targeted, everyone he's killed or attempted to kill - Massoud, Marcony, the Earth Mother, the Waffle - they all had one thing in common. They were authority figures. They had power and influence over the lives of many others. I believe that is the element he's targeting. He has no interest in the weak or defenceless. Instead, he's obsessed with the destroying only the most powerful among us. Right now, that's you. You are by far the most attractive target to him in the Underground. We have to get you out of here now."

"If that's true, then I'm not the only target here. Look around, there are scores of powerful people." As PRNC spoke he pointed to different sections of the crowd. "Toland has a private booth in the bleachers, the leading thloggers of the Underground are in the media balcony, that kid in the front row is the world free-style frag champion and some of the best bands in cyberspace are backstage. Any one of these people could be targeted."

"But you have the most authority out of anyone here, so you are the most obvious target," said Arthur.

"So if I leave, then he'll pick someone else. Won't he?"

"More than likely," said Arthur.

"I'm not going to run away and let someone else die in my place."

The lights in the theatre slowly dimmed and another judge came over to pull PRNC back to his seat.

"I'm sorry sir but I must insist," said Arthur as he nodded to Blue. Blue stepped towards PRNC with a smile on her face. PRNC read her well. He wasn't going to have a choice.

"If you take me away now," said PRNC as he motioned with his thumb to the crowd, "they will know something is wrong. And once they know, they will panic."

Arthur looked worriedly at the crowd. PRNC pressed his advantage.

"You think he's coming after me right?"

"Yes. You fit his M.O."

PRNC turned to Blue. "Can you stop him?" he asked her.

She didn't hesitate. "*Yes,*" she croaked in her broken whisper.

PRNC turned back to Arthur. "Then use me as bait. Let me go to my seat and judge the contest. Wait for the killer to approach and then take him down."

"We're not gambling with your life," said Arthur. "We've got to get you out of here."

"You've already gambled with our lives," said PRNC as he shot a glance up at Mmorpg. "The risk might as well be mine."

Mmorpg floated down beside Arthur and motioned him aside. Blue stayed with them but kept a wary eye on PRNC.

"He's right," whispered Mmorpg.

"What?" whispered Arthur underneath the noise of the crowd.

Mmorpg kept his voice low. "He doesn't know that we've disabled the logout function. Nobody knows but us. Imagine what he'll do when he finds out that he's trapped in here with the killer." Mmorpg glanced up to the rafters at the millions taking their seats. "Imagine what all of them will do when they find out."

Arthur looked up at the crowd. "Massive panic," he whispered.

"That's right. Once the Spectacle ends, they will know as soon as they try to log out. And then all *heck* will break loose. If you're right and Undecided is here to kill PRNC, then we have to stop him here. It is our last chance. Otherwise, we'll all go to jail."

PRNC called after them. "Is there something the three of you would like to share?"

Arthur winced as he pulled away from Mmorpg. "Alright," he said to PRNC, "we'll play this your way. Take your seat. Blue I'll need you right beside ..."

Blue shoved Arthur out of the way. "*Amateur. Form a triangle around the pencil-neck. Blend into the crowd and mark anyone approaching him.*" Blue turned towards Mmorpg. "*You got a fancy lens that'll do that?*"

"Yeah, we could use green lens for that," said Mmorpg. "We can tag him with our eyes and you'll get a marker pointing to his position."

"*Do it. If you spot him, just mark him and stay out of my way.*"

"He's fast," said Mmorpg. "You'll get one shot."

"*Don't worry,*" said Blue, "*I don't miss.*"

"I'll keep an audio line open as well," said Mmorpg. "If you see him, give a holler. We'll be able to hear you."

While Arthur and Mmorpg took their positions, Blue escorted PRNC to his seat. As they reached his chair, PRNC turned towards Blue and threw her a smile.

"I guess my life is in your hands," he said as he extended his hand.

Blue grabbed his thumb and index finger and squeezed. PRNC's body shuddered in pain.

"*Your funeral,*" said Blue. She shoved him down into his seat. He gasped, looking up at her with both admiration and fear. Blue took her place behind him, just out of sight.

The lights faded to black. Silence. A spotlight appeared and shone upon the stage. The capacity crowd roared as the clamshell opened to reveal Avideh. It was her time to shine.

****

Arthur was immediately struck dumb. He had seen her face on holographic screens, synaptic relays and on posters plastered all over the Underground. But to see her in person was another matter entirely.

The moniker of Goddess for which Avideh and Vanessa were vying was more than just a title. To be in their presence, unconstrained by the limitations of broadcast media, was a spiritual revelation. Underneath Avideh's luxurious pitch black hair lay a face of Persian perfection. Light cocoa skin framed large, expressive eyes and soft, supple lips painted with light crimson. Her neck was regal, stretching down to a torso that was symmetrically unparalleled. Every aspect of her body was perfect. Every part fit together into a larger whole.

Her black dress accentuated her ample bosoms, lean waist and hourglass hips. She carved a silhouette across the night sky that left everyone before her completely enchanted. What Arthur found most exhilarating, however, were her ankles. Framed by a glass slipper, the heels accentuated her slender calves and the chiselled marble that was her ankle bone.

Arthur watched Avideh stroll across the stage. Like everyone else, he had fallen completely under her spell.

****

In the darkness, the spotlight and the eyes of four million people watched Avideh as the music began to play.

With the opening bars of Howard Blake's "Walking in the Air" began, harmony washed slowly over the audience. Blue felt her tense muscles loosen just a tad. From behind Avideh, English mist streamed out and surrounded the crowd, separating each person from their surroundings. A series of xylophone strikes matched the sparkling of stars as they appeared one after the other in the sky. By the time the ominous woodwinds sounded, Blue found herself standing alone with Avideh, an audience of one.

As Avideh started into the floating chorus, hitting each note with the soft touch of a mother's hands, Blue realized that she was no longer in the arena, but levitating high alongside Avideh above the moist clouds. With the lyrics "moonlit sky" escaping from her lips, Avideh turned to an abnormally large and full moon that rose from the mist and pushed high up into the night sky. From there, the two of them began to move with the moon, floating high in the sky while the village far below slept off the day. Blue had foregone simply floating through the air and had joined Avideh as she raced with the moon across the night sky. Together, they skirted the tops of clouds in their lunar pursuit.

With the second verse, Avideh came close and joined hands with Blue's outstretched palm. To her own surprise, Blue did not seem to mind. They left behind the clouds and the moon and soared high above the lakes glistening below. With the instrumental intermission and the mists far behind, Blue could look down to a multitude of clear lakes, unblemished by human contact and up to the unclaimed stars above. The lakes led to a vast forest, replete with tiny villages peppering the landscape.

As they flew across the globe, the villages seemed to go by like dreams, matching the soft lyrics emanating from the perfect vocal chords of Avideh. The music became less of a performance and more ingrained with Blue's own thoughts and consciousness. She was no longer watching or listening to it; she was becoming the song itself. Memories of her job, Mmorpg, Arthur and Undecided seemed to drift away like a bad dream. For the first time in many years, she felt pure and unselfish joy. She felt it not from death and destruction, but from an almost childlike playfulness she had long ago lost.

Forests, hills, streams and rivers all beckoned below, a far more alien world than Blue had ever known. They beckoned her to fly closer. To smell the needles of the firs, to feel the mist spray off the churning river, to fight the western wind soaring off the crest of the hill. The land called Blue lower. Together, Blue and Avideh dropped into the natural world.

A village hid behind the hilltop, full of children escorted by their mothers and fathers. As Avideh moved into the vocal intermission of the piece, accompanied by the rising and falling of the woodwind section, the children looked up and gaped open-mouthed at the pair flying effortlessly above them. Some tried to get their parents' attention, but the adults, for whom such magic of the imagination had long since passed, ignored the pleas of their offspring and plodded on towards home.

With the next verse, they rose up again to the coldest, highest reaches of the sky. Continuing to ascend, they scaled the snow-covered peaks of a spectacular mountain range. Precipice after buttress after mount greeted them as they skimmed the mountaintops, allowing Blue to brush her hands against a great cliff as the second instrumental intermission ensued.

Suddenly, as the next verse began, they swooped down past the mountains and across a great glacier lake, rousing a grizzly bear from its slumber and frightening the poor beast into a retreat back into the forest, barking its scolding growls along the way.

Then, as the music built up for its final climax, the full brunt of Blake's orchestra came together, filling the melody with more power and poise than ever before as the flying pair soared just above the rooftops of a Victorian city. The moon, having caught up to them, stood resolutely large and proud in the night sky. This time, everyone below saw the angels, one of beauty and the other of death, and greeted them with shouts as they flew past.

Blue and Avideh split their hands as they came upon a massive clock tower, advanced in antiquity. Together they flew around the tower in opposite directions, like children playing tag. Pulling away from the chiming clock, Blue noticed that she was once again standing, no longer floating upon the air. Rising above Blue in crescendo, Avideh struck one last final and powerful rendition of the chorus. The English mists again enveloped them as Avideh brought the piece to a close with the soothing words *"We're walking in the airrrrrrrrrrrrrrrr. We're walkinng inn thee airrrrrr."*

As the spiralling instrumental finale cut off and lights came on, Blue found herself back in the arena with a triumphant Avideh standing before her on the stage. Applause roared from all directions. Facing slightly off to the left, the Persian princess tilted her head back and stretched her palms out in a dramatic pose, soaking up the love of millions.

The chanting continued as the clamshell stage closed upon the preening Avideh, leaving the crowd wanting more. The audience was in complete rapture. Blue seethed about having dropped her guard so easily. Had she missed the killer? She looked over at Arthur, hidden in the crowd. He shook his head. She turned towards a translucent Mmorpg. He shook his head as well. The killer had not shown. But there was another act to come.

The lights dimmed. A soft murmur spread through the crowd. Vanessa, the pop princess of the Underground and the woman they had come to see, was up next. They all waited with anticipation.

CHAPTER TWENTY-FOUR

THE BIRTH OF A GODDESS

The audience, four million strong, sucked in their breath impatiently. Only a minority among them had ever seen Vanessa before. They had tried to describe the experience to their friends, but words failed them. Words could not explain the stoppage of pulse and thought that accompanied that first gaze into her crystal blue-green eyes, the emptying of mind that came from looking upon her vivacious hips, the hush of breath that stemmed from a single glance at her elegant exposed neckline. The experience extended far beyond simplistic lust into the realm of the divine. This was the day that would complete them, that would satisfy the unexplained yearning which had so dominated their thoughts. This was the day they would fall in love.

In the darkness, the clamshell stage swung slowly open to reveal a huddled figure hidden in the shadows. The audience fell into a stony silence, holding their breath for the once-in-a-lifetime spectacle they were about to witness. The spotlight, dim at first and then slowly brightening, left the crowd hanging with anticipation.

Yet Vanessa was nowhere to be seen. On the floor of the stage lay a caressing cocoon of brown hair. Strand by strand, the cocoon unravelled to reveal Vanessa inside, crouching on her knees, arms hugging her torso. She looked at the floor. Her hair flowed behind her like a gigantic sail, catching the virtual wind crossing the stage. Her olive Chilean skin absorbed the light perfectly, highlighting her elegant features and supple cheeks. Her white dress sparkled with the allure of diamonds, as did her eyes when she smiled sheepishly at the crowd. At that moment, four million people fell in love with Vanessa. Arthur watched Vanessa turn her head and their eyes met. He smiled meekly but she returned her gaze to the floor and to her performance.

The words rolled off her tongue smooth as silk. In a soft whisper, she slowly began the chorus without background instrumentation, establishing a connection between herself and her audience.

For once, when we came from disharmony
These wounds are deep, and they burn in eternity.
Touch me now, I'm here in Evermore
Hold me closer, closer, forever more.

Four million pairs of hands reached to hold her, to embrace her, to love her. She was not perfect, her hips were wider than Avideh's and she possessed a soft belly. But rock-hard, perfect bodies were a dime a dozen in Evermore, requiring little more than a thought. But that was what set her apart, that was what made her different. She wasn't a supermodel or a pinup. Arthur sighed.

She was someone who from the moment you laid eyes upon her, he felt, you yearned to pull closer. You dreamed of being with her and taking her home to meet your mother. You imagined spending the rest of your life basking in her presence. She was the lady every woman wanted to be: a idol endlessly haunting the minds of men. She was a woman everyone could love without anger or judgement, without fear or loathing, without pain or bitterness. She was love at its most pure. Next to her, all else faded away.

Arthur's face slumped. *She was so close,* he thought, *and yet so very far away.*

With the second rendition of the chorus, her hair stretched down to the floor and hoisted her up into the air. As she rose above the stage, the light flowed over her sparkling dress like a river, accentuating curves that stopped the hearts of millions.

> Our lives are not what we wanted
> For our dreams and our hopes have been discarded.
> Touch me now, I'm here in Evermore
> To remain, remain, forever more.

Suddenly the arena fell into darkness, save for a narrow beam of light from a star far above. Vanessa reached out to the light with her right hand, full of longing. Arthur thought her differences with Avideh on the stage were obvious. Whereas Avideh had eliminated the crowd to make a personal connection to each individual, Vanessa was using the crowd to build an atmosphere of belonging, an aura of home. With each fluid movement that came from her body, shivers shot through the arena.

> You see the light, it's not a star.
> It's your destiny, upon the horizon.

The beam of light spread across a fictional horizon and formed a sun. As the sun rose behind Vanessa, its light threw her figure into silhouette. She continued to sing.

> Here with me, and me with you.
> Until the end, 'til our spirits have rise-en.

As the pace of the stanza quickened, so too did Vanessa's dance. She moved with ease and power, carving out her presence in the audience's consciousness. The strands of her hair swept across her face in time to the beat. Her hair remained in front, selectively hiding parts of her body. Through the strands, her gaze remained on Arthur, but he didn't let that fool him. He know that her personal gaze was the mirage of the performance; everyone felt that they were the star of her attention; everyone thought she was looking only at them. It was a trick. Yet deep down, Arthur didn't care. He let himself believe, just for a moment, she was looking only at him.

Touch my heart, feel it beat
Wipe the scars from off your feet.
Cry your tears, hold your fears
The memories of old always sear.

The intensity of the verse increased with its speed. Bumping up
the beats per minute, Vanessa continued to selectively hide her body
with her hair, forcing the audience to focus on her eyes, her lips and
legs at the exact moment of her choosing. The light shining from
behind her changed in colour and hue as it moved to the beat of the
song. The resulting kaleidoscope of light spilled into masses
surrounding her. The audience leaned back in awe. They tried to
scream in adulation, but their voices were lost before the pervasive
chime of Vanessa's voice as she sang.

A cry of anguish, a scream for hope
You just want to hide and mope.
To live a lie, to live a dream
To live our lives in ecstasy.

With the chorus returning once more, even stronger than
before, an explosion of light came flying past the floating singer.
Left behind was no longer the rising sun, but a glimmering pool of
water holding impossibly vertical, stretching high into the sky. The
vertical pool altered colour with the tone of the song: diving to blue
for the quiet and morose parts, red for the crescendos and green for
the pulsating stanzas. From Vanessa's powerful lungs came the
chorus, pulling her vocal cords to their limits.

For once, when we dream of our destiny
Our lives are full, complete, and without meaning.
Touch me now, I live in Evermore
Don't take me away, away, forever more.

The background changed around them. No longer were the
audience mere spectators in an arena. They were freed into the
Downtown Core, confronted by a spectacle they would never be
allowed to see again. Menacing skyscrapers rose up on all sides,

trapping them inside the heartless metropolis. Darkness fell across the city, leaving only a small circle of light at Vanessa's feet. Bowing her head, Vanessa's hair blew across her face as she sang.

> My nightmares grow, they steal my light.
> The darkness spreads, across my soul.

She knelt to the ground as if falling, her voice trembling with emotion. Hands on the ground, eyes closed, Vanessa slid her head just off the ground, allowing the pavement to caress her cheek. The crowd pulled towards her, eager to help, eager to touch her, eager to hold her.

> Reality calls, with a voice of dread.
> Pulling me back, making me whole.

The darkness faded away as Vanessa pulled herself to her knees, revealing the rotting wood of a dilapidated home. The smell of green mould suffused the air. Vanessa knelt before a small tattered bed, its faded bedsheets filled with ponies. A small army of faded and broken stuffed animals sat on top.

> I can't go back, I can't go home
> I just want to be left all alone.
> Hear my screams, hear my words
> Reality is the land of broken dreams.

Then with a defiant raising of her hands, she rose into the air propelled by her hair as it morphed into the wings of a butterfly. The force of her lungs belting out the final verses knocked the old building down around them. Up, up she floated, high into the metropolitan sky. As the music built to its final crescendo, so did she, butterfly wings fluttering far above the beat. As she rose like an angel into the sky, the light of a thousand suns surrounded her, basking her in the fury of a supernova.

> Burn it all, nuke it all
> The mirage will soon come to fall.

Feel the rush, feel the brush
Of the end of the superlative crush.

And with the final word of the verse, Vanessa exploded. From the epicentre of the blast came the shock waves, crushing every building and skyscraper in their path. Arthur was thrown back with the wave. Struggling for life, he grasped at the remains of a twisted rebar foundation and held on as tightly as he could.

The whirlwind of destruction pulled on his body, urging him to let go, to join the others crushed in the devastation. But Arthur would not let go; he held fast and tight. The instrumentation of the chorus beckoned him to hold on.

As the remaining pieces of civilization and order flew past, Arthur grimaced and strained at the effort. He was spent, he could hold on no longer. Accepting his own doom, he released his grip of his own volition, expecting to be blown apart like the others into the eye of oblivion.

But he wasn't. Arthur simply fell to the ground as the storm abruptly ended its dance of destruction. The world around him lay in ruins. Wreckage was everywhere. Every trace of man had been wiped out. Then, out of this wasteland, Arthur heard a voice. A soft, hopeful, but melancholy voice, calling to him. As the final verse of the "Call of the Nocturne" played, Arthur watched Vanessa descend from the sky, eyes on him.

For once, when we lived in a paradise.
Our dreams destroyed, and dashed for all eternity.

Her bare feet landed on the wasteland without discomfort. She reached down in front of Arthur and pulled up a pink flower he had not seen before. She caressed his weathered cheek and then cupped the flower in her hands.

Touch me now, I lived in Evermore
Where I'll be, always, forever more.

A tear rolling down her face, she uncupped her hand to reveal a pink butterfly. It fluttered with the exuberance of life, floating softly into the sky to reveal a sun reborn, shining its rays of life down upon the death below.

Then the lights dimmed again and Arthur found himself back in the arena, surrounded by millions of screaming fans. Vanessa was back on the stage, revelling in the crowning achievement of her life. Nothing else that she did in her life would ever compare to this moment. Arthur watched her hold the applause for as long as she dared. The crowd was more than accommodating and expressed their approval with applause lasting long after the lights had been extinguished. When she had finally had enough, Vanessa shot the crowd a smile, turned and walked gracefully back behind the stage.

Arthur watched her go, wondering if this was the last time he would ever see her. He dropped his eyes to the floor in pain. She belonged to a different world now, a world where he could never be accepted. She was far beyond him. In the deepest recesses of his mind, he made a wish he would never admit to. He wished that in some small way, she would remember him. Arthur raised his eyes to take one last look at her as she walked away. Instead, he saw the killer.

He recognized the killer clear as day. Brown leather jacket, Akkubra hat, it matched the memory of the dying Waffle. The killer walked past him without a second glance and moved towards the stage, towards the judges table.

"Yellow lens," said Arthur. He had to be sure.

A golden hue invaded the world before him as yellow names popped up above the heads of the crowd. But Arthur ignored these. He was only interested in one name. As the killer drifted into the crowd, his name appeared in gold above his head: [JTF6.0]Undecided.

"Green lens," said Arthur. He had to mark him. A green shade slipped over his vision. But it was too late, Undecided had slipped back into the crowd.

Arthur moved forward. He could catch glimpses of the killer, but not enough to mark him for the others.

"I have him," said Arthur.

"Where is he?" asked Mmorpg.

"I can't get a clean shot at him, said Arthur. "He's unmarked and moving towards the judges.

****

Blue moved up alongside PRNC. The crowd before them moved in a constant state of flux. Blue couldn't see anyone in this mess. This was not a good place for an ambush.

Blue grabbed PRNC by the shoulder.

"*Come with me,*" she said. PRNC did not argue. Together, they moved through the crowd and went behind the stage.

"*Is he following me?*" asked Blue.

"Yes," she heard Arthur. "He's moving past the judges table and towards the stage."

"Where is he?" came Mmorpg's voice. "I can't pick him up."

"*Follow behind him. Make sure he comes to me.*"

Blue kept walking with PRNC in tow. She eyed her surroundings. The back stage area was full of people celebrating the end of a successful show. There were too many people to get in the way and too much space to maneuver. Blue needed a kill-space, a long narrow corridor, to set up an ambush. To her right, she saw a door marked "Hotel".

"*That'll do.*"

She entered the door, dragging PRNC behind her.

They found themselves in a hotel corridor. It stretched out in both directions as a long narrow passageway. It was perfect. There would be nowhere to run. Blue moved with PRNC past the elevators and down the hall. Twenty metres past the elevators, the corridor turned a corner to the right. Blue pulled PRNC behind this corner and shoved him to the ground.

"*Stay down. If anything happens, run.*"

PRNC held up his hands in surrender. "You got it," he said.

Blue put her shoulder to the edge of the corner. She would have to wait for the precise moment. Too early and the killer could escape. Too late and the killer would be on top of her. Ten metres away would be just about right.

"*Where is he now?*" asked Blue.

"I lost him backstage," said Arthur.

"I think he went into the hotel," said Mmorpg.

"What makes you so sure?" asked Arthur.

"There's a series of footprints stomped into the floor by the door. That's our guy."

Blue held her breath. Footsteps, hard and heavy with an accompanying crunch, came closer. She waited and listened. The footsteps were fourty metres away. Blue slipped the safety off. The footsteps were now thirty metres away. Blue remembered her training: two shots to the chest, then one to head. She had to be sure. Twenty metres away. The killer was at the elevators. The muscles in her legs throbbed with excitement, ready to turn that corner and open fire.

But the footsteps stopped. Blue took a breath and listened intently. She heard the groan of bending metal.

The elevators.

Blue popped around the corner, ready to fire. She saw the killer jump into the elevator shaft. Blue ran towards the doors and found them twisted into an awful shape. As she reached the shaft, she stepped out in front of the doors slowly, her sights searching for a target.

Instead, she heard the snap of a cable and a whoosh of air from the elevator shaft. When she looked inside, the shaft was empty. Blue stepped forward to the edge and looked down. She saw an elevator car falling to the basement. She looked up and saw Undecided riding the detached cable up into the darkness. Footsteps came from behind her. It was Arthur with Mmorpg floating in behind.

"Where is he?" asked Mmorpg.

"*Up*," said Blue. She threw Arthur an angry look. "*PRNC was not the target.*"

"Then who was?" asked Arthur.

****

Vanessa could hear the crowd giving its seal of approval as she rode up in the elevator. She had known once the final note had passed her lips that the competition was over. She would be the next Goddess of Evermore. All that was left now were the formalities.

The elevator stopped with a cheerful ding.

As she stepped out of the elevator, she found herself surrounded by a mob of thick-necked men in nice suits. The well-dressed goons made no movement towards her. Instead, they nodded politely and stepped out of her way.

She walked quickly to the entrance to her suite and found Henry, as always, standing guard outside.

"Who are all those people by the elevator," she asked.

"They say they're security, but I've never seen them before."

"Should I be worried?"

"No, just go inside. I'll handle them."

"Thank you," said Vanessa.

She entered her suite and immediately changed her dress. The sparkling white dress was indeed stunning, but it did not suit her. It was far too glamorous, far too inviting. She changed into a medium skirt and a white shirt, casual and comfortable. She felt like a rainstorm, and wished for one. The rainstorm appeared naturally outside on her balcony, dripping heavy droplets of water onto the patio.

Stepping outside into the storm, she let the raindrops stream down her face, washing away all her tension and her guilt. She loved the spiritual side of rain, how it seemed to renew and redeem her, to clean away all of the ugliness that consumed her, leaving only beauty behind. She loved the rain.

Now soaked, she walked to the railing and leaned on it. She looked out onto a skyline created just for her, deeply lost in thought. She thought about PRNC. He was as handsome as she had been told. The status he held was obvious. Many thought he would be the next sovereign, but Vanessa had never been much interested in politics.

He would make a fine match, a match that would certainly please Lamare. She fantasized about PRNC, dreaming of first dates, engagements and a wedding yet to come. But for one moment, just one moment, she thought about Arthur. She had no interest in him. She was far above him now. He must let his feelings go. And yet, deep down, Vanessa hoped he wouldn't.

She smiled innocently and twirled her hair as she stared out across the skyline. The lights of the cityscape twinkled like stars in the night. It was so beautiful out here. Above her, the moon escaped from a cloud, casting moonlight across the balcony. The pale light illuminated Vanessa's face with a soft caress.

Below her, muffled by the stone and wood beneath her feet, came a joyous celebration. The results were in and she had been announced as the next Goddess of Evermore. All those years of planning, of preparation, of practice had finally paid off. She would be leaving this land forever and taking her rightful place with the elite of the Downtown Core. To sip the finest wines, to dine on the most succulent food, to hobnob with the most powerful and beautiful people. She had earned her place with them.

But what to wear? Which dress would be the most appropriate for the ceremony? Something classical, perhaps: elegant, refined, fit for a princess. Something with gold and a touch of black and white. As she dreamed, her clothes morphed and changed, tailoring themselves to her wishes.

Looking down, she could see the golden gown, trimmed with white strips along each of her legs. It came up to a black bodice that covered her torso and most of her neck, leaving only her shoulders bare to the elements. She had dressed her arms with long white gloves and diamond rings upon her fingers. Soaking wet, the colours of the ensemble glistened even more brightly.

She felt beautiful, but how did she look? She turned with a smile to enter the suite and look at herself in the mirror, but stopped with a gasp of fright.

Lying before her, stretched across the threshold of the opened balcony door, lay Henry. From his crushed and broken body, a dead hand reached out for her. His mouth, lying uncomfortably ajar, was frozen in the middle of a scream.

Vanessa felt a harsh cord slip over her head and wrap around her neck. It drew tighter, forcing the air from her throat. Vanessa tried to struggle but the cord only drew tighter, spreading the taste of death into her mouth. Her legs were lifted from the ground, leaving her feet to dangle. She scratched at the rope, tore at it in desperation, praying for just one gulp, one last breath of air. Just one, that was all she needed. She tried to kick back at her attacker, to knock his legs out from underneath him. When her wayward kicks finally connected, they met only hard rock that bruised her heels. The world around her blurred. The rain did not stop. The realization that she was going to die finally struck her slowing brain. It retorted weakly that such a thing was impossible.

The monster turned her towards him, but her vision was so far gone she could not make anything out. She could only see a blurry outline of arms around her throat. She never thought death would be so painful.

But the figure recoiled upon seeing her face. The cord loosened and she collapsed to the wet pavement, gasping for the breath. She heard footsteps moving away from her as she coughed viciously. Her vision returned, slowly but assuredly. Soon, she was able to pull herself weakly to her feet.

Help, she thought. She must seek help. She staggered into the suite, stepping over the body of her dear friend. Avideh, she thought, Avideh must be behind this. If Vanessa did not show, the title of Goddess would surely pass to the Persian beauty.

Slowly regaining her strength, Vanessa passed through the broken shards of what used to be her door. The oxygen returned to her lungs more forcefully with each successive breath. She turned right and went down the hall, the world pulling back into shape as she approached Avideh's executive suite. The door was open. Vanessa stepped inside, eager to confront her long-time rival.

She expected to find Avideh lying innocently on the couch, with an innocent look upon her face.

But she wasn't on the couch.

She was on the floor, her head twisted around so grotesquely that both her back and eyes faced up towards the ceiling. Vanessa's body went cold. Her legs froze with fear. She had no explanation, no idea of what to do and no way to protect herself. Her eyes fell upon Avideh's twisted neck. Encircling the Persian beauty's throat was a vicious scar that hung like a necklace upon her neck.

Vanessa sagged with pity at the sight. A woman's neckline was a symbol of her femininity: clean, clear and perfectly smooth. Imperfections on the arms and legs could be hidden, but not the neckline. Even if Avideh had survived, no one would want her now. In Evermore, there was no room for flaws.

Tears welling in her eyes at the desecration of beauty before her, Vanessa finally looked away from the body and came upon a sight far more frightening: a broken mirror. Within its shattered remains stood pieces of her reflection, mocking Vanessa with delicious irony.

No. It could not be.

Vanessa looked for another mirror but all of them had were broken into pieces. She ran back to her apartment and threw herself into the bathroom, closing the door behind her. Staring at the back of the bathroom door, Vanessa closed her eyes and took a long breath to steady herself. Mustering her courage, she turned and looked into the unbroken mirror.

Upon her neck lay the same grotesque scar.

No.

Vanessa touched the scar to make sure it was real. Following the line around her neck with her fingers, she felt at the back of her neck an odd indentation that was jagged on one side and straight on the other.

Dropping her shaking hands down to her sides, Vanessa looked again into the mirror and focused. She wished the scar away, trying to change her skin as easily as she had changed her clothes.

The scar remained.

She rubbed the scar with her hands, trying to smooth it out, to rub it away.

The scar remained.

She ran into the washroom, washing it with soap and water in the vain hope she could scrub it away.

But the scar remained, everlasting and permanent.

The soapy water dripped away and Vanessa saw her career sink with it. Who could love a deformed creature like herself? She was no longer perfect, no longer pristine. If a woman's body was a temple then hers had been desecrated. She was no longer a goddess. She no longer belonged in the Downtown Core.

Why hadn't he killed her? she thought.

Death would have been far more compassionate. To crush her dream as she was on the cusp of realizing it was cruel. She buried her face in her hands, the tears gushing down her cheeks.

What was she to do? Who could love her now?

She pulled her hands away from her face and looked at herself in the mirror. With a thought, she was dry but the scar remained. Vanessa took a deep breath.

"I can do this," she said.

As she watched, the remnants of her clothes cracked and crumbled into ash. Her hair stretched and pulled across her body. It surrounded her, covering her more completely than any ensemble. Moving smoothly and loosely over her naked skin, it formed a pliable cocoon that no eye could penetrate. But it was not static. Vanessa's mane flowed and curled and swept as if directed by some unseen wind, but it never left her body exposed. It was protection - a stylish suit of armour more at home in a magazine ad than an armoury. The hair almost seemed to blow with a purpose, covering enough to be discreet and yet little enough to be daring.

Vanessa looked at herself in the mirror. Her neck was hidden. Her gown of hair was beautiful.

"Perfect," she said. She was ready.

She turned around, opened up the door, and screamed.

****

Blue sprinted up the stairs. Arthur and PRNC lagged behind. She reached the top of the stairwell and crashed through the door. She turned towards the elevator doors and paused.

She had stepped into the aftermath of a great battle. Bodies were strewn across the hallway. Their well-dressed corpses crumpled inwards in the most sickening of ways. Impact craters were visible everywhere, even on the walls and the ceiling. One of the victims was still embedded halfway inside a wall.

Adrenaline rushed to Blue's heart. A twinge of excitement ran up her spine. Her breathing grew longer and deeper. She stepped through the thong of bodies while small pieces of the ceiling fell down around her. Blue kept her sights trained for the slightest movement. But there was none.

To her right, she saw the broken remains of a door hanging off its hinges. Pieces of wood lay across the threshold. As Blue approached, she heard a scream.

She ran forward, crashed through the doorway and pulled up her gun to fire.

Blue found a woman wrapped in her own hair stepping away from Mmorpg as he rose through the floor.

"Ms. Vanessa," said Mmorpg as he viewed the wreckage. "Are you alright?"

Footsteps came from behind. Blue turned and saw Arthur and PRNC running down the hallway.

Blue turned back and saw the body of Henry by the balcony. "*Where is he?*" she asked.

"What's going on?" said Vanessa.

"You saw nothing?" asked Arthur.

"I was in the washroom getting ready for the ceremony," she lied. "I was using the hair dryer."

"If he attacked here, then ..." said Mmorpg. He looked to the left wall and his eyes turned red. Without another word, Mmorpg floated through the wall.

Blue, with Arthur by her side, crouched down to examine Henry's body. The bloodless corpse had collapsed in on several sides, like giant dents in fibreglass. His legs had been broken, his arms dislocated and his torso crushed.

Vanessa spoke to PRNC. "How could this happen? I thought nothing could hurt us here."

PRNC sighed. "Believe me, it's a long story and not suitable for a soul as sweet as yourself."

Vanessa shrunk back. "No," she said, "I suppose you're right."

Mmorpg pushed his head back through the wall.

"We have another body in the next suite," said Mmorpg. "It's Avideh." He disappeared back through the wall. Blue and Arthur stood up immediately and moved towards the adjacent suite. Vanessa and PRNC followed.

"Excuse me my lady but you don't have to see this," said PRNC.

"Yes I do," said Vanessa.

The four of them entered Avideh's suite. There they found Mmorpg kneeling over the body of Avideh. Her head was backwards. Her eyes lay wide open, the dead irises capturing her final moments of terror. Vanessa stifled a gasp at the grotesque sight.

"She was so beautiful," she said.

Blue and Arthur bent down to take a closer look at the broken neck. Blue followed the ribbon scar of the cord until she found what she was looking for - another indentation, just like the one on the little girl, Marcony and the leader of the Waffle.

But this time there was only a circle with a gap at the bottom and the numbers 3 and 9 in the middle in reverse. Once again, Blue removed the green plasticine from her coat pocket. Lining up the marks from the other victims carefully, Blue pressed the plasticine into the indentation. Satisfied that the marks had been captured, Blue pulled the plaster away from the body, turned it around and looked at the completed mould.

It was a key. Two edges, one straight and one with jagged grooves, were connected by a triangular lip at the bottom. Standing parallel, the two edges stretched up to a circular head with the number 1394 etched upon its face.

"It looks like a key," Arthur said.

Blue restrained the urge to break his jaw.

It was a key, but what did it unlock - a door, a box, a locket? Blue searched her mind for an answer but the number 1394 gave few clues. What did the number represent? Was it an address, a combination, or some sort of secret code? The complete picture remained beyond Blue's grasp. There were still too many missing pieces.

No matter, she thought, putting the mould carefully back into the yellow can. She would find him. Blue returned the yellow can inside her coat pocket. Out of the corner of her eye she saw Vanessa huddling with PRNC. Blue turned to face them.

"What is she still doing here?" she asked. Vanessa gasped at the sight of Blue's face. Vanessa reached up for her own neck but stopped herself. Blue snorted.

"Get used to it princess. The real world is an ugly place."

Vanessa pulled her hand slowly away from her throat and dropped it to her side.

PRNC raised an open palm towards Blue in agreement. "It is now about 2130 hours my lady," said PRNC. "The audience will be expecting you. It is time to accept your crown."

"Would it be possible to delay it for a while?" asked Mmorpg. "Perhaps you could buy us an hour?"

"Whatever for?" asked PRNC.

Mmorpg paused.

"No reason," said Mmorpg. "Never mind."

"My lady," said PRNC, "please come with me."

PRNC and Vanessa moved towards the door.

"Don't trip over the others," said Blue.

"What others?" asked Vanessa. Blue ignored her.

"I get his reasoning," said Arthur, "but not his methods. He usually crushes his victims like poor Henry back there. Why did he strangle Avideh and Burke and no one else? It just doesn't fit."

"He strangles his victims," said Blue. *"He destroys his obstacles."*

"But only three of his victims were strangled," said Arthur, "How can you be sure that's his M.O.?"

"*Four. The little girl was strangled, Massoud escaped while his bodyguards were crushed.*" She paused to suck in air. "*Burke was strangled while his followers were smashed, Marcony was choked, Terra ...*" her voice lost its strength momentarily. "*... was bludgeoned, so was Henry, but Avideh was strangled.*" Blue drew in another long, painful breath. "*That's your pattern.*"

The look of shock upon Arthur's face was incalculable. A long silence followed Blue's summary.

A scream came from the hallway. Vanessa had found the other bodies.

Arthur's jaw, dropped in confusion, closed slowly. His eyes regained their focus. When he spoke, it was as a question, clear and cold as rain.

"What little girl?" asked Arthur.

Blue looked at him impatiently, "*The first victim, in the alley, strangled.*"

Arthur looked like he had just been shot. "No one told me about her," he said. "I thought the attack on Massoud was the first."

Blue grabbed Arthur by the throat.

"*Amateur. I'm not here to play twenty questions. Stop wasting my time.*" She tossed Arthur to the floor.

Arthur stammered as he pulled himself to his feet. "Okay, I'm sorry. I'll ... check out Henry's body again. Maybe ... maybe there's something we missed."

"*That's better.*"

Arthur moved quietly towards the door. Mmorpg waited until he left the room.

"You've failed, Blue," said Mmorpg.

"*He hasn't gotten away yet.*"

"It's too late now," said Mmorpg. "The Spectacle is over. Millions of people will soon be walking towards the exits. It will not take long for them to notice they can't log out."

"*Tell them it's a glitch. You're good at lying.*"

"And how much longer will it take them to find out they can die? Especially with that monster running around. The one that you were supposed to catch."

"*Kill,*" corrected Blue.

"The one you have failed to kill," said Mmorpg."

"*Not yet I haven't.*"

"And how many more people have to die before you do?"

"*Who cares?*"

"Arthur was right. This was a mistake. We'll pull everyone out and shut everything down. Once they find out, the authorities will do it anyway."

"*I'm not done yet.*"

"Oh yes you are. Arthur!" called Mmorpg as he walked towards the wall to Vanessa's suite. "This has grown way beyond our control. It's over."

Mmorpg disappeared through the wall back to Vanessa's suite, leaving Blue alone with the body of Avideh. Blue heard a soft chirping sound from the doorway. She turned and found a gopher smiling at her. When she approached, the gopher chirped happily to her in binary. Blue didn't need to translate the ones and zeros. She knew what the critter had found.

Mmorpg walked back through the wall.

"Where did he go? I can't find Arthur anywhere."

"*We don't need him anymore.*"

"What do you mean?" Mmorpg looked down and saw a gopher smiling up at him.

Blue drew a violent smile upon her face. She felt the anticipation growing in her voice.

"*We've found him,*" she said.

CHAPTER TWENTY-FIVE

THE CULL OF THE COVENANT

The antiseptic smell of the monochrome bathroom struck the nostrils of Luther. Not a speck of dirt or grime marred his vision of the lavatory. It was a perfect bathroom, the hallmark of modern domesticity. Before him lay the sinks - black and white, spic and span, three in total scrubbed on the hour, every hour. A row of bathroom stalls stretched off towards the right. All of them looked exactly the same, save for one. The third stall, marked with the number three, stood uncomfortably upright on broken hinges. While it was painted the same colour as the others, it somehow felt darker. It wasn't the colour that had attracted Luther; it was the screams. He could hear them from across the cyberscape. Barely audible, the sound fell upon his ears like a whisper on a distant wind. He could not make out the words, but they called to him, drawing him in like a siren's song.

As he approached stall number three, the indistinct voices became clearer, rising in intensity. Luther faced the door while his breath came out in short shallow bursts. He felt foreboding before him, the hairs on the back of his neck rising in warning. He reached out his hand, eager to enter yet afraid to touch the cold, steel frame. Still the voices implored him to enter, to take that fateful plunge into unknown depths. He reached out further, extending his hand ever closer to the door. The stall door shivered in expectation, waiting to be opened.

The door creaked open from his touch. Inside, Luther saw a gaping hole in the wall. The hole appeared to have been made with the crudest of tools. Tiles were ripped out in haste and left upon the floor. Deep grooves in the wall converged upon the hole, disappearing into the pitch-black tunnel. Above the hole, words were scribbled in solid black crayon.

Dearly Beloved … wHY CAN'T ii FEEL ANyTHiNg? … I love my dolls, I love to dress them up and play house. I H@TE YOU! But it's so hard to reattach their heads. TWISTING, TWISTING, ALL THE EVIL OUT, ALL THE EVIL OUT. …we are gathered together here in the sight of God… Little Joanna is very sick with gangrene; we'll have to amputate the leg. h1DE AND Se3K IS mY F@V0rIte GamE. The furnace is always the best spot. BURN, BURN LITTLE JOANNA, BURN THE EVIL OUT, BURN THE EVIL OUT. …is the union of husband and wife in heart, body and mind… Nothing, just playing dolls … and soon the house was empty … Close your eyes, think of the beach, think of the beach … it is a means through which a stable and loving environment may be attained … it'll be over soon … What — therefore — God has joined together — let no man pull asunder."

Moving slowly forward, Luther stepped into the stall, the broken door slamming shut behind him.

****

At the stroke of 2130 hours, the crowd roared in idolatry as Vanessa strode gracefully to centre stage. Instead of gracelessly grinning like a beauty pageant contestant and wiping away dry tears like so many goddesses before, she moved slowly and demurely, almost shyly to the stage. This was a far different Vanessa than they had seen before.

Bowing her head respectfully to the audience, she glanced at PRNC as he walked towards her. However, nobody in the audience saw him approach, spellbound as they were by Vanessa's hair.

Her mane of stunning brown hair blew around her face and neck, covering everything but her large, soft eyes, which peered out vulnerably from beneath the cocoon. The hair focused the audience's attention on her eyes. Peering into her blue irises, the audience felt that they were staring into her soul. She was at once hidden and open, covered yet naked. The millions watching Vanessa felt a connection with her they could barely comprehend. Inside and out, she was breathtaking. Some of those present began to weep at the shift they had just witnessed. Vanessa had gone from being a mere contestant in a competition to being the embodiment of a living dream - a dream of true beauty that all must pursue.

PRNC gave her a congratulatory kiss on an exposed cheek and she began to slowly rise. To rise above the hopes of her followers and the dreams of her predecessors. Now and forever more, she was a goddess.

****

Jonah held Indira from behind as they watched the ceremony projected onto the glass skyscrapers surrounding Malon Mall. They didn't have the money to get tickets to the Spectacle but this was the next best thing. Surrounded by people watching the projection, they still felt a part of the event.

"I like her," thought Indira.

"She's ok," thought Jonah. The crowd around them began to celebrate.

"Do you think she's pretty?"

"Not nearly as pretty as you."

She turned to him laughing.

"You are a liar," she laughed.

"I am not."

"You honestly think I'm prettier than her?"

"Yes I do."

Indira looked down at her feet and grew silent.

"No I'm not. I ... don't really look like this you know," she thought.

"I know."

"I mean this is how I feel like I look but in the real world I look like someone else."

"Me too," thought Jonah.

"So how can you know that I am pretty or not?"

"I know."

"Do you?"

"Yes, no matter what you will always be beautiful to me."

"Are you sure?"

"Yes," thought Jonah.

Indira stepped away from him. As he watched, her facade slowly faded away. Whereas before there had been a shapely Indian women, there was now only a short fat one. Her long legs and narrow arms had been replaced by stubby limbs and fingers. Her smooth coffee skin had been replaced by acne, blackheads and blotches. Her hourglass figure gave way to a pear. She was ugly and she was fat. She looked up at Jonah with pleading eyes.

But he did not see the acne, or the belly, or extra chins. He saw only her eyes. They were the same eyes that had stared into his soul so many times before. In them, he saw all of the hopes and dreams that she had for her life. Her eyes owned him.

He smiled. "I love you," he said out loud.

With those words, his facade melted away. The muscle fell from his limbs. His torso shrank and curled in on itself. Freckles invaded his face. Indira saw nothing more than a scrawny little teenager smiling at her through his braces. But she could see none of that. She only had eyes for his smile. It was the same smile that had brought her so much joy. It reminded her of how he would laugh at the most innocuous little things and how that laugh would infect her and bring her joy. She loved his smile.

"I love you too," she said.

They kissed as the crowd around them danced in joy. They held the kiss as long they dared and then held one another as the celebration on around them. It was getting late. It was almost time to go.

"I should get you home," thought Jonah.

"We have a couple of hours left on the pass," thought Indira, "we can stay for a little while."

"What about your father," asked Jonah.

"He can wait."

As Jonah closed his eyes and bent in for another kiss he heard a voice come from behind. "Kernel: logout," it said. More voices surrounding him repeated the phrase. People were logging out, he thought. With the Spectacle over, there was nothing left to see. *Let them leave,* he thought to himself. He didn't want to share this moment with anyone else. He kissed Indira like he was never going to see her again, holding each kiss for as long as he could. The air around him went still. Not a sound could be heard.

He pulled away and opened. "Finally," he thought, "we're by oursel..." Jonah's voice trailed away. Indira opened her eyes and saw Jonah looking past her. His face was white.

"What's wrong?" she asked and turned around.

Surrounding them stood hundreds of people frozen in place, their heads curled to their sides. Indira gripped Jonah's hand. Covered in Spectacle paraphernalia, the crowd stood silent and still. Together they moved through the crowd, peering into scores of open eyes. Emptiness stared back. They were surrounded by living statues. Indira paused and let go of Jonah's hand. Approaching one of the bodies, she reached out with her hand and gave it a soft push. The body tilted away like a pendulum and then swung back firmly into place. Indira pushed harder. The body fell over, collapsing to the ground in an unconscious heap. Like a herd of cows, the crowd was sleeping standing up. Indira stepped back slowly.

"They didn't log out," she thought.

Jonah shook his head.

"No, they couldn't log out."

"Gray lens," he said as the gray thlog portal came up to meet him. He had to tell the world about this. This was too big to keep to himself. But as the incoming posts overwhelmed his sense, he soon learned the truth. Everybody already knew and they were scared.

****

The word spread like a virus throughout Evermore. For reasons unknown, nobody could log out. Theories and explanations flew around like flies. Some thought it was a glitch. Others believed that the logout function had been disabled. A small minority wondered if they were in Evermore at all. But nothing stuck because there was one element missing: why?

Try as they might, debate as they did, the Evermore public could not figure out why they would be stuck inside the world they loved. And they asked the Consortium and when no answer came they demanded with louder and louder voices. Finally the answer came from the Office of the Sovereign. They had encountered a glitch, they explained, and were working around the clock to fix it. Trust them, they promised, and soon they would get everyone home. The anger subsided, but not the worry. The crowds sat back and wondered. Such a glitch had never happened before. *They would tell us if something was wrong,* thought the masses. *Wouldn't they?*

And so they waited patiently for an answer. But in the back of their minds, they could feel the fear scratching lightly on their skulls.

****

From a balcony, Klein watched the fearful masses pour into Market Square. He could hear a dull buzz following the mob. The crowd massed around the elevator and looked up at the Consortium. They were anxious. They were fearful. And they were looking for answers.

Jie approached Klein from behind, a clipboard in her hand.

"I have a lot of concerned people up here, Richard," said Jie.

"There's a lot of concerned people down there."

"They want to know why nobody can log out."

"There's a glitch in the system," said Klein. He pointed his finger to the sky. "They've said that they'll have it fixed soon."

"We never have glitches, Richard," said Jie.

"I know."

"Then why have we trapped everyone in here with the killer?"

"May I ask you a question?" asked Klein.

"Yes."

"Over the past five years, we have accomplished a lot in power. We've given the Underground a voice, reformed the government and built an economy the size of Canada. But our greatest accomplishment is not a program. It is not a law. It is a principle: No matter who you are, no matter where you're from, you will have a place to belong in Evermore."

"A home for everyone," said Jie.

"That's right. Now if everyone out there knew the truth, then everything we've worked for, everything we've accomplished would be gone."

Jie said nothing.

"If the outside world knew people in here could die, they would shut everything down. Then where would be our home?"

Jie remained silent.

"So I must ask you. How many lives would you sacrifice for a principle? How many people would you kill to save our home?"

Jie thought for a moment.

"All of them," she said.

****

Blue sprinted towards the Cathedral, Beretta drawn and the Chrysalis disappearing over her shoulder. Once she had received the location of [JTF6.0]Undecided from the gopher, there had been little point in waiting. She had lost Mmorpg a couple of blocks back, but no matter. She didn't need him anymore. Blue now had a bead on the killer and with each step her blood boiled with exhilaration. She had been cooped up within the bars of civility for far too long. She longed for the freedom of ultra-violence and the thrill of torn flesh. Following the green arrow, Blue turned a corner and raced the wind.

The arrow guided her to the entrance of the Cathedral. Since she had been there before, it was not difficult to find again. This time, the massive oak doors were broken and ajar. The left half of the entrance lay splintered off to the side.

Blue entered the Cathedral, weapon drawn and ready, looking for something to kill. The bodies of clerics lay everywhere, often in painfully contorted positions. Some of them were missing their skulls. Others had their chest cavities ripped out, but without the grime of blood or internal organs strewn across the floor. To her left, Blue could make out the remains of a golem that had been constructed from the stone tiles of the floor.

Blue snorted in disappointment. Not even their summoned creatures could save them.

To Blue's right were pieces of what appeared to be a bull built out of the Cathedral's wooden benches. Staffs of various shapes and materials were strewn chaotically around the floor, weapons dropped from the hands of the vanquished. The signs of battle were everywhere: nicks and scrapes in the floor, shattered pillars, smashed stained glass windows and gaping holes in the walls. The scale of destruction progressed towards the inner sanctum, as the majority of the bodies were concentrated around the entrance to the Caliph's chambers.

Blue moved deliberately, her Beretta primed, always assuming that in the next instant the killer would step from the shadows and into her sights. She moved slowly up the steps to the entrance of the inner sanctum.

She saw another golem on her right, this one desperately made from the staffs of the fallen. Its body lay shattered in half. The creature's jasper eyes wore a twisted look of agony in its final pose. Looking up, Blue noticed the body of a giant snake wrapped around an arch in the ceiling. The snake had been constructed from the banners that had lined these halls.

The doors to the Caliph's chamber had been pulled apart like a tin can. Inside were the bodies of two more clerics and the Caliph herself. Her final protectors had put up a good defence, trying to use the infinitely long red sheets of the Caliph's bed to bind the intruder.

"Whelps. Your magic couldn't save you."

The Caliph was dead, her eyes bulging up towards the Deity who had failed to protect her. Matching the vulgarity of her eyes was her tongue, stretched out in its quest for breath down to the tip of her chin. Just below her outstretched tongue stood the now-familiar scars around the neck born of the lethal cord. The Caliph had died defenceless, at the mercy of a butcher, with none left to protect her fragile frame.

"Too late, too slow," Blue said to herself as she scanned the ceiling for intruders. The killer was long gone. There was no monster to stop, no battle to fight, just the broken remains of a massacre long since passed. The gopher had brought back the location of where the killer had been. That was useless. Blue needed to know where he would be.

There were no more leads, no more paths to follow. Her quest for [JTF6.0]Undecided had hit a wall. Blue looked back at the body to find the Caliph looking right back at her. But the Caliph's eyes were still dead, looking blankly off into space. Her mouth still rested disturbingly open, her flaccid tongue hanging out. But as Blue convinced herself that the body before her was indeed dead, a voice seeped out from the still lips and unmoving jaw of the Caliph. With her final breath, the Caliph had saved a message for Blue, a message that only she would be able to hear.

"You are not ready to face him," the voice whispered. "He is too strong and you are too weak. Wait for when the time is right. Wait for the Nocturne." The voice whispered off into oblivion.

A flash of anger and indignation spread up her spine. Too weak? Not ready? Did the Caliph think Blue was a child? Nothing was going to stop her. Nothing was going to break her like the helpless old woman. Blue was going to find this killer and bring upon him great vengeance. She was going to break [JTF6.0]Undecided into small pieces and crush them under the soles of her boots. She only needed someone to show her the way.

She heard a small buzzing sound to her left. Wheeling around, she brought her gun sights upon Mmorpg as he floated through the wall.

"Why didn't you wait for me?" he asked.

"*Because you're slow,*" said Blue.

Mmorpg saw the bodies strewn across the room.

"My god," he said, "did you find Arthur?"

"*Who cares? The killer's not here. The trail's gone cold.*"

"If you had just waited for me, you would've gotten your shot."

Blue turned towards Mmorpg. Her eyebrows arched in curiosity.

"I received the message just after you took off. The striders. They've engaged Undecided."

CHAPTER TWENTY-SIX

THE ORDER IS BROKEN

Just inside the Great Gate stood eight striders of the Order. Always focused, ready and prepared, they lay in wait for the moment they would be called into action. The striders felt neither anxiety nor fear. Their intense training freed them from frustration and anger. The Order had been given a single task, protect the citizens of Evermore from harm.

Their search for the killer exhausted, Hiru's squad of six had returned to the Great Gate to join the two gatekeepers. The Underground was simply too vast, too infinite to search properly. Their only chance, Hiru had decided, was to focus their efforts in one strategic area.

The dual lands of the Underground and the Downtown Core were connected at a single point: the Great Gate. If the killer was targeting figures of authority, as Arthur had theorized, then soon he would have to move into the Downtown Core where the Evermore elite resided. To do so, he would have to pass this point and the combined strength of the Order.

The striders had taken up a defensive position at the bottom of the large stairway leading up to the Great Gate. The area was well suited to defence: it gave them a bottleneck they could control and no space for their target to maneuver. An army could not drive them out of their entrenched position.

Strider Hiru, as always, took the point. For him, leadership meant facing the danger first, each and every time. Flanking Hiru were his two strongest warriors, Strider Eva on his right and Strider Siegfried on his left.

Behind the trio stood the remaining five members of Hiru's squad. While not as spectacular or creative as the striders in front, they were nonetheless technically perfect. Their emotions never wavered and they never made mistakes. They stood motionless, blades sheathed upon their backs, supremely focused on the task at hand. No matter who stepped out from that hallway, no matter how strong or fast or smart they were, they would never reach the Great Gate. The killer's reign of terror would end here.

The lights in the tunnel before them faded to black.

The Order remained calm. No doubts entered their minds, no fear clawed at their souls. They simply waited for the killer to show himself. Then they would unleash their justice.

From the blackness came the slow, harsh beat of solitary footsteps, each one giving a loud crunch that echoed down the hallway. Hiru drew his blade from his back and his disciples followed suit, readying their weapons.

The crunching footsteps came closer. With each step, the sheer force and power of the killer's movements became more apparent. But the striders did not waver. They did not panic. They had fought too many battles to be rattled by the sound of footsteps.

Still, the hidden killer drew closer, the sound of his feet crushing the floor grew louder and louder. Finally, a figure took shape in the shade of the tunnel. He was not as big as they had imagined, not as fearsome as they had been led to believe. In fact, the killer appeared to be of below-average height. For a brief moment, the striders, save for Hiru, minutely let down their guard.

But as the figure emerged into the light, their discipline returned. The figure was indeed of below-average height, but not of average build. His bulging shoulders and legs fought against the confines of his brown jacket and blue jeans. The killer moved with a slow grace and power that was painfully evident. The crunching sound grew more forceful as he approached. The walls began to shudder. With each step he took, chalk-like dust coughed up into the air. The striders searched for his face, eager for any sign of weakness. But they would find neither. The killer's head was bent towards the ground, hiding his face behind the lowered brim of a dark brown, Australian Akubra.

At Hiru's command, the striders moved into position and surrounded the approaching attacker. But the killer paid no attention to them. When they were ready, all the Order save for Eva switched on their blades and their eyes turned to bright emerald green. But Eva held her yellow lens upon the killer for one extra moment. She had to know for sure.

As if on cue, the killer stopped. Slowly he raised his head. The collar of his jacket stretched far up above the norm, covering nearly his entire jaw up to the bridge of his nose. His jacket was unzipped, leaving a gap from the high collar down the middle of his torso to his belt. This revealed a white shirt underneath, giving the killer's head the appearance of an imposing Hoplite helmet, but with the dorsal fin replaced by an Akubra. From beneath the brim of his Akubra came the raging glare of his propane blue eyes.

The killer glared straight at Eva. Her answer came in an instant, a yellow word floating just in front of his chest. "[JTF6.0]UNDECIDED." With a flip of her finger, Eva's irises turned green. Bringing her sword above her head, Eva took her place in her comrades' formation, eager to defeat the monster.

In an instant, the battle was joined.

The Order attacked as one, choreographing their movements perfectly in tune with one another. They parried, swung and stabbed as one entity, united in mind as well as body. They attacked and defended from all directions, slashing with the sharp edges of their blades while simultaneously using their resonance trails to shield their comrades from any possible counterattack. They gave Undecided no chance to fight back, no room to regroup, no time to breathe.

He didn't need any.

Undecided's defences were impermeable. Each blow of a striders' swords was either dodged or easily deflected by the killer's bare hands. No matter how quickly or intricately the Order attacked,

Undecided always found a way to escape harm. Streaks of resonance trails whirled around him as he dodged every dangerous assault.

His speed and agility surprised the Order. The Order had always fought as if the world stood still, yet this opponent could match their speed, perhaps even exceed it. The sound of whistling air echoed off the tunnel walls, fuelling their intensity. They were at a stalemate. No matter how ingeniously the striders attacked, Undecided would emerge unharmed. They would fight forever, until one side made a mistake.

Undecided slid underneath a charging swing and rolled away from a series of uppercut strikes towards the towering stairs. Eva could see the younger striders growing impatient and careless.

"Stay in formation!" yelled Hiru.

The renowned discipline of the Order returned. The young striders pulled tight their emotions and fell back into formation.

In the midst of the spectacular battle, Hiru changed tactics and the Order followed. The striders pushed Undecided back towards the stairwell, restricting the space in which the killer had to move. *It was risky*, thought Strider Eva, they were pushing Undecided closer to the exit. But they had no choice, they needed to pin him down.

With their quarry, the striders shifted the battle into high gear. Moving with a speed and grace they themselves had never known, they attacked with the force of a hurricane, determined to take the killer down. In the middle of the whirling shards of steel, in the midst of a shimmering sea of green resonance trails, stood Undecided: ducking, bobbing and weaving away effortlessly from the relentless attack.

The striders backed Undecided up the stairs, but as they did so Hiru discovered that the advantage had shifted. The iron railing in the middle of the stairs allowed the killer to divide the Order. Moving quickly from one side to the other, often by swinging underneath the bar, Undecided gained the only thing he needed - time. The Order's attacks grew more desperate, less coordinated. More and more frequently, a strider would have to come to the aid of his comrade milliseconds away from getting clobbered by Undecided's fists.

The Order quickened the pace, bouncing off walls, somersaulting over the railing, anything to catch the killer off guard.

But despite the speed and ferocity of their assault, Undecided remained untouched.

Splitting from the main group, Siegfried and Eva came after the killer in tandem. While Siegfried kept Undecided off balance with a series of ranged attacks, Eva moved in for the kill. Coming in underneath Siegfried's zigzagging slices, Eva spun a tapestry of slashes with her whip-like everblade.

Undecided blocked all of the difficult cuts, save for one. Eva's final slash, coming from behind her back as she retreated, shredded open a gaping gash in Undecided's jacket. The wound was purely superficial, failing to break the skin. But it rallied the Order.

Emboldened by Eva and Siegfried's successful departure from the coordinated attack, the five young striders pursued their own individual attacks.

"Stay in formation!" yelled Hiru but this time, his disciples ignored him.

The youngest among them, eager and inexperienced, saw what he thought was an opening on Undecided's backside and leapt towards the killer with reckless abandon, everblade poised to swing through the midsection with a cleaving blow. But the opening had been a feint. A millisecond before the young strider could cut him in two, Undecided pushed off his outside foot, charged inside the arc of the swing and smashed the strider's faceplate with a open-palm strike. The armour protecting the strider's jaw broke into chips and fell to the stairs below. As he knocked the inexperienced warrior unconscious, Undecided tightened the palm around the warrior's face, pivoted and threw the body to the ground, bouncing it off the side of the railing.

The fall of the first strider caused a chain reaction among his teammates. The collapsing young warrior tripped up another strider as he jumped forward to attack. As the tripped strider stumbled helplessly towards the waiting Undecided, time seemed to slow to a painful crawl. The vulnerable warrior, struggling to raise a last-second defence, seemed to hang up in the air forever. Undecided struck full on with an uppercut into the strider's jaw, shattering his face armour and bouncing him harshly off the low ceiling above and then off the iron railing below. The unconscious body of the second strider slid limply down the railing to the base of the stairs.

Their numbers dwindling, the Order could no longer keep up the pressure on Undecided. They had to give him more space, and therefore more time. Strider Siegfried tried to catch Undecided off guard with a boomerang strike from his ranged everblade, but the killer was wise to him. Undecided caught the extendable chain, yanked backwards to bring his attacker into range and caught Siegfried with a right cross that dropped him to the floor. With only five striders remaining, Undecided went on the offensive.

The rest of the Order formed a wedge, regrouping to defend themselves against Undecided's counter-attack. Undecided seemed to strike at them all at once, using all four of his limbs in a blistering barrage of punches, kicks and attempted grapples. He forced Eva and Hiru to one side of the railing and the three younger striders to the other, often using the railing as a pommel horse to attack both groups simultaneously. As he reached across the railing to fend off an attempted counterattack from Eva and Hiru on the right, a strider on the left raised her sword to strike at his exposed backside.

The other two striders, recovering from Undecided's previous strike, were late in granting her cover. With nary a warning, Undecided pushed backwards off the railing. Slamming his backside against her exposed torso, he smashed the strider against the stairway wall, pinning her helplessly against it. Then he delivered a rapid-fire series of crushing elbows to the face that crumpled her.

As he let her slump to the floor, the two remaining junior striders attacked. Undecided ducked the swing of the one on his right and then stepped on the strider's foot to pin him in place. The killer then blocked the low strike of the strider to his left with his free steel-toed boot. Spinning around, he swept the legs out from beneath the strider on his right, stepped inside the arc of the resonance trail and then slammed the strider's head backwards into the railing with his left hand. The railing snapped in two from the force of the impact.

Before Eva or Hiru could react, Undecided stepped inside the last junior strider's downward strike, grabbed the strider's left wrist, twisted it over to dislodge the everblade and then forced the strider's head down into the hard concrete. With a violent crunch, the strider's body went limp and dropped to the ground. Undecided turned to glare at the remaining defenders of Evermore, Eva and Hiru, who flanked the killer cautiously. Now, there were only two.

In the calm before the final storm, no one attacked, no one defended. Undecided slowly led the striders up to the top of the stairs, all the while making sure not to come between them. At the top of the staircase, the killer paused on the landing before the Great Gate.

Hiru came up slowly on the left side of the railing. Eva came up cautiously on the right. This time, Undecided allowed them to flank him. A long moment of peace followed, Undecided's eyes were locked onto the irises of the more dangerous Hiru while his body faced Eva.

****

Minutes away, Blue ran towards the Great Gate. Her weapon drawn, her instincts honed, she thirsted for the sweet narcotic of adrenaline. She prayed to a god in whom she did not believe that the killer would be a match for her, that he would be her equal. Nothing else mattered but the fight moaning from her stomach. She was ready

****

Eva stared at the back of Undecided's head, watching for the slightest movement upon which to attack. But Undecided kept staring at Hiru. Deep and vicious breaths blew from the killer's nostrils and passed through the high collar of his jacket.

Then, without warning, Undecided turned his head and looked straight at Eva. In a momentary lapse, Eva was captivated by the killer's beautiful blue eyes.

The attack came quickly, the fury roaring from Undecided's fists. Eva straightened her blade and fended them off with balance and grace. Hiru counter-attacked from the other side, bearing his blade with masterful precision. Undecided returned his attention to the master strider.

The killer deflected Hiru's blows and struck back with a sweep kick to knock the master off his feet. Hiru easily somersaulted over the kick and stabbed downwards at the prone killer.

Undecided rolled away from the sword as it impaled the concrete, delivering a ramrod kick to the backside of Hiru's head. The master strider bounced off the wall, leaving a crater, and fell like a rag doll against the railing of the stairs. Hiru's legendary sword fell harmlessly to the floor.

Letting her sword slack into its whip-like form, Eva began an assault fuelled by hot anger rather than the cold precision of her training. She slashed deeply at the retreating Undecided, ripping his jacket into shreds. She came closer and closer, stepping over the cratered footprints of the killer as she poured out her rage.

The steel tiles of the walls and ceiling, damaged from the battle, hung from the sides of the hallway. Undecided pushed away from Eva, grabbed three of the tiles and threw them one after another at the last strider. Spinning forward, she used her resonance trail to deflect the first two projectiles and then cleaved the last in half with a spinning uppercut of her sword. As the fragments bounced harmlessly down the stairs, Eva wasted no time in continuing the offensive. She spun and swooped, swinging her everblade behind her back, over her head and in every direction imaginable to slay the killer. Eva ducked and deflected Undecided's attacks masterfully, somersaulting over his kicks and sliding beneath his roundhouses.

Finally, she caught a break. Surprising Undecided, Eva threw her blade at him, the chain stretching from her wrist. The blade nicked the killer as it passed him and embedded itself into the wall.

As Undecided glanced back at the blade behind him, Eva retracted the chain upon her wrist, whipping herself forward towards the killer. She swept Undecided off his legs as she slid towards her sword. Pulling the blade from the wall, she attacked the rising killer with both speed and precision. Off-balance, Undecided could only put up a meagre defence, parrying her blows weakly as his sleeves were cut to shreds.

It didn't seem possible that he would recover, but recover he did. Undecided renewed his furious assault against Eva, forcing her to retreat into the corner. Feeling the pressure, Eva sought to escape. Surprising him again, she threw her blade straight up. As her sword impaled the ceiling, she caught the killer off-guard with a left cross. With a right kick to the knee, Eva retracted the chain, pulling herself up and over Undecided. Rising gracefully above him, Eva reached for the hilt of her sword, eager to end the battle as fast as she could.

But she was not fast enough.

[JTF6.0]Undecided reached up and grabbed her thighs as they arched over his head. He pulled them down and over his shoulders. Grabbing Eva's hips, Undecided slammed her back repeatedly into the wall. As her consciousness drifted away, the killer grabbed the back of her head, pivoted and slammed her face into the floor, kicking up pieces of broken metal and dust as the limp body came to a stop in a crater of concrete.

Despite the beating, Eva resisted the darkness. Exhausted, bruised, battered, it took every ounce of strength she had left to keep her eyes open. Undecided walked towards the gate. She reached out to try to stop him, but the chain attached to her wrist drew tight. Her strength spent, Eva's arm collapsed, but did not hit the ground. Instead, it was held aloft by the taut chain. Eva stared at the killer as her vision slowly blurred. It was the only thing she could do - witness her failure.

Undecided stopped in front of the Great Gate. The barrier towered above him, daring him to breach its impermeable walls. He felt the steel of the gate. It did not yield to his touch. He struck the doorway with a powerful punch, but it merely bent backwards to absorb the blow. Undecided tried to pull the gate apart from the middle, but the Gate simply stretched to parry the pressure. Eva smiled weakly. The lockdown of the Great Gate had been successful — Undecided could not penetrate the barrier. The Downtown Core was safe. In response, Undecided turned and punched the wall in frustration. The wall shook.

Undecided stopped.

A chain was rattling. Turning around, Undecided saw a chain stretching up from Eva's wrist. He looked at the chain for a long moment and then following it, looked up.

As Undecided reached for the chain, Eva felt the darkness overtake her. The world faded to black.

CHAPTER TWENTY-SEVEN

THE VEIL OF IGNORANCE

The Consortium rumbled with the news that the striders had been defeated. Representatives from both sides pounded their s in orchestrated bravado, seeking to draw over the undecided delegates and with them gain control over the darkened chamber.

Asa leapt on the news with both a partisan glee and a tempered anxiety. "It has come to the attention of this Consortium that the Order of the Strider, supposed defender of life and liberty in Evermore, has been defeated by the killer that threatens our existence. We are troubled to learn that the killer known as [JTF6.0]Undecided has breached the Great Gate and is about to enter the Downtown Core.

"The time for deliberation and debate is past. We must activate the JTF project. With their regenerative and adaptive capabilities, they are our last chance to halt the monster's advance. But we must act quickly. It will take minutes for the JTF squadron to form and be deployed. These precious moments are vital to our survival. We must act now to end the fear that has consumed our society."

Asa paused, drowned out momentarily by the applause.

"Do not waste your time on applause. The moment for action is at hand. Don't waste the few minutes we have remaining when our very way of life is at risk."

Asa sat down as the Corporate Coalition roared its approval. On the other side, however, anxiety reigned. As Klein rose to speak, he articulated these concerns.

"While I thank the honourable member for his candid evaluation of the situation, there are numerous concerns he has failed to address. Implementing the JTF project is extremely reckless. Once activated, they are immortal. Every time they are killed, they re-format themselves, evolve and come back stronger than ever. Their ability to adapt and regenerate means that ultimately, they cannot be controlled. We could be unleashing a horror upon the world that is far more dangerous than the killer plaguing our shores.

"What happens if the JTF, as they evolve, no longer listen to our commands? What happens if they become accountable only to themselves? Who watches the watchmen then? We could find ourselves in a police state of our own design. I ask the members of the Consortium to consider this decision with the greatest of caution. Do not rush headlong into a decision we may one day regret."

The Klein Coalition applauded with cautious reserve. Asa rose from his seat with calculated abandon. "How would the honourable member propose we protect ourselves from the killer? Are we to flee? Are we to shut ourselves in a hole and pray he leaves us alone? The honourable sovereign has sent two groups after the killer. Both have failed to apprehend him, or even to slow his progress. The JTF are the only option left. We cannot be concerned about issues like freedom when our lives are at stake. [JTF6.0]Undecided must be stopped by any means necessary. Only the JTF can stop him. They are our last hope."

From there, the debate raged back and forth. Those who favoured implementing the JTF wanted a quick end to the debate and an up-or-down vote. Those who opposed the tactic delayed as much as possible, hopeful that the impending crisis would pass over without need for such extreme measures.

From her seat beside Sovereign Klein, Jie realized that the proceedings were getting bogged down in minutiae. The two sides were deadlocked, with neither coalition able to gain the support needed to make a decision. The Corporate Coalition pushed to have the JTF put into the field while the Klein Coalition struggled to add amendments and limitations to the motion.

To Jie, the debate was a losing one. With no other options remaining, the JTF would have to be deployed. With a simple glance at his face, Jie could tell Klein had reached the same conclusion, but he would be trapped politically by the fears of his constituents. The Underground had always been suspicious of any extension of the Consortium's authoritative powers, ever since the Great Strike. Klein himself had used that issue to lead the Rouge Revolution and permanently install representatives of the Underground into the Consortium.

The citizens of the Underground only had one third of the seats, and were thus naturally cautious about any expansion of the Consortium's legislative and executive power. If Klein supported the implementation of the JTF, his credibility with his base of support would be damaged beyond repair. Nonetheless, the situation demanded something drastic had to be done. The killer had to be stopped. Jie could see only one way out of the deadlock.

Jie rose to her feet and waited. At first, the Consortium continued their bickering, but one by one they noticed that Jie wished to speak. Slowly, the partisan rancour cooled to a simmer. The representatives sat back into their seats, ready to listen.

Stiffening her spine, Jie began her speech.

"Members of the Consortium, we are trapped in deadlock between two contrasting but equally valid views. We must act quickly and decisively, but we must also ensure that the rights and liberties held by the citizens of Evermore are never in question. In these most crucial of times, I am forwarding a motion to refer this matter immediately to the Original Position to adjudicate the deadlock. If they are able to make a decision, then I, as a member of this Consortium, will abide by it."

The roar of approval came from all sides of the assembly. The Corporates liked it because it would likely lead to the deployment of the JTF far more quickly. The Klein Coalition trusted the Rawlsian institution of the Original Position because it was the first act initiated by the Klein government. The ISPs were happy to see an proposal that might break the deadlock.

Since the three parties always had an equal number of representatives in the Consortium, a mechanism had been created to resolve deadlocks that would inevitably occur. The Original Position ensured an avenue of escape where decisions could be made void of values, beliefs, socio-economic position or ideology. Only cold-blooded rationality held sway for the patrons of the Original Position - a rationality that had never before been summoned.

Asa rose without delay. "I will second that motion to ensure this crisis is handled quickly."

"I will third the motion," came Klein's reply, "to ensure the rights and privileges of the people of Evermore are protected." The members of the Consortium rose in unanimous consent and applauded the decision, consolidating all the seats into a single omnibus bloc of support.

Together, Jie, Asa and Klein stepped down to the floor and walked towards the empty centre of the assembly. Before them, the ice floor melted away to reveal a spiral staircase descending down into the basement of the Consortium. To the cheers of their supporters, the three of them walked down the steps and into a room that none had laid eyes on before – the Original Position.

The Original Position was a square room of ice, much like the rest of the Consortium. It bore no colours or decoration. Only the translucent sheen of its frozen walls illuminated the room. In the middle of the square chamber stood a thick cylinder of ice stretching from the ceiling to the floor. Jie, Klein and Asa approached the icy cage.

"Where are the ignorant philosophers?" asked Asa.

Jie breathed deeply in anticipation. No one had seen the philosophers in five years. This was because the philosophers of the Original Position were bound by the Veil of Ignorance, which deleted their knowledge of their own socio-economic position or philosophical biases. The philosophers were logic unbound and rationality unconstrained - the ultimate in judicial deliberation.

When the Original Position was created upon Klein's ascendance as sovereign, the six wisest intellectuals in Evermore volunteered to enter this frozen chamber and serve as unbiased adjudicators for the rest of their natural lives. When asked why they were willing to dedicate their entire lives to the venture, the volunteers had simply stated that they wanted to brush away their irreconcilable social biases and reach a nirvana of logical rationality. For them, the Original Position was the culmination of deductive reasoning humanity had been striving towards for centuries – a grail of truth. That day, the six of them had walked down into this chamber and were never heard from again.

Until today.

"Philosophers," said Klein, "I am the Sovereign of Evermore. I require your wisdom to adjudicate a dispute."

As Klein's words echoed off the chamber walls, the icy cylinder began to melt. It melted slowly at first, but as the streams rushed down from the top, the pace quickened. From the melting ice, a ring of decapitated heads appeared around the surface of a cylindrical monolith. The heads were frozen, but as the ice melted around them, their faces began to twitch. The heads stretched to the left and right, loosening muscles that hadn't been used in five years.

Asa and Klein looked at what remained of the shaven heads of the original six. Their eyes had been put out and their sockets were clean and empty. The ears of the philosophers had been sawed off, leaving unsettling chunks of flesh hanging from their aural canals. The noses of the philosophers had been hacked away with what could only have been a butcher's knife. The original six had been robbed of every human sense save for the sense of touch. All other senses that could introduce a philosophical bias were harshly removed. The desecration of their bodies was necessary to attain the philosophical Veil of Ignorance. It was a high cost to pay for logical perfection.

The six heads were now fully awake. The trio of politicians stood in awe at the spectacle, unsure of what to do. Despite their deformities, the ethnicities of the original six could be ascertained. In a clockwise circle from the front, the heads appeared to be Aboriginal, Hispanic, Chinese, African, Arabic and Slavic.

"If they only have the sense of touch, how can we give our question?" asked Klein.

"Write it in braille?" said Asa.

"Maybe they can hear our thoughts?" said Jie.

The Aboriginal spoke to them. "Greetings, honourable members. Do not concern yourself with our ability to understand you. We can feel the sonic vibrations of your words upon our skin. We can understand the content of your words, but we are unable to unconsciously evaluate the message in the manner in which your message is presented. It helps to protect us from bias. In accordance with the procedures, I am to assume that one of you is the sovereign."

"That would be me," said Klein. "Don't you remember me? I shook your hand before you entered this room not so many years ago."

"You must forgive me. Our memories, our links to our past, can intrude upon our logical deductions and introduce irrational bias into our thoughts. Thus, the only logical conclusion was to remove our memories completely. We have no memory of who we were, what we did, or anything else that is irrelevant to our present duty. In fact, I am liable to forget this conversation not long from now, as it is unlikely it will have anything to do with our deliberations. Now, please give us the disagreement in question so that we may deliberate over the matter and give a proper and efficient verdict."

"Of course," Klein said apologetically. "Permit me get straight to the matter. A killer we cannot control has broken through the Great Gate and entered the Downtown Core. The killer has easily defeated our greatest warriors. An urban mercenary we dispatched to apprehend the suspect has been unsuccessful."

"If your citizens are in danger, why not simply log everyone out until the killer has been found?" asked the Aboriginal. "That would be the simplest and most logical recourse."

"Unfortunately, we have encountered a software glitch in the kernel. The glitch has disabled the logout function for the time being."

"That is unfortunate," said the Aboriginal.

"To protect the citizens trapped in Evermore, one side in this dispute has suggested that we engage the JTF. The other side of the debate is terrified that the activation of the JTF project would severely curtail the freedoms and liberties of the citizens of Evermore."

"Who are the JTF?" asked the Aboriginal.

Asa spoke, "They were a project initiated under my government. They are a physical army that can materialize out of any surface and move with tactical precision and efficiency. They would be more than sufficient to stop the killer."

"What tools do they have access to?"

"In developing the JTF project, we created a wide assortment of weapons, vehicles and tools with which the JTF could be deployed. These include firearms, explosives, RPGs, APCs, tanks, planes - all the way up to the airship *Chasse-Galerie*. They can be provisioned any tool we can imagine. Their only limitation is our courage."

"And what is the concern with their deployment?" asked the Aboriginal.

"They cannot be killed," warned Klein. "When mortally wounded, a member of the JTF will fall to the ground, quantify the results of its tour of duty, make adjustments to its source code and then regenerate as an improved fighting machine. Once unleashed, they cannot be fully controlled. If we're not careful, we could be freeing a monster far more terrifying than the killer Undecided."

Asa stepped in front of Klein. "The JTF are programmed to only follow orders directly from the Consortium. This is known as Directive One. A directive is deemed invalid if it comes into conflict with any of the directives above it. None of the lower directives can override Directive One. If an order is given anywhere in the JTF chain of command that contradicted the decisions of the Consortium, the JTF would be forced to disregard it. The JTF will be fully subservient to the authority of the Consortium. You have my word on it."

"Your word means nothing to us," said the Aboriginal. "It suggests trust, of which we six are no longer capable."

"The people fear the JTF," said Klein. "They fear it may lead to a police state they may never escape. Many of the people who now call our land home come from places where their every move was monitored, where their every choice was questioned, where they had no freedom to express themselves openly. Activating the JTF could annihilate that freedom and give these people nowhere else to turn. Please consider that in your ruling."

"It will be noted," said the Aboriginal. "Now, based on your lines of debate, it is logical to assume that both sides have exhausted their arguments. Is that correct?"

Klein and Asa looked at one another for a brief moment and said together, "Yes."

"Now, you do realize that all decisions are binding. Once you have referred a matter to the Original Position, you are bound to accept the results of our adjudication, even if you disagree with them. Are you both prepared to accept this condition?"

"Yes," Klein and Asa said at the same time. Klein continued, "In the interest of non-partisanship, we will accept any decision you make.

"Excellent," said the Aboriginal. "Then we will begin our deliberations."

The debate between the six philosophers of the Original Position was ensued. As each philosopher spoke, the table swivelled so that the politicians could view the speaker up close. The first was the Aboriginal. Jie remembered that when the philosopher had first entered the Original Position she had been a woman. Jie could no longer tell if Aboriginal was still female, as all indications of gender had been stripped from her face. Her skin, while holding its brown hue, had faded to a sickly gray.

"Without freedom," said the Aboriginal, "there is no security."

The next head, the Hispanic, swivelled into place. "Without security," he warned, "freedom is only an illusion."

And on they went, each head speaking in turn. The only one that failed to speak was the Chinese female. She seemed completely isolated from the others, making no effort to contribute to the discussion. The debate went through various arguments for and against. It took only a minute to come to a general agreement on the course of action. The JTF would have to be activated; the security of the nation demanded it. Next, the philosophers discussed what limits that would be placed on such a deployment. What weapons would they be given? Should a time limit be placed on their deployment? What orders should follow Directive One? The discussion reached such an intense pace that the heads spun in a blur, their words spilling out so fast that neither Asa, Klein or Jie could understand them. Finally, after two more minutes, the spinning halted and the face of the Aboriginal was again before them.

"We've come to a decision," said the Aboriginal.

"Excellent," said Klein.

"It is our decision that the JTF must be dispatched immediately. To maximize the probability of their success, given the severity of the threat you have described to us, it is our logical conclusion that no limits should be placed on their deployment."

The three politicians jolted in surprise. Jie knew that all three of them had expected that some limitations would be placed on the JTF. Asa would be hoping for less. Klein would be hoping for more. Asa was the first to recover from his surprise and speak.

"No limitations. So they will have access to tanks?"

"Yes," said the Aboriginal.

"Gunships and APCs?"

"Yes, anything that is necessary to stop the threat before anyone else is harmed."

"What about the *Chasse-Galerie?*" Klein asked nervously.

"Our logical deduction," said the Aboriginal, "is that if the JTF fail, then the only recourse will be to evacuate as many people as possible from the killer's path. Since the logout function is unavailable and the killer is grounded, then the safest place in Evermore would be the sky. The only vehicle capable of carrying out such an evacuation on a sufficiently large scale would be the airship *Chasse-Galerie*. Thus it must be deployed, immediately. Are there any questions?"

"No," said Klein, his shoulders slumped in resignation. "Thank you for your service to Evermore." Klein and the beaming Asa walked back up the staircase. Jie began to follow. But from behind, she heard a soft voice.

"Help me," pleaded the voice. She turned and saw the pained face of the Chinese woman front and centre. In a split second, her face swivelled back to the rear of the circle. The Aboriginal retook her position at the front.

"Is she alright?" asked Jie.

"Yes." The Aboriginal sighed. "She hasn't been herself lately. She's been ... emotional. I apologize for the inconvenience."

Jie nodded worriedly and walked back up the stairway. She began to wonder if the philosophers had made things better or worse.

CHAPTER TWENTY-EIGHT

THE TRUTH REVEALED

In full sprint, Blue entered the hall of the Great Gate. Mmorpg trailed behind, struggling to keep up. The unconscious bodies of the striders were strewn about everywhere. As she sprinted up the stairs, her eyes came to rest on the Great Gate. The door was intact, firm to her touch. As Blue pushed, the Great Gate simply bent back to absorb the force. It remained sealed; the killer could not have passed under its arch.

Turning around, Blue's eyes fell upon the body of Eva, lying face-down upon the floor. The strider's hand hung suspended above her body, held in mid-air by a rigid chain. Blue followed the chain upwards and discovered a gaping hole in the ceiling.

Mmorpg followed her eyes and read her mind.

"Don't go out there," he warned.

Grabbing the chain, Blue pulled herself up towards the sword embedded in the ceiling. Reaching the sword, she reached hand over hand towards the opening. With a final swing of her arms and feet, her body swung through the hole and into the area above.

Below her, Eva's body suddenly stirred with life. Opening her eyes from a deep slumber, the strider lifted her face from the floor as fragments of concrete fell from her jaw.

"Father?" she said groggily.

The loss of perspective disoriented Blue, causing her legs to buckle and her stomach to launch up into her throat. At her feet, she could make out the ceiling of the tunnel before the Great Gate. But as she moved her head, the objects before her smeared across her field of vision. The original afterimage of each object stayed in place while successive images blurred themselves across Blue's eyes. It was like watching a long exposure photograph in motion. The end result was that the more Blue moved her head, the more disorienting her vision became.

She heard Mmorpg buzz through the ceiling.

"*What is this place?*" she asked.

"It is the place without places," said Mmorpg. "It is the null space."

"*What's it for?*"

"Nothing. Absolutely nothing. Do you think that the hosts use every inch of space that is available to them? Of course not. They use only what they need. The rest remains as nothingness."

"*It blurs,*" said Blue. She was almost fascinated by the smearing world around her. It was like petroleum jelly smeared over your glasses. It was almost beautiful.

"That's because we built the engine not to render it. If no one was supposed to see than what was the point in showing it? What you're seeing right now is your mind's reaction to the paradox. It knows that something is there but it can't see it. So it gets confused and tries to render it"

Blue took a step forward. She was now outside the defined walls of Evermore, far beyond the imaginary pieces that made up their world.

"No," said Mmorpg. "Come back inside. If you get lost you'll never find your way back."

Blue ignored him. She held her vision steady, being careful not to move her eyes, and stepped forward. She moved carefully, her vision becoming more and more incapacitated with every step.

"Come back!" called Mmorpg. He reluctantly followed, but fear pierced his voice.

Blue continued to walk forward. By now she was almost blind. Her body grew cold from exposure. It was so peaceful here, she thought. She could stay in this place forever. No one would ever find her here.

With another step, her feet felt the edge of a hole. The spell broken, Blue kneeled down and dropped through the opening. She was back in the tunnel, but beyond the Great Gate.

"Where are you?" yelled Mmorpg.

"*Keep moving forward,*" said Blue. "*You'll find me.*"

Soon enough, Mmorpg floated down through the ceiling. He was frightened but unharmed. Landing beside Blue, Mmorpg turned back and looked up at the hole in the tunnel roof.

"So that's how he got through the Great Gate," he said.

But Blue ignored him. Instead, she was examining a series of footprints, caked into the concrete, leading away. Up ahead, Blue heard the swoosh of a train leaving the station.

****

Strider Hiru moved through the passenger car quietly as the train barrelled through the tunnel. He kept himself in a low crouch as he walked, reluctant to give away his position. His sword was drawn at his side, ready to strike at a moment's notice. Hiru approached the door connecting to the next passenger car. He ducked below the window and took a deep breath. Slowly, the strider pulled his head up to look through the window.

In the next car, he saw Undecided. Undecided was standing in the middle of the car with his back turned to the strider.

Hiru slid open the door slowly.

Undecided kept his back to Hiru.

Hiru raised his weapon.

Undecided did not move.

Strider Hiru took a single step forward. His foot stepped on the dividing line between the two cars, but then he froze.

Undecided perked his head up as if smelling something in the air.

Hiru's foot began to tremor. The shaking spread all the way up into his hands. Strider Hiru was trembling.

Undecided turned around and stared at the master strider, his silver blue eyes etched by the brim of his Akubra into a flame of violent exuberance. His manner invited Hiru into his car, to beckon the strider to another beating.

But Hiru did not step forward. Instead, with heavy eyes, he lowered his weapon.

Undecided snorted his disgust and turned away. The train hit a junction and the cars were divided. Hiru watched as Undecided's car darted up another tunnel and towards the Downtown Core.

His body shuddered. Hiru placed his hand on the wall to steady himself. His body, weak and weary, hung with guilt. He was alone with only his shame to guide him.

****

Arthur stared at the body of the little girl. Protected from disturbance by a fake wall, the first victim lay exactly where Mmorpg and Blue had found her. The force of the asphyxiation had turned the little girl's face the light colour of chicory. But it was not her bulging eyes that distressed Arthur; it was the physical desecration of the child's body. There was something there only he could understand, only he could see. And it sickened him.

The words dripped from his mouth like syrup. "I understand now," he whispered to himself, "it all makes sense to me."

Arthur bent over and coughed in revulsion. As he steadied himself against the heaving in his chest, Arthur's eyes focused on something at his feet.

Arthur reached down and picked up three little dolls. He shuddered and cradled them in his arms. Pulling himself upright, Arthur cast one last morose glance at the body at his feet.

"I know who I am," Arthur said. He turned and walked away into the shadows.

CHAPTER TWENTY-NINE

JTF3.0 VERSUS UNDECIDED

The birth of the JTF began not with a bang, but with a metallic moan.

Jie heard it, soft and distant, through the icy walls of the Consortium. Curious, she stepped outside onto the Consortium's veranda, a porch usually reserved for ceremonial occasions. As she walked outside, the sun rose above the horizon and spread its morning rays upon a city lost in slumber. Jie knew the rise and fall of the sun was purely Forsythian. If you preferred the night, then all you would ever know would be the mysterious danger of the black sky. If you preferred the sunrise, you would know nothing but. More and more, Evermore was giving people what they wanted instead of showing what was actually there. Jie was normally a night person, but this was not an ordinary day.

She heard the groaning again, this time off to the starboard side of the veranda. Jie peered over the railing and down the great ice walls of the Consortium. A metallic slime protruded from the Consortium's side. Like a cancerous tumour it grew and spread, sucking the mass away from the white, icy walls.

With each passing second, the whining became louder and more mechanical. Two more tumours began to grow near the front and back of the Consortium. Fusing together, the three pieces became one, an oozing, unformed mass almost a kilometre in length.

Finally, the blob stopped growing. Hanging off the side of the Consortium, the mass turned its efforts inwards. Slowly its features grew more defined. The sides snapped into symmetric precision, forming the rough outline of the blob's final form.

The mass created command towers on its base, jet engines at its rear and bottom and airstrips upon its flat top. Jie soon realized she was watching the creation of a flying aircraft carrier. From its flight deck, jet fighters grew up. Soon APCs and tanks joined them. Right before her eyes, Jie watched a transport chopper form around the largest battle tank, encapsulating it within the helicopter's cargo bay.

Into her ears rose a pounding military theme led by powerful trumpets. The music instilled in her a sense of awe at the army that was building itself right before her eyes.

As fourty engines on the hull roared suddenly to life, the vessel surged out of the ice. Watching the airship slide across the walls of the Consortium, Jie saw the name written upon its bow come into view. The *Chasse-Galerie*.

But the great ship was empty. There was nobody piloting the massive vessel. Jie peered closer at the flight deck of the great airship. From the runway, she could make out the rising forms of faceless humanoids, bowed down in the fetal position. As the forms rose into a standing position, the features drew themselves as if from clay. A variety of fatigues, boots and helmets adorned their bodies. Within moments an army had been born. Its forces complete, the *Chasse-Galerie* pulled away from the wall and cut its last umbilical to the Consortium with a waking moan.

With only one texture mapped to their face, the JTF wore only a single expression. Jie felt a chill on the back of her neck as she stared at their lifeless faces and still eyes. Never blinking, never breathing, the JTF came to life.

Jie had little time to quell her uneasiness. The fully armed troops loaded into the helicopters. Once full, the choppers took off from the deck and flew towards the financial district to the south-east.

Jie watched the army deploy with worry written upon her face.

"Deity help us," she said.

She lowered her head and saw the growing crowd at the base of the Consortium. After a moment's hesitation, Jie left the balcony and moved to the elevator.

****

Indira eyed the mass growing on the side of the Consortium with apprehension as Jonah led her towards Ridley Station.

"I'm sorry," thought Indira. "I know we have some time left on the pass, but I don't feel safe here."

"It's ok," thought Jonah. "We had a pretty good day, but there's nothing to worry about. Nothing can hurt us here."

The stairs leading down to the station were just ahead.

"I know, but something is wrong."

"I know. I know. Perhaps there's a way out in the Underground." Jonah looked back at the growing tumour on the side of the Consortium. It worried him.

"Let's get you home," he thought.

"What is that crunching sound?" asked Indira.

"What?" thought Jonah. His ears focused on the noise. It sounded like snapping bones. He couldn't place its location.

As they came to the stairs, a figure rose to meet them. Indira gasped in surprise, letting go of Jonah's hand. Even by Evermorian standards, the stranger's clothes were peculiar. He wore a brown leather jacket with the collar turned up to cover his jaw. A cowboy hat of some sort was pulled down over his eyes. Regular blue jeans led down his legs to a pair of simple brown boots. The man looked liked he belonged on a ranch, not in a city.

The stranger did not break stride, advancing towards them without a second glance. Jonah stepped back politely to let the stranger through.

But Indira froze. As the stranger drew closer she raised her hand and waved. Smiling she said, "Well hello, my name is ..."

The stranger reached out his hand and grabbed her by the throat. He wrenched her head sideways with an awful crack. As Indira's body slumped, the stranger tossed her aside and kept on walking.

Jonah moved to Indira's side.

"Honey?" he thought. "Are you ok?"

She said nothing.

"Come on now baby," he thought. "Say something to me."

Her body did not move.

Jonah reached down to his soul box - the one that was always connected to her. "Did you re-spawn somewhere else?"

Silence. She was no longer in Evermore. No matter. He could speak to her no matter where she was.

"Is it your father?"

Silence.

"Come on Indira. Your father doesn't know we're connected. Think something for me."

Nothing.

"Baby, come on now. *Think something*. Please."

No thought came. Jonah looked down at her body and finally understood.

She was gone.

His chest began to spasm. "No," he thought. "It's not possible." But it was. His love lay still in his arms, her thoughts silenced.

Jonah looked back at the stranger. The killer walked into the centre of the Downtown Core – towards the Xchange, the Consortium and the approaching *Chasse-Galerie* in the sky.

Jonah motioned with his fingers, and a thlog portal opened at his command. Before him, thousands listened intently for his next post.

"We can die," he thlogged.

****

Jie stepped out of the elevator just as the news hit the thlogs. "We can die," was all that was said. The crowd erupted in anger. They screamed at the Consortium above with furious words and terrified looks.

"What's going on?" asked one. Numerous questions of similar meaning followed.

Jie spoke as loud as she could. "We advise you to evacuate the centre of the Downtown Core. Evacuation teams have been dispatched to assist you in this matter."

"Where are we supposed to go?" asked another.

"We can't leave," said a third.

"Once again," said Jie, "please move away from Market Square in a calm and orderly fashion. Everyone will be fine."

"Who is killing people?" asked someone. "How do we know what he looks like?"

"It is imperative that you move away from this building now," said Jie, "We will explain everything soon, but for now ..."

"GIVE US SOME ANSWERS!"

The crowd surged upon her without warning. Jie fell to the ground as the mob kicked at her. Blows to her head drowned out the screams around her. Jie pulled herself to her knees and crawled through the legs of the advancing mob. After a couple of seconds, the crowd lost track of her amid the sea of legs. Jie crawled to the edge of the crowd and pulled herself up to her feet. She looked back at the mob, now cursing the Consortium with their every breath. They wouldn't listen to her. She couldn't save them.

"Klein," she thought, recording a thoughtmail. "We need to evacuate this crowd. The killer is heading straight for them."

"We know," replied Klein. "We've redirected a section from Squad Alpha. They'll be there in two minutes."

Panting, Jie turned away from the crowd and rested her eyes upon a building constructed out of a waterfall. Light poured from inside. The Xchange was still operational.

"My god," said Jie. "They're still in there."

Jie ran towards the Xchange. She may not able to save the people behind her, but she could save the traders. Off in the distance, she heard explosions. She didn't have much time. Luckily, in the Xchange, there was no such thing as time.

****

Having lost Undecided's track in the sprawling subway tunnels, Blue and Mmorpg finally surfaced at Lucas Station. They found themselves alone, surrounded signs of looting everywhere. Store fronts had been smashed, light poles had been toppled, everything of perceived value had been ripped away.

"Look what they've done to my beautiful city," said Mmorpg.

Blue scanned the streets for any sign of her quarry.

"It doesn't make any sense. Why would you steal a virtual object? It doesn't have any value. You can't take it with you. And the owners will just recall it once they realize it's gone. It's unnatural."

"*It is natural,*" said Blue. "*This is who we are. When the chips are down we will eat our young. We are rancid, horrible creatures. Always have been, always will be.*"

Gunshots rang out from the south. Both Blue and Mmorpg turned towards the noise. They saw helicopters floating above the skyscrapers

"That came from Ridley Mall. More rioters?" asked Mmorpg.

"*No,*" said Blue, "*it's him.*"

Blue broke into a sprint and ran towards the helicopters. Mmorpg floated after her, struggling to keep up.

****

Once Undecided was in range, the rotor-blades of half a dozen helicopters began to swirl on the deck. As trumpets played triumphantly from loudspeakers of a battle soon to be won, the helicopters took off from the flight deck in two squads and flew towards the killer. In Alpha Squad, there were three transport choppers to evacuate the citizens lying directly in Undecided's path. Beta Squad had two attack choppers and a transport. Each of the attack choppers carried eight soldiers and a full assortment of missiles and chain guns mounted on each wing. They would receive no fast-moving air support as the area was considered too densely populated for air strikes. Two attack helicopters would have to do.

Beta Squad stopped five blocks ahead of the approaching Undecided. The choppers hovered five stories above the intersection. The cabin doors of CG1, the lead attack chopper, slid open and the squad commander dropped out, the bungee cord attached to his belt the only connection to the safety of his vehicle. As he fell, the commander kept his weapon trained on an unseen target far off in the distance. He paid no attention to the asphalt coming up to meet him.

At the last moment, the bungee cord drew taut and sprung the commander up from his fall. Sights always trained on the objective, he reached back with his left hand and uncoupled the bungee cord from his belt. He landed in a perfect kneeling firing position, covering his troops as they dropped to the ground. As each of the troops reached the bottom of the bungee, the cord kicked them up and forward, giving them time to unhook themselves while landing in an ideal firing position. Two helicopters, two bungees per chopper and four soldiers per bungee. Within three seconds of the commander stepping out of CG1, all sixteen troops had taken up positions at the intersection of Ridley and Tourian.

Their human cargo dispatched, the attack choppers retracted their bungees and retreated to an aerial support position. One street over to the west, the transport chopper landed softly with its rear cargo hatch open. A set of treads roared to life, throwing the tank excitedly onto the street. The transport took off again immediately, moving away to aid Alpha Squad in the evacuation. The tank came to a stop around the corner from Ridley and Tourian, ready to serve as backup.

Slowly and methodically, Undecided stomped towards the JTF3.0. The JTF took up covered positions around the intersection, using the surrounding skyscrapers as cover. Undecided had no weapons other than his hands, so the cover sought by the JTF was not really necessary. The JTF, however, were not sentient beings: they were programs, binary constructs bound by the limitations of their code. They could only do what they were told to do. Thus, they were compelled to seek proper military positioning. It was both their greatest strength and their greatest weakness.

Undecided approached the ambush slowly with his head lowered, the Akubra covering his face. Each step he took pancaked the asphalt beneath and left a clear trace of his footsteps. The JTF3.0 and their assault rifles did not concern the killer. His hollow eyes were focused on one thing only - and nothing would stop him.

The commander radioed back to base, "Mother, Beta Squad in position. Target approaching."

The response came back quickly, "Roger Beta Squad, you are cleared to engage."

"Is the host in the red zone?"

"Negative, host is out of range. Weapons free. Repeat, you are weapons free."

"Roger that," the commander turned his attention to the approaching killer. "Halt!" The commander's voice rang out like the mechanical drone of a military radio. "You have been found in violation of the Evermore Code of Conduct. You are to cease and desist your activity and surrender yourself to our custody."

Undecided kept walking.

"This is your final warning. If you do not surrender, we will be forced to neutralize you."

Undecided ignored him.

Over the radio, the commander gave the order. "Engage the target."

The recoil from the barrels of sixteen rifles punched the shoulders of the JTF as hundreds of rounds reached their target.

But the target kept coming, the bullets simply refracting around his body. The smoky whispers of bullet trails bent around his unharmed form like water over a rock. Windows in both skyscrapers cracked and shattered from the refracted rounds. The squad's grenadier fired off an RPG. The explosion engulfed Undecided in flames. His body disappeared behind a wall of fire and smoke.

"Seize fire," ordered the commander. All firing stopped. Their unmoving eyes searched for the target but all they found was a gray fog that smelled like ammonium.

"Advance and locate target," ordered the commander.

The JTF moved in formation into the expanding cloud of smoke. As they entered, the combination of smoke and dust blocked out the sun, engulfing Beta Squad in a false dusk. Encased in the smoky darkness, the JTF could barely see the man in front of them, let alone search for the target. That was when Undecided struck.

Radio chatter came over the com, "Enemy spo—" but was quickly cut off. From the smoke came the killer, attacking the middle of the group. He slapped away the commander's weapons, broke his arm and snapped his neck all in one motion. The chain of command broken, the junior officers hesitated. Undecided moved like a Valkyrie on speed, throwing an officer over his shoulder and crushing his neck with the steel toe of his brown boot. There was no wasted motion; the killer's dispatch of each soldier led him right into his next victim, like an epic combo from an old video game.

The element of surprise gone and the smoky black dissipating, Undecided grabbed a soldier's wrist, twisted his body around and used him as cover. The JTF were confronted with another paradox of their programming. They were ordered to neutralize the target no matter the cost, but their 'Friendly Fire Directive' forbade them from consciously harming one of their own.

This hesitation allowed the killer to get close enough to throw his hostage through the group on his left, decapitating three of them. A fourth he slammed through a broken window and a fifth was killed by confused cross-fire. In their confusion, the remaining JTF banded too close together. Their proximity to one another made it impossible to organize an effective counter-attack and left them vulnerable to hand-to-hand combat.

Undecided wasted no time. Swooping in underneath the confused shots of his quarry, he slammed into the very centre of the group. The soldiers' rifles were useless at such close range. Many of them dropped their primary weapons and tried to use handguns and knives to attack the killer. In a flurry of punches, kicks and grapples, Undecided painted a masterpiece of broken bone, crushed cartilage and smashed skin. Within seconds his masterpiece was complete, the bludgeoned corpses of the JTF lay strewn across the crumbling street.

With the infantry annihilated, the choppers were immediately ordered to move in and destroy the target. CG1 looped around into the middle of the intersection behind Undecided and released a barrage of air-to-ground missiles. The resulting storm of flame and shrapnel did not harm the killer, refracting harmlessly around his body and shattering the remaining windows of the surrounding skyscrapers.

The concussive force of the explosion, however, knocked Undecided back through the air. He hit the pavement about a block away, bounced off once and then skidded across the pavement. Leaving a deep groove in the asphalt, his body slid hard through an intersection and slammed into the bottom of a tall glass building on the corner. CG2 came out of its backup position to lend support to CG1 on the search and destroy mission. Together, the two choppers circled the skyscraper, searching for any signs of the killer, but they could not see his body. A radio message from the cockpit was transmitted back to the *Chasse-Galerie*, "The target is neutrali—"

At that moment, Undecided jumped through the window of the twenty-seventh floor. Mere metres above chopper CG1, he fell feet-first towards the swirling blades of the helicopter. Impossibly, his right foot landed on one of the rotors, braced and pushed off in a nanosecond to clear the blade. The blade bent from the impact but continued to spin. The left foot touched down on the next rotor, braced and pushed off again. In this manner, Undecided ran on the spinning blades of the helicopter towards the mast at the centre.

CG1 immediately dispatched a mayday. CG2 circled around the building to provide covering fire. As Undecided reached the spinning hub of the revolving helicopter blades, he reached down, ripped out a screw from the mast and somersaulted off the blades in one single, devastating motion. Centrifugal force ripped the blades apart just before the killer fell headfirst through the rotors. Completing the somersault, Undecided landed feet-first on the street, smashing an impact crater deep into the asphalt.

Crouching down as if in prayer, Undecided lowered his head as the helicopter crashed in a storm of shrapnel behind him. One of the rotors bounced beside him as the second chopper, CG2, came around the building into view. In a single motion, Undecided grabbed the bouncing blade, spun around to build momentum and threw the improvised javelin through the tail fin of CG2. The second chopper spun out of control. It slammed into a building and exploded in a fireball, propelling glass shards in all directions to the street below.

When the tank rolled around the corner half a second later, it found only devastation. Undecided was gone, lost to the failed forces of the JTF.

CHAPTER THIRTY

WELCOME TO THE XCHANGE. MAY I HAVE YOUR TIME PLEASE?

As Jie approached the entrance to the Xchange, mist struck her face but her cheeks did not get wet. She passed easily through the wall of falling water, leaving her hair dry and her dark suit untouched. The waterfall walls were simply a Forsythian aesthetic, dry water designed to be marvelled at. They would not affect her. On a normal day, she would stay and admire the spectacle, but today she simply didn't have the time.

On the inside was an overly cheerful woman sitting at a desk comprised entirely of water. Each side of the square desk was a still pond, its surface affected only by the vibrations of footsteps or the sounds of voices. The woman was in her mid-20s with blond hair, amber eyes and the grin of an over-achiever. The glowing exuberance of her eyes and the sparkling whites of her smile left no doubt about her joy. She wore a professional black power suit and a name tag that read "Hello, My Name is Jacquie" with a red heart for the dot on the letter 'i'.

"Hello, my name is Jacquie," said the greeter happily. "Welcome to the Xchange. May I have your time, please?"

Jie did not have time for the usual formalities. She made an attempt to walk past the pointless greeter.

The greeter moved decisively to block her way, hands clasped respectfully in front of her. Her smile grew even larger, squeezing her eyes into tiny slits. "I'm sorry," she said, "I must have been not very clear. I can be very forgetful sometimes. Giggle. May I have your time, please?"

"This is an emergency," said Jie as forcefully as she could muster. "I must speak to the chairman, immediately."

"I must have been not very clear. I can be very forgetful sometimes. Giggle. May I have your time please?"

Jie gave Jacquie a look of incredulity. She glanced down at her watch. "Uhh, I have 2316."

"Thank you, it is so important that you check your time when you enter the Xchange, to make sure your time is correct. Sometimes the time transition will throw your internal clock off a few nanoseconds, but not to worry, all will be adjusted accordingly. Now, how can I help you today?" The head of the greeter tilted abruptly from her right to her left.

"I need to speak to the chairman. We have a serious threat approaching this building and we need to evacuate everyone immediately." The stress was getting to Jie. They had only minutes to get out of there, if they had any time at all. There was really no way of knowing exactly how much time they had left. Jie nervously looked at her watch again. It read 2316.

"I'm sorry, but the chairman is in a meeting right now. May I take a message?"

Curse words sprang to Jie's mind in at least three different languages, but she held her tongue. It would have made no difference anyway. If she had tried to swear, the Evermore language filter would simply change it to something harmless like "Fudge", or "Shucks, Gee-golly-whiz-that's-not-swell."

"Sure," growled Jie through gritted teeth. "Tell him the Proxy of Finance is here. If he is unable to meet with us at this moment, we would consider that very unfortunate and would reassess our continued legislative support of the Xchange."

Jacquie's head twitched back to the right, followed by a long pause. "Oh, I see the chairman's schedule has just had a cancellation. You may go up and see him now," said the greeter, motioning to a green arrow that had suddenly appeared on the floor. Jie followed the arrow with great haste, eager to leave the smiling psycho behind. She looked at her watch again. It still read 2316 hours.

The green arrow led up to a grand balcony made of flowing white ivory. The balcony overlooked the trading floor, where a fantastic flurry of movement could be seen. The four waterfall walls surrounded the chamber, but it looked completely different from the inside. From the outside, the four walls of water appeared as torrential waterfalls. From the inside, there were millions of separate water droplets falling in slow motion. It was a sight Jie could never seem to get used to. It shattered her suspension of disbelief, reminding her she was walking through a virtual landscape. By the same token, it was a sight that could never be matched in the real world. Jie watched in awe at the incredible beauty of the falling drops of water as they hung almost motionless in the air. Nowhere else on Earth, real or virtual, could she see such a sight. The falling waters of the Xchange were the very pinnacle of Forsythian architectural theory.

The loud footsteps on the promenade gave away the chairman's presence. He was of above-average height, with a sensible black-and-white business suit and salt-and-pepper hair.

"Good morning, Ms. Wan. We are honoured by the presence of a member of the Consortium at our fine establishment," said the chairman with a formal grin.

"Thank you for seeing me on such short notice, Chairman Rice," said Jie. "I would not have called on you if the matter wasn't urgent."

The chairman nodded. "Don't worry about it. Everything here is on short notice. Now, what can we do for you today?"

"Evacuate," responded Jie firmly. "A killer is approaching this building from the south, destroying everything that crosses his path.

We must move your people out of here immediately and onto the *Chasse-Galerie.*"

"But of course," replied the chairman coolly. "We have been aware of this threat for quite some time. There is no need to evacuate yet; we still have plenty of time before he arrives."

"No matter how much you slow it down, you're stilling running out of time."

"You underestimate us, Ms. Wan."

"The killer will be here in a matter of minutes."

"Well, they are minutes to you, but to us it's more like hours. As you must be aware, time in here runs a thousand times slower than it does outside the Xchange. We could talk for what seems to be an hour, and only a few seconds will have passed. And in the pit," said the chairman, motioning to the mass of wheeling and dealing below them on the trading floor, "time is slowed down another thousand times. Time passes in the pit at one millionth the rate it passes in the rest of Evermore. So you see, Ms. Jie, we have a lifetime of deals still to make."

"A second, an hour, a lifetime, it doesn't matter. Undecided is coming. We have to get all of you out of here - now. It's not worth risking your lives over."

"Risk," said Chairman Rice. His grin disappeared and his voice grew cold and vicious. "Let me tell you what risk is, Ms. Wan. Risk is leaving behind everything you have and everything you own to create a business that doesn't physically exist. Risk is moving from a real economy, based on goods and services, to a virtual economy based on data and information.

"All the men and women below you have taken this risk, Ms. Wan. They've gambled with their life's savings, supported only by the conviction that no matter where you are, the rules of commerce apply. They run businesses, they sell stocks and today they are watching it all fall apart.

"Look around you, Ms. Wan. Everyone is selling. Your inability to protect the good people of Evermore has shaken investor confidence in our economy. As we speak, investors are pulling their money out of the city. It is taking everything we have to hold enough foreign investments here to keep the virtual economy afloat.

So you see, Ms. Wan, it is risk that compels us to stay. We cannot leave."

"Close the Xchange," said Jie. "If you close the market, the foreign investors can't pull their money out."

"We are the biggest stock market in the world. We don't stop. We don't sleep. We don't close. If we shut down the Xchange now, it would be a sign of weakness, an admission to our investors that their money is not safe here. Our clients would move their investments to other, more traditional exchanges, like the TSX. We have worked too hard and too long to lose everything because of some punk in a cowboy hat.

"That punk has taken out both the Order and the JTF."

"We cannot leave."

"We can't protect you here."

"You can't protect us anywhere. We'll be just as vulnerable on the *Chasse-Galerie* as we are here."

"The *Chasse-Galerie* is mobile and airborne. The killer won't be able to follow us."

"Yes, but where will you land? Do you plan to stay in the sky forever? What are my traders to do while we're stuck in the clouds? Play cards? You may have grown accustomed to living in the sky, Ms. Wan, but rest assured we have not. Our home is here, in the pit, making a deal."

"He'll kill you all," warned Jie.

"Or, he might pass us by," said the chairman calmly.

"He hasn't passed anyone by yet," said Jie. "I can't take the risk."

"I'm afraid we have to."

"You must leave."

"Make us," said the chairman.

Jie could not think of anything to say. She could not force them to leave.

"You must forgive me, Ms. Wan," said the chairman, "but I must bid you adieu. I have urgent business, understandably, to attend to."

"You're making a big mistake. I'll have the JTF standing by to evacuate you when you change your minds."

"There's no one who can help us now, Ms. Wan. Good day."

Jie walked back to the entrance, brushing past the annoyingly cheerful Jacquie on the way. As she left the Xchange, the slow cascade of water droplets became a torrent of falling thunder behind her. She glanced at her watch. The time read 2317.

She heard a soft, crunching sound off to her right. Jie turned and looked down the Ridley Mall. Off in the distance, kicking up a trail of asphalt dust with each slow step, came the killer. [JTF6.0]Undecided moved with efficiency and purpose. His path of destruction would carry him directly through the Xchange and on to the pinnacle of governance in Evermore – the Consortium. Looking back to her left, Jie saw the massive *Chasse-Galerie* docking at the Consortium to rescue the government. At the base of the elevator, the JTF were trying to evacuate the crowd. It was their responsibility now. Jie ran to the elevator, fleeing from the approaching onslaught.

CHAPTER THIRTY-ONE

THE RESURRECTION OF THE JTF

Blue came to the crossing of Ridley and Tourian and marvelled at the destruction surrounding her. Wreckage of the two helicopters lay burning in the middle of the intersection. Mangled bodies of the supposedly invincible JTF were strewn about like discarded action figures. On the corner, the entrance of a skyscraper appeared to have been punched in by a giant. Everywhere around her, Blue found nothing but chaos and annihilation. She loved it.

Her pace quickened as she moved cautiously through the wreckage. Her blood boiled as she stepped over broken bodies of soldiers with lifeless eyes. She breathed in the carnage. Step by step, Blue made her way through the wasteland and back onto the street, where the towering monolith of the Xchange and the Consortium lay before her. That's where the killer would be, but she could not resist. She turned around and took one last longing glance at the destruction that had eluded her.

"Spectacular isn't it?" came a voice from the right. Blue pivoted to see Toland step out from behind the wreckage. "The power violence has to transform a society. Just this morning, everyone felt safe and in control. Now they flee in terror."

All around her, well-dressed men armed with electric whips appeared. She was surrounded. She drew her pistol.

"You won't need that. We're not here to fight you. Instead, I'm here to make you an offer."

"You want the gun."

"No, I want you. I want you to work for me."

"Already like my job."

"Yes, but it holds you back from your true calling. They hire you to kill, but they keep you reined in. You are a wolf in chains. You deserve to be set free, to be who you truly are."

"You would give me that?"

"You and I are so similar. We are both drawn to violence. I approach it from a business perspective, but for you violence is a way of life. It feeds you. It sustains you. It gives your life purpose. You need it just like an animal needs the hunt. Come work for me and I will feed your hunger."

"Thought you wanted Undecided."

"We did. Thanks to the Graduate's assistance, we knew the killer was going to attack Vanessa, and so we waited for him. Contact was made, entreaties were offered but Undecided wasn't interested in making deals. His mind is beyond reason. He can't be controlled and he can't be trusted."

"And I can be controlled?"

Something beyond the circle of goons caught her attention. Pivoting her gaze towards the wreckage of the helicopter, Blue saw the metal slowly heal itself. Twisted pieces of useless shrapnel straightened and re-fused themselves to the frame. Blue watched the helicopter rebuild itself piece by piece.

"You can be trusted. You understand the concept of mutual advantage. With me, there will be no shortage of people to kill. Together, we could own this town."

"Not interested."

Blue looked at the bodies of the JTF lying on the ground.

"You live for death. It's part of who you are. All that I'm offering is the freedom to be who you want to be - a killer."

An arm moved. The broken bones, collapsed torsos and crushed skulls healed themselves as she watched. Within a few seconds, soldiers began to rise from the ground, weapons in hand. Neither Toland nor his men noticed. Their attention was focused on her.

"I may be a killer, but I'm not a monster."

The faces of the undead soldiers still showed only a single expression, but this time their eyebrows were far more arched and serious.

"With all due respect. I'm not inclined to take no for an answer."

"Perhaps you could ask them?"

Toland turned around to find a JTF soldier pulling himself to his feet. One of his arms lay harmless at his side, dislocated at the elbow. His head hung flaccidly on his shoulder with a viciously broken neck. With a crunch, the elbow popped back into place. The head seemed to rub on every vertebra with a horrible grinding sound as the soldier snapped his head back into its socket.

A patch on the soldier's right shoulder flashed, the words across its crest morphing from [JTF3.0] to [JTF3.1]. With his head back on straight, the soldier opened his eyes, looked past Toland and saw Blue.

"Target acquired," said the JTF soldier in his metallic radio drone, making a move to draw his pistol. One of the Toland's men tackled him first. The thug pinned the undead soldier to the floor, hyper-extended the soldier's pistol arm and then smashed down upon it with his elbow.

But there was no crack.

The blow should have broken the elbow, popping the bone out. Instead, the elbow joint reversed itself like rubber. The goon marvelled in shock. The JTF soldier twisted his head around, bent his elbow backwards and shot the thug in the head.

The man dropped dead to the ground. As the JTF soldier pulled himself to his feet, dozens of his comrades rose behind him. They looked at Blue. A flicker of recognition crossed their eyes.

"Engage target," they said in concert as they reached for their guns.

"Protect the boss," yelled one of the goons. They leapt forward to protect Toland. Blue stepped back, looking for cover. To her left, a glass-roofed convention centre exploded in a fireball of broken concrete and shattered glass. Through the smoke rushed a tank. It turned its turret towards Blue with a mechanical whir. A radio voice chattered from an external speaker on the side of the tank. "Engage target!"

Blue instinctively threw herself backwards as the ground in front of her exploded. The blast kicked up grey powder, chunks of pavement and enough concussive force to send her rolling away from the battle.

Jumping back to her feet, Blue found herself in front of a collapsed convention centre. The screams of Toland's dying men surrounded her. She had to retreat. She had to run. She didn't have the equipment to take on a tank and a fully armed squad. She ducked into the ruins of the convention centre just as another shell exploded above her. Behind her, she heard the mechanized voice of the JTF.

"Pursue target," they said.

Blue dug her way through the remains, ducking under collapsed columns and squeezing through the ever-shrinking passageway as the dying building fell in upon itself. She heard the march of the JTF as they stepped among the broken cinderblocks behind her. Her journey led her into what had formerly been a ballroom. The walls tilted perilously to the side, leaning towards the ground under the weight of the collapsed floors above.

All the exits were blocked.

She was trapped.

The radio chatter of the JTF came closer and closer. Blue hid behind the shattered remains of a grand piano. The garden of broken keys, wires and wood gave her a good view of her approaching pursuers. They were different than the bodies she had seen before. They looked bigger, stronger and more agile. They carried higher-calibre weaponry and far more gear than before. She was outmanned and outgunned. She dreamed of going down with guns blazing, lead tearing through her flesh until her lungs filled with bile and her blood spouted acid.

But before Blue could act out her suicidal fantasy, the debris around her began to move. The blocks of rubble rose into the air and back into the missing sections of the spiral staircase to her left.

All around her, the room was being repaired, not by carpenters or tradesmen, but by what seemed to be the hand of God. Like a room collapsing in reverse, the building reconstructed itself piece by piece. A rising pillar caught a JTF soldier and crushed him into the ceiling above. A broken window, rebuilding itself shard by broken shard, eviscerated another soldier as its jagged pieces flew across the room.

The reconstruction of the room took about thirty seconds, and wiped out a quarter of the squad. Rising from behind the refurbished grand piano, Blue took care of the rest. Twelve headshots later, she found herself alone again, in a room full of dead JTF soldiers who had a lot on their minds.

Mmorpg floated through a wall.

"We've got problems," he said in exasperation.

"*What now?*" asked Blue.

"I just received a status report from Undecided's battle with the JTF."

"*They lost.*"

"I know that. Their guns were useless. The bullets simply refracted around Undecided's body."

"*So?*"

"That's impossible. There is no way that should happen with my physics engine. Something is wrong. Something is seriously wrong."

"*Sending amateurs to do a professional's job. That's what's wrong. Incompetent whelps. Mistook me for the target. I will handle this.*"

"No. You don't understand. The bullets in their weapons were authorized to kill by the sovereign, just like yours. If their bullets bent around the killer's body, then yours will, too. We have no way to take down Undecided."

Blue stepped towards Mmorpg and she raised the pistol. The muzzle rested barely an inch away from Mmorpg's translucent forehead.

"*No time to bend from point blank range.*"

Blue returned the gun to the holster and turned to leave.

"And what if that doesn't work? What do you do then?"

Blue stopped and looked back.

"*Do you have any ideas?*" she asked.

Mmorpg's eyes darted from left to right frantically, searching his brain.

"*Perhaps Arthur would know?*"

"We can't find him. Nobody can. He's disappeared off the face of the earth."

Mmorpg fell into silence as a slight grin crossed his mouth. Index fingers out, his fists shook together in rhythm. He had an idea.

"The logout function," said Mmorpg.

"*What?*"

"The logout function. Undecided may not have realized it's been disabled. If you can force him to call the logout function, then the subroutine I've replaced it with will trick him. It'll make him think he's woken up in the real world. The killer will think he feels tired. He'll go to bed and sleep. Meanwhile, his mind will still be here in Evermore. He'll be trapped."

"*How can I make him log out?*"

"Pain. No matter how strong he is, he will feel pain. Inflict as much punishment on him as you can. Keep on him until he can take no more. Drive him out of Evermore."

Blue smiled.

"*Pain. I can do that.*"

****

At that very moment, no more than five blocks away, Undecided came upon the crown jewel of the Evermore Downtown Core – the Xchange. The killer did not stop to gaze at the wondrous work of art before him. He was not captivated by the falling water, the majesty of its droplets or the soft touch the rising mist. Undecided simply marched forward, step by crushing step, towards the next obstacle in his way.

Not a single trader evacuated the building. As the doubleclock ticked to 11:55 and 2332, Undecided entered the building. A couple of seconds passed, and then Undecided exited out the other side. He was inside for only a moment.

Undecided did not turn back. He moved forward into Market Square. At the other end of the massive park, he saw a great crowd screaming to the heavens as they surrounded an elevator tube. Undecided followed the tube a hundred metres into the sky as it stretched to the ice palace of the Consortium. There lay his final target and the end of his quest – the death of the sovereign and all those who would protect him.

CHAPTER THIRTY-TWO

FATEFUL DECISIONS

The flurry of activity in the Consortium threatened to overwhelm Jie when she stepped out of the elevator. People moved haphazardly from room to room, clearing up their affairs before the evacuation. Guarding them were the remaining troops of the JTF, and three striders led by a woman in a white cloak. Jie recognized Strider Ryu immediately. He stood behind the woman in white, deferring to her authority.

The woman in white glanced harshly at a staffer as he crammed his little pocket computer with as much data as it could carry. Taking her cue, Strider Ryu stepped forward. "Leave it," he said. "It will be here when you return." The young staffer, his eyes glimmering with dreams of power and privilege, ignored his order and went back to downloading the material.

Through every corridor she walked, Jie saw the same scene play out. Everyone was grabbing as much data as they could. *Information might be power,* thought Jie, *but time was life and they had precious little of it.* Another corner, another strider coaxing people to move to the ship. Jie rushed towards the Office of the Sovereign. A radio command came up from the lieutenant of the JTF squad.

"Five minutes," said the lieutenant.

They had five minutes before the killer reached the frozen walls of the Consortium. There was no more time.

Jie burst into the sovereign's office with barely a knock – discarding formalities in favour of efficiency. Inside, she saw three people sitting at the table to the right: Klein, Kinsella and a young woman who seemed strangely familiar.

"Jie," called Klein, "I want you to meet someone." Jie strode over to the table and sat down. "This is Ms. Gibson," said Klein. "She's volunteered to help us in a very important way."

"Nice to see you again, Ms. Gibson," said Jie. The young Ms. Gibson, looking barely eighteen years of age, nodded nervously, focused on something else.

Kinsella, his hand placed supportively on Ms. Gibson's shoulder, asked, "Now are you sure you want to do this? You can still back out. There will be no shame, nobody would question you."

The young woman shook her head. "I want to serve the coalition," she said bravely, "and this is the best way I can help right now."

At that moment, Jie finally recognized her. Her name was Molly Gibson, a party activist of Indian and British heritage who had served in the Klein Coalition since the tender age of sixteen. She had started as a political staffer, but had moved up to become president of the youth commission. Following a two-year stint where she was responsible for instating the youth wing as a fully fledged partner in the coalition, she had taken her seat on the back benches. Since then she had worked on the Consortium's economic committee, where she had been instrumental in blocking the passage of the R3X initiative. This victory had led many insiders to dub her one of the party's rising stars.

When Jie had struggled during the budget debate, she had almost been able to feel Molly sneaking up behind her. That image of growing influence and confidence was unrecognizable in the cowed woman before her. Molly looked terrified. She was trying to put on a brave face for her superiors, but she was clearly rattled about what was going to happen next. Molly's terror felt far greater than Jie had seen from anyone else that day. Everyone was afraid of the killer who stood less than five minutes away, but in Molly's face that fear was amplified. *What could be more horrifying than death?* Jie wondered.

"When we come back to the Consortium," said a labouring Ms. Gibson, "this information will put us at a major advantage over the Corporates. It is important that this data be protected at all costs. Just please, please, take good care of my memories."

"Of course," soothed Klein. "I will hold onto them myself. Now, are you ready?"

"Yes." Molly nodded. "I am ready."

"Ok," said Kinsella. From the desk, he picked up two different earphones. One was red and the other was blue. He put the red earphone in Molly's left ear, traced his fingers across the thin cord, then connected the data plug to a small silver disk drive. The blue earphone he attached to her right ear and connected the other end into the network mainframe located on the table itself.

His preparations complete, Kinsella stepped in front of the shivering Ms. Gibson, looked straight into her face and said, "Begin recording." The colour of his pupils clicked to white while the rest of his eyeball turned black. "Now," Kinsella continued, "Ms. Molly Gibson, are you aware of what is being done here and do you or do you do not authorize this action."

Molly looked into the camera of Kinsella's eyes, found her strength and said with a bold voice, "My name is Molly Gibson. I, of sound mind and body and in full command of my capacities, fully and willingly authorize without duress the swapping of the memory, audio-visual and motor functionality components of my mind for the complete party database of the Klein Coalition. My original cranial data will be stored on disk until such time as it can be safely restored to me. I take full responsibility for any damage to my cranial data or my physical body resulting from this procedure. This disposition has been given under the supervision of a lawyer, Mr. Kinsella, and the Sovereign of Evermore, Mr. Richard Klein."

"End recording," said Mr. Kinsella. His eyes clicked back to their normal hue. "Are you ready?" he asked Molly.

She nodded her head and anxiously followed with her eyes the slow movement of Kinsella's hand to the red button on the table's touchscreen panel. With a click of the virtual button, Ms. Gibson's eyes rolled back into her head and she began to shiver. Her skin crawled with goosebumps and her mouth, hanging ajar, made a moaning sound as if she were trying to shout an alarm but could not put together the words. The light on the disk drive blinked green. Almost as suddenly as it had begun, the process was over. Molly's arms had become a vein-like shade of blue, and she was shivering profusely.

Kinsella looked at the disk drive, made sure that it was finished and then pushed the blue button. Molly shook even more violently than before. The blue shivering of her arms instantly turned to sweat. From her lips came the high-pitched whine of a dial-up modem, an endless river of data pouring through her ears into the empty container that was now her mind. After almost a minute, the data transfer came to an end and Molly's sweat-covered body slumped in the chair. Kinsella checked to ensure she was still breathing.

After reviewing the table's touchscreen to ensure that the transfer was successful, he detached the plugs from Molly's ears. From the disk drive, he pulled out a small blue card about the size of a fingernail and handed it to Klein.

"Take good care of this," said Kinsella.

"Rest assured," said Klein, "this data will be well protected."

"We have about two minutes," said Kinsella. "It's time to go."

"I'll meet you on the *Chasse-Galerie*," said Klein. "I just want to take one last look at the office and have a word with Jie."

"Very well," said Kinsella, picking up the sleeping Molly and cradling her slight frame in his arms. "I'll see you on board." Kinsella carried Molly out of the room. Klein and Jie were alone.

"We have to go," said Jie.

"I'm not leaving," said Klein, "I'm staying here."

"What do you mean, you're staying here? That monster will be here any minute."

"I know," said Klein. "Believe me, I don't want to die. But I see I have little choice."

"You have a choice. Get on the ship," said Jie.

"I am the one he's after," said Klein. "He has no interest in the rest of you. If I get on that ship, he'll just keep coming after us. I can't put all those people at risk again. Too many people have died today because of me. I will not add any more needless deaths to my conscience."

"But you'll die!"

"Yes, but that's responsibility, Jie – the willingness to pay for your mistakes. At least it will be at a time and place of my choosing. At least it will mean something."

"It will only mean you're too stupid to get on the boat."

"Ahh, Jie. You have to understand that being sovereign means the needs of others come before your own. Never forget you're serving a greater community. It is for them you must sacrifice your time, money and possibly even your life. It is your duty as a public servant."

"What do you mean?" asked Jie, tears struggling down her face.

"You are now the Sovereign of Evermore, Jie," said Klein. "I have made a deposition with Kinsella to name you as my successor and as sovereign in the event of my demise. Once I am dead, it will up to you to lead."

"I don't want to be sovereign," said Jie.

"Yes you do," corrected Klein. "You have always wanted to become sovereign, and now is your chance to make something positive out of it. Don't cry. I have faith that you will do us all proud. But you must leave now. The killer is coming up the elevator as we speak. You must leave now before it is too late."

Jie nodded and backed away towards the exit, torn between staying with her mentor and retreating to the safety of the *Chasse-Galerie*.

"Wait," said Klein, "take this with you." He handed the blue storage disk to Jie. "Guard this well, Molly has a wonderful future with the party. Who knows?" he said with a grin. "She too might one day be sovereign."

Jie accepted the disk, took one last tearful glance at her life-long hero and ran out the back door of the office towards the haven of the *Chasse-Galerie*. Klein, standing tall, turned towards the front entrance and faced his oncoming death.

****

Arthur found himself looking at the monochrome door of stall number three. He hesitated, almost afraid to take that final, deliberate step. But the voice in his head, full of a certainty Arthur had never known before, urged him on. He pushed open the stall door gingerly and came face to face with the gaping void. From the black hole, he could hear a mother's screams, calling for it all to stop. Black handprints surrounded the hole on the chipped and broken tile, like someone had been dragged in against their will. Into the stall stepped *Arthur* and the door slammed shut behind him.

****

Undecided marched towards the crowd surrounding the elevator. Nobody in the tangled mob recognized him. The JTF were too busy struggling to evacuate the protesters to see the killer coming. It was only when he broke the neck of the first person in his way that people began to scream. The mob scattered in all directions, crushing an unfortunate few beneath their feet. Undecided did not pursue them. They were not his prey. The JTF attempted to engage him, but he made short work of them.

Approaching the elevator, he found a young man cowering on his back, petrified by fear. Undecided ignored him and stepped into the lift. A small indistinct face appeared on the glass before him.

"Welcome to the Consortium," it said in a cheerful voice. "To what purpose do we owe the pleasure of your company?"

Undecided punched the reflection, cracking the glass walls of the elevator.

"Very well," replied the voice. "Access denied. This elevator is restricted to authorized personnel. Have a pleasant day."

Undecided grunted at the cracked walls of the elevator. This lift had eyes. Stepping out of the car, he reached down and grabbed the terrified boy by his throat.

"Please don't kill me. There's so much more I want to do," pleaded the boy.

Undecided dragged the boy into the elevator and slammed his face into the glass. The message was clear.

Klein's face appeared on the glass walls. The message was received.

"Let him go," said Klein. "It's me you want."

Undecided nodded in agreement. He tossed the boy outside. Klein dissolved and the indistinct face reappeared. It had a new message.

"Access granted," it said cheerfully. "Have a pleasant day."

****

Blue and Mmorpg came upon the entrance of the Xchange. She stopped and looked at the wall of falling water. Above the Xchange towered the Consortium.

"*He's in there.*" said Blue.

"How can you be sure?" said Mmorpg.

"*Because I can smell death.*"

"If Arthur was right, then Undecided's ultimate target would be the sovereign."

"*Then get him out of here while I deal with the killer.*"

Mmorpg nodded.

"Good luck Blue."

He floated up and over the Xchange and moved in a diagonal line towards the Consortium.

Blue stepped forward into the waterfall. The wetness did not strike her. She was not surprised. She had seen that trick before. As her eyes adjusted to the interior light, she saw a body with a cute name tag and limp legs protruding out of the tiled floor.

Blue kept moving towards the centre of the complex, well aware of the time constraints she was under. For some reason, she felt quicker, stronger, nastier than before. It was like someone was burning natural gas inside her heart. Entering the main trading floor, she felt the adrenaline kick into overdrive as she rounded the corner and found … death.

Hundreds of bodies were strewn like rag dolls across the trading floor. Bodies were flung over banisters, embedded in walls and layered in contorted positions upon the floor.

Blue gazed at the bodies.

"*They don't bleed,*" she said. "*Everything is supposed to bleed. It bleeds everywhere. It seeps into carpets and wood. It drips down drains and ducts. It can never be washed or cleaned away. Blood is life. Without it, there is nothing.*"

Off to her right, Blue heard the patter of a ticker tape. Curious, she turned and moved towards the machine. Such machines had become outdated long ago, but the Xchange kept one for nostalgia.

The chairman, impaled upon a fountain with the familiar red ring around his neck, had felt the ticker tape machine was a connection to a golden age of capitalism unrestrained by responsibility. He had wished to remind the traders that with daring and intelligence, anything was possible. The ticker tape machine was an ornamental piece. It had never before been used. Yet there it was, spitting up ribbon after ribbon of tape. Blue shifted through the pile until she found the beginning and began to read.

Once upon a time there was a young lady named Cinderella. Cinderella's mother had passed away when she was too young to remember. Her father, wishing for Cinderella to have the guidance of a proper mother, decided to remarry. Soon Cinderella had a whole new family to call her own. One day, her father got very sick. Many doctors were brought in to examine him, as Father was well respected in the community due to his inherent kindness. The doctors were perplexed. Despite their training and best efforts, they could not figure out why Cinderella's father was sick. They instructed Cinderella's stepmother to keep him warm and feed him a steady diet of soup. But poor Father kept getting worse, and worse, and worse until one day he moved no more. After her father was buried, Cinderella moved into her stepmother's old farm home, far away from the warmth of Father's land. Once there, Cinderella's stepmother and her two stepsisters became very cruel. They forced the young orphan to clean the floors, wash the dishes, mow the lawn, scrape the gutters and take out the trash. They never let people see her, hiding her in the basement with the mice when company arrived. They never stopped poking fun at her, mocking her for the old rags she was forced to wear. They called her names, like 'Cinderfella' or 'little whore' or 'fat pig'. But Cinderella did not cry. She only hung her head and continued on diligently with her chores. One day, a proclamation went out through all the land. A fantastic ball would be held, where the prince would pick his bride-to-be from all the belles of the kingdom. The stepsisters were brimming with joy. They went out and bought the nicest clothes, the most expensive hats and the most glimmering jewellery. Cinderella had no money, but she did have the pile of old rags her stepsisters had thrown away. She worked very hard and sewed those old rags together into a beautiful dress. Wearing the dress, she approached her stepmother and asked if she could go to the ball in the dress she had made. The stepmother simply laughed as the stepsisters ripped her dress into pieces. Her clothes torn, Cinderella cried and ran out into the garden as her step-family laughed themselves to sleep. She sobbed for many minutes before she realized she was not alone. Looking up, she saw an elderly woman with a wand and soft butterfly wings. "Who are you?" asked Cinderella. "I am your fairy godmother," responded the old woman, "and I am here to make your dreams come true." "My dreams come true?" said Cinderella. "Yes," said the fairy godmother. "Now, what would you like more than anything else in the world?" "I want to go to the ball, said Cinderella, "but my stepmother and stepsisters won't let me." "Well," said the fairy godmother, "that is easy enough to fix." "It is? How?" asked Cinderella, looking at the fairy godmother's magic wand. "Yes, look over there," said the fairy godmother. "Have you ever used that before?" Cinderella turned to see an axe wedged into a log. "Yes," said Cinderella, "my stepmother makes me chop wood here." "Excellent," said the fairy godmother. "Take the axe, go into the house and chop up your stepmother and your stepsisters. Start with the neck so they don't wake up and scream; that's the best way." Cinderella picked up the axe, walked into the house and came back a few minutes later, covered in blood. "Excellent," said the fairy godmother. "Now go back in and put all the pieces in a big sack." Cinderella did as her fairy godmother commanded and came back out with a dripping sack. "Do you have pigs on this farm?" asked the fairy godmother. "Why yes, we do," said Cinderella. "Good, now feed your stepmother and stepsisters to the pigs. Make sure the pigs eat every piece." Cinderella nodded and came back in a few minutes with the empty sack. "Now," said the fairy godmother, "take the sack, your clothes and anything else that has blood on it and burn them in the fireplace. After that, wash the floors and take a bath so that all the blood is washed away. Remember, blood is bad. Then put on the nicest dress you can find in your stepsisters' closet and meet me back out here." "Okay," said Cinderella and she went back inside the *house. A couple of minutes later, smoke rose out of the chimney. Soon enough, Cinderella reappeared in her stepsister's red dress, with her hair up, gold jewellery around her neck and glass slippers on her feet. Her fairy godmother smiled at Cinderella. "Now go," she said. "Go to the ball and don't look back." With an exuberant smile on her face, Cinderella bounced off to the ball. She met her prince, got married and lived happily ever after.*

TLG

Blue stepped away slowly as the ticker churned out more messages. She had no interest in reading further. She felt oddly disturbed by the story, but pushed those feelings to the back of her mind as she looked towards the back wall of the Xchange.

The killer was not here. There was only one place where he could be. Through the back side of the building, she could see the elevator stretching up to the Consortium high above. She switched on her red lens. Through the still cascade of falling water, she watched the killer slowly rise towards the Consortium.

Had Mmorpg gotten to the sovereign in time? A quick scan through the red lens broke her hopes. Mmorpg was still floating up slowly towards the Consortium. The killer would beat him to the sovereign.

They were too late. There was no more time. Blue broke into a full run towards the Consortium and leapt through the wall of water.

****

Safely aboard the *Chasse-Galerie*, Jie nodded to Kinsella as she moved into the aft compartment of the bay. She sat down near the strategist on the other side of a large bulkhead. Buckling herself into her seat, Jie could no longer see Kinsella and he could not see her, but Jie could see the muttering Molly sitting limply across from her.

"Klein's not coming," said Jie morosely.

"I know," said Kinsella in a world-weary tone.

An empty silence followed. Then Jie heard the docking locks disengage and felt a sudden lurching that told her they were free and airborne. They were safe now. The monster could not reach them here.

Safe and now sovereign. Jie tried to wrap her mind around the title. It was her title now. For so many years she had served in the background. For so many years she had gone to bat for the coalition under trying circumstances. And now the prize was hers. Jie felt queasy. How could she be happy? She had left her mentor, her greatest influence, to be ripped apart by that monster. Now that she was sovereign, would she be his next target? She could not worry about that now. She had been entrusted with the leadership of the country in what could be its most difficult hour. It was now her responsibility to stay calm and collected. The hopes and dreams of a nation now weighed upon her mind.

Soon enough, her thoughts moved to different concerns. Jie remembered the many battles Klein had fought against those who wished to replace him, not just from other coalitions but often from within his own party. Now that he was gone, would they accept her as sovereign, or scheme to overthrow her? Klein had been their spiritual leader for so long, and yet even he had had his hands full with dissidents. And Jie was no Klein. How long would it take her enemies to organize? How long would it take them to plot? Weeks? Days? Possibly hours? They could be hatching their plans right now, right under her nose, in the midst of this crisis.

There would be no better time for it. Chaos was everywhere. There was no longer a clear sovereign, as her ascension had not yet come before a vote. No, once they had the chance, they would strike and she would not be able to stop them. Her tenure as Proxy of Finance had been scandal-plagued. She had struggled to overcome the opposition's taunts and accusations. To all concerned, she was vulnerable.

She needed leverage to secure her position. Jie pulled out the storage card from her pocket and looked at it for a long moment. The *Chasse-Galerie* hit some turbulence, shaking the cabin with a dull metallic groan. At that moment, under the noise of the shaking airship, Jie snapped the card in two. Without hesitation, she dropped the pieces into a vent to be blown away. Kinsella, his vision blocked by the bulkhead and his hearing filled with the rattling noise of the cabin, did not react.

Jie relaxed her tensed shoulders and looked at Molly. Molly looked right back at her. Molly's eyes, so vegetative just moments before, glared at Jie with the flame of a pyre. Molly's lips moved to speak, but no words could escape, the knowledge of speech lost along with the card. Her only reaction was a tear that slid slowly down her cheek. Molly's chest heaved as if she were sobbing, but no sound came from her lips.

Jie put her head down and stared at the floor, ignoring the mountain of condemnation that her conscience heaped upon her mind. She was sovereign now. Her actions would serve the greater good, and for the greater good sacrifices would have to be made.

****

Klein, waiting for his death to arrive in the office of his greatest achievements, took in every breath as if it were his last. The building was completely silent.

Klein found that on the brink of certain death, the world around him adopted a far more agreeable hue. Things he had considered ordinary or boring were now beautiful. All the memories of his time in this room floated to the surface. The sweet victories, the discouraging defeats, the long nights working closely with his dearest friends; he had years of memories in this office. Klein felt honoured to be able to die here.

He did not have to wait long. Excruciating silence gave way to the distant sound of heavy footsteps on ice. Louder and louder they crunched as the killer drew closer. Finally, the steps stopped outside his main chamber door.

"Come in," commanded the sovereign.

The large oak door splintered into fine pieces as Undecided ripped through the entranceway.

"Here I am," said Klein with his strong, deep voice. "Come and take me."

Undecided obliged. The killer stepped over the broken door and grabbed Klein's neck with his left hand. Klein felt the breath squeezed from his throat. He raised his arms to his neck and gasped in protest. With his right hand, Undecided reached for the cord that hung around his neck.

From his left, Klein suddenly sensed a flutter of movement. Through the wall of ice crashed Blue. Driving her shoulder straight into the broad torso of the killer, she knocked loose his grip on the sovereign's neck. Klein fell the ground and began to cough violently.

Blue drove Undecided back and through the opposite wall into open space. Locked together, they fell at terminal velocity towards the city of skyscraper steel and asphalt earth below. Undecided struggled, but Blue held her advantage, keeping the killer between herself and the rising ground.

A hundred metres from the earth, they collided with the side of a short skyscraper. Together they slid down the building like a sled through snow. The skyscraper began to collapse from above them, from top to bottom, as they stripped the front side of the skyscraper on their descent. As Undecided's body smashed into the pavement with a resounding thud, Blue kicked off and rolled away from the collapsing building above them. Her Beretta came free from its holster and disappeared from her sight.

Rolling to her feet, Blue skidded to a stop, kicking up pieces of black pavement as she faced the fallen killer. She spotted her gun. It was between her and Undecided, just ten metres away.

Undecided had only enough time to get to his knees and shoot a glare at Blue before the building fell on top of him. Within seconds, both he and Blue's Beretta were buried beneath the rubble. An exploding cloud of dust and debris consumed her, knocking her to the ground. Bracing herself against the raging wind, Blue shielded her eyes and pulled herself to her feet as swirling dust scraped against her skin.

The cloud of debris blotted out the sun, pitching the area into a dirty dusk. Everything around her, including her clothes, was covered by a soft layer of drywall powder, like a fresh snowfall.

The air began to clear, giving Blue a chance to survey her surroundings. Debris was strewn all around her, but nowhere more than in the large pile where the building had collapsed. Blue breathed anxiously through the gray ash, staring at the mountain of crushed concrete, broken drywall and twisted steel.

The wreckage moved. Climbing out from the top of the pile came Undecided, rising from the ashes. Caked with dust and burning with rage, he glared at Blue, setting his sights on his newest obstacle.

Framed by the doubleclock tower far behind her, Blue stood before the mighty killer with only her fists to protect her.

"*Fine*," she said. "*We'll do this the fun way.*"

She was ready to rumble.

CHAPTER THIRTY-THREE

RUMBLE IN THE RUBBLE

Undecided glared at Blue with propane blue eyes. Her breathing deepened as adrenaline poured into her veins. The moment had finally come. No longer would Blue be restrained by the civilities of society, prisoner of their flaccid moral codes. She was finally free.

Her hands shook with anticipation. She clenched them into fists to control her excitement. Undecided merely stood still, sizing up his newest obstacle.

Blue moved first. She broke into a run towards the killer. Undecided rushed to greet her, kicking up dust as he ran. His visage was stony and resolute. Hers brimmed with joy. She smiled as the ecstasy of violence overtook her.

They met in the middle of the rubble of the fallen building, its girders sticking up like ribs off a rotting carcass. Undecided delivered punches with such force and speed that air was sucked into the vacuum left behind. He threw punch after punch at Blue, but Blue expertly deflected and dodged the crushing blows. Unable to find an opening, she took her time and used whatever space Undecided gave her. Adrenaline would sustain her edge.

Undecided did not have the patience for another long fight, instead coming straight at her with a full-fledged assault. Running out of room, Blue jumped behind the ribbed girders for protection as a kick skimmed her cheek. Doing so freed up her range of motion while restricting Undecided's space for attack.

Undeterred, Undecided tried to punch straight through the steel girders. Instead of holding firm or breaking in two, the girders bent over backwards, trapping Blue as Undecided reached through. Blue ducked out from beneath the collapsed girders and delivered a series of body shots underneath Undecided's outstretched arm.

An elbow forced her to retreat, but she failed to withdraw in time, and Undecided's right hand forcefully grasped her left arm. Without hesitation, Blue rotated her left wrist clockwise, locked in Undecided's exposed wrist and bent it against the ligaments. She forced him to his knees, where her boot greeted his cheek. The crunching blow knocked him back hard through the rubble, the girders falling away from his rolling body. The first strike belonged to Blue.

Blue felt goosebumps rise against her skin. The wait had been worth it.

Slowly, with a glint in his propane eyes, Undecided rose again from the rubble.

He came straight at her again, never bothered by concepts such as strategy. Only the satisfying sound of breaking bone filled his mind. Without warning, he delivered a right cross that should have ripped her head off. Blue calmly deflected it to the right, punched him in the face, stepped into his torso, swept her leg behind his knees, grasped his shoulder and threw Undecided hard over her hip down to the pavement. As he hit the jagged earth, Undecided responded with a weak sweep to gain some space. Blue backed off and waited for the next volley.

****

Sovereign Klein gave a yelp in surprise as Mmorpg rose through the icy floor.

"Sovereign," said Mmoprg, "please come with me. I need you to clear the zone."

****

Undecided charged at Blue with the ferocity of a bear, ripping out the girders that got in his way. There was no doubt in Blue's mind that Undecided was far stronger. To finish him, she would have to be quicker and smarter.

This time, Undecided attacked with a series of short jabs Blue couldn't counter, followed by a straight-on kick she ducked. Behind the collar of his jacket, Blue saw the edge of a grin on Undecided's face. He was starting to make adjustments. She would have to be care—

Undecided attacked as Blue's eyes blinked, moving into range in the nanosecond her eyes were closed. She slid underneath the left cross and moved into position behind him. Undecided countered with a left elbow at her nose. She blocked the elbow with her left arm and punched Undecided square in the face with her right.

While he was momentarily stunned, Blue grabbed the killer's wrist, bent it back behind his shoulder and forced his back to the ground. The steel-toed brown boot smashed into her jaw, dazing her momentarily.

In a single continuous motion, Undecided freed himself from her grip, pivoted and swept her legs out from underneath her. Building up momentum, Undecided spun around again on the same pivot, and delivered a rising kick to Blue as she fell to the ground. Her body slid violently into the rubble, kicking up clouds of dirt and shrapnel. Through the slit of his collar, Blue could see Undecided grinning sadistically, savouring every scraped knee and broken tooth.

A long moment passed. Then finally, Blue rose slowly from underneath the rubble. She held her side gingerly as she sucked in air.

She felt pain. And she loved it.

The two of them faced one another, caked in ash, surrounded by the desolate ruins. The land was still and quiet.

Undecided made the first move. As he restarted his assault, Blue threw dust she had picked up while on the ground into his face. The dust caught in his eyes and blinded him for a split second. When he recovered, he saw the grooved soles of Blue's black boot exploding towards his head.

He followed the path of the grooves down, down into the darkness until he discovered a bed – covered in white sheets in a sea of black. As the bed rotated, it became evident there was a mob of young boys around it. Screaming and shouting with morbid excitement, the boys, bound by cruelty, pounded the small lump beneath the sheets with large white pillows. To them it was only a piñata, something fun to hit. But from the bed a small whimper could be heard, scarcely audible beneath the sound of the blows. And from a small breach in the covers, the eyes of a little boy could be seen – filled with tears and looking out into the distance for help that would never come.

The world fell into one salty eye and re-emerged from the iris of Undecided as he delivered a vicious kick, forcing Blue to retreat.

The dust popped off of their clothes as they traded punches and kicks. Back and forth they moved, endlessly defending, effortlessly dodging, until one finally made a mistake. Slipping under a feint, Undecided delivered a harsh uppercut to Blue's jaw, spilling dust and sweat up, up, up into the air.

Higher and higher the world spun until Blue saw a white bed sheet stretching up into the air. It was wrapped around a fan that hung from a faded green ceiling. The ceiling fan spun, twisting the sheet endlessly around itself towards the bottom. When the knots reached the bottom of the sheet, the world spun out of control.

It spun and spun until it became Blue's spinning hip, flowing out a sweep kick that Undecided somersaulted over effortlessly. He landed with a thud and a pair of soft explosions at his feet, kicking up clouds of dirt in his wake.

The pair danced around, throwing punches and feints but leaving no opportunity for a counter-attack. Blue found that Undecided was becoming more unpredictable and difficult to counter. He was getting smarter. She would have to move fast before he grew too comfortable.

His confidence on the rise, Undecided threw a lunging cross. Blue moved with a purpose that surprised her attacker. She stepped into the punch before Undecided could get full extension, blunting the fist with her open palm. A quick jab to Undecided's face knocked his head and dazed him momentarily, giving her just enough time to grab his wrist. Bending the wrist back into an awkward position, Blue tried to force her adversary down onto his belly. But Undecided was having none of it. To stay on his feet, he kept rolling forward to relieve the pressure on his wrist. Blue kept up the effort, twisting the wrist and elbow into a menagerie of painful positions as she threw Undecided around the rubble. Finally, like a chess grandmaster, she pressed her advantage until Undecided ran out of options. Struggling to stay on his knees, he growled like a bear as Blue shoved his head into the shattered asphalt. He was pinned.

Blue twisted the arm against the socket. Undecided grimaced.

"*Say it.*"

Undecided's shoulder pushed against the twist. His teeth ground against one another in protest.

"*You want me to stop? All you gotta do is say the words.*"

Undecided continued to struggle. His shoulder began to shake.

"*SAY IT!*"

Undecided turned his head towards her. His eyes brimmed with joy. Through the slit on his collar, Blue could see a smile uncurl upon his lips. Undecided shook his head.

He knew.

Against the laws of nature, Undecided spun on his shoulder in a final bid to escape. Blue heard an unsettling pop and a dry snap as his wrist and elbow broke in her hands. A rising roundhouse kick snapped across her cheek, spilling her end over end into the rubble.

Blue rose quickly, ready for the killer's next attack. But Undecided remained where he was, mere feet away, glaring at her with a cold viciousness in his hollow propane eyes. He grabbed the injured wrist and pulled with his good arm. The joints popped back in place with an unsettling crunch. Blue saw the hellfire in his eyes, a sea of brimstone burning within him. He arched his torso and rolled his shoulders back, towering over the smaller Blue. In an instant, he delivered a kick from the dust at his feet. Blue blocked as the dust kicked off his brown boots and sprayed across her face, spilling the particles past her at a dreamlike pace.

The dust painted Blue a room in which a little girl was watching television. The show was a comedy, but the little girl did not smile. Off to her right, the door to a green bathroom lay ajar. Hearing the creak of an opening door, the little girl looked up with fear to her left as a shadow enveloped her.

The room blurred past her and became the sand etched into the black fabric of her shoulder as Blue cut loose with a fury and intensity she had never known before. She moved faster, struck harder and fought with an intensity that curled her tongue in excitement.

Suddenly, Undecided lowered his arms, dropping his defences. Blue didn't think twice. She moved in and delivered a flurry of jabs to his nose. Undecided didn't react. Blue followed it up with a group of crushing blows to all corners of his face. Again, Undecided did not move. His eyes were as blank as the sky, like he had withdrawn deep behind them. He could no longer see his assailant; he could no longer see the world around him. Blue never hesitated. She crushed his head with whatever she could muster, whipping it back and forth like a speed bag.

"*Come on! Log out!*"

Her punches rose in frequency and intensity, spilling the dust off Undecided's head with the power of a piston. Undecided's face was battered and bruised, but Blue would not stop. Again and again she pounded, each blow rising in power and pitch as she pulverized his face. The final left cross twisted Undecided's head awkwardly around and knocked his hat clean off his head and to the right.

The world dimmed and Blue saw the hat morph into a bus, shaking as it chugged along its merry way. Two people sat on a seat near the middle: a young man and a young woman. The young woman spoke animatedly, voicing her disapproval in the young man's ear. But the young man did not react. Instead he stared straight ahead as his shoulders slumped slowly forward. The skin on his face sank as we fell into the darkness of his sunglasses…

And rose from the searing pupils of the killer. Undecided roared to life and flew again at his adversary. With both speed and strength, he unleashed a barrage unlike anything Blue had ever seen. Again and again, Undecided threw his force against his adversary, pounding her faltering defences with his jackhammer strikes. Blue bobbed and weaved, allowing the blows to glance off her sides, but she was running out of room.

The fist smashed into her left cheekbone, knocking her off balance. Staggering back and desperately trying to regain her balance, Blue felt her ribs bend painfully inwards from another blow. She threw up her arms in defence, only to have them knocked aside as another fist pounded her face. The world reeled, causing everything to blur and grow indistinct. Blue felt her mind struggling to focus. *Keep moving,* she thought, *keep fighting and don't go down.*

Undecided moved in closer and unleashed a furious assault, bashing everything he could lay a hand on. Blue's face, neck, joints, everything was put through the grinder. Blue tried to counter with a weak cross. Undecided deflected the volley and delivered a sharp strike to her throat. A wet squishing cough squirted out of her lungs. Her vision blurred, looking aimlessly for something on which to focus. Her arms, refusing the confused commands of her mashed brain, dropped helplessly to her sides. A sharp kick to her knee brought her down to all fours, as Undecided continued to heap punishment on her from all sides.

Blind, weak and incoherent, she reached frantically around in the rubble for something, anything that she could use. Undecided kneed her in the head. The blow knocked her backwards into the dust. She staggered to get back to her knees, turning her back to her killer. Her hands grasped something in the hazy darkness. Undecided approached, clenching his fists in preparation for another workout. Her hands felt grooves and cold steel – rebar. Blue's hands closed tightly around the rebar rod as she put together what was left of her strength. Undecided reached out for the back of her neck.

Spinning around, Blue swung the bar like a bat into his crotch, doubling him over. Blue swung the bar back and forth, again and again, smashing across the killer's face. Undecided staggered.

She pulled the bar up and behind her. Undecided looked at her with dull flaccid eyes. Pivoting her hips, Blue brought the rebar down and then up in one mighty swing. This final blow caught Undecided in the chin, knocking him back into the rubble. Undecided tumbled end over end until he finally came to a rest. He didn't move.

Exhausted and barely conscious, Blue collapsed onto the dirty pavement. She could not move, she could not think and she could barely breathe for the splitting pain in her ribs. Lying on her back, she stared into the sky. Her vision blurred in and out of focus. There was nothing above her but a shrinking blue sky, slowly consumed by the growing clouds. Her vision faded away again just as blurry objects began to pass overhead. Pulling her swollen head together, she began to make out broken wreckage flying past her: glass, plastic, steel. She raised her head.

Piece by piece, the building that she and Undecided had annihilated was rebuilding itself. She turned away from the reconstruction of the tower and back to where she had knocked Undecided. He was no longer lying in the rubble. Instead, he was raising himself deliberately to his knees as the rubble blew past him.

****

Mmorpg led Klein through the streets of the Downtown Core, looking down at the street as he floated.

"Where are you taking me?" asked Klein.

"I can't help Blue until I clear the zone of civilians." Mmorpg eyes widened as he spotted a small red line stretching across the pavement. "There it is."

Mmorpg led the sovereign across the red line.

"Please stay on this side sir," said Mmorpg. He turned around and headed back towards the Consortium.

"Where are you going?" asked Klein.

"She needs my help," said Mmorpg.

****

Blue collapsed on her back again. She was done. She could fight no more. She did not care what he did to her; she no longer had the will to fight. Her mind drifted away, seeking to remove itself from the pain and suffering that was sure to follow.

"*Let me go,*" she said. "*Let me go.*"

The world began to fade into nothingness, and she welcomed it.

Until she heard the sound.

Her mind snapped to attention. She knew that sound. It wasn't glass. It wasn't concrete. It was hollow steel, clicking as it bounced off broken concrete. She knew that sound.

She looked off to the right at the rising rubble. Slowly, the wreckage pulled itself off the fractured pavement, leaving nothing behind but a gun. It was her gun, the 9mm Beretta that had been buried underneath the collapsing building.

Her muscles screaming from the acid pouring into her veins, Blue pulled herself onto her front and crawled towards her new hope.

Undecided remained on his knees. He did not move when the rubble rose up around him. He did not move when Blue crawled past him to the right. He stared only at the ground as raindrops began to lightly bounce off the pavement.

Undecided reached behind his head and pulled off his jacket like a sweater. He dropped the coat at his knees, placed his hands on the back of his head and bowed forward. His torso, stout and broad, was filled with muscles and cleansed of fat. His ripped physique clung to his frame with the tautness of a bodybuilder. There were also signs of great fatigue, like a soldier who had fought for far too long. In deep grooves where there should have been only ribs, there were scars. Four on each side of his torso, the long scars stretched diagonally across his hips. They moved up from the centre and towards the outside, forming a dark V around his belt. Undecided's body was both fit and sick, both strong and weak.

Blue quickened her pace, gaining strength as she approached her Beretta.

Undecided leaned back, dropping his arms to his sides and staring straight up into the rainfall. Slowly, he rose from his knees, his face gazing up into the sky.

The last chunk of wreckage rejoined the tower. The city square was now whole again, as if nothing had happened. *Just a few more feet*, thought Blue, *just a little more.*

Fully erect, Undecided continued to stare up into the sky, water dripping down his face. His voice came off his tongue like a soft whisper. "Raindrops," he soothed, raising an open hand towards the retreating Blue. Turning his head, Undecided looked at his palm as it collected the falling water. His palm closed into a fist and his face tightened. "Like tears from heaven."

Blue's wet fingers felt the groove of the grip. She grasped the Beretta and rose in single motion. As she turned the pistol towards her tormenter, though, she saw only a flash of movement. She fired from point-blank range and watched the bullet trail bend harmlessly around the oncoming blur. A great force smashed into her chest.

Blue felt herself flying backwards. Her back hit something hard. A gaping hole in a building opened up before her as she crashed through each one of its walls. Thrown completely through the building, Blue saw the world tilt and the street came up to meet her.

The wet pavement skidded past and soon came to a stop. It took her a dazed moment to realize she was now lying on her side in the middle of the street. She could not feel the grooves of her Beretta; she must have lost it again as she crashed through the building.

She looked up in time to see Undecided stepping through the gaping hole, his broad shoulders scraping against the crumbling marble. Blue staggered to her feet to face the killer, but she could no longer see him.

Instead, she found herself in a field of daisies, butterflies a-flutter with hope and life. The smell of fresh pollen struck her nostrils, causing saliva to drip from her tongue. Blue grinned as the sunshine beamed down upon her. Off in the distance, in the middle of the meadow, stood a little girl in a white dress. The little girl was fearful of Blue, the whites of her eyes wide in terror. Blue thought this strange. *Why would the little girl be afraid of her? She was not a bad person. She was not dangerous.*

Wobbly from the pollen, Blue held out her hand as she staggered towards the little girl. The little girl's fear disappeared, quickly replaced by a rage that flared from her eyes and nostrils. The little girl sprinted towards Blue at a gallop, her propane blue eyes glaring at her intruder.

Her mind spinning, Blue saw the world transform around her. Bright daisies bathed in sunshine became a dirty street drenched in rain. The sweet taste of pollen in her mouth turned to bitter sweat. And the little girl was no longer small and harmless, but a full grown man stepping in for the kill.

THUD. The dull, terrible thud of bone hitting bone rang through Blue's ears as she collapsed on the ground. The world around her spun into darkness.

She saw a bookworm sitting at his computer, writing an essay that would never be finished. Outside, she heard a party of students pass by on their way to the next bar, chattering away about their exciting stories and their brimming hopes. The bookworm peered up, watched them go by and then returned his hopes towards his computer. The click-click of his keyboard dropped on the beat like a drummer. He kept typing, the same pattern, again and again as life walked on by.

Pulling herself from the darkness, Blue found herself in a crawling position. She ordered her legs to stand, but they would not listen. Her body shook with exhaustion. She turned towards her aching limbs.

"*Get up and fight you little wimp,*" she said.

Just then, she felt her ribs cave in.

****

Mmorpg floated through a building just in time to find Blue lying on the ground. Undecided stood above her, kicking in her ribs with glee.

"Let's even this up," said Mmorpg. "Kernel: activate god mode."

"God mode activated," said the kernel.

He began to draw a cube with his two index fingers. But before he could finish, someone stepped in front of him. Mmorpg stopped in surprise and yelled at the stranger. "Clear the zone!"

But the stranger, skinny and freckled, didn't hear a word. He carried a limp woman in his arms through the battlefield. Her dark brown skin contrasted with the empty whites of her eyes. Raindrops dripped from her short plump fingers.

"Get out of here!" screamed Mmorpg.

Instead, the thin pale kid let the dead woman slide from his fingers and drop to the ground. He reached down and picked up a jagged piece of glass that was sliding across the pavement. He stared at Undecided.

But Undecided, joyfully kicking the life out of Blue, did not see the thin kid walking up behind him. He smashed his boot into Blue's cheek. She rolled over towards the dripping curb. The thin kid came up behind Undecided and swung the glass shard in his hand.

Undecided turned around just in time to block the blow with his left hand. With his right, the killer gave the kid an uppercut. The kid's head snapped back with an awful crunch and he dropped dead to the crowd.

"Dear God," said Mmorpg.

Undecided walked over to Blue, picked up her head and placed on the curb. She could put up no resistance. Undecided raised his foot.

"No," said Mmorpg. He drew a cube with his index fingers. The cube glowed green as Mmorpg grabbed its sides and turned.

****

Helpless to fight back, Blue watched Undecided lift his foot up above her head. He was going to curb-stomp her. It was a horrible way to die yet she was ready for it. Better here than in a hospital bed.

But Undecided stumbled backwards as the ground shook beneath them. Undecided turned to the right and Blue followed his gaze. She saw Mmorpg, struggling to turn a green cube in his hands.

"Wow this is a big one," said Mmorpg. He turned towards her and their eyes met.

"BLUE! GRAB ON TO SOMETHING!" he screamed.

Turning away from Undecided, Blue spotted a sewer grate. She grabbed its grill with both hands. She heard the rumble of sliding earth and saw the world in front of her lift up.

****

Mmorpg strained as he turned the cube. The cube mimicked the weight of the massive weight of the zone as he spun it. The world around him rotated clockwise. The streets, the buildings, the lights swung up into the air on one side of the axis and down into the ground on the other. He was literally rotating a piece of the city. Mmorpg gasped in awe at his own doing. To his left and rising fast where Blue and Undecided, hanging on desperately to the street as it tilted up into the air.

****

Debris slid past her as the ground in front tilted upwards. Blue looked off to her left and saw skyscrapers turning in place. To her right, it was the same.

She heard an odd crunching noise behind her. Looking down the street, she saw Undecided. As he climbed up towards her, he punched through the asphalt with his fists, creating steps for his feet.

Blue tried to rain kicks down upon him but he held fast. He was simply too strong.

With a monstrous thud, the city came to a stop. The street was now completely vertical. The skyscrapers, glass and steel monoliths that once stretched up into the sky, now hung across the falling rain.

Blue look up to the tower above her and listened to the frame moan against the weight.

She felt something grab her leg. Looking down, Blue saw Undecided pulling her down towards him. Rage danced in his eyes. She held fast to the grate as their combined weight strained her body.

Another giant moan from above and a deafening crack. Blue looked up to see the horizontal skyscraper collapse under its own weight. The windows shattered first, spilling glass shards down on Blue and Undecided as they struggled. The steel frame held for only a second longer. With a painful moan, the frame bent and twisted down towards them.

Undecided had pulled himself up to Blue's belt. She kneed him continuously in the chest as he reached for her neck.

She heard a series of sharp snaps. She looked up in time to see girders tear away from the building's base. The huge steel frame rolled down the pavement towards them. Blue hugged the pavement as fingers wrapped themselves around the back of her neck. The steel girders grazed her back as they rolled past. She heard the frame smash into the skyscrapers below.

Blue felt the fingers pull her head back and smash her head into the pavement. She pushed back with her arms but no longer had any strength. Her head was smashed into the street again and again. The world around her blurred into nothingness. Her body relaxed.

****

Mmorpg held the cube in place as he stared up into the sky. He prayed that Undecided would fall from the asphalt cliff, but the killer held tight. He could not be shaken loose. Mmorpg watched helplessly as Undecided slammed Blue's head again and again into the rotated street. Mmorpg felt useless. There was nothing that he could do to help her.

High above him, Undecided pulled the unconscious Blue from the cliff face of the street and held her by the neck over empty space. Staring down at Mmorpg, the killer grew an awful smile across his scarred face.

He released Blue and let her fall.

"No!" said Mmorpg as he twisted the cube back into place. As Blue fell, the street rotated back down and underneath her. She hit the pavement on a slant and rolled down the incline. Bouncing off the broken remains of a skyscraper, Blue crashed through a massive pile of debris and disappeared from Mmorpg's view. He brought the street back to level and dissolved the green cube.

"Kernel: deactivate god mode."

"God mode deactivated."

"Blue!" Mmorpg yelled as he searched through the rubble. "Where are you?"

****

Blue tried to pull herself back to her feet in the rainy street, her clothes soaked with water. Her mind fought for only a moment, then surrendered. Her weary body collapsed to its knees. She could fight no more.

Blue felt strong, stubby fingers slide through her hair and grab hold by the roots. There was a terrible pain in her scalp and she felt her body lift into the air. Opening her eyes, she looked straight into the face of her killer. For the first time, she saw the scarring on his jaw. Red and swollen, it was like he had a thousand cold sores that never healed, growing and multiplying all over his jaw. Blue tried to knock away the hand that was hoisting her up, but she was too weak. All she could do was grab his wrist, but only for a moment. Her strength completely spent, her grip loosened and her arms fell limply to her sides.

Blue slumped there for a long moment in mid-air, trying to stay conscious, struggling to keep her eyes on her attacker. For a long moment, Undecided simply held her there.

He reached back with his free arm.

The punch took forever to reach her. In dead silence, the fist moved slowly through the frozen rain towards her face. The last thing her left eye saw was the iron ring on his little finger.

The fist smashed into her face like a bull, crushing her eye and knocking her backwards through the air. As liquid oozed out of her socket, her hair stretched taut and swung her body back towards the killer. She was met with a vicious backhand that ripped open the scars on her right cheek. Blood splattered onto the wet pavement. Undecided dropped her to the ground. Legs shaking, Blue pulled herself to her feet. She would not go down.

Again and again Undecided beat her face, spraying blood across the falling rain. But Blue would not go down. He levelled a blow at her that crushed her already damaged larynx. But still she stood.

Finally, Undecided stepped aside and stomped his boot down upon the back of her knee, snapping her lower leg like a chicken bone. With no more strength or bone on which to stand, Blue fell onto her back. Undecided straddled her and delivered crosses to her already destroyed face. As her head whipped back and forth to each side, crimson splattered everywhere, forming a collage of blood and flesh upon the street.

His bare torso spray-painted in poppy-red, Undecided rose and admired his masterpiece. His breathing was calm and subdued, but this violence wasn't enough. He needed more.

Standing over the broken body of Blue, Undecided raised his steel-toed boot and stomped on her chest. The angry crunch of snapping ribs awoke Blue from her stupor. She raised her arms helplessly in defence as Undecided continued to stomp down viciously on her body. She absorbed blow after blow until her left arm snapped into two. It bent awkwardly two inches below the elbow.

Undecided stomped on her teeth and then on her chest again. This time, Blue grabbed the boot with her one good arm. Undecided tried to pull it free, but Blue did not relent. Her face covered in red grime, Blue curled up as close as she could to the killer and spat out her words through missing front teeth.

"*Fuck you!*" she seethed, spattering blood out of her mouth and onto Undecided's steel-toed boot.

Undecided narrowed his eyes and pushed down with his foot. All around Blue, concrete creaked and shuddered. With an awful crack, the pavement broke into chunks. Down, down, down Blue sank into a crumbling morass of sand, tar and asphalt. The pavement snapped into even smaller pieces, all covering Blue as she sank further into the street.

Blue reached out in vain to grab Undecided's jeans. She sank into the broken street until only her outstretched hand remained. Her hand reached frantically for something, anything. Then, as seconds passed, it shuddered and went still. Her fingers drooped forwards while her arm poked out of the ground like a tombstone.

As the hands of the doubleclock tower struck twelve, Undecided watched over the grave. As the chimes rang, Blue's hand remained still. Satisfied, Undecided removed his foot from the street, grabbed his clothes and continued on his way.

CHAPTER THIRTY-FOUR

CALL OF THE NOCTURNE

A few minutes passed with Blue's outstretched arm jutting out of the grave. But though she remained still, the dirt above her began to shift. It slid out, down and then underneath her body. More and more the dirt built beneath her, pushing her up to the surface. Daylight broke upon her face as her head was pushed out of the grave. Her limp body followed, flopping to the side as the pavement continued to repair itself.

Still Blue did not move. The skin around her jaw began to flutter. Protrusions stretched out from her cheek for only a moment, then withdrew. Blue's lips shuddered, and then were forced open by dirt pouring out of her lungs. The soil drifted across the concrete street and flowed back into the closing hole. As her lungs emptied of dirt, air rushed in to fill the gap. In an instant, Blue's eyes popped open. Her body instantly vomited, pouring out shards of plaster, concrete and dust from her stomach.

Lying on her face, dripping with sweat, blood and puke, Blue watched, fascinated as the street rebuilt itself. A flicker of remembrance crossed her eyes and she reached into the open grave with her one good arm. The street tried to push her out as it healed its gaping wound, but she held fast. Her arm searched the grave by touch.

Then she found it. She felt her fingers caress its steel grooves. Blue grasped tight and pulled, but it resisted. She pulled again, trying to get whatever leverage she could muster from her broken body. But creaking in outrage, the street would not yield. Instead, the street pushed up against her arm, trying to force her out of the hole. But Blue held fast to the grooves. Together, with her strength and the force of the healing grave, the bar began to move upwards. Blue wrenched with her back, burning all of the swollen muscles on her body. With a snap and a cloud of dust, her arm exploded from the grave, the rebar rod clutched in her hand.

Using the rod as a crutch, she pushed herself to her feet. Blue scanned the street for any sign of life, but it had been evacuated long ago. There was only her now, alone.

Something caught her eye for a moment, then disappeared. She hobbled over to the place where she thought she had seen it, but found nothing. She closed her eyes and breathed in deeply, clearing her battered mind. When her eyes reopened, they did so with renewed purpose, scanning the street for any sign of life.

They found a single drop of blood - her blood.

She looked around the street again and found another drop. Blue hobbled to the next spot and followed the line to the next red stain upon the pavement. With each drop she found, her will returned. Broken, defeated, she still had purpose; she still had something to do. As the ringing in her ears stopped, she heard a voice call from behind.

"There you are," said Mmorpg. Blue hobbled around to see Mmorpg floating through of a building. "Oh my god. Are you alright?" he asked.

"*I'll live.*" Blue's voice was even fainter and raspier than before. With each syllable, her larynx spasmed painfully, Every few seconds, she was forced to swallow the bile inching up from her stomach. She continued to follow the drops.

"What happened? Did you get him to log out?"

"*He knew.*"

"And the Beretta?"

"*Useless, even at close range. It just bent around him.*"

Blue continued to follow the blood trail.

"Where are you going?"

"*Following his trail.*"

Mmorpg finally noticed the drops of blood Blue was following."

"Is that his blood?"

"*No, it's mine.*"

"That violates the obscenity filter. That-"

"*-shouldn't be happening, right? Because of your rules? Face it whelp. Your rules have failed.*"

"I just don't understand it. The security protocols, the obscenity filter. My code is bulletproof. It can't be overridden."

Blue stopped, her eyes fixated on the ground. She reached down and picked up her Beretta semiautomatic.

"*We are animals. We can't be controlled by good intentions. Only way to control a vicious animal is to put it down. Only way to keep people safe.*"

Propping the rebar pole under her armpit, Blue tucked the gun between her legs and pulled back the slide with her one good arm. A bullet ejected from the chamber and tumbled to the ground. Blue examined the weapon, but found no damage. It would still fire. She returned the pistol to its holster, grabbed her pole and limped along the blood trail.

"Stop," said Mmorpg.

"*I can't,*" said Blue.

"It's over, Blue."

"*Not until I kill him.*"

"You can't be serious. You can barely walk."

"*I will finish this.*"

"No you can't. He's too strong."

"*I'll find a way.*"

"No you won't. We've exhausted our options. The bullets simply bend around him and you can't force him to log out. There is no to stop him unless ..." Mmorpg paused.

Blue stopped and looked back towards Mmorpg. Mmorpg bit his tongue.

"*I have to beat him,*" said Blue. "*I need to beat him.*"

Mmorpg, head lowered, said nothing.

"*Please. Give me a way.*"

Mmorpg raised his head and looked at Blue. Her moistened eyes pleaded with him.

"There is a way," he said. "Gibbs and Chiu found it."

"Arthur mentioned them before. Who were they?"

"Jeffrey Gibbs and Kevin Chiu were my original partners. They helped me design the very first version of Evermore."

Mmorpg sat down on the curb.

"We were brilliant. Together, we created something special: a virtual playground where everything was possible, where the only limit was your own mind."

"What happened to them?"

"We were all fans of first-person shooters. We jumped at the chance to recreate these games in Evermore. We created bots, we staged shootouts, it was a blast. We had programmed the guns to use rubber bullets, so we thought it would be safe. One day, bored of bots, we decided to try fighting each other. Kevin served as the host. He recreated the old Main Library at UBC, filled with row upon row of green stacks. It was perfect for a gunfight. As the host, Kevin slept embedded in the wall while Jeff and I battled it out. We ran from row to row shooting at one another. We set up ambushes. We staged heroic escapes. We had fun. Well, everything went well until one of my stray bullets struck Kevin in the temple."

"That's a kill shot, even for a rubber bullet."

"In real life it is. You see, we didn't understand that the mind can't tell the difference between virtual death and real death. When you die in a virtual world, your mind convinces itself that it's dead too. It turns itself off. How were we supposed to know that?"

"So what happened?"

"Once the rubber bullet hit Kevin in the head, his mind shut down. The world around us started to collapse. We had only seconds. I knew immediately that something was wrong and I logged out. But Jeff, he hesitated. He ran out of time and was trapped inside Kevin's dying mind. When I came to I tried to wake them but it was no use. Their minds were dead. I had killed them both."

Mmorpg drew in a gulp. His voice heaved as he spoke.

"The authorities thought they had overdosed on drugs. I didn't correct them. The next day, I began work on the security protocols so it could never happen again."

"*So there is another way.*"

"Yes, there is, but we can't take it. You handgun is exempted from the safeties. If you could trap Undecided inside a zone and kill the host, the zone would collapse. In response, the security protocols would automatically call the logout function to kick you both out of the collapsing zone. The subroutine that I've replaced it with would trap both of your minds inside Evermore until we could find Undecided's body in the real world. Once we had him in custody, we would be able to free your mind. It would be the same plan as before, we would just carry it out in a slightly different way."

"*There's one problem.*"

"Yes, and that's why we can't use it. To stop Undecided, you would have to kill the host. You'd have to kill an innocent man."

"*That's not the problem.*"

"Like hell it isn't. He's done nothing wrong. He doesn't deserve to lose his mind."

"*We never get what we deserve. That's the problem. Stopping Undecided is not enough.*"

"Once he's arrested, he will face justice."

"*Did I?*"

Mmorpg was silent.

"*I killed seven children. Yet here I am. Did I receive justice?*"

Mmorpg could not respond.

"*There is no justice in this world but what we take for ourselves.*"

"But..."

"*Can you guarantee that if arrested, Undecided would never kill again?*"

"He'll spend the rest of his life in jail. He's murdered dozens of people."

"*In a fake world. How many ways can a defence attorney tear your case to pieces. Who's to say that the victims even exist?*"

"We have bodies," said Mmorpg.

"*With no physical trace to Undecided,*" said Blue. "*How do you prove a virtual crime?*"

Mmorpg paused, deep in thought.

"You can't," he said.

"*Then give me a way to kill him,*" said Blue, "*or everyone, would have died for nothing.*"

"What about the host?"

"*While he lives, Undecided will never stop. He will kill again. It's your choice. Save one or save a hundred.*"

Mmorpg hesitated.

"*If we want to save lives, then we have to finish it now.*"

"Can you live with that?"

"*Yes. Can you?*"

"I've doomed so many people today already. One less won't save my soul."

"*So there is a way?*"

"Yes, we go directly into the kernel and disable the security protocols completely."

"*What good would that do?*"

"If you kill the host with the safeties disabled, Undecided won't be automatically logged out when the zone collapses around him. He will be trapped inside the host's dying mind. His mind will disappear along with the host. It won't kill him but it will leave him a vegetable for the rest of his life."

"*So it won't kill him?*"

"No, but it will leave him vulnerable, to a fate worse than death."

"*That'll do.*"

"But there's one more problem. You'll be stuck in there with him. You'll suffer the same fate, trapped in a coma for the rest of your life."

"*I have to beat him.*"

"You're willing to sacrifice your life?"

"*Nobody beats me and lives. Are we agreed?*"

"Yes. Locate Undecided. I'll quarantine the area and turn off the safeties. Find and kill the host and it will all be over."

"*Done,*" said Blue. She turned and hobbled after the blood drops on the ground. Mmorpg floated after her.

Blue stopped.

"*Stay here.*"

"But..."

"Can you shut off the safeties from here?"

"Yes but..."

"Then stay here."

"But I need to help."

"You don't want to see this. Killing an innocent. That's not something you ever forget."

"I know."

"No you don't. No, you don't."

"Fine. I'll keep an audio link open. Give me a shout when you're ready."

"I will. And when the police come looking for you, blame me. Tell them that I forced you into this. With my past, they won't have any trouble believing you."

"No. This is all my fault. When Undecided is dead, I'll turn myself over to the authorities and take responsibility for everything. Gibbs and Chiu deserve that much."

Mmorpg held out his palm.

"Good luck Blue."

Blue eyed his hand warily. Then she wedged the rebar pole underneath her armpit and extended her hand. She wrapped her hand around the outline of his hand and shook. Mmorpg shook her hand in return. She turned around and hobbled after the drops of blood.

The trail led her to a subway station. Blue limped down the steps and moved to the edge of the platform. She waited. The first set of cars zoomed to a stop. The doors opened before her, but she did not see any blood so she let it go. After another minute, another set of cars arrived but with the same result, no blood on the inside. She waited again as the second train zoomed away. Finally, a third train arrived, the doors opening with a whoosh before her. Blue looked inside the car and found blood everywhere: on the floor, on the seats, even on the roof. She limped inside without a word. The doors closed behind her. As the train lurched forward she moved to the only seat that wasn't covered in crimson. An outline of blood had formed on the seat like a chalk outline at a crime scene.

She sat down in the bloodless void, filling the silhouette completely. Mmorpg remained standing. He watched her as she sat quietly, neither moving nor speaking, framed in her seat by death.

The train snapped to a stop, but Blue took her weary time. Using the rebar as a crutch, she limped out of the car and again came face to face with the Great Gate.

It had seemed so impressive the first time she saw it – so grand and powerful. She had been struck by the feeling of security and safety the Gate seemed to radiate. Now when she faced the gate, she felt only broken bones rubbing against her chafing skin. The Gate created a mirage of security. It had failed to protect them from the monstrosity she now followed. They were never safe. They had never been safe. They would never be safe. That was the way of the world.

She passed through the Gate easily, feeling no resistance. The Gate had given up, resigning itself to failure as she passed beneath its arches.

The staircase was deserted. The walls and floor bore evidence of a great battle that had taken place, but no one remained. As she limped down the grand staircase, Blue ran her fingers across the craters and sighed.

The trail led her into a village. The western European townhouses exuded a soft serenity she had not noticed before, a sense of home and community, but there was nobody there. There were no children playing in the streets, no families arguing behind the windows, no music playing over the loudspeakers. The land was silent and peaceful. Blue paused to enjoy a moment of respite. There was nobody here to bother her.

Blue followed the trail of blood to an old shack. Its rotting walls seemed out of place with the surrounding architecture. Blue recognized it immediately. She knew where it led. She opened the door, letting it creak ajar and entered. But instead of leading to the forest like before, it led her back to the monochrome world. Stepping through the door onto the street, she glanced around at the various hues and shades of gray that surrounded her. She had been here before, but it looked different this time. It felt colder.

The black trail of blood drops stretched out in front of her towards an old diner. She remembered the diner, framed in a sea of 50s nostalgia and dreams of yesteryear. This time, the street was deserted, not a person stirred. Nor was there any wind. The world around her seemed frozen in time and devoid of life. She entered the diner slowly.

The diner was abandoned. Plates of food remained untouched, a coffee pot boiled with a shrill whine. In the back, a burger was burning to a crisp on the grill. There was no sense of panic, no dropped utensils or plates, no signs of chaos or struggle. It was as if everyone had simply stopped what they were doing, stood up and marched calmly out of the diner.

The blood led into the back.

Bracing her weight against the wall, her shoulders scraped against the narrow halls as she limped towards the back. Blue followed the trail into the men's washroom. Stalls lined the left side of the room. The trail led straight ahead, then turned and passed under the awkwardly unhinged door of stall number three. Blue remained at the entrance of the bathroom, suddenly wary. There was danger here, but she had to follow. She held her breath and took one step forward.

A trail of blood flowed slowly out from beneath one of the stall doors, pooling into a black crimson puddle just outside the stall. Blue froze, a chill crawling up her spine. Breathing in softly, Blue limped into the puddle and faced the broken door of stall number three.

She heard voices, but could not understand what they were saying. She heard pleading, begging, but could not hear to whom and for what. As she reached out with her good hand to the stall door, she heard a quiet sobbing from within.

The aluminum door creaked open. Inside, Blue saw a gaping hole in the tiled wall. She had seen this hole before, and yet she was filled with a renewed sense of dread. This time, the hole bled. Black blood flowed slowly down the porcelain wall behind the toilet and collected in a pool at her feet. The hole shrank and grew before her, as if it were breathing. Her breathing became more laboured, and so too did the hole's. She held her breath and the hole froze.

Blue stepped on the toilet seat and peered into the wound. All she could see was a narrow light at the end of the tunnel. The walls of the tunnel were wet and moist. From the hole, she heard long and painful breaths.

Blue climbed headfirst into the hole.

The fit was tight, especially when she breathed in. Her breathing pulled the tunnel in tight around her until she exhaled. She slid through the tunnel using her one good arm and leg. The rebar crutch remained locked in her fingers.

About halfway through the tunnel, she felt pressure on her legs. She breathed out, but the pressure increased. Glancing back, she saw the light from the bathroom shrivelling up.

The tunnel was closing in behind her.

With renewed alarm, Blue struggled to slide her way through the rest of the tunnel as it collapsed in on her. The light at the end grew larger and larger as she approached, her pain growing with each breath she took. Finally, she slid out of the opening at the other side and fell into a small utility room. Standing up painfully, Blue watched as the hole closed up completely, cutting off her only escape.

The utility closet was small and square. Floor of steel, walls of brick, the room contained an aluminum shelf at one end and a wooden door at the other. Above her, a hanging light bulb on a simple chain swivelled in the stillness. Its shadows fluttered as it moved. The shelves contained all sorts of odds and ends: used paint cans, dirty shovels and open packages of plaster and drywall mix. A mop and bucket, old and mouldy, lay at her feet. Bracing herself against her rebar crutch, Blue moved forward and opened the door.

The door opened onto a stairwell that descended into shadow. Blue stepped forward, squinting in the glare of a bare lightbulb hanging from the cracked ceiling of the landing. The door clicked behind her and she whirled around and yanked on the handle, but it was locked. With no choice but to advance, Blue started to move down the stairs. With each step came a mournful creak, letting her presence be known to anything that awaited her in the darkness.

A voice chimed in her inner ear. It was Mmorpg.

"I've finally managed to structure the spider's IR code. All I have to do now is to simply generate the source code and match the variables with their corresponding register."

"*Doesn't matter*," said Blue. "*We already know who the killer is.*"

"Where are you?" Mmorpg asked.

"*I'm inside a stairwell, going down. Do you see me?*"

"Yes," Mmorpg said, "but you're heading into a server that I've never seen before. It's buried under a layer of placeholder zones."

"*He's in here.*"

"Yes, but what's strange is that this area only has one link to the rest of the world. Every other zone has dozens, sometimes even hundreds of links to adjacent zones to facilitate movement around —"

"*Follow the plan. Seal me in,*" said Blue.

There was nothing but silence.

Behind her, the walls twisted and creaked. The floor morphed, climbing up the walls to the ceiling. As the floor met the ceiling, they fused together into a barrier of wood, plaster and paint.

"*Mmorpg?*" called Blue. For a long moment, she heard only silence.

"Yes, I'm still here," he finally responded. "I've kept a small port open for communication. I'll cut it if I pick up any outbound traffic. But for now, no one can pass through this link."

Blue made her way down the stairs, hugging the wall to reduce the pressure on her broken leg. After about twenty steps, she reached a landing, with another flight of stairs continuing down to the right. Another hanging light bulb illuminated the way. Blue heard a soft, shrill noise, but she could not figure out what it was.

She continued to descend into the darkness. The lights grew further apart and fainter as she stepped. The noise continued to grow in pitch and volume. Blue could hear it more clearly now, but still could not discern what it was. Down and around she descended the stairwell. There was something written on the walls but not enough light to read it. The voices could be heard clearly now. They were screaming in terror, they were crying in despair and they were laughing hysterically. All three sounds merged together into a symphony of misery, filling her heart with melancholy - and dread.

Behind her, the walls closed in again, cutting off the only light bulb in sight.

"*Was that you?*" Blue asked.

"No," Mmorpg responded, "that was not me."

She heard chains rattling as they stretched across the collapsed way. Blue could hear the chains tighten and dig themselves into the wood.

There was no going back.

Blue was now lost in the dark, blind and helpless. She groped her way along the walls. The screaming and crying and laughing grew more and more pronounced.

Without sight, the screaming symphony filled her thoughts with the most horrible evil. Her imagination, freed from the bounds of reality, pulled the most terrifying visions from the nether regions of her mind. In the darkness, she could almost see the demons dancing around her. She could almost feel their hands reaching out to pull her into the black.

Blue's breathing grew more laboured, her mind more focused. She let the fear turn her into a weapon of viciousness no monster could match. Her eyes flared and her molars began to grind.

Malevolence and fury oozed from her pores. The threat of monsters reaching out for her was replaced by a fantasy of her doing wonderfully horrible things to their twisted corpses. Things that stretched beyond the bounds of human decency, actions that would revile the most heinous criminal. The monsters before her melted away, terrified of the demon in black.

Sobs, cries and screams filled her ears. Rather than deter her, the sounds now cheered her on. Blue lusted to cause those screams, to break those sobs, to bring pain and suffering to all who crossed her path. Her mind in a ready state of war, she brushed past a thin chain hanging from the ceiling. Reaching for it without hesitation, the lady of death pulled the chain and lit the lamp.

Before her stood a door - oak and strong. Upon that door she saw words, some etched with a kitchen knife, others written in blood. She followed the words, watching them stretch out over the door and across the walls and ceilings. The writing started off concise and neat on the door, but grew more frantic as it stretched across the room.

Mary had a little lamb. Day 133, I found mr bunny today. Where's the chopsticks? I wanna be an astronaut. mr bunny made me cry. Quiet, not during his program. Pretend like you're asleep. London Bridge is falling down, falling down, falling down. London Bridge is falling down, my fair lady. Just play quietly. I can read under the covers with my flashlight. Just pretend it's hide and go seek. Under the bed. Don't let him find us. Just pretend it's a game. I don't like my flashlight any more. Why do you look at me like that mr bunny. It's not my fault. Come out and play mr bunny. I promise I won't do that again. Help me with the sheet, I promise it'll be fun. Spin. WEEEEEE. FLUSH. Spinnning round round and round and down and down you go. SHHHH. I don't want to be found. Please please don't let me be found. If I should die before I wake, I pray the Lord my soul to take. I didn't break it, it was an accident. RUN! HIDE! PRAY! Please don't let me be found. Kuwabara. Faith no more, faith no more. Run mr bunny, I'll protect you. Kuwabara. Dear God, make me a bird. So I could fly far. Far far away from here. KUWABARA. Alone. KUWABARA. Pretend. Pretend. KUWABARA. Help me. KUWABARA. Why have you fors... me? Run away, run away, run away with m..........

The letters disappeared in a dishevelled scrawl upon the floor. Limping forward, Blue moved to the bottom step just in front of the door. Placing her one good arm on the thick oak, Blue pushed, but the door would not move. At the tips of her fingers, Blue felt something cold and hard. Wiping away the grime, Blue uncovered a number – 1394 – stretching diagonally across the oak frame.

Blue paused.

Reaching into her coat pocket with her right hand, she pulled out the yellow can and popped open the green lid. The mould lay at the bottom of the can, forming an outline of a key with the number 1394 etched into its base. Blue looked down at the doorknob and saw a small silver key protruding from the handle. Dropping the yellow can, she reached out and grasped the key, its long nylon lanyard brushing against her wrist. The smooth, cold surface greeted her fingertips as her thumb rubbed the raised number upon the key's face – 1394. Turning the key, Blue heard a soft and satisfying click.

The wooden door creaked open to reveal a dimly lit apartment with faded green ceilings. Soft, gray carpet lined the floor. Blue entered and walked down the hall, passing by empty picture frames hung on the walls.

The hallway opened up into a den with a large television in the corner and a large couch on the other side. In the middle lay a green, circular rug marked with a series of brown concentric rings. In the middle of the rug was a shallow impression from something left there far too long. The TV, always on, cackled with the static of a lost station. To her right, in between the television and the gray couch, the door to the bathroom stood ajar. Blue walked over to it.

The bathroom had a colour design straight from the 1970s. The sink and toilet were a dirty green and the walls were covered in tiles with tessellated patterns of squares and circles. The shower, on the other hand, was brand new and stood off in the corner with its soft serenity of beige cleanliness. The sink overflowed with running water. Blue turned off the tap and pulled the plug. She watched, mesmerized, as a dozen yellow pills swirled down the drain. A discolouration on the toilet caught her eye. She moved towards the toilet and lifted up the seat. Inside the bowl rested two razors that bled the water red.

The crackle of the TV static stopped. Out of her line of sight, on the plasma screen, a pair of short, pale arms popped up. One was clenched in anticipation and the other was holding a razor blade. The razor blade cut into the forearm like it was fresh bread. Crimson liquid oozed out of the gash and dripped down into the bowl. Blue closed the lid and the screen returned to static.

Limping back to the den, Blue felt a gust of air upon her cheek and looked up. Above her, a ceiling fan spun at an easy pace. Again, the static on the screen disappeared. In its place was the image of a little girl hung by her neck, spinning lifelessly in circles as the fan turned. Blue swivelled her head towards the television, but saw only static.

Sensing movement to her left, Blue turned and watched a door opposite the TV open slowly. After a moment's hesitation, Blue limped towards the open door. Behind her, a new image flashed on the television screen. It was a low-angle POV shot of the television screen as it slowly backed away into the distance, as if the camera was being dragged just behind Blue.

Blue passed through the doorway and found herself in a bedroom. Along the wall were plastered scores of movie and pop music posters. The shelves were filled with movies and CDs. Along one wall was an overturned basket of Barbie dolls, clothes hanging loosely over their plastic bodies. Hanging on a third wall was a big-screen TV. Blue turned to the final wall and stopped. Where the bed should have been, there was only a large gaping hole in the wall. A pink bunny doll sat on the floor beside the hole. Its soft, fuzzy head had flopped forward and was resting on its legs.

The hole appeared to have been ripped open by sheer force rather than skilled carpentry. Splinters of broken planks and torn plaster lined the opening. Blue limped painfully towards the opening. The door closed slowly behind her. She held herself steady against the wall and peered into the hole. There was nothing but black emptiness. Beside her, the pink bunny doll, raised head, turned towards Blue and smiled.

Back in the main den, the TV came to life again. On the screen, there appeared the door to the little girl's room. The camera moved slowly towards the door, shaking with each step. Pushing the door open, the image moved in quietly behind the distracted Blue. Blue wheeled around just as the image rushed in on her, pushing her backwards and through the hole. Blue fell into the darkness, her muffled screams disappearing into the blackness.

The television returned to static. The small pink bunny laughed with the mania of a hyena.

– CHAPTER THIRTY-FIVE –

BEAUTIFUL THINGS

Blue fell into shadow, crashing through planks of rotten wood as she tumbled into nothingness. She hit the ground with a thud, the stone floor knocking the wind from her lungs. Her broken limbs ached while she struggled to her hands and knees.

The taste of blood lined her tongue. Salty sea air with a hint of formaldehyde pricked her nostrils. Pushing the pain deep inside, Blue pulled herself to her feet using the wall for support. The air felt damp, like a cellar in summer. But she could see little, only a hallway ahead with three beams of light crossing her path. The beams came from above and to the right, piercing the room at fourty-five degree angles. The hallway opened up into a circular rotunda illuminated by a single ray of light shining down from above.

Slowly and painfully, Blue moved forward and limped into the first ray of light. She expected a trap to spring like in the movies she had seen as a kid, but no trap was sprung, no menace jumped from the walls. She only felt the light heat of sunshine upon her skin. It made her feel better about her pain and her mission. The light filled her with warmth, like hot chocolate on a cold day. She stepped forward and out of the first ray of light. The darkness enveloped her, pulling her soul into cold despair. But she continued, limping forward towards the next light.

She passed into the second ray of light. Again, no trap was sprung. She felt only sunlight. But her spirits improved and she limped with a little more strength on her broken leg. Her shattered arm, throbbing so viciously just moments before, now caused little concern. She felt the caress of a mother's hand brush past her cheek, but there was nobody there. The light implored her to stop, to remain here, to stay away from the dark. Briefly, she considered its siren call, but something in the darkness was calling her, too, and its call was more dangerous, more seductive. So again, she stepped back into shadow.

The coldness of the dark struck her. Gone were warmth and love. Gone was the mother's caress. Gone was the call of the siren. Instead, she shivered, trapped alone in the darkness.

The light giveth, the dark taketh. When she had stepped under the light, her limp had improved, the dull ache of broken bone receding into her memory. But when she returned to the dark, the pain intensified. Anguish wracked her body, agony consumed her mind. The sanctuary brought by the light only served to intensify the suffering rendered by the dark. Broken bone grated on broken bone. Torn muscles pulled at bruised skin.

She limped forward towards the third ray of light, eager to feel its warm touch again. Back into the light she hobbled, letting the light soothe her like a warm bath. She felt so young again, reborn without sin. She did not want to leave its warm embrace. The darkness called her forward but she ignored it. It pleaded with her to continue, but she held fast. She would stay here forever more. She closed her eyes and gave in to the light.

The darkness promised her the truth.

Her eyes opened and her pulse quickened with excitement. She had to continue. One foot in front of the other, her feet plodded forward and back into the black.

In front of her, the circular spotlight of the rotunda began to flicker. As she came to the edge of the light, she could look up for the first time. Above her, a giant fan started to spin, splitting the light into the frames of a film. On, off, on, off, again and again it went. Like a cheap horror film, the light illuminated Blue one moment and darkened her the next. Her emotional state flipped back and forth like a light switch. Each time the light breached her form, Blue felt the joy of a thousand birthdays and weddings rolled into one. With each passing shadow, she dipped into the deepest pits of her despair. Into both heaven and hell, her emotions rose and fell like Icarus on a feedback loop. Between the two, she could neither rest in contentment nor wallow in misery.

Mmorpg's voice spoke directly into her ears, breaking the loop with words drenched in fear. "Blue, I've regenerated the source code and fed in the data I pulled from the spider's registers. There was a variable that stored the user's name, the name of the person who dispatched the spider, the one who has blocked us at every turn. I am truly sorry, Blue. I should have seen it coming. I ... I should have known. I knew we couldn't trust him."

"*Who sent it?*" asked Blue.

"I did," called a voice from the darkness. Behind her, she heard a door close and footsteps approach. Looking back, she saw a darkened form approach the first ray of light. From the emptiness, the figure spoke.

"It took me so long to understand," called the voice.

"*Who are you?*" asked Blue.

"Of course, I should have known. Multiple avatars per user is a tradition that stretches back to the very beginning of online worlds. Since the dawn of Evermore, individuals have sought not only to rebuild themselves to their ideals of perfection but to build multiple ideals of the self. To build not just a self that fits their dreams and desires, but to build a community of the self, a community with its own characters, its own plots, its own themes. The community of the self is in essence a creation of our own mind, a narrative of the lives we wish to be a part of. Its superiority to reality is inevitable. Rather than being held hostage in a community of one's peers, over whom we have no control, we have the ability to create new friends, new foes, new lovers, all of whom are crafted to suit a particular purpose in the narration of our minds. Given the unpredictable real, which rarely fits our emotional needs for narrative and dramatization, we prefer to impose a story on our own lives. Even in the real world, we see ourselves not as individuals, but as protagonists, with our own set of antagonists and supporting characters. We impose the structure of a narrative on our existence to make sense of it, to make the meaningless meaningful."

"*Why are you here?*" Blue demanded.

"Why?" the voice chortled as Arthur stepped into the light. "Without narrative, we would see our lives for what they truly are – a blink in time without rhyme. Without our personal three-act plays, we would find little reason to carry on. We spend our entire lives struggling, but for what? We won't be remembered, our pathetic little lives will not grace the pages of historic tomes. We are nothing, a simple speck of dust drifting through a universe of cosmic scale."

Blue felt her stomach sinking. Arthur had changed. There was a much harder edge to his voice. His eyes sang with intensity. He stood taller, bigger, stronger. There was something different within him, something dangerous.

"We are compelled to create narrative, we are forced to create stories, to mythologize ourselves so we can get up from bed each day and live our decrepit little lives. But our means are limited. It is difficult to create a myth of heroism and valour about yourself when you work a minimum wage job. It is difficult to see yourself as a princess when you can't get a date to save your soul. That's what makes Evermore so precious and popular. I had originally thought its allure lay in the fact that one could create an ideal self - a perfect conception unlimited by what Mmorpg would call the arbitrary justice of genetics and social station. I thought the ability to create a perfect avatar was what suckered people in and compelled them to spend their entire lives in this virtual prison. But I was wrong. The unconscious purpose of Evermore is not to create the one, but to create the many. People want to be more than perfect individuals; they want to be part of a larger world where they feel welcome, accepted … and not alone. Because the truth, that we are always alone, is always too much to bear. So we create not just one avatar, but many, all of whom are subconsciously designed to fill a psychological need. Some give us the friends we so desperately want. Others give us the foils against whom we can define ourselves. For we need antagonists, we need foes and we need conflict to make our narratives interesting. A story without conflict is a boring tale to tell. So we create these characters, we construct these conflicts and we compose these stories to build a narrative of the self inside a universe of one, always revolving around our needs, our dreams and very often our fears."

"*What do you want?*" Blue asked.

"I want what I have always sought and have only recently found," responded Arthur. "The truth. The truth of who we really are and what we really want. I have always dreamed of understanding why people do such horrible things to those who are good and kind."

Arthur stepped forward into the darkness, disappearing again from Blue's sight. "My questions stemmed from my inadequacies, my inability to win love and acceptance from my peers. Wherever I went, I found only those who would mock and reject me. No matter what I did, I could never find the bond of friendship or the love of a beautiful woman. I blamed my genes, for God made me short, stout and ugly. Nor was I blessed with a charming personality that could turn vinegar into wine. The only thing God has given me is my mind. So I used it. I searched for answers, to find out why people did such horrible things to me, to understand why I could never know true love at the hands of another."

She could see a rough outline of a figure moving towards the second ray of light, but it no longer fit Arthur's profile.

"But of course," Arthur continued, "that was a myth, a construction of my own design. I had constructed a narrative of my life - with an essential conflict, a goal and a supporting cast. I had always understood I was creating a narrative to mask my inadequacies, to bring order where there had only been misery and chaos. I had assumed I was at the centre of that narrative, that the universe revolved around me. I was wrong."

She held her breath.

"I am not the protagonist. I am merely a supporting character, sidekick to another's star billing. I was created to fulfill someone else's psychological needs. I was given my own background, my own motivations and my own character traits, as if they were written in shorthand for an actor. Only now do I understand my purpose."

"*What is your purpose?*" she asked.

"I am a catalyst, someone who serves no other role than to move the plot forward, to push the protagonist towards her goal. To bring her closer to facing her conflict, overcoming her climax and finding her resolution at the end of a self-composed tale."

"*Who are you talking about?*"

"In one way I am speaking of myself, but I am only one part of the puzzle. I am only one character in the universe of one you have created. For my entire existence, for how long I do not know, I have searched for my place, to understand who I really am.

"In reality, the truth was always there. But my subconscious would not let me see it. So it remained just out of sight, in the corner of my mind, scraping against my skull. That is why I led you all on a wild goose chase, moving from dead end to dead end. That is why I invented a false motive for the killer, distracting us from his real target, from his true motive. And that is why I dispatched the spider – to stop myself from discovering the truth.

"But I failed. The gopher survived and led us to the monster. More importantly, it led me to her. When I looked upon the body of the first victim, the one you forgot to tell me about, I realized the truth. When I looked upon her still form and her lifeless eyes, I understood for the very first time."

Arthur stepped into the second ray of light. "I understand now who I really am."

Blue herself looking straight into the burning propane eyes of Undecided, fully clothed in brown Akubra, coat and boots.

"*You're the killer?*" asked Blue, her breath coming in short quick bursts.

"Not quite. I am both hero and villain," said Undecided. "I am both knight and maiden. I am the jester and the bard, the painter and the muse. I am a traveling troupe of contradictions and clarity, creating questions wherever I sleep and answers wherever I go." Once again Undecided stepped into the darkness. She stepped back towards the edge of the rotunda of light.

"*So who are you then?*"

"Who am I?" repeated Undecided. He laughed at the question. His voice had changed again. This time it was lighter and yet harsher, like he was gargling water as he spoke.

"*Why must you insist in asking all the wrong questions,*" he said, stepping into the third ray of light. She was surprised to be looking into her own blue eyes. Before her stood Blue, the lady of death.

The vicious woman struggled mightily to breathe as she hobbled forward. The copy wore a devilish grin.

"*The question*," said the lady of death, "*is not really who I am, nor who you are.*" The lady of death passed through the third ray of light and stepped back into shadow. Blue retreated to the very edge of the circle of light. From the darkness, the words continued.

"The real question," came the voice, this time male and strong, "is not who we are, but who we will both become." And with that, the shadowy figure stepped into the rotunda of light.

Blue saw a middle-aged man staring at her with fatherly affection.

"Welcome home my darling," said the middle-aged man.

CHAPTER THIRTY-SIX

WELCOME HOME

The middle-aged man looked upon her with pride. He had the harsh hollow eyes of Undecided, but the soft soothing voice of Arthur. He wore a softly rumpled polo short and a pair of khaki pants. His hair was neatly trimmed and groomed, but the creases on his face gave away his age. He was almost fourty, but his eyes bore many more years of experience, not all of it good.

"I have missed you," he said, "so very much."

The middle-aged man reached out to touch her.

Blue raised her pistol and fired five shots. Their trails bent and refracted around the middle-aged man. Just like Undecided, bullets could not touch him.

Blue paused for a moment as the man approached. Then her eyes turned upwards. She raised her weapon to the ceiling and fired three more shots.

With the crash of an exploding lamp, the rotunda of light disappeared. As Blue felt her way through the darkness, she heard a voice call out from behind.

"Hide and seek. Good. I love to play."

Blue ducked into the first room she found and locked the door behind her. She rested her back against the wall, her broken bones throbbing painfully as fluid dripped from her useless left eye. Mmorpg's voice came into her ear.

"Fighting him is useless. Find the host and kill him. It is the only way."

Blue turned and found herself in an old, abandoned classroom. Upon the walls hung blackboards filled with the ramblings of children. The desks stood silent, covered in dust while a doubleclock gazed down upon them from the wall. Soft blue moonlight illuminated the room through an open window that led nowhere. In the middle of the classroom, surrounded by desks, was a bed.

Blue limped over to the bed. It was small, pink and covered in hearts. Inside its covers lay a little girl lost in a deep, peaceful slumber. She clutched three dolls tightly to her chest.

Blue put the gun down on the bed and touched the little girl on the cheek. Her skin felt cold. Her hair stretched down to the ground and merged into the floor. The strands of her hair continued onwards to form the walls, the ceiling and every object in sight. The room was growing out from the little girl's body, like branches from a tree.

"*I've found the host,*" said Blue. "*Pull the safeties.*"

"Are you sure it's the host?"

"*I'm sure. Pull it.*"

"Kernel: disable security protocols," said Mmorpg.

Blue heard the voice of the kernel come through the audio link. "Are you sure you want to do this?" it asked.

"Yes, I am sure," said Mmorpg.

"Security protocols disabled," said the kernel.

"The security protocols have been disabled," said Mmorpg to Blue. "Finish the job."

Blue heard scratching on the wall. She turned and saw white chalk marks appear on the blackboard. The chalk was writing a message.

I CAN'T SEE YOU. WHO ARE YOU?

"*My name is Blue,*" said Blue to the blackboard. The chalk wrote back in response.

ARE YOU HERE TO PROTECT ME?

"*From who?*"

FROM HIM.

An arrow pointing to the door appeared on the chalkboard. It shivered.

The door handle to the classroom rattled as a shadow passed underneath. Blue heard a voice call from outside.

"Hush little baby don't you cry,
Daddy's going to buy you a butterfly."

The door rumbled. More scratching came from the blackboard.

SAVE ME FROM HIM. PLEASE.

Blue brushed the little girl's hair softly.
"*Hush,*" said Blue. "*He won't hurt you any more.*"
She picked up the pistol and pointed it at the girl's head. She heard the voice call from the doorway.

"And if that butterfly isn't fun,
Then Daddy's going to buy you a rabbit bun."

Claws stabbed through the doorway. The sound of teeth gnashing poured through the splintering wood. The blackboard quivered along the wall. The pistol in Blue's hand began to shake. Blue's eyes narrowed in concentration. Her finger twitched, struggling to pull the trigger. Another message appeared in chalk.

I'M SCARED.

"*Don't worry,*" said Blue. "*It'll be over soon.*"
Sweat poured down her brow as the gun continued to shake. She heard the voice call yet again.

"And if that pink bunny can't sing,
Then Daddy's going to buy you a special thing ..."

The song trailed off into the darkness but the room remained still. Blue listened intently. Nothing could be heard.

Blue relaxed the grip on her pistol. As her body relaxed, so did the child. Blue glanced at the blackboard.

HE'S COMING FOR ME.

The door exploded into fragments. The middle-aged man stood in the door with violent joy written across his body, but he was no longer a man. Instead, he was a body covered in teeth and claws. Blue's finger slid along the trigger.

"I've found you at last," spoke the razor-sharp teeth. The hideous creature advanced towards them.

Blue pulled the trigger. The gunshot ran out as the child slumped into stillness. Letting the body roll onto the floor, Blue turned to face the monster. The blackboard held one final message.

THANK YOU.

Blue dropped her weapon to the floor. Snakes slithered their way out of the man's many crooked jaws. The snakes wrapped themselves around Blue's broken body and pulled her towards the maelstrom of jagged teeth. His eyes glistened as she felt the warm sickness of his breath upon her skin.

"*You're welcome,*" said Blue.

As the doubleclock struck 0110, the world around them came to a stop. The monster was on the verge of devouring her, his teeth grazing her skin, but they stayed frozen in place. Together they remained in a horrifying embrace while the world around them began to crumble. The walls, the desks, the chalkboard, everything broke into pieces. Like ashes they blew apart, from top to bottom, the shards disappearing into thin air as the electronic whine of a modem screamed into their ears. The whine grew in pitch and volume as the zone collapsed in upon itself. Finally, the arms and legs of both Blue and the monster began to disintegrate. It spread to their torsos, then to their heads.

As she watched the monster's face fall apart, Blue heard one final thought pass through her mind.

I'm free.

While the world screamed in agony, she dissolved into nothingness.

****

Mmorpg listened as the audio link in his ear fell into silence. The dark school was gone. The killer was gone. Blue was gone. The job was done.

"Kernel: logout," said Mmorpg. He felt the sensation of falling backwards and found himself back in his alcove, sitting in his usual chair. On the glass wall before him read a single message:

UNKNOWN ZONE DISCONNECTED.

Mmorpg slid the dermals from his temples and buried his face in his hands. He was so tired.

He rose from his chair and removed the dermals from his temples. His thoughts turned to the soft leather couch in the director's office. His face sagging from exhaustion, Mmorpg wanted nothing more than to curl up on that couch and sleep the rest of the day away.

But he couldn't, not yet. He had one more thing to do first. He had to see Blue.

Mmorpg walked towards her makeshift bed against the wall. She was sitting so quietly there. Brain dead though she was, she looked like she was sleeping peacefully, waiting for someone to wake her up. Mmorpg turned to his right and looked out into the Womb.

Beyond the glass walls of his office, dozens of hosts slept. They were dreaming up worlds for the pleasure of others. None of them would understand the danger they were in, or the sacrifice others had to make.

He turned back towards Blue and closed his eyes in prayer.

"Rest in peace Blue. May you find your nirvana."

Mmorpg opened his eyes and his mouth dropped in horror.

Blue's body melted away like wax before him.

Mmorpg ran outside his office and saw the hosts melting as well. Their bodies spilled onto the floor as Mmorpg ran to the laboratory. As he stormed in, he yelled, "What's going on?" at his staff. But he stopped, his face locked in shock.

His entire team was frozen in place. The supervisors, their interns, the programmers and the technicians, none of them moved a muscle nor blinked an eye. Mmorpg approached the nearest one, an Asian woman of strikingly fine features. Her mouth stood gaping open as if to yawn, but no air came in or out. Mmorpg reached out to touch her. Her skin felt muted and lifeless, like paper.

And then, right in front of him, she crumbled apart.

The rest of his staff underwent the same trauma. Bit by bit, they fell into pieces that disintegrated before hitting the floor. Bewildered, Mmorpg looked back towards the big screen. A torrent of silvery liquid poured down its face.

His own words returned to haunt him.

"What each user sees in Evermore is a creation of their own mind," said the Mmorpg from this morning. "The images placed in front of their eyes, the sounds they hear, the scents they smell are all pulled from their subconscious. Their memory forms the RAM of Evermore, reconstructing the world in their own image. But that memory can be accessed more directly."

These were the words Mmorpg spoke to the director. He gulped at their memory. *No*, he thought, *it couldn't be.*

"Let's imagine we have one person who really wants to leave. Let's imagine that instead of allowing her to actually log out, we only make her think she's logged out. Instead, we pull out the right images from her memory so she thinks she's back in the real world. From her perspective, she'll believe she's logged out. She'll stand up, feel tired and then go to the bedroom to take a nap. A few hours will pass by, we'll find and fix the problem and then we'll log her out. She'll wake up in her bed or chair with her dermals on her head and think that she forgot to take them off."

Mmorpg slowly understood the truth, the awful truth. "My god. What did you make me do?" His memory answered.

"We don't make them do anything. They think they're doing something, all the while staying safely here in Evermore. When it's all over, they'll think they were dreaming or that they fell asleep after logging out. They'll never know the difference."

The truth overwhelmed him. Tears streamed from his eyes as he buried his face in his hands. As the world fell apart around him, his conscience ripped his soul to pieces.

"It was all my fault," he cried. "It was my fault."

A collapsing wall snapped him out from his self-pity. Pulling every last ounce of moral strength from his broken will, Mmorpg raised his soaked face away from his hands and said the one thing that would put everything in perspective, "Kernel: logout."

Nothing happened.

As the world came crashing down around him, panic swamped his mind. Where was he? Was he still in Evermore or back in the real world? He couldn't be in the real world, the real world didn't melt. But if he was in Evermore, then why couldn't he log out? Looking down at his hand, Mmorpg saw his fingers disintegrate, their fragments disappearing into the air. His feet were the next to crumble away. Mmorpg felt his body go numb. He was dying.

But his memory saved him.

"How can you be so sure the killer is still here?" asked the director two hours ago.

"I've disabled the logout function," said Mmorpg's memory.

At that instant the answer flashed into his mind.

"Kernel: re-enable logout function!" he commanded.

"L0gaout funktioooon 3n@@bleeeeeed," came the tortured reply of the kernel.

"Kernel: logout," said Mmorpg.

Adam felt himself pulled through the eye of a needle and thrown back into his chair. Everywhere around him, alarm bells rang ominously. Before he could catch his breath, Alice leapt into his sight and screamed, "What the hell were you doing?"

Adam pulled the dermals from his temples.

"How long have I been logged in for?" asked Adam.

"Since you got here this morning. We've been trying for the last hour to log you out but for some reason you disabled the logout function."

"Why didn't you contact me?"

"We tried but you didn't respond."

"So you panicked."

"No. Disabling the logout function made us curious. Turning off the security protocols, that made us worried. We didn't start panicking until one of the zones began collapsing."

"Which one is crashing?"

"T3e3l1g3E. It's in the underground."

"How many are inside?" asked Adam.

Alice stopped in front of a large screen. It read 43,282. "That's high," she said.

"How many have died?"

"I'm not letting anyone die." She typed commands into the computer. The screen flashed in response:

EXECUTING KICK(T3E3L1G3E, ALL);
LOGGING OUT ALL USERS IN ZONE T3E3L1G3E.

"No," said Adam. "Earlier. How many victims did we have earlier today?"

Alice threw him a confused glare. "None."

Adam smiled in relief. His security protocols had worked after all. They had always been working.

Alice leaned in closer. She spoke in a grave tone, "The safeties are off and the zone is crashing. If we can't get those people out, then we'll have more than enough victims to deal with. Now wake up."

Shaking his head, Adam turned and looked out into the white room. Despite the noise, all the hosts in the white room were sleeping peacefully. Supervisors were everywhere trying in vain to wake them up.

Adam stepped towards the glass door. It opened as he approached.

"Don't wake the hosts up yet," ordered Adam. "Wait until the users get out first." The supervisors nodded their assent. Adam turned back and saw a blank wall where Blue's bed had been.

"Where is she?"

"Who?" asked Alice.

"The woman with the scar on her face," said Adam. He pointed to the empty space alongside the wall. "She logged in with me this morning."

"No." Alice's eyebrows arched with concern. "There was just you. No one logs in from this terminal except for you. For security reasons. Don't you remember? You made that rule."

Adam stepped back towards his chair. The doors slid closed behind him, revealing a large computer screen upon the glass wall of the alcove.

The big screen cycled through the vitals of all of Evermore's users as they were automatically logged out. None were fatalities. Adam breathed easier. His security protocols had worked after all. They must have always been working.

There was a number on the left side of the screen that Adam turned his attention to. The number started at 43,282, but it quickly dropped in large chunks. Soon it fell into the hundreds. Adam stared at the number as it fell: 456, 341, 159, 104, 103, 89, 45, 30, 22, 17, 11, 5, 4, 3, 1, 1, 1.

"Come on, come on."

The number remained stuck on 1. Everyone had gotten out safely except for one.

"Who are you?" asked Adam. He tapped the number on the glass. The number expanded into a blue box, listing the user's information:

Login Name: multiple accounts
Status: Guest
Registration Keys: TLG0001, TLG0002, TLG0003
Address: 4774 West 6th Avenue, Vancouver, B.C., V6T 1C5

"That's just outside of campus," he called to Alice. "Call UBC Hospital. Have them dispatch an ambulance immediately to the site and bring the victim to the Urgent Care Centre here," said Adam.

"They're going to want to know why," said Alice.

"Let us handle that. Call the director and have him meet me at the hospital," said Adam.

"What?" asked Alice, a puzzled look on her face.

"The director," shouted Adam. "Do I have to repeat myself?"

"But sir, you're the director."

Adam froze in surprise. He stood still for a moment and stared into space, thinking. Then he shook his head and ran for the exit.

He sprinted from the room and dashed up three flights of stairs. Using the airborne glass tunnels to avoid the relentless rain, Adam made his way towards the hospital, all the while trying to reconstruct the day in his mind. He needed to understand what was real and what was fiction, but with each attempt he grew more confused. Nothing lined up or made sense. Finally, a sense of doubt overwhelmed him. He stopped in the last passageway before the hospital and looked around in a panic.

"Kernel: logout," he said.

Nothing happened.

"Kernel. Are you there?" he asked.

There was only silence.

Satisfied, he moved through the last door and stepped outside the building. The rear entrance of the hospital stood before him. An ambulance pulled away.

Moving through the sliding doors, Adam sprinted through a series of antiseptic white hallways until he came to the hospital's reception desk.

"Hello," panted Adam. "There was a patient that was brought in from 4774 West 6th Avenue. I need to see him."

"4774 West 6th Avenue," replied the nurse calmly, glancing at a large circular clock beside her that read 12:31 PM. "Yes, just admitted a couple of minutes ago. May I ask who you are?"

"My name is Adamska Romanenko," replied the programmer. "I may have information that pertains to his condition. I must see the patient."

"I will have someone escort you up," replied the nurse firmly. Within seconds, a security guard appeared and led Adam up to the third floor. Past door after door they marched, moving straight into the ICU. The nurses on station directed them to room 379.

The security guard waited outside the door while Adam entered the room. There were two beds in the chamber, flush to the wall. The first one was empty and open. The second was closed off with a long, white cloth divider. A doctor waited outside the curtain.

"Mr. Romanenko," said the doctor sombrely. His white hair, round glasses and salt-and-pepper goatee gave him an air of serenity and authority.

"Please, call me Adam."

The doctor ignored his request. "Mr. Romanenko," he repeated, "your laboratory notified us you would be coming. What is your involvement in this case?"

"I work for a firm that allows people to enter a virtual world through the use of sub-dermal transmitters. Through our security protocols, we could see the client's brainwave patterns were outside normal parameters, so we immediately sent for an ambulance. We wanted to be on the safe side."

The doctor scratched his head. "Well, physically, the patient is in perfect health."

Adam took in a deep breath. "What about mentally?" he asked.

"Well, mentally is a different story," said the doctor. He removed his glasses and lowered his voice to a whisper. "There is no cranial damage, no pressure, no haemorrhaging. The mind is in perfect shape. But the patient will not wake up."

"A coma?"

"Not quite. There is no diffuse pathology to explain the condition, nor are there any supratentorial injuries. Focal infratentorial lesions that would account for the state of the patient are also not present. Physically, there is nothing wrong. It's like her brain simply decided to shut itself off."

"Her?" said Adam in surprise. "Would I be able to see her?"

"Not right now, her father is with her."

"Her father?" asked Adam. He looked again at the cloth divider. A silhouette rose and moved towards him. The cloth divider was pulled aside and Adam found himself staring at the middle-aged man. Their eyes met, Adam struggling to speak.

"Hello there," said the middle-aged man politely as he reached out his hand, "I understand you're from that Evermore company."

"Yes I am," responded Adam, taking the outstretched palm. The iron ring on the man's little finger chafed against Adam's skin as they shook hands.

"I'm glad you got here so quickly. Do you know what happened to my little girl?"

378

"Well, that's what we're here to figure out," said Adam. "You have my word that we will not rest until we found out what happened to your daughter. We will also cover all of your expenses to ensure her continued good health."

"That's mighty kind of you, sir. I just want her to get better. She's all I got."

Adam steadied his breath and looked at the girl lying still on the bed. Breathing through a tube, the little girl appeared so tiny next to the menagerie of machines standing guard beside her. Adam could hear the oomph and puff of the machines as they breathed for her in perfect synchronization. Her blonde hair, recently brushed, lay neatly upon the bed. Around her neck hung a golden cross. Her hands rested together on her chest, holding a little doll.

Adam looked closer at the doll. The doll was dressed in a cowboy hat, authentic leather jacket, blue jeans and brown boots. It looked just like Undecided.

"That was one of her favourites," said the father.

Adam turned towards him, "What?"

"One of her favourite dolls." The father reached underneath the bed and pulled out a cardboard box full of dolls.

"I brought them with us in the ambulance," he said. "I thought they might help her. She adores them all so much."

Adam looked down into the box. The dolls were dressed like everyone he had met that day. There was Jie with her round glasses and pouty demeanour. There was Lamare with her wrinkled face. He saw Klein and Palette and the 733t and their mounts. He saw PRNC and the Caliph and the clerics and the striders with aluminum foil swords taped to their backs. There was Toland holding a baseball bat, the JTF with their plastic guns and Vanessa covering her face with her long flowing hair.

"She played with all of them but there was one that was her personal favourite." The father reached into the box and fished around. Scores of dolls bubbled to the surface. Adam recognized them all. Reaching down into the box, he brushed aside a skinny doll with freckles and a cubby one with dark skin. He picked up one dressed in a CANADA T-shirt and dark shades and regarded it carefully. It was Arthur.

"Now I know it's here somewhere," said the middle-aged man.

Adam saw a piece of newsprint poking up from the pile of dolls. "What's that?" asked Adam.

"Oh, that's just some old news story she held on to. I'm not sure why. You can take a look at it if you like." The father pulled out the crumpled paper and handed it to Adam. Adam unfurled it to find a photo of Blue. She looked younger, healthier and was missing the vicious scar on her cheek.

"Kids save the darndest things," said the father as he continued to rummage through the box. Adam read the story accompanying Blue's photo.

VPD IN SHOCK FOLLOWING OFFICER'S RAMPAGE

The Vancouver police department is still in shock following yesterday's startling events. As first reported by the Star, seven children and two police officers are dead following a shootout yesterday afternoon in Burnaby. According to witnesses, Constable Gabrielle Duchene, a seven-year veteran of the VPD, drew her pistol and opened fire on a group of seven children as they walked home from school. Constable David Manchester, her partner and 14-year veteran of the VPD, intervened and wounded Ms. Duchene but was killed by gunfire during the exchange. Constable Duchene was later found dead at the scene along with the seven children. When asked what may have precipitated the incident, some witnesses believe they saw one of the children pull a water pistol on the officers as they walked by. Police Chief Anne Leung promised the victim's families that a full investigation would be conducted into the incident. Commentators have questioned-

"Ahh here it is," said the father. He pulled out a doll and handed it to Adam.

It was tall and lanky, like a Barbie doll, but it was not beautiful. Instead, it wore a black coat with black hair and ...

Adam turned the doll's head.

... a blue scar painted on its right cheek.

She loves these dolls," said the father. She would spend every last minute playing with them, creating these crazy stories   only she could understand." The middle-aged man fought back tears. "She's going to be a wonderful storyteller one day." He looked longingly at his daughter with both a tear in his eye and a smile on his face.

"Yes sir," said Adam, his lungs fighting for air. He handed the doll back to the father. "She is an amazing storyteller." Adam looked one final time at the little girl's face. She looked so peaceful. Her eyes, closed and still, were narrow. It was as if she was looking at something far, far away.

****

Her clip empty, the exhausted woman in black fell back down to the ground. She had emptied every last round at the stranger, but had only managed to break a couple windows in the short, dank alley. As she collapsed to her knees, her eyes caught the lifeless eyes of all the small children she had just slaughtered. Blood streamed down in buckets from the open hole in her cheek. It filled her throat, forcing her to cough it back up. The Beretta was now empty and useless, she let it drop into the red puddle at her knees. The world blurred and faded. She was losing consciousness. She heard mumbling in front of her.

She concentrated, bringing the world before her back into focus. There was a sandalled figure there, approaching her. The figure reached out a forgiving hand and spoke in a soft, reassuring voice, but the woman in black could only hear a mumble. She concentrated, letting the world blur again so she could hear the words.

"…it's okay." continued the sandalled figure. "I understand why you did what you did. I understand everything now. You have my forgiveness, my child. And I would like to thank you for everything you've done for us. But we don't need you anymore. Your time has come. You have earned your peace in a better place." The sandalled figure placed a hand on the woman's shoulder. The woman in black looked up at the figure as torrents of tears streamed from her eyes. She smiled while the world around her faded.

"Thank you," she said.

"Welcome home," the voice said softly as the darkness enveloped her.

The Consortium rose in applause as Klein entered the chamber. The sovereign waved to the crowd as he had done so many times before. A standing ovation befitted a man of his stature and service to Evermore. There were neither cheers nor jeers; protocol dictated that class be maintained.

Taking his place at the lectern for the last time, Klein gripped its oak surface with a gentle caress. He looked around the chamber wistfully, recalling his many years of service here. He smiled at the memories.

Up into the sky his podium lifted, up into the rafters. As he rose, the representatives of the Consortium of Evermore lifted their heads and listened intently. From the top of the chamber, Klein gave his final speech as sovereign.

"It has been a long road, my friends. And we have traveled it together. As this wonderful country has grown and matured, so have we. I have watched the boys and girls that came into these halls so many years ago grow into men and women before my eyes. Oh, how have we grown." Klein paused for applause.

"When we came here, we came as representatives of the people, the people who lived their lives completely in Evermore, the people who worked, slept and prospered in our realm. For five years, we brought their dreams into these halls. For five years, we met their nightmares head-on in our laws and protocols. For five years, we have built a new nation."

He paused again, letting the awkward silence hang in the air. "Yes, Yes. We are a nation. We are nation not of colour or blood but of a dream. A dream that causes each and every one of us to look out towards the horizon, towards the nation we are becoming, towards a future for all, no matter how weak or small. It is a dream we have sought for five long years, but were too scared to acknowledge, lest it be crushed by our expectations. And now, more than ever, the people of Evermore see this as our true home. We see this land as being more accepting and welcoming than any place we've known before. We see this land as representing the values we feel deep within our hearts. We hear words that have always been on our tongues but have for too long gone unsaid. We have found a home here in Evermore - a home that will stand forever more. As the people of Evermore, we have grown into something more than the sum of our parts. Ladies and gentlemen, we have become a nation." Rapturous cheers greeted his words.

"And yet, there is still so much to do. Now that we have built a home for the people, we must furnish it. We must endeavour to give the people of Evermore the tools and skills necessary to fulfill our own destinies. To give ourselves the ability to live our entire lives here if necessary. To allow us to work, live and prosper within our safe borders, to never again have to visit the barren lands outside of this realm. Economic self-sufficiency is now our biggest challenge. We have the opportunity to build a virtual economy independent of the real world. To create jobs, to buttress industry, to build an economic foundation for the future, that must be our goal.

"And with new challenges come new leaders - men and women who have the skills and the will to hold up the torch. Ladies and gentlemen, we are fortunate to have such a fine generation of young leaders ready to take charge. They will lead us to the stars and back again. There is one I want to introduce you to again, although I'm sure you're very familiar with her. I have known her ever since she entered the Consortium as a newly chosen representative, her eyes wide as the sky and dreams bigger than this hall. She was young, green and inexperienced, but even at that age you could see echoes of the leader she has become. In the three years she's been in my cabinet, she has taken every tough assignment I've given her, smiled and gotten the job done. She has had many rough times, but with each challenge I have had the pleasure to watch this young lady grow and mature. And unfortunately, I began to realize that I needed her more than she needed me." Laughs echoed off the chamber walls. "She has certainly earned her spot here within these halls. She has done more for the people of Evermore than any other member of this chamber, myself included." More laughter came from the crowd.

"Needless to say, when the time came to decide to move on with my life ..." A collective groan filled the room. "Oh no, it's alright, it's time to move on. When the time came, there was only one conceivable choice to succeed me. There was only one person who had the fortitude, the vision and the principles to lead Evermore into the new age. Please join me in welcoming our new sovereign – Ms. Jie Wan."

The Consortium rose in standing ovation for the new sovereign. Jie stood silent in a calm pose, careful not to look too eager or intimidated. The applause lasted for a minute, then slowly died as Klein prepared to make his finish.

"Dear citizens of Evermore, I stand before you now without power, without authority, without an office or a title. I stand here now as one of you. And I must say that this is the happiest moment of my life." More applause. "Thank you, good night and good luck Evermore. May your future be as bright as the people who lead you. Good night and à la prochaine."

The standing ovation lasted for ten minutes. Klein's soaring popularity kept his podium floating at the top of chamber. Finally, remorsefully, the podium returned to the floor. Klein stepped out from the lectern, waved a final goodbye and left the public spotlight forever.

****

Vanessa's eyes shot open as the morning sun hit her face. Within an instant, excitement overwhelmed her body. Finally, the day she had been dreaming about for so long had arrived. With a joyful grin on her face, she leapt out of bed, grabbed a comb and began brushing her hair. With her anticipation bubbling, she had difficulty getting it right. Who could concentrate on a day like this?

Her hair twisted itself into knots as she tried to comb it. This would not do. *Focus,* she thought to herself, *this is important.* Never again would she get a day like today. Never again would she feel like this. She refocused her attention, turning towards the mirror.

She saw the scar.

She gasped as the memory of the attack came rushing back. Her hair frizzled out in shock at the imperfection that stared out at her from the mirror. It hadn't gone away. It was no bruise. It was there permanently.

No, she thought to herself, *it could not be.* She grabbed a wet sponge and tried to rub it away. She washed and scrubbed and scraped to no avail. Her eyes filled with tears. Her mouth desperately wanted to cry but she dared not let it. She dared not, lest anyone know. Vanessa looked again at the mirror, hoping against hope that this was all a bad dream from which she would soon wake.

As the tears streamed down her satin cheeks, she brushed her hand along the scar around her neck. Vanessa could feel the imperfection closing around her throat, choking her of air. The tears dripped silently.

Vanessa took one final look at herself in the mirror, one more look to remind her of who she truly was, of who she could have been. And then slowly, her flowing hair covered her body in a cocoon. Never again could anyone see her true self. She was entering a world where she would be a princess among mortals, but could never be held. It was the life she had always dreamed of and always feared. Finally, it was hers.

She left the room and approached the base of a giant stairway. Her soft toes caressing the ivory floor, Vanessa walked to the bottom of the stairs. Along each side of the stairway stood the greeting party. Two per step, they congratulated Vanessa as she passed between them. At the very bottom of the ivory staircase were her oldest friends, who had known and loved her when she was nobody. She continued to move up the stairs. In the middle of the staircase were the people most responsible for her crown. Vanessa's former competitors from years past smiled proudly as she passed. Some cried with joy, some cried with sorrow and some cried for their own broken dreams.

At the end of the middle section, Vanessa saw Lamare for the final time. Lamare could not accompany Vanessa to the Downtown

Core, but her crinkling cheeks beamed with pride and joy. Finally her chosen protégé would ascend to where Lamare had always belonged. Vanessa allowed herself to reveal a hint of a smile to her adopted mother – a small gesture of appreciation for the time and sacrifice Lamare had given her.

Finally, in the highest section, Vanessa came upon her new peers, the members of the Evermore Elite. During this final phase of her ascension, she passed dukes and earls, princes and princesses, the most beautiful and eligible men and women in the land of Evermore. But she barely noticed them, for she only had eyes for one man.

Smiling down upon her with a million-dollar grin, PRNC waited for Vanessa with the poise of a gentleman. Extending his hand, he called her name. Vanessa wasted no time in taking his outstretched palm. For the longest moment, they stared deeply into each other's eyes as if searching for an answer to a question they had not yet asked.

Hand in hand, PRNC turned to the golden door before them, placed his fingers upon the handle and pulled. The door opened and bathed the pair in a warm and loving light. Vanessa felt all her troubles drift away and she grinned giddily behind her cocoon of hair. Together, PRNC and Vanessa walked into the light.

****

Toland sat despondently at his desk. Hope had long ago left his eyes. A group of well-dressed men approached.

"Did you find Undecided?" asked Toland.

"No sir," said one of the goons. "There's no sign of him."

"Did you locate Blue's pistol?"

"We've scoured the battlefield in the Downtown Core," said the goon. "It's nowhere to be found."

Toland's eyes dropped to the table. Despair overcame him.

"But we found something else," said the well-dressed goon as he placed an object on the table.

Toland reached down and picked up the bullet. He rolled the cylinder in his fingers until he saw the letter "X" etched into the casing. He grinned.

"Boys. We're in business."

****

The midday sun streamed through the crystal clear windshield of Adam's '89 Chevy. He had been driving all night from the coast, and the blazing sunshine was lulling him towards a dangerous sleep. He needed a break.

Adam pulled his pickup truck and his trailer into a small lookout point. Surrounded by soft savannah hills, the rest stop overlooked a long, green lake. Adam put his vehicle into park and stepped out for a short walk. A crow in a short tree watched him.

Much time had passed since that fateful day, and yet to Adam it all felt like yesterday. Again and again, he saw the face of the sleeping child who would never dream again. Staring out over the great green lake, he lost himself in his own thoughts as he traced the line of the lake to the small city upon its banks. It was here he would stake his future.

No longer concerned about margins or profits, or the ground-breaking realm of technological marvel, Adam thought about his new job, as a teacher in a small community college. He was returning to the basics, teaching the fundamentals of ones and zeros and how to use them to carry out your will. A slight smile curled his lip as the sun beat mercilessly down upon his skin, deathly pale after a lifetime in the city of rain.

Placing his hand over his eyes and squinting, Adam saw the world around him coming alive. Grasshoppers hopped through the savannah weeds, great eagles soared high and a fat marmot poked its head out from beneath a concrete divider.

Adam turned and looked at the marmot with the same inquisitive curiosity that the marmot gave to him. The marmot cautiously stepped out of its hole and approached Adam. It sniffed its nose, looking for food. Adam reached out with a gentle hand. The marmot squeaked in surprise and bolted away. The fat around its belly jiggled humorously while it sprinted down the hill towards the water.

Adam laughed with an ease he had long ago forgotten. He laughed long and hard, only stopping when he heard a bus pull away.

Adam turned his attention back towards the city that would become his home. He saw a little girl facing away from him, looking towards the city beyond. The girl had dirty blond hair stretching down to her toes and a white dress adorned with innocent little flowers. She stood perfectly still, as if waiting for the city to come to her.

From behind, she looked just like the victim. But that could not be.

Adam watched her for a long moment and then turned away. He looked towards the east end of the lake and its complete freedom from human habitation. The memory of the victim weighed heavily upon him. His responsibility for her coma pulled on his conscious. It was now his burden to bear for the rest of his life. Finally, he could resist no more. Overcome by guilt, he turned back towards the child.

But she was gone.

The crow took off and flew past Adam to the north. Over the lookout and over the cliff, it floated away. It soared across the great green lake and over a long white beach where a lonely woman with flowing brown hair walked as if lost in a dream. Over orchards of apples and forests full of life it fluttered and flew, towards a bright horizon of infinite possibility.

Not everyone had such a bright future. Trapped in a cold, dark dungeon of her fears and miseries, suffocating in a sea of oil that oozed out of the dank, black brick that surrounded her, the woman in black struggled eternally to stay afloat amongst the crude. There were no exits to escape and no ladders to climb out of the abyss. She would remain trapped there, forever more, with only her screams for company. But her screams could penetrate those walls, filter up through the ground and be faintly heard among the population above. And when people asked about the faint scream, they were told the tragedy of Blue and to beware the call of the Nocturne.

The End